W9-AGB-635

SIGNIFICANT OTHERS

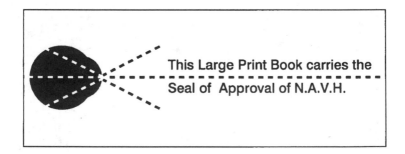

This Large Print Book carries the
Seal of Approval of N.A.V.H.

SIGNIFICANT OTHERS

SANDRA KITT

Thorndike Press • Thorndike, Maine

Published in 1997 by arrangement with Dutton Signet, a division of Penguin Books USA Inc.

Thorndike Large Print ® Romance Series.

The tree indicium is a trademark of Thorndike Press.

The text of this Large Print edition is unabridged. Other aspects of the book may vary from the original edition.

Set in 16 pt. Bookman Old Style.

Printed in the United States on permanent paper.

Library of Congress Cataloging in Publication Data

Kitt, Sandra.
   Significant others / Sandra Kitt.
     p.   cm.
   ISBN 0-7862-0920-8 (lg. print : hc)
   1. Large type books. I. Title.
  [PS3561.I86S57 1997]
  813'.54—dc20   96-41772

*To my sister, Donna, and brothers
Jerry and Warren; our love
and respect for each other
are unconditional.*

I want to thank my agents, Ling Lucas and Edward Vesneske, Jr., for their patience and guidance; my editor Danielle Perez for her clarity and insights; and John Paine for teaching me a thing or two about continuity . . . and football.

Prologue

Patricia Gilbert heard the commotion before she'd even turned her car off from Rugby Road. The high-pitched sounds combined with the repetitive motion of her windshield wipers. Whatever was going on it had already escalated to an intense pitch.

Patricia knew it wasn't unusual for a group of the Duncan students to be vocal and noisy, even at seven-thirty in the morning. Her experience had shown that teenagers had zero reverence for time and place. They were always loud. Four blocks from the high school, there were at least three dozen students clustered in a circle, most of them black. Their screams of excitement were not like fooling around, but contained sudden bursts of reaction: cheers, grunts, shrieks, raucous laughing.

There was a fight in progress.

Patricia peered through her red-framed glasses and proceeded slowly down the tree-lined street with its old wood-framed homes. It was raining lightly and the neighborhood seemed eerily deserted of residents, but infested with the riotous energy of adolescents. They filled part of the sidewalk and spilled carelessly out in front of her car. She tried to keep parallel to the action, but it was shifting and swaying on the sidewalk, the circle of onlookers moving in unison to keep up. Patricia pulled her car over, stopped, and shifted into park. She quickly opened the door and stepped out. The rain was just heavy enough to be inconvenient, dampening her hair and clothing and fogging her glasses. She walked around the hood of the car and tried to penetrate the thick bunching of bodies.

"What's going on here?" she shouted. Only one or two of the students even bothered to look her way. "Let me through . . ." Patricia insisted. When the kids recognized her, they reluctantly allowed her space. Still she was jostled and bumped.

"It's Miss Gilbert . . ." was whispered through the gathering.

"So what?" a male voice responded

with scathing indifference.

Patricia forced her way to the center and found two young boys squared off in a struggle, fists and feet flying. She knew one of the boys. Kamil Johnson. A sophomore, he was bright but precocious and troubled. He had transferred to Duncan in his freshman year, from a school in which he would have been forever lost, but his maturing progress had so far been slow. He still resorted to bullying and fights when he got angry or wanted attention.

The surrounding audience of classmates had already chosen a side to root for, and their preference became clear when Kamil grabbed the front of the hooded sweat cardigan worn by the other boy. Kamil swung vigorously, flinging his opponent to the ground. A cheer went up.

"Get him! Get him!"

"Kick his ass . . ."

"Oreo nigger . . ."

For a second Patricia stood mesmerized. Her progress had been impeded by bigger students who refused to give way. She tried to see over their shoulders or past their arms. Her rain-speckled glasses hampered her vision. The

9

physical intensity of the two boys' battle seemed surreal, an unexpected explosion in an otherwise peaceful landscape. They were trying to hurt one another and Patricia wondered, as her stomach knotted, if either of the boys had weapons.

"Stop it," she shouted. "I said, stop it!"

When the fight continued, Patricia backed away and retreated quickly to her car. She leaned inside and pressed the car horn several times. The sharp noise began to have the desired effect. Slowly the cluster broke and a handful of students began heading toward the school building. They were disinterested now that the fight was ending. Patricia leaned on the horn and kept the pressure on for an earsplitting ten seconds. She stopped and hurried back to the fight.

"Cut it out, Kamil."

Kamil paid her no mind until Eric Patton, a grade higher and two years older, and taller than Kamil, suddenly planted his body right in front of him.

"Hey, back it up." Eric instructed in such a booming authoritative tone that even Patricia watched to see if Kamil would obey. He did.

"Motherfucker gonna be *toast*," Kamil threatened, glaring at his opponent.

"You the one with the burnt ass, nigger," Eric scoffed. Everyone laughed. But the fight was over and the crowd began drifting away.

"Don't be trippin' on me, man. This ain't none of your business."

Patricia gave a brief glance to the other boy, on his knees and starting to stand up. "Well, it's *my* business," she said to Kamil.

"This ain't school," he said impertinently to Patricia. Kamil muttered to himself as he straightened his sweater and jacket, readjusted his cap. "Nothin' better be tore, else I'll have to fuck you up," he said, gesturing with a threatening point of his hand.

"Come on, man," Eric said to Kamil, trying to push him away from the confrontation. "You won, man. You won. Leave the nigger alone."

"Enough," Patricia said to the boy. "All of you, out of here. You have two minutes before the first bell."

"Fuck that," someone returned, but the students began to disperse and head toward the school building a few blocks away.

In a half minute Patricia stood alone on the wet sidewalk with the other boy. There was blood on his knuckles and he was bleeding from a corner of his mouth and his nose. His navy-blue sweat top had been half pulled down his arms and back. He tried to shrug the now wet cardigan back on. Patricia touched his arm.

"Are you hurt?"

He didn't answer, but shook her hand off and bent to retrieve his knapsack. The contents had been emptied, intentionally or in the heat of the confrontation Patricia couldn't tell. But all his personal things were strewn about the street, wet and dirtied. He methodically began picking everything up, his breathing still labored from the fight.

"I said, are you hurt?" Patricia repeated in a tone that expected an answer.

"No," the boy said grudgingly, but he didn't look at her.

Patricia walked a few feet away to pick up a textbook, some pens and pencils, a soiled paperback novel. It was Stephen King's *The Stand*. She silently handed everything to him. He silently took them, haphazardly dropping them into the knapsack.

"What's your name?" she asked, as he glanced around for anything he might have missed. He didn't bother with the notebook pages that had come loose and now were plastered to the wet sidewalk.

"Kent."

"Kent what?"

"Kent Baxter."

"Are you a student at Duncan?"

He took time to zipper the bag. He'd finally caught his breath, but Patricia could see that his hands were shaking and his breathing was still uneven. She saw him swallow, lick his lips, and run his tongue into the corner of his mouth where blood was smeared and drying. He nodded, wiping the blood from his nose indifferently on the sleeve of the sweater.

Now that the adrenaline rush of the encounter had dissipated, Patricia took a moment to examine the young boy who stood before her. She couldn't say if she agreed with Eric Patton that Kamil had been the victor in the fight with Kent Baxter. Kent was uncowed, and still surprisingly self-possessed.

He was a good-looking teen, solidly

built and slightly taller than herself. She guessed that he was older than fourteen. He didn't slouch, like so many of the boys did, rounding their shoulders unnaturally as if trying to hide within themselves. Already the soft roundness of an adolescent face was receding and he was developing planes and angles to his cheeks and jaw. His complexion was like linen, now a kind of washed-out ocher in the unflattering light of the cloudy day. His hair was curly, and slightly unkempt because of the fight. She watched as he tried to set it right with his hand and fingers.

Patricia couldn't recall ever seeing the boy before, but knew he was too old to be a freshman. She wondered, too, what the fight was about, although Kamil Johnson's vile insults were certainly specific enough. Kent Baxter suddenly glanced at her furtively, and in his expression Patricia saw the expected defiance, but also some uncertainty. His dark eyes told her that this boy was not characteristically insolent or stubborn, just that he wasn't sure he could trust her . . . or anyone else.

She remembered that her car was double-parked with the engine still running. Off in the distance was the faint ringing of the school bell. She was wet, and her hair was becoming frizzy and beyond redemption.

"I'll drop you off at the school," Patricia offered. She headed to the car. "Get in." When the boy hesitated, she turned to him. "I'm Patricia Gilbert. I'm a counselor at Duncan. If you had been luckier, you could have gone the whole school year and never met me. Get in."

Still Kent showed ambivalence.

"Look, you don't have to be seen with me. I park on the street near the track field. I'll let you out there. Make up your mind, Kent Baxter. I'm getting wet."

He looked off toward the school but the streets were practically empty now. Kent got in the passenger side of Patricia's Chevy Cavalier. Patricia got in as well and pushed her glasses to the top of her head. She slowly pulled into traffic. At the corner the light turned red, and she stopped again. She sighed and glanced closely at her passenger, who stared sullenly out the window.

"I think you'd better use the bathroom before going to class, and wash up a bit. If any of your teachers give you a hard time about being late, tell them to

15

speak with me."

He gave no indication that he was even listening. His gaze was unblinking, trancelike. Patricia wondered what he was thinking. One thing that did occur to her was that there had been an imbalance of power in the sidewalk encounter with Kamil. No one had been rooting for Kent Baxter.

"What was the fight about?" she asked.

It was a moment before the boy reacted. He shrugged. The light changed and Patricia stepped on the accelerator. She drove the remaining three blocks to Duncan High School . . . and continued right past. She could detect Kent's confusion and his rapid blinking when he turned a puzzled gaze to her. Patricia chuckled softly.

"Don't worry. I'm not kidnapping you. I just thought you could use a little time to get your act together."

"I'm okay."

"Fine. But I don't want to hear that the fight continued later." She gave him a hard look. "I don't particularly want to haul you into my office with threats, either, and I don't want to have to call your parents."

Kent silently looked out the window once more. Patricia drove almost a half mile through the Midwood section of Brooklyn, circled a block, and headed back north toward the school.

"I've never seen you before. First year at Duncan?"

"Yeah."

"Sophomore?"

"Yeah."

"Okay," Patricia sighed. He wasn't going to make it easy. "Have you had other fights with Kamil Johnson?"

There was a pause, but finally Kent shrugged again.

"I'll take that to mean yes," she said dryly.

At the school she quickly found a place to park and turned off the engine. The sudden silence in the car was uneasy. The rain was making gentle pat-pat sounds on the hood and roof. She swiveled in her seat to look earnestly at the teenager.

"I don't think I have to tell you that I don't approve of students fighting. Teachers and counselors are strange that way. We feel a responsibility not to let anyone get hurt. I've got your number, Kent Baxter, and I'm going to be watching you. I hope I don't have to . . ."

Patricia never got any further. Suddenly Kent Baxter slumped forward, resting his forehead on the top of the wet knapsack. And he began to cry. She was stunned into silence and could only watch as the boy's shoulders shook. Patricia wisely didn't touch him, but let the purging continue for more than a minute.

Patricia felt herself go soft with sympathy. The adult posture of responsibility and control gave way to wanting to comfort this child. His sobs were wracking bursts of raw emotion that seemed to stem from the very center of his being. It spewed out a pain that couldn't have had anything to do with the recent fight.

"It's going to be all right, Kent," she promised quietly, and just let him cry. But Patricia didn't have a clue what "it" was.

Kent Baxter wasn't hurt physically. But listening to the pitiful sobs of the boy huddled in her car suggested to Patricia that something much deeper than just protecting his ego or budding manhood had been at stake in the fight with Kamil Johnson because he hadn't backed down from that.

Almost as quickly as the crying started, it stopped. Kent sniffled and discreetly resorted to the sweater sleeve again to wipe his nose. Patricia waited another few seconds before speaking.

"Feel better?"

"No," he muttered rudely.

She pursed her lips thoughtfully. "My office is on the first floor, around the corner from central if you ever want to come and talk, just you and me." She doubted that he ever would. Patricia glanced at the time. "You have fifteen minutes before the next class."

Kent nodded, sniffed again. He sat still for another long moment, as if gearing himself up for the rest of the day. Finally, without another word, he opened the car door, stepped out, and slammed it shut. Without an acknowledgment or backward glance, he headed into the high school.

Patricia sat for a little longer, puzzled. Not over the incident of the fight, but over the silent pain of a teenager who bore more than he obviously thought he could handle. And Patricia was aware of how oddly familiar the boy's turmoil had seemed. She'd experienced it in her stomach, recognized the pain evoked through his sobs; she had a flashback of her own. Patricia sensed that Kent's troubles had to do with feeling isolated and alienated . . . and he was very angry.

She blinked through the rain-streaked windshield and wondered what it was that made this boy believe that he couldn't trust anyone . . . and why she felt like the weight of it could break his heart.

"I'm going to report you to the principal for being late," Jerome Daly threatened with a grin when Patricia walked into their office.

Patricia grimaced at her colleague as she continued on to her half of the divided space. She dropped her purse and tote onto her chair and shrugged out of her leather coat.

"Morning . . ." she murmured, digging a mirror out of her desk drawer and frowning at her image. She poked and prodded at her wildly curled hair and quickly gave up.

"Bad hair day," Jerome observed, leaning casually against the partition that separated their offices. He sipped coffee from a mug that had CROOKLYN printed around the side.

"It's raining, in case you haven't noticed."

"Don't you own an umbrella?"

"Where are the files for the students who are new this year? I don't mean freshmen," Patricia asked, putting the mirror away and wiping off her glasses before perching them on her nose.

Jerome ran his fingers through his thinning blond hair. He peered sheepishly at her through his wire-rimmed glasses. "On my desk. There's only a dozen or so."

"Can I see them?" Patricia asked, already heading for Jerome's cubicle.

He followed her, taking a seat at the desk and rocking forward on the spring action. "What's up, Pat?"

Patricia accepted the handful of manila folders from Jerome and, leaning against the edge of his desk, began leafing through the names printed on the tabs. She quickly came to the last one. She was disappointed.

"Is this everything?"

"What are you looking for?"

Patricia hugged the folders to her

chest, thoughtfully rubbing her chin on the top edges. "I broke up a fight this morning . . ."

"Really? I didn't hear anything."

"It was off school premises, near Avenue J. Kamil Johnson was one of the boys."

"I'm not surprised," Jerome responded dryly.

"And a kid named Kent Baxter."

When Jerome didn't respond Patricia glanced at him. Jerome shifted uneasily. He leaned across his desk, dug out another folder, and handed it to her.

"Kent Baxter," he said.

Patricia opened the folder, found a copy of the photo the students were required to have on their bus and train passes, and recognized the boy. He was staring straight into the camera, his expression totally blank. She flipped the photo over and underneath found a few more pages, mostly transcripts of school records from Colorado Springs.

"Colorado . . ." she murmured in surprise.

"Right. He started in September."

She began reading the last page in the folder. It was clear that Kent's parents were not together, possibly divorced.

22

He'd been living with his mother, Melissa, in Colorado. A Brad Heflin was listed as stepfather. But there was virtually no information on the father, Morgan Baxter, with whom the boy now lived. She glanced at Jerome.

"There's almost nothing in here. Wasn't Kent Baxter interviewed and evaluated at the start of school? Didn't his father come in for an orientation?"

"Would you like a cup of coffee?" Jerome asked, getting up and heading for the corner of the outer office where a coffee machine was set up on the table.

"Jerome . . ." Patricia began on a warning note.

"Look, he got lost in my paperwork. Yes, the kid was interviewed. No, I haven't written up my notes yet. Yes, the father was called for a meeting. No, he didn't come in. He's canceled two appointments."

Patricia waved the file in his face. "It's the end of October. When were you going to finish this?"

"Christ, you get pushy when your day starts badly." He took the folder. "There are fourteen hundred kids at Duncan. Can I be forgiven for missing one file?"

Patricia took the folder back. "Never mind. I'll handle it."

"What was the fight about?" Jerome asked, not even attempting to dissuade Patricia from taking over the case.

Patricia fell silent. Suddenly she found that she didn't want to share her immediate impressions with her colleague. It wasn't that she didn't trust Jerome. He was more aware and sensitive than other counselors she'd worked with. But Patricia knew that she couldn't adequately explain her intuition about Kent Baxter. For the moment, it seemed too personal. He was much more than a new kid in school, or new to New York, an environment that had to be drastically different from Colorado Springs. All indicators were that he'd been primarily raised by his mother. Which made Patricia wonder why the abrupt move to New York to be with his father. And in the brief time she'd spent in the boy's company, she realized that he was not like the other Duncan students in some very significant ways.

But the thing that really made Patricia cautious was recalling the awful sounds of Kent Baxter crying as he sat in her car. She had no intention of subjecting that secret to Jerome who was prone to sarcastic observations. Patricia couldn't remember the last time she'd seen a Duncan student cry about anything.

"It was a fight." She shrugged indifferently. "But I'd never seen this boy Baxter before."

"Well, as long as you're so interested . . . in my latest attempts to finish the evaluation I was supposed to meet the elusive Morgan Baxter this Thursday. He called yesterday to ask if I could possibly come to *his* office. I said yes. Can you?"

Patricia nodded her head. "Sure. I'll go."

"Thanks, Patty. I owe you one."

"You owe me more than that, so don't think I'm going to forget. And don't call me Patty."

"What is it about the kid?" Jerome asked.

Again, Patricia hesitated. She'd thought about that, too. Thought about the way Kent's momentary loss of control had struck a cord of recognition. She didn't want to explain that either.

"I don't want him to fall between the cracks," she answered smoothly.

Chapter One

"I never want to be fifteen again," Patricia murmured as her eyes scanned the odd but very specific grouping of students who were enjoying an hour's worth of freedom. It was lunchtime at Duncan High School, and for the first time in more than a week, it wasn't raining. Everyone wanted to enjoy the last gasp of fall weather before winter set in.

"Personally, I'd rather have a paper cut," came back a drawling caustic reply. It made Patricia laugh. "High school was strange. I used to get into some weird stuff."

Patricia's gaze rested on her lunchtime companion. A smile formed slowly on her face, the color of coffee with too much milk in it, with her image of Jerome Daly at fifteen.

"You? I don't believe you were ever fifteen," she scoffed, teasing him. "Did

26

you ever smoke, Jerome?"

"Of course not. It's a nasty habit that will kill you."

"I thought so. You're so logical. You don't strike me as the kind of person to do something unhealthy or stupid, even when you were their age." She nodded in the general direction of the high school's freshmen and sophomore classes.

Jerome adjusted his glasses and grinned. "I had my moments," he muttered. "But I never had the kind of baggage the kids here have to deal with. I remember when girls had to wear skirts and dresses to school and cared about how they looked."

Patricia smiled. "They care. I don't think girls wear dresses at all anymore, but they do care how they look. We just don't like it."

"I remember when the biggest trash you could talk about someone was calling them stupid . . ."

"Uh-huh." Patricia shook her head. "Talking about someone's mother."

"Now that was nasty. How about getting on them 'cause they were a nerd."

Patricia glanced at him. "No. If you were an immigrant, black, or poor."

He nodded. "You're right. I forgot about that. It hasn't changed, has it?"

"Yo, Ms. G. You're looking fresh."

Patricia glanced around sharply at the giant male approaching. His face was covered with a growth of uneven blond facial hair. His hair was Marine length except for a straggling rat's tail. The jock had two silver loop earrings in each lobe, with a Star of David dangling from one of them.

"Are you looking for me again?" she said, grinning.

"I ain't in no trouble. I passed first quarter. Ask Mr. Daly."

"Barely . . ." Jerome reluctantly confirmed with a short nod of his head.

"Good. I'm glad to hear you're trying harder, Peter. I'm hoping not to see you in my office at all this semester. Stay out of trouble."

The boy dared to wink at her. "I might come by to see you anyway," he said audaciously, taking the next two steps in one leap as he headed into the building behind them.

Patricia shook her head and laughed.

"What are you so pleased about?"

"Peter Connors just made a pass at me."

"Well, he'll never be a Supreme Court judge, but he's not blind," Jerome said.

"I know he's lazy and precocious and not very motivated, but at least he comes more often than not to class. Pete's good at sports," Patricia offered. "He still has time to get serious and find himself. We still have time to work with him."

"He's also late more mornings than not, probably won't survive biology —"

"Is biology still required?" Patricia interrupted.

". . . and he started a food fight in the cafeteria last week. And you want me to take him seriously? And where are his parents? How come they're not motivating him?" he asked reasonably.

"Well, what do you suggest? More phone calls? More meetings? In the meantime we have to be there for them."

Jerome shook his head and grunted. "The thing is, nobody here trusts me to do things my way. The administration is so constipated, with its rules and regulations, I wonder who it is they really care about. The students or job security. Why can't we just . . . *do* things instead of theorizing about them?"

"I think you would have made a great revolutionary," Patricia teased him.

Jerome looked quickly at her, his smile ironic. "And you make a great cheerleader."

Patricia squirmed uneasily under the sly compliment. She put the remains of her lunch in her oversize tote and hugged it to her chest. "What's that supposed to mean?"

He shrugged, sensing her caution. "Take it easy. You know I think you're pretty special, but I haven't forgotten where we stand. It just means you're the perfect role model. You're in the groove. You connect. You know the pass words and the code to reading the kids. Let's face it. I'm just pond scum to most of them."

"Don't exaggerate," Patricia ordered. "I don't have any special dispensation just because I'm black, Jerome. That doesn't always cut it with the students. I'm still an adult who tries to tell them what to do. I know you think they razz you because you're white, but maybe it's because sometimes you try too hard. Try not to act like them," she advised.

"I couldn't. They're all weird. And I'd

look pretty damned silly with my hair in dread locks." Patricia laughed lightly.

The hollow clanging of the interior bell erupted in the air, ending the lunch hour. There was a collective groan, lots of foul complaints, but the students broke from their groups and made desultory progress toward the school building.

"Do you have anything this afternoon?" Jerome asked as he and Patricia found themselves engulfed in the oncoming wave of students.

"I have to go see the father of Kent Baxter. Why?"

"I need you to help me out. Can you see a transfer student for orientation?"

"I guess. Who is it?"

"Girl from Spain. Gabriella Villar, a freshman."

The five-minute warning bell rang.

"The information is in a folder on my desk somewhere . . ." Jerome said, heading toward the street and digging for car keys in his pocket.

"This appointment of yours better be important, Jerome. I hate it when we're not available for the kids."

"This *is* about the kids. I'll explain later . . ."

Patricia sighed, and was about to trail behind the last of the students into the school when she became distracted by sounds she couldn't immediately identify. There was loud music from someone's boom box, and students shouting. But something else was going on as well. She could sense tension and wondered what was wrong. Patricia slowed her steps and looked in the direction of the noise. She hurried toward the dozen or so students, milling about near the corner.

"Why are you all still out here? The bell rang already."

The students grew quiet but no one answered. Some of them began to walk away. The volume on the boom box was lowered. In the group Patricia spotted Kent Baxter. He was pulling on his jacket and picking up his knapsack. She glanced around, but couldn't really tell what might have been happening. Kamil was not among the students leaving the scene. Patricia turned back to Kent. He was walking away.

"Wait a minute," Patricia called out. He reluctantly stopped and turned to face her. Patricia walked up to him, trying to see if there were any signs of what might have been going on. "Were you fighting again?"

He shrugged, a convincingly puzzled expression spreading over his face. "I wasn't doing anything."

"What were you doing, then?"

He grew fidgety. "We were talking about . . . about one of the classes," he said.

Patricia watched Kent closely, but had to admit he seemed unfazed by her questioning of him. Still, her gaze narrowed speculatively. "I want to see you this afternoon in my office," she suddenly announced.

He looked aggrieved. "I didn't do anything."

"I didn't say you had," Patricia reminded him quietly. "But I'd still like to see you. Two o'clock. You can get a pass from the office on your way to class."

Kent made an impatient gesture, but turned and went into the building. Patricia followed behind, finally losing sight of him in the crowd.

Patricia took in the bobbing heads and faces of the student body of Duncan. She felt both hope and trepidation in knowing that these were the faces, and colors, of the future. When she'd started at the high school the students had been mostly white from middle to upper middle class families. Kids of working professionals. But in keeping with the changes in the city and community ethnic makeup, Duncan now more or less realistically reflected the population. Academically it was still considered a strong school. But it now also offered opportunities to those students, like Kamil Johnson and Eric Patton, who showed promise but needed discipline. She'd been hired to encourage that promise.

As she reached the sanctified corner of administrative and faculty offices Patricia found the corridor quiet and all doors tightly shut. Except for the counseling office, which she insisted remain open at all times during school hours. The office didn't allow for much privacy, so she and Jerome never scheduled appointments at the same time.

Patricia retrieved the manila folder from Jerome's desk, bearing the name of Gabriella Villar on the tab. She took it to her own desk, removed her coat, and, sitting down, began leafing through the information. It was a straightforward orientation of a new student, and took only a moment or so to read.

The fourteen-year-old was the daughter of an economics scholar from Spain, in the U.S. to work as a consultant with two corporations in the city. The girl had already attended schools in England and Tokyo.

"Is anyone here?"

"Yes, Mrs. Forrest," Patricia said vaguely as she finished reading and closed the folder. She stood up as the middle-aged woman came in escorting a young girl.

"Good morning, Pat," the older woman drawled.

It was a familiarity that bordered on the disrespectful and had always been a minor irritation to Patricia. "Morning, Mrs. Forrest," she nonetheless returned politely.

In the seven years Patricia had worked at Duncan, Mrs. Gertrude Forrest had never addressed her equally as a professional, and had always grudgingly accepted her as part of the school administration. Patricia knew that Mrs. Forrest had been in the first wave of black employees to be hired at Duncan. She had begun as a classroom teacher, but had quickly learned the rules of advancing upward. Through district and political connections she had boosted her position to Dean of Students at Duncan. Patricia was just irritated that her colleague treated the position as a right rather than a privilege, forgetting that her role was to serve the students, not herself.

"When are you going to cut off all that hair?" Mrs. Forrest asked as she adjusted her half-frame glasses.

"I did," Patricia quipped smoothly. "This is what's left."

"You need to do something with it," the woman said quietly.

Patricia ignored the comment. Her wavy red hair had been her nemesis, even as a child, and a ready target for ridicule and speculation. Mrs. Forrest was an attractive woman, in a matronly sort of way, and had always reminded Patricia of those proper church ladies she met at services, when she went with her grandmother. Patricia suspected that Gertrude Forrest's attitude toward her wasn't much different from a lot of other black people she'd encountered over the years who somehow believed she'd gotten to where she was through her light skin and *good* hair.

Mrs. Forrest had even once been presumptuous enough to say to her, "You can get anything you want, Patricia. Just look at you . . ."

Patricia transferred her attention to the young girl standing silently behind Mrs. Forrest. She didn't seem to be paying any attention to the adults' exchange. "Why don't we just sit out here?" she said, pulling several chairs together. "It's less crowded than my office."

"This is Gabriella Villar," Mrs. Forrest introduced. "I don't think she speaks much English. She hasn't said a word all morning."

Duncan was not a bilingual school, and Patricia suspected that she wasn't really needed at all to interpret for the dean. She studied the girl more carefully but didn't ask Gertrude why she'd made no attempt to speak with the young student.

When they were all seated, Mrs. Forrest turned to Patricia and peered over the top of her glasses.

"I really don't like the idea of students starting in the middle of the semester."

"Her file says she's an overseas transfer. That's a little different, don't you think?" Patricia asked easily.

Mrs. Forrest maintained her poise and reorganized the papers she held. "There was a lovely little girl in September from Haiti whose parents tried to get her into Duncan. Mr. Boward wouldn't let her enroll. Said she'd have to go to the school up in Flatbush. He's so obvious, if you know what I mean."

Patricia smiled pleasantly. "I know it's predominantly black, but it's every bit as good as Duncan, isn't it? Isn't that the school you came from?"

Mrs. Forrest pretended not to have heard. "Would you mind acting as translator until I get these forms filled out?"

Patricia looked at the young girl. She was very pretty. She had an exotic aloofness and carriage that clearly stated she wasn't an American teen. Her hair was dark and cut short, unlike the girls at Duncan who still actively cultivated long permed hair, or who wore braids and extensions. Her eyes were a soft hazel color and slightly slanted, giving the girl a feline look to her delicate facial features.

"I have to warn you," Patricia began, "my Spanish is pretty rusty." She held out her hand to the young girl. *"Hola. Yo me llamo Patricia Gilbert."*

The girl took the proffered hand, showing mild surprise at Patricia's use of the language. *"Hola,"* Gabriella said in a soft voice.

"Bienvenida a la escuela."

"Grácias . . ."

Mrs. Forrest nodded in approval. "Good . . . this shouldn't take long."

But all through the interview Patricia noticed that the girl was quiet and uninterested in the process. It was only near the end of the hour, when she thanked Gabriella for an opportunity to practice her Spanish, that Patricia won a half smile and a blush from the girl.

Ten minutes after the administrator left Patricia's office with Gabriella, Kent Baxter walked quietly in. Patricia bent her head around the partition of her office and smiled at him. She could see he was indecisive about being there at all. He made a half turn out the door.

"Hi. You made it," Patricia said. "Come on in."

When Kent appeared in the doorway of her small space, he looked around with disinterest. Patricia pretended busyness by stacking books and papers as she studied him. She suddenly realized that he'd cut his hair from when she'd first met him. It was layered very close to his scalp. Peter Connors and some of the other boys cut their hair in imitation of whoever the current reigning rock group was. Patricia had the distinct feeling that Kent Baxter's severe cut had been an act of insurrection. She wondered . . . against what?

His clothing was neat and everything fit. No jeans that were too long in the legs or seat, that sat on his hips. No sweater two sizes too large so that hands retracted inside the cuffs. No fancy sneakers with gimmicks that were left untied with the tongue hanging out. Kent Baxter didn't copy his peers. And he was handsome, which was bound to draw attention and create problems for him.

"Sit down," Patricia coaxed. He obeyed, eyeing her suspiciously and boldly for a long moment. "Is something wrong?" she asked.

He quickly averted his gaze. "You don't look like a guidance counselor."

She grinned wryly. "I've been told I look like a lot of things, so I don't think I'm going to ask if that's a compliment or not. I've been reviewing your record since the start of school in September. So far it hasn't been great. You're late for classes, or you cut. You don't participate in discussions, forget homework assignments, and" — she glanced briefly at him — "get into fights . . ."

He slid down in the chair, just enough to demonstrate a lack of interest. "My grades are okay. I'm not failing."

Patricia raised her brows. "It's early yet, but you're getting close. You started high school in Colorado an honor student. What happened?"

He shrugged.

"I'd still like to know about the cuts and lateness."

Kent's knee began to bounce in nervous tension, as he pressed the ball of his booted right foot rapidly on the floor. "Sometimes I miss the bus."

"You could get up a little earlier," Patricia suggested, but she already suspected that oversleeping wasn't the real problem. "What about the cuts?"

"I got sick one day. I had to go home."

"That doesn't explain the other" — Patricia looked quickly at a page — "eleven cuts. That's a lot in just two months of school."

41

"I guess," he responded vaguely.

"We can always change your home-room, give you a different schedule."

"I don't care. It doesn't matter to me."

"Of course it does. It's going to be a very long school year if you don't like your program."

"It's okay," he insisted, somewhat impatiently.

Patricia turned a page in the folder. The next was blank. "Are you happy here?"

Kent looked confused. "What difference does it make? I probably don't even belong here."

"Really? Where do you belong?" she asked, surprised by his answer.

"I don't know. Nowhere."

"Maybe you just miss Colorado."

"New York is okay."

Patricia stared at the boy for a moment, guessing that he wasn't being evasive; he simply had no real answers. "Well, when you make some friends, it'll be easier. Especially if you like sports. Where do you go during lunch? After school?"

"No place. Home."

"Do you have a favorite sport?"

"Football."

"We have a team here at Duncan."

Kent suddenly chortled. "Yeah, I know. I'm on the team and I've seen them practice."

Patricia was alert. "You don't think they're very good, eh?"

He lifted a shoulder, seemingly bored. "I was on a better team last year, only coach hasn't played me yet. Connors is okay, but he's just big. The team just expects him to take the other players out. Patton doesn't think about what he's doing out there all the time. He shows off 'cause he's fast."

"Ummmm," Patricia observed. "Why has the coach benched you so far?" Kent got a stubborn set to his chin and stared silently past her. Patricia nodded knowingly. "For fighting, right?"

Kent gave her a furtive glance but remained quiet. Suddenly there was a growling sound and she realized it was noise from Kent's stomach. She reached for her tote bag, on the floor next to her desk, and pulled out a Ziploc bag of raisins and nuts, and an apple. Patricia handed them to Kent.

"It sounds like you didn't eat lunch."

He shook his head, declining the offer.

"Go on. You can't go through the rest

43

of the day with the urry-ups."

Kent reluctantly grinned and took the food. He put the bag into his pocket, but bit into the apple.

Patricia was alert again to the excuse even though it was legitimate. "Wouldn't your father like to see you play?"

"I don't know."

"Have you asked him?"

"No."

"Why not?"

Patricia could see the boy's growing unease with each new question. She was somehow probing too deeply. But she didn't believe that Kent Baxter was a youngster who was prone to trouble.

"Want to tell me what's going on with you and Kamil?"

"Nothing," he said shortly. He stared at the half-eaten fruit.

She kept her attention on Kent's face, watching for other nuances of response. "He said some pretty raw things to you the other morning. He drew blood. Didn't that make you mad?"

"He was just snapping."

She pursed her mouth at that. She really hadn't expected that Kent would give Kamil up. The kids had a strange code of honor in that regard. They settled their own scores and didn't squeal on each other. The black students were usually harder to penetrate because they were mistrusting of anyone new in their midst, and they pretty much stuck together as a group. They had different rules to live by that had strict parameters. But the way many of them seemed to have targeted Kent suggested something deeper and more worrisome that Patricia detected.

"You know, I don't think your father would be too happy about that fight. Or the one that almost happened at lunchtime."

Kent finished the apple and then looked straight at her, a challenge in his dark eyes. He threw the core of the apple into the wastebasket, and it made a rattling thump in the empty bottom. "You going to tell him?"

"If I have to. If I think it's important. My decision would be a lot easier if I knew it wouldn't happen anymore." She sat back in her chair and frowned slightly at the boy. "Why did you leave school in Colorado?"

Kent's knee was still bouncing. "I just didn't like it anymore."

"Was your mother upset that you wanted to come and live with your father?"

He grew uneasy, restless in the chair. "I guess so."

"But I bet your dad's happy."

Whatever she'd said suddenly seemed to make the boy uncomfortable. He got up abruptly.

"Am I going to get suspended or something?"

Patricia pushed her glasses up her nose. "Why would you think that?"

"You told me you wanted to see me. I thought I was in trouble."

"No suspension. I'll give you the benefit of the doubt and assume you'll try to do better in class."

Kent looked confused. "Is that it?"

She laughed lightly. "Why? Were you expecting to be flogged?" Patricia stood up. "I think you're still settling in here at Duncan. Think about joining some other groups. There are lots of special interest clubs that meet after school. You don't have to feel left out.

"We'll talk again in a week or so, see how you're making out, okay? And I'd really like you to try to be on time for school the rest of the month."

The request brought Kent up short as Patricia walked him to the door of the office.

"But that's only until the end of next week."

"Right," she said, nodding.

Kent thought about that, considered the degree of severity of the request, and realized he was getting off pretty easy. He relaxed momentarily. "Right," he repeated, walking out of the office.

Patricia smiled to herself as she watched him go. It would be great if all Kent Baxter needed was just to make a few friends, and try to do better in class. But whatever his problem was it had little to do with Duncan and even less to do with being new to New York. Patricia sighed and turned back to her office. She fully expected the meeting with the father to be equally as interesting as the one with the son.

Chapter Two

Patricia hated driving in downtown Manhattan.

And yet, downtown was vibrant and towering, even if it had little charm. She'd never been able to master the narrow streets in the financial district bordering the World Trade Center. She invariably got lost in the one-way streets that were never going in the direction she needed. Factored with the slow commuter exodus toward the bridges and tunnels, and trying to park her car, Patricia was a half hour late for the appointment with Morgan Baxter. And it had begun to rain.

His company, Ventura, Inc., was in one of the new buildings off Battery Park City, diagonally across from the World Trade Center complex. The elegance of the setting, with all the smartly dressed young men and women, was enough to set Patricia's teeth on edge.

She didn't think she was going to like Morgan Baxter, but she also hoped that he wasn't going to fulfill her perception of him as a CEO type who'd spent more time building an empire than raising a son.

Patricia had worked with enough kids to know that when there was a problem with an adolescent, there was usually something wrong at home. So, when Patricia took the elevator to the thirty-fifth floor and got off, she was already on the offensive.

The reception area of Ventura was unpretentious and soberly quiet. Patricia swung through the door a little too forcefully, drawing attention to herself. She was already nervous with anticipation.

"Can I help you?" a black male receptionist asked.

"I'm here to see Mr. Baxter."

The receptionist raised a brow in a superior manner and gave Patricia a quick once-over, as if she were in the wrong place. "You mean . . . *Mr.* Baxter? The president?"

Patricia smiled thinly, peering at the man through her glasses. Her impatience began to show. "Is there more than one Mr. Baxter?"

"Your name, please?"

"Patricia Gilbert."

"Just a moment . . ."

He dialed through to the office and announced that Mr. Baxter had someone waiting to see him. He then indicated a corner of black leather chairs and the ubiquitous glass coffee table with copies of *Fortune* and *Business Week* magazines on top.

"Mr. Baxter's secretary will be right out to meet you," the receptionist said, dismissing her.

Patricia nodded but elected to remain standing and glanced around. She sensed an efficient hum to the office. There was no one loitering about, and everyone passing along the corridors seemed to have a purpose and destination. She was suddenly curious about what kind of business Morgan Baxter was in. He was certainly among a short list of black men in New York who had founded businesses successful enough to command such a well-appointed office. Morgan Baxter had obviously done well for himself.

"Miss Gilbert?"

Patricia turned at the pleasant but

formal announcement of her name. There was an efficient-looking, middle-aged woman waiting alertly. Her dark brown skin was smooth and she wore only lipstick. Her short crisp hairstyle was beautifully shot through with gray. She had a presence that reminded Patricia of her favorite fourth-grade teacher, Mrs. Hicks, who had been a much needed surrogate mother. She looked like the kind of woman who would welcome children climbing into her lap.

"Yes." Patricia stepped forward as the other woman eyed her with interest.

The woman held out her hand. "I'm Constance Anderson, Mr. Baxter's assistant."

"I had an appointment to see Mr. Baxter. I'm afraid I'm very late."

"Mr. Baxter was prepared to see you" — she glanced at the wall clock — "forty-five minutes ago. I know you called to say you were going to be late, but I'm afraid he's gotten very busy in the meantime."

"But he does understand why I was coming."

"Of course."

"This will only take a few minutes,"

Patricia stated calmly. "Can you please just tell him I'm here?"

"He knows you're here," Mrs. Anderson said. "Come with me. Mr. Baxter will see you when he can."

Patricia followed through a short maze of corridors until they reached a clearing before an impressive set of closed oak doors; another reception area with Mrs. Anderson's desk, and corridors of more offices.

"Do you have any idea how long I'll have to wait?" Patricia asked.

The assistant raised her brows. "None."

An intercom interrupted them and Mrs. Anderson answered. Indicating a chair for Patricia to sit in, she excused herself and walked to the oak doors. It was opened just long enough and wide enough for papers to exchange hands, a word or two spoken, and the doors closed.

Patricia could feel her patience dissolving into a low, steady burn. She was disliking Morgan Baxter more and more, and she hadn't even met him yet. She hadn't come to discuss a contract, after all, but his *son*. With a sigh of resignation, Patricia walked to the area of comfortable chairs, where she'd been relegated, and sat. A half hour later she was still there. Impatience won out over prudence and she again approached the desk.

"Look, it's getting very late and I . . ."

"Perhaps you can tell me what the problem is."

Patricia's mouth tightened in annoyance. "I insist on speaking with Mr. Baxter personally," she said quietly. "It's important and I don't understand why you can't manage a few minutes for me to see him."

The secretary glared at her and the cool remoteness of her demeanor turned frosty. "Young lady, I've worked for Mr. Baxter for more than ten years and I know best how to manage his time."

"I could care less about his time. I'm concerned about his son. Even Mr. Baxter would have to agree that his son's welfare is his first priority. Or it should be."

Mrs. Anderson stood up. She was nowhere near as tall as Patricia, but her authority was felt. "You will have to wait."

Patricia opened her mouth to protest

but the intercom sounded again. This time when Mrs. Anderson left her desk, she walked the length of a short corridor and into another office. Patricia turned her attention back to the closed oak doors. She didn't hesitate as she stepped around the edge of the desk and headed to the executive office. She tapped on the door. From within came a brusque "Yes?" Patricia opened the door slowly and walked in.

A man's back was to her. He was in shirtsleeves and was bent forward over the papers, now spread out over a conference table. There was an arrangement of easy chairs, and a sofa to her right, placed in front of a window through which a dreary Hudson River spread out to the shoreline of New Jersey. Patricia took a step forward.

"Mr. Baxter? I'm from Duncan High School. I wanted to talk to you about Kent . . ."

The middle-aged man stood up and turned quickly around, surprise and bewilderment furrowing his brow. He was gray, balding, and paunchy.

"What the hell is going on?" came an angry voice, so sharp and deep that Patricia visibly jumped as she turned to face a trio of men she hadn't noticed before. They were standing around a light table upon which was scattered color transparencies.

She had no idea which of the men had spoken, but they all were looking at her with disapproval. Patricia pushed her glasses up her nose as the youngest man came forward. It wasn't until this instant that Patricia realized she hadn't considered what Kent's father would look like. It hardly seemed relevant, after all. But the moment her startled gaze settled on the man coming slowly toward her, she knew that he was Morgan Baxter. There was too much of a resemblance between father and son, except that Kent's coloring was much lighter than that of his father.

He kept coming toward her, his dark appraising gaze commanding Patricia's attention. There was a controlled patience in his eyes that was intimidating. It made Patricia sense that this man was not one to be indifferent about anything. His glance swept her from head to toe and seemed, to Patricia, to hold a brief but hard censure. She watched as Morgan Baxter's eyes veiled as he stared at her face. She took his suspicion personally.

Morgan Baxter had a sophisticated air: chiseled, precise, and masculine. Sardonic eyebrows hinted at a trace of humor. Yet his mouth and chin were strongly sculptured, the former with an ironic tilt at the corner — hiding a smile, perhaps — the latter with a shallow cleft. All in all, it was clear that the elder Baxter had passed along quite a lot physically to his son.

He stopped less than two feet away from Patricia. His eyes narrowed as he quickly assessed her, looking her over so deliberately that she felt furious with him. His attention came back to her face and silently studied it . . . and her hair. A brow arched.

Patricia had never cowered before anything or anyone in her life. But she was tempted to touch her hair, to fool with it and try to set it right. She knew the humidity had played havoc with it. She knew that it was, unfortunately, all over the place. Still, she met his challenging gaze straight on.

"I'm in the middle of an important meeting."

"Yes, I'm sorry to interrupt. I came about Kent."

"I hope you're not one of his class-mates," he said dryly.

Patricia clamped her teeth tightly, knowing that the statement had been meant as a put-down. "I'm a guidance counselor, Mr. Baxter. My name is Patricia Gilbert, here in place of Jerome Daly. I called."

Morgan turned to the men in the room. "Gentlemen, I apologize. I'll only be a moment."

The three men all nodded and discreetly moved to another corner of the office to converse among themselves.

"I know I'm late and it's my fault, but . . ." Patricia launched into a whispered speech.

"Is my son all right? Is he hurt?" Baxter cut in.

"No, of course not," Patricia assured him, taken off guard by the question.

"Is he in trouble?"

"Well . . . not exactly."

"Then this conversation can wait."

Patricia narrowed her gaze at him. "I'm sorry, but it can't."

"I know that Kent's having problems adjusting to a new school. I expected that. I got the letter to attend a parents' night. I'm sorry, I had to be in San

Francisco at the time."

"That only explains the first meeting you missed," she said.

"So you decided to take matters into your own hands? Didn't you believe that something important might have actually come up to make me cancel at your office?"

"You did reschedule a meeting for this afternoon. I'm here to accommodate *you*," Patricia said defensively. She was beginning to feel anger at his sarcasm, as well as an underlying resentment that Morgan Baxter's presence had distracted her. He wasn't anything like what she had expected.

"Then you might have waited until I was finished," he said, nodding his head in the direction of the other people in the room.

"I'm really sorry I just barged in," she said stiffly.

He pursed his mouth. "Are you?"

She shrugged. "Well, maybe I'm not, really. I thought I had a good reason. It wasn't Mrs. Anderson's fault . . ."

"I would never assume it was."

Morgan suddenly took hold of Patricia's arm and gently propelled her out of his office. She didn't resist, although she was surprised by the abrupt action.

Mrs. Anderson was standing by her desk, waiting. At the sight of the two of them she retook her seat at the PC and instantly became busy.

"I appreciate your concern about Kent. I realize you came with good intentions, but this could have been handled differently." Morgan spoke low, just for Patricia's hearing.

Her smile was tight and unforgiving. "You're right. You could have kept the appointments made for you, and *this* could have been avoided."

She wasn't about to let him know she was feeling somewhat chastised. Yet, she felt mesmerized by his piercing gaze.

"It's my job to help the students feel like part of the school," she said firmly. "And to help with problems that come up about classes and teachers and . . . and things. I thought talking to Kent's parents — his father — would help me to know and understand him better. It's you who hasn't exactly cooperated, Mr. Baxter. There are some problems. Small ones right now."

Morgan's jaw tensed. "I agree we should talk. But not now. Can we try and make it next week? Mrs. Anderson?" He turned to the secretary. "Do I have an opening?"

She quickly flipped through the calendar, pencil poised. "How is Friday, at two-thirty?"

"That's fine." Patricia nodded.

"Your office or mine?" Morgan asked.

To Patricia the question seemed surprisingly intimate, and she blinked at him. Her glasses slipped a notch down her nose. "Mine," she quickly responded.

"I'll see you there."

She'd been dismissed and she had no choice but to leave.

"I appreciate your coming," Morgan Baxter tacked on as she turned to the exit.

"You don't mean that," Patricia challenged, facing him again.

"Then you'd be wrong. But you could use a lesson in protocol. You can't control my office the way you can one of your classrooms. Or your students."

Patricia's cheeks warmed with embarrassment. "I said I was sorry. If I hadn't been so late . . ."

"That's not professional, either."

He was unrelenting. Patricia had a

feeling this was a skirmish she wasn't going to win, but she was determined to have the last word. "Your time isn't more valuable than mine, Mr. Baxter. I was with a student. Quite frankly, they are *my* priority."

He tilted his head thoughtfully. "I appreciate that. But you should be careful not to start behaving like them as well."

Patricia's mouth dropped open. She stood speechless. Once again, his gaze swept over her, coming to rest on her hair. She watched as a corner of Morgan's mouth lifted, but she didn't know into what. A smile? A sneer?

"Nice meeting you," he murmured dryly and walked brusquely past his secretary.

"Likewise, I'm sure . . ." Patricia murmured as he reentered the office behind the oak doors and closed them.

Patricia looked at the secretary whose upright posture and punching of her keyboard bespoke righteous vindication. Patricia realized now that she'd handled the situation all wrong. She wanted input and consensus from Morgan Baxter on what was right for his son. And she might need this woman as an ally, not an enemy. Slowly she

61

walked back to the secretary's desk and cleared her throat. The keyboard went silent.

"Is there anything else?" Mrs. Anderson asked in an impervious tone.

Patricia took a deep breath. "Yes. I'm very sorry if I was out of line. Of course Mr. Baxter relies on your judgment and good sense. I shouldn't have tried to overstep that."

The secretary's expression did not immediately change. If Patricia was looking for instant forgiveness she was not about to receive it. She knew she'd probably done irreparable damage in just the few minutes with Kent's father as well. She turned to leave.

"And I think . . ." came the calm voice behind Patricia, "Mr. Baxter is going to rely on your judgment and good sense where his son is concerned."

Patricia turned back to Mrs. Anderson, startled.

"Truce?" Mrs. Anderson asked briskly.

Patricia nodded. "Truce. Thank you. Next time I won't be so presumptuous."

Mrs. Anderson almost smiled. "I can tell you're genuinely concerned. Next time I'll understand."

The moment Patricia was outside the

office and waiting for the elevator, however, her thoughts were less on her poor handling of the encounter than they were on Morgan Baxter's reaction to her. Or, more precisely, what she imagined his reaction to be.

Patricia pensively boarded the elevator. On the slow descent she caught a blurry glimpse of her reflection in the brass moldings. She saw someone with a pale thin face, large glasses, and a *lot* of red hair. That's what Morgan Baxter saw. That he might have judged her based on appearance began to bother her, as it always did. Patricia sighed in annoyance, wondering if it was going to start all over again. The need to set him straight. The need to prove herself.

As the elevator arrived on the ground floor, Patricia took a deep breath of determination. She thought that perhaps the best thing to do, under the circumstances, was to give Kent's father the benefit of the doubt until he proved *her* wrong. But experience and painful memories told Patricia that the chances were slim and none that she was.

The meeting had been over for twenty

minutes, and all the clients were gone. They had invited Morgan to join them for drinks and dinner, but he had declined, thinking of the other obligations that awaited him that were not business related. But he hadn't left his office yet to see to those either. Instead, Morgan sat on the sofa in the conference room, considering the encounter earlier with Patricia Gilbert. The one thing that kept playing in his mind was that she had been concerned enough about his son to force a meeting, a confrontation actually, in order to gain his attention. It had worked perfectly. He'd honestly been meaning to get over to the school. Sooner or later. He hadn't thought there was any urgency beyond the usual school formality of parents' night. Morgan now suspected it wasn't quite that simple.

He tried to resolutely keep his mind from conjuring up all the ways in which Kent might be having trouble in school. Morgan's gut tightened briefly in apprehension. He knew the list was endless.

In irritation he got up abruptly from the sofa and restlessly paced his office. He was reluctant to admit that when his son left for school each morning he ceased to think about him for most of the day. Kent was in one of Brooklyn's better public schools, and Morgan assumed that the environment was structured, and safe. But he considered the counselor's urgency as he finally stopped in the middle of his office. Her presence had done nothing to allay his fears that he might not be going about this business of parenting in the right way.

Then, in an absent way, Morgan visualized Patricia Gilbert again with her wild improbable hair, the surprising gray eyes. His immediate reaction to her had made him uncomfortable because he found her . . . ambiguous. And he wasn't sure he trusted her. But that was his fault. He'd let her looks get in the way at first, but her attitude had set him straight. That's what had finally given her away. Set her identity. Her lack of fear and reverence, her show of spirit. Nonetheless, almost everything about Patricia Gilbert made him edgy.

Still pensive, Morgan finally gathered the notes and other reports relating to the meeting and walked to his secretary's desk. Constance Anderson turned from her PC when she heard

Morgan approaching. She was as alert and efficient at six in the evening as she had been at eight that morning.

"Yes?"

He gave the papers to Mrs. Anderson and stood with his hands pushed in the pockets of his trousers.

"I'd like copies of these notes sent to each of the participants of today's meeting."

"Certainly," Mrs. Anderson said, accepting the stack.

"And can you pull the minutes from the last meeting with Sager?"

Mrs. Anderson quickly lifted a stack of folders and found the one she needed. She passed it to Morgan.

"Did Tanner or anyone else from Sager management call?"

"Mr. Tanner did call yesterday but he wanted to speak with Mr. Sullivan."

"Did he?" Morgan asked with mild curiosity. "Did you mention that *I* want to talk to him?"

"He said he'd get back to you, but he still wanted David. He said it had to do with their meeting two weeks ago."

Morgan thoughtfully slapped the folder against his leg. "David said it was a so-so meeting," he murmured.

"Mr. Sullivan is in Washington. Shall I try to get a message to him?"

"No, don't bother. This will hold."

But she kept her attention on Morgan's face, aware of his distraction. "Is there anything else I can do?" she asked carefully.

Morgan pursed his lips and grinned at her ruefully. He relaxed his shoulders. "My feelings must be showing. You always ask that when I look like I don't know what I'm doing."

Her smile was both understanding and patient. "Well, that's certainly rare, and I only ask after five o'clock. I know it's none of my business . . ."

Morgan chuckled softly. "Not that that's ever stopped you. I'm not complaining, Connie. I appreciate your concern."

"I can see you're worried and confused about your son."

He tugged on an earlobe. "You've been with me too long. You're starting to read my mind."

"Oh, it's not that. I know that suddenly having your son with you, after all these years, is hard to adjust to. But I've raised children. I know they can be difficult."

Morgan sighed. "I could use some advice right about now."

"I'm not exactly an expert. I made mistakes, had plenty of sleepless nights, and had enough surprises pulled to curl the hair on my head . . ." Morgan chuckled. "Somehow it works out. Be patient, but firm. Don't be afraid to discipline, but don't put a stranglehold on your son." She gave Morgan a sage, sharp glance. "And keep that appointment with the counselor next time."

"Yeah, I think I'd better."

"I think she really cares. She storms her way in here and embarrasses herself trying to get your attention. I was impressed. Unusual woman . . ."

"Ummmm," Morgan uttered vaguely.

"Hi, everybody," a husky but feminine voice said.

Morgan and Connie turned their attention to the woman entering the reception area.

She was stylishly dressed for business and her entire appearance stated confidence, good taste, and a penchant for expensive things. Her sienna complexion was expertly made up to diminish the squareness of her face, the slightly

68

too full mouth, the widow's peak. But the finished product invariably drew attention and admiration.

She gave Connie a charming but distant smile.

"Good evening, Ms. McGraw," Connie murmured, turning to her desk.

Then the woman turned to Morgan giving him her complete attention. Her gaze become softly direct and the smile more personal as she arched a brow and waited.

"Hi, Bev," Morgan murmured, pleased to see her.

Morgan, however, did not find it appropriate to show open displays of affection for his lover in front of his secretary. He knew that Beverly expected it, as if it would confirm her place in his life. He merely placed his hand on her arm and squeezed gently in acknowledgment without going over the edge into the too familiar. It would have to do, for now.

Morgan had never thought of Beverly McGraw as a classic beauty but she'd made the most of her natural gifts. She was stunning in a practiced and carefully planned sort of way. She worked at it. And her background was similar to his own. Lower middle-class upbringing except that Beverly had been raised in Chicago in one of the nation's housing projects that had been little more than residential warehouses. And like him, Beverly had found the drive and ambition to pull herself out of a situation in which she could have been trapped to become a very good negotiating attorney. She loved to argue, and she loved to win.

"Did I interrupt something important, or is this five o'clock chitchat?"

Connie smiled and began preparing to leave for the night. "Discussing children and the fear of failure," she murmured with humor. "What a beautiful pair of earrings," she said, glancing briefly at Beverly.

"Thank you, Connie. I treated myself to a trip to Tiffany's after that god-awful case with American Express. What do you think?" she asked, directing the question to Morgan.

"Very nice," he said with a nod, turning away to his office. "Let me get my coat and close my office. I'll be right with you."

Beverly watched him disappear, a poutish smile rounding her full lips.

She turned to the secretary. "So, what's this about children?"

Connie chuckled, putting on the jacket that matched her dress, and reached for her handbag under the desk. "Just how they can drive you crazy. You can't let down your guard for a minute. And the worst begins when they become teenagers." Connie shook her head in wry humor.

Beverly had already turned away, wandering to the leather chairs. "I wouldn't know about any of that," she murmured. "What's new and exciting with Ventura these days?" She sat gracefully and crossed her legs.

"As you know, Sager is at the top of the agenda."

"Yes, Morgan did mention something about that company but he's been pretty closemouthed about the details. Secret deal?" she asked smoothly.

Connie's smile was still friendly, but now guarded. "The negotiations are complicated."

Beverly raised her brows expecting more, but Connie was silent. Beverly examined her manicured hands. "Is David involved?"

"Oh, yes. Mr. Baxter has given him a

71

lot of responsibility on this project."

"Is he in? Maybe I'll go back and say hello," Beverly said, although she made no move to get up.

"Mr. Sullivan's on the road this week."

Morgan stepped out of his office, suit jacket on and a soft leather attaché case in hand. "Good night, Connie."

"Good night. You two have a nice evening," she said.

Morgan extended a hand to Beverly and she stood up to precede him through the exit. Only when they reached the isolated area of the elevators did Morgan smile at her with any degree of intimacy.

"You look wonderful, as usual," he said quietly.

"I would have preferred if you said you were glad to see me."

"That, too."

They boarded the empty elevator and as soon as the doors slid shut Beverly sidled up to Morgan and planted an inviting kiss on his mouth. Morgan's lips responded naturally but briefly, ever conscious of his surroundings. The rest of his body had less control and he felt the start of arousal as Beverly's sensuality and appeal wafted from his brains to his glands. Her perfume was like an exotic aphrodisiac. He knew she was aware of her effect by the way she smiled into his eyes.

"I'm giving you a choice. We can keep the reservations for dinner, or we can go to my place."

Morgan felt his decision-making process slow to a crawl as his nostrils flared with her promise. "Why can't we do both," he reasoned, nonetheless.

Beverly shrugged as she lowered her gaze demurely. "I don't know about you, but I don't want to wait that long."

Her eagerness was contagious. Morgan let it sweep over him, blocking out the more practical considerations of his son. He knew he couldn't stay with Beverly for the night, as he might normally have done. He had to get home to Brooklyn at some point. He quickly grabbed her mouth with his in an intense show of desire. The elevator bell pinged and the doors slid open to the first floor.

"Let's take a rain check on that reservation."

When they reached Beverly's co-op on Central Park West, the anticipation had reached a fevered pitch between them.

Morgan was never sure how Beverly managed to do it. With his ex-wife, he was always conscious of being careful, of turning any hard-core lust into softer romance. With Beverly, they just got to it. She reminded Morgan of some of his first crude affairs as a teen when he didn't know from slow or foreplay.

They had a routine.

He would undress her first until Beverly's rich brown curvaceous body was stark naked. She was large-breasted, the chocolate aureole tips drawing his attention. She had a good body that was lean, but more muscled than soft. The body of a woman that had come from being a tomboy too long. Beverly was agile and comfortable with her physical self, and not afraid to enjoy or encourage the pleasure he got from her.

Morgan let Beverly rub her bare breasts against his chest. She pressed her pelvis and thighs against his hard erection. All the subtlety and coyness she used during the day vanished.

"Damn . . ." Morgan mouthed between his teeth. Her assertiveness always threw him off. Until he got back into the game . . . and gave as good as he got.

There was no tenderness, nor pretense. He'd never felt that they were making love so much as having unforgettable sex. He'd gotten used to reveling in the pure release that took the tension out of every part of his body. Which allowed Beverly to take him in deeply and hold herself to him with her shapely legs. She rode with him thrust for thrust and it only heightened Morgan's pleasure. It was so different from Melissa. And he had loved her . . .

Afterward Beverly grew soft and mewling. He lay atop her, his mind slowing, like a carousel at the end of the ride. She stroked his back with just the tips of her fingers, knowing full well that with almost no effort she could arouse him to readiness again. He rolled heavily to the mattress next to her.

"You enjoy that, don't you?" he murmured against her throat. He kissed her shoulder, and the skin was cool with a nongiving firmness.

"That I can turn you to jelly? Of course," she admitted with a throaty laugh. "I take no prisoners."

Morgan smiled in the dark. He found her analogy grating. Hard. Beverly's hand wandered down his torso to play boldly with his penis to bring it back to life. Morgan groaned. His body flexed . . . and suddenly stiffened. He grabbed Beverly's hand to keep it still.

"Don't."

"What?"

Morgan's sigh this time was different. "I can't. I'd better get up."

Beverly released him and watched Morgan swing his long legs from her bed. "Your son," she said flatly.

"Yes, my son. Dammit . . . I should have called him that I was going to be a bit late."

"He'll be okay," Beverly said. "He's a big boy."

"He's fifteen years old," Morgan said rhetorically as he suddenly remembered Patricia Gilbert's visit to his office that afternoon. "I don't even know if he's home, if he has homework. If he's had dinner . . ." He began dressing urgently.

"Morgan, we just got here."

"Come on, Bev," Morgan muttered. "Don't give me a hard time."

"I thought that's exactly what you wanted."

Morgan didn't respond. He stepped into his slacks and pulled them up. Beverly sighed and got out of bed, reaching for a black silk flowered robe.

"All right. You have to go. Any other black boy his age would deal with the fact that his divorced father dated women."

A frown drew Morgan's brows together. "Don't blame Kent. And it's not that simple."

"I'm not blaming him," she said carefully. "It's just that . . . it's very hard for you and me to be together any more like we used to."

"Well, it can't be like it used to. I have a different responsibility now. I'm still adjusting. So is Kent. You have to." Morgan stared at her. "Why not start by being friendly to him. Get to know him. Then we'll take it from there."

She grimaced and turned away. "We'll sec."

"Yeah, we'll see," he repeated dryly. Beverly followed Morgan to the door, watching as he picked up his personal things along the way. He opened the door and then faced her once more, his expression contrite and annoyed all at once.

"Sorry . . ."

"When do I see you again?"

"Maybe the end of the week."

"Let me know beforehand if you have to clear it with your son," she said, quietly closing the door on him.

Morgan tried to figure out if that was sarcasm or a straight remark from Beverly. The fact that he had to consider it at all put him in a bad mood. By the time Morgan reached her lobby the brief euphoria of their lovemaking had left him feeling empty.

Chapter Three

"How did the meeting go?" Patricia asked. Jerome was kneeling before the last drawer of a filing cabinet in their office.

"Not bad. I'm trying to arrange a field trip to Maimonides Hospital, to the neo-natal unit with some of the kids. I want them to see what a newborn baby looks like whose mother took drugs or drank too much alcohol."

Jerome stood up and turned around with papers in his hand. "What do you think about me getting Eric into a pro-gram for teen fathers? I happen to know that . . ." His wry smile faded. "What did you do to your hair?"

"You don't like it this way?" she asked.

"I hate to say it, but you look like Mrs. Lechter the chem teacher. Why the bun? Or I should ask, why the bird's nest? And why are you dressed all in black?"

Patricia was not insulted. "It's Halloween. Doesn't it make me look serious and smart? Mature?"

"You look demented. I like it when your hair is loose," Jerome said, and then added coyly, "On second thought, there is something mysterious and sexy about basic black. Maybe if you added a little accent, like a long string of pearls . . ."

"Shut up, Jerome," Patricia responded good-naturedly, remembering the way Morgan Baxter had looked at her a week earlier in his office. She was used to the observations about her hair, and almost everything else about her. She frowned as she unexpectedly remembered Theresa Handy in sixth grade accusing her of acting like she was white, because she had light skin, and Mrs. Monroe, her teacher, asking her where'd she'd gotten that red hair, as if it had been purchased somehow.

Immediately after meeting Morgan Baxter Patricia had wondered if he was doing the same thing. She could see the instant assessment in his eyes; the curiosity and puzzlement. If he couldn't figure it out, would he make it up?

Patricia also remembered that Morgan didn't so much make her uneasy as just defensive. His whole demeanor had annoyed her. How dare he find her amusing?

"God, I hope this doesn't mean you're going to start changing the way you dress."

"I'm just trying to look my age."

"I know women who would kill to have your looks and assets. Live with it," Jerome muttered unsympathetically, opening his file again. "Next you'll tell me it's a black thing."

"It is. It's about . . . hair."

"It's a hang-up."

"Thank you, counselor, for your insight," she said as Jerome kicked the file drawer shut and returned to his desk. "Are you thinking of leaving Duncan and setting up private practice?"

"Okay, okay. Sarcasm doesn't become you, you know" — Jerome glanced at her furtively and grimaced — "Look, Patty, I know what you've been through."

"No you don't."

"Okay, not *exactly*. But you've told me about some of the men you've been out with."

Patricia lifted a shoulder dismissively.

"What does my hair and dress have to do with men I've dated?" she asked, trying to keep her annoyance in check.

Jerome's gaze was direct, and understanding. "It would be a lot easier for you if you looked more . . . you know, black."

Patricia moved restlessly. "Jerome . . ."

"We're friends. Friends care about each other. I like you the way you are. So should anybody else."

Patricia deftly changed the subject. "What is this about Eric and a parenting program?"

Jerome adjusted his glasses and sat on the corner of his desk facing her. "Well, it's too late for preventive maintenance. If Mr. Boward had let me give out that stuff from Planned Parenthood and have a serious talk with the guys . . ."

Patricia sighed impatiently. "You know it will never happen. Don't forget our late departed former commissioner who got bounced right out of his job over the issue of sex education. We can't tell parents what to do about their kids and sex."

"We're educators. Why can't we educate about things that are, in my opinion, a bit more important than second-year French and advanced calculus?"

"Why can't you just do what you're supposed to do and stop looking for reasons to bring yourself to the attention of the front office? I consider it an accomplishment that Eric stays in school and acknowledges that he has a daughter."

"And I'd like to see to it that he graduates with only *one* kid, not two."

Patricia frowned. "Is there someone else he's involved with?"

"Not yet."

"I thought you might have been thinking of Kyra Whitacre. I've seen them together."

Jerome shook his head. "I wouldn't worry about it but I'll keep an eye on him."

"Well, as long as you're in the let's-do-something mode, do you think we can get Kent Baxter off the bench and into some of the football gaines?" she asked thoughtfully.

"That's up to Coach. You know he doesn't like it when some kid breaks the rules and is difficult. Baxter is lucky he wasn't kicked off the team for fighting. Why should he get any special favors now?'"

"This is a special case. Kent Baxter has played football. I bet he's good, and I think the team could use him in play."

"Hmmmm . . ." Jerome said absently.

"You owe me," Patricia reminded him.

He squinted at her through his glasses. "I know. But the coach doesn't owe me a thing. I'm telling you he's going to say no."

"According to my calculations, Jerome, I'm good for at least half a dozen favors from you."

"What do you want me to do?" he gave in with a shrug.

Patricia smiled sweetly. "Talk to Coach. Tell him it's your specific recommendation that Kent Baxter be allowed to play. There's only a month left to the season anyway. Still time for him to get into practice and make the last three games. Tell him what a therapeutic benefit it would be to the boy."

"He's not going to care about that."

"Well, then lie. Tell him Kent was outstanding at his other school."

"Enough," Jerome groaned in disgust. "Next you'll have the kid walking on water."

"Kent needs to make friends. He's

having a rough time with some of the students."

"Kamil Johnson," Jerome supplied. "You met with Kent's father. How did it go?"

Patricia chuckled nervously. "He practically threw me out of his office. I interrupted an important meeting."

Jerome chortled. "I bet he wears yellow suspenders."

"No one wears suspenders anymore and I don't think he's that superficial," she said, finding herself defending Morgan Baxter.

"Did he throw you out of his office before or after the information about his son?"

"Well . . . before."

"Hmmmm . . ." Jerome uttered again, rocking back in his chair as if to say "I told you so."

"But he did schedule another appointment for this afternoon. *And* he's coming here." Jerome looked skeptical. "Whose side are you on?" Patricia asked her colleague in annoyance. "You admit you think some of our students are in crisis but you dump on the parents as well."

Jerome looked unrepentant and answered in irritation. "I'm down on parents who haven't parented. There's more to raising a kid than having them and then sending them to school. Is he good-looking?" Jerome asked with sudden curiosity.

"Who?" Patricia blinked.

"Baxter."

"What kind of question is that?"

"Just asking. You sound a little nervous every time you mention him. Is he black?"

Patricia glared at him. "What is your problem this morning?"

"It's probably relevant. I overheard Sylvia say once that there wasn't exactly an overabundance of black men she could relate to out there."

"I'm not looking," Patricia said stiffly. The hall bell rang as another period ended, sparing Patricia the need to respond. "Lunchtime," she said quietly.

Jerome grabbed his knapsack and got up. "I've got a date for lunch." Patricia raised her brows. "I'm not going to tell you who it is, but I'll be back before the afternoon bell. Besides, you're sure to spot just a few students you want just a few words with, and I'll eat alone anyway."

"I'm sorry about yesterday. I'm a little concerned about Kyra Whitacre. She's a nice girl. Comes from a close family, but there are problems. The father left and when I talk with the mother I hear a lot of bitterness. She's tightened her reins on Kyra and that could be a mistake right now, when she's just starting to learn how to be independent and make decisions on her own."

"I know," Jerome conceded. "Just don't let these kids take advantage of you, Pat. Sometimes they have to work things out on their own."

Then the phone rang. Patricia and Jerome exchanged looks.

"I'll bet that's for you," he said and closed the door as he left the office.

Patricia hated when Jerome was right, but even as she answered the phone she knew Morgan Baxter was canceling his appointment. Actually, it was the efficient Mrs. Anderson making the call for him.

"He's very sorry to disappoint you, but he had to fly-out to Chicago late yesterday afternoon."

"How sorry?" Patricia asked.

"I beg your pardon?"

"How sorry is Mr. Baxter about canceling?"

"He's in the middle of very important negotiations. This couldn't be helped."

"When is he going to have time for his son?" Patricia pressed.

"Mr. Baxter understood that his son was not in any sort of trouble."

Patricia sighed. "Mrs. Anderson, I'm trying to see that it stays that way and Mr. Baxter is not cooperating."

"I don't think you want me to tell him that," Mrs. Anderson finally responded. "Mr. Baxter is concerned about his son but he understood that there was no emergency."

"No, of course not. I was probably being rude again. What you can tell Mr. Baxter is that he owes me."

"Can I ask, what?" Mrs. Anderson asked, astonished.

"A meeting, time to be determined later. And you can tell Mr. Baxter that I think he's a coward for not calling me himself."

Mrs. Anderson, surprisingly, laughed. "I'm not sure I'll tell him that, either. Good-bye." The line clicked silent.

Patricia grimaced. Had she gone too far? Probably.

She frequently found that communicating with parents could be more frustrating than working with their children.

Patricia sighed in frustration, disappointed in Morgan Baxter. She lifted a history text from the chair next to her desk and leafed through it idly. Kent Baxter had inadvertently left the book with her the day before, and had not yet returned for it. Patricia blinked now, drawing her attention from the book to focus on the small orange pumpkin placed next to her desk phone. She stroked it idly with a finger, wondering again who had left it for her. She'd found it that morning after returning from an administrative meeting. There had been no note or message, just the pumpkin nestled in a box of shredded paper and with a yellow bow tied around the stem. She'd forgotten to ask Jerome about it, and wasn't sure he would have admitted to it. It wasn't his style . . .

Patricia debated holding on to the book until Kent returned for it, but decided instead to use it as an excuse to seek him out. She was curious as to where she'd find Kent during the

lunchtime break and who he'd be with
. . . or if he'd be off alone.

She got her lunch and coat, intending
to eat outside the building again if it
had warmed up any since she'd arrived
that morning. Once outside she spotted
Kent sitting on a low retaining wall.
Nearby was Pete Connors, and Brit Harris, Eric Patton, Boomer, WeeGee, and
Tip Top. Connors was the only white
boy among the group, a wannabe who
had shown he was down enough to be
part of the school group, if not the real
neighborhood one. There were other
boys about, the ones Jerome referred
to as "rough cuts" because they were
the black and Latino teens who everyone else was afraid of.

Patricia had learned to recognize long
ago that it wasn't fear the kids wanted
to instill in people but respect. They just
didn't know how to do that. The black
males at Duncan had a swaggering gait,
a side-to-side movement with their
shoulders as they aggressively made a
space for themselves. It didn't allow for
them to be overlooked. It was deliberate, meant to intimidate other people . . . white people, out of their way.
The boys at Duncan kept their emotions

locked up tight, or cultivated not having any. Kent was not as good at it as they. Patricia recognized that Kent's posturing was protective, but for the boys at Duncan it was necessary to their survival. They didn't allow themselves weaknesses. They weren't introspective.

Patricia approached Kent and the other boys, quickly finding a reason to stop and talk.

"How's it going?" she said to no one in particular. The other boys made a glancing acknowledgment of her presence before returning to their own conversation. "I have a question about one of your classes, Kent. Can I have a quick word with you? You can come back to your friends in a minute."

He reluctantly got up, accompanying her some distance along the wall. Patricia sat but he remained standing.

She handed him the textbook. "You left it in my office."

Kent looked at it blankly, finally taking it. "Oh. Thanks."

"I see you got to classes on time this morning. And yesterday."

"My father dropped me off." He hesitated.

"Good. Have you told him about the

football team?"

"I forgot," Kent said indifferently.

Patricia watched him settle into the lie. Why would he be reluctant to talk about a school varsity team? Most of the Duncan parents pushed their kids to be competitive at sports. And much of the student socializing revolved around games, tournaments, and the heavy partying afterward. She merely nodded and opened her large bag. She rummaged inside the cluttered depths.

"Well, I hope you talk to him soon. I think you'd be great." She extracted from her bag a turkey sandwich and a banana. She unwrapped the sandwich and extended half to Kent. "Can we have lunch while we talk?"

Kent looked at the offering. "Look, you don't have to feed me."

Patricia kept her hand out. "Did you eat lunch?"

Kent grimaced impatiently and took his half of the sandwich. "What do you want to talk about?"

"About you. What do you want to get out of your time here at Duncan?"

He reacted with impatience. "Look, what's the big deal? I just wanted to be with my father. This school is no different than the one I came from."

Patricia quietly watched him. "Did you get into fights there, too?"

He stared at her. "I can take care of myself."

Patricia thoughtfully considered her sandwich. "You realize I'm going to have to speak with your father sooner or later. Either about your grades, your lateness . . . and why you're so un- happy."

"I don't care." He had almost finished his half of the sandwich.

She heard the despair in his voice and felt for his difficulty. "What? That your father might come to talk to me . . . or that he won't?" Predictably Kent said nothing. "Don't you want to be happy here?"

"Why does it matter? Lots of kids don't like school or their parents."

"Is that what your problem is? You don't like your parents?"

"I don't have a problem," he said ob- stinately. He suddenly tossed the rest of the sandwich away. "Look, I haven't done anything wrong. I wish you'd stop picking on me."

"I'm not picking on you. I'm just trying to . . ."

"I told you. I can take care of myself. I don't need you."

Eric Patton trooped past with the other boys. "Hey, Baxter. We're going to the field. You coming?"

Patricia watched Kent as he looked after the retreating classmates. He seemed both surprised and hesitant. "Friends?" she asked. He made an undecipherable sound. "You'd better go on."

He turned to follow the other boys.

"Kent . . ." He reluctantly looked over his shoulder at her. "It's my job to make sure you're okay at Duncan, and that you don't get . . . hurt. That doesn't mean I don't really care. I understand more than you think I do."

He looked at her for a second, as if trying to judge her sincerity. He seemed about to say something but changed his mind. Kent made another impatient sound and started slowly after his classmates.

In the middle of the afternoon Patricia went to check out the preparations for the Halloween party the student council had tried to organize in the gym. Just outside the gym she encountered Kyra Whitacre and Eric Patton. Standing too

94

close together and talking too earnestly.

Kyra spoke up first. "Hi, Miss G."

Eric Patton lounged against the wall and said nothing. He smiled easily at her. For Patricia, danger bells immediately sounded in her head. She knew Eric's reputation. She knew Kyra's vulnerability. She was barely fifteen years old and a freshman.

"Hi," Patricia responded. "Are you helping with the decorating of the gym for the party tonight?"

"No," Kyra answered somewhat petulantly. She looked at her companion.

"Party's gonna be lame," Eric predicted lazily.

"If you go, you can help get it on," Patricia suggested.

"Yeah . . . right." He chuckled skeptically.

"I want to see what's going on anyway. Don't you, Kyra?" The girl looked hesitant and glanced at Eric for guidance. "Come on, Eric . . ." Patricia said playfully to the boy. "Walk us over."

He pushed away from the wall and trailed behind her and Kyra. Patricia kept the conversation easy, although it was mostly just between her and the girl.

She kept glancing over her shoulder to Eric. Patricia could see from his faint smile that he knew what she was up to. But it didn't matter. As long as she kept Eric from what *he* was up to.

The trio walked through a short passageway where music and youthful voices could be heard coming from the gym beyond. Eric immediately deserted them and made his way across the floor to some of his friends who were standing around goofing on the setup.

"Kyra?" Patricia got the girl's attention as she stared off after Eric. "I'd like to know how your classes are going."

"Okay," Kyra answered with a lack of enthusiasm.

For the next hour, Patricia tried to keep Kyra engaged in conversation. But it was clear that the girl was not going to talk openly about anything that included Eric Patton.

"You made the cheerleader squad this year," Patricia said.

"My mom doesn't like it too much. She says she needs me at home to help out. Somebody's got to watch my little sister and brother 'cause she works late every day. The squad practice takes up a lot of time."

"It's only two afternoons a week."

"She just doesn't want me doing it," Kyra said with annoyance. "She doesn't want me to do anything that's fun."

"Well, maybe I can speak with your mother. Maybe there's a way of getting some assistance to help at home . . ."

"Don't do that," Kyra said quickly. "It's not so bad. It's just that sometimes I feel like she wants me to be unhappy like she is 'cause my father left us. I just want to be like everybody else in school."

"I understand," Patricia said to Kyra. "Maybe you and I can work something out. I don't want you to have to give up the squad. And I certainly don't want you to start doing worse in school." Kyra looked guilty. "You're not going to make it through freshman year unless you do better. A few of your teachers have already spoken to me. Your mother's not going to like that."

"I know."

"So why don't you come see me next week? We'll put our heads together and see what we can come up with. Okay?"

Kyra nodded. "Okay."

By four-thirty the work for the party was done. Patricia suggested that Kyra go on home if she hadn't changed her mind about the gym party, and then she hoped that the girl would listen to her. Patricia was stopped at the exit by a petite young girl who was in charge of the Halloween party arrangements.

"Miss Gilbert, could you stay for tonight?"

"You need a chaperone?"

The girl rolled her eyes. "Please don't use that word. You make it sound like we can't be trusted." Patricia merely grinned. "It's just that . . ." She looked over her shoulder to make sure there was no one around. "Mr. Daly was assigned to stay but we know he doesn't really want to."

"That's not true," Patricia countered as she turned to the door. "But if you want me to be here, I'll be happy to."

"Great," the student enthused and then wrinkled her nose. "Ah, Miss Gilbert . . . do you think maybe you could, you know, change your hair. You sort of look like . . ."

Patricia raised her brows behind the red-framed glasses. "I know what you're going to say. What if I tell you this is part of my costume?"

"You're wearing a costume? Oh, bet! This I gotta see."

* * *

It was after eleven when Patricia entered her apartment in Park Slope and gratefully closed the door on the world, the week, and the strains of rock and rap music that persisted in her head. The school Halloween party had been loud, surprisingly well attended, and fun. Now she had a terrible headache as payment for her sacrifice to the evening.

She kicked off her black low-heeled pumps, dropped her tote of school papers and books on the floor just inside the door, and walked into the living room to put her pumpkin on the mantelpiece. The uppermost thought in Patricia's mind just then was taking some aspirin and going to bed. But the phone started to ring.

Patricia knew that the one person she was most likely to get a call from was her grandmother. But they had a routine. Gilly called on Sunday mornings, and Patricia called on Wednesday evenings. The timetable rarely changed, and they would never call one another so late. Unless something was wrong.

Patricia forgot her headache and hur-

99

ried to the phone in the bedroom, just down the hall beyond the living room.

"Hello?" she asked softly.

There was no answer at first, but Patricia knew that someone was on the other end. She could hear sounds in the background; the caller was on a public phone.

"Hello?" she repeated.

"It's me. Kent."

"Kent," Patricia said blankly. "Kent Baxter?" She could hear his breathing, and a moaning sound like distress. "What's wrong?"

"Can you . . . come and get me? I'm . . . sick. Please?"

"Me? Why didn't you call your father?"

"He's not home. He's . . . in Chicago, I think."

"Where are you?"

"I . . . I don't know. Flatbush Avenue somewhere . . ." He moaned again.

Patricia grew apprehensive. "Kent? How come you're sick? Are you alone?"

"Could you just . . . come and get me? I can't . . . get home."

He sounded close to tears, and his voice was unsteady and thin.

"All right, all right. Tell me where you are."

100

She had trouble understanding him. Kent didn't seem to know exactly where he was or what were the nearest cross streets. But Patricia wrote down what she could.

"I'll be there as soon as I can," she promised, hanging up. She grabbed her purse and stepped back into her shoes as she rushed out the door.

She thought the worst. He was hurt. He was high. She cursed herself for not asking more specific questions. Had Kent gotten into another fight somewhere? Had he been beaten? Patricia's stomach knotted with fear as she thought up every scenario imaginable.

When she reached the intersection given her by Kent, she saw no sign of him. She checked all four corners and found no one who matched his physical description. Patricia drove another block south. And another. In the middle of the next block she came upon a Jeep Cherokee pulled halfway up on the curb. The two front doors of the vehicle were wide open, but there was no driver or passenger. There were two squad cars and a number of policemen surveying the scene and asking questions of bystanders. She couldn't tell if there had been an accident or not, but Patricia immediately suspected that Kent was somehow connected to the scene.

One officer tried to wave rubberneckers past the obstruction. She was forced to wait until he'd given her clearance to proceed. While she waited there was suddenly a knocking on the passenger side window of her car. Patricia turned her head sharply and found a face pressed against the glass. It was Kent.

She leaned over and unlocked the door. Kent awkwardly climbed in, slamming the door behind him and slumping in his seat. He seemed clumsy and weak. Apprehension again flared up within Patricia, and then faded when she leaned toward him. Kent wasn't hurt. He was drunk.

Or at least he'd been drinking. He reeked of beer and cheap wine. His clothing smelled of marijuana.

"Are you hurt?" she asked nonetheless. He shook his head, and leaning his head back, he closed his eyes.

Patricia felt her stomach churn. She stared, speechless, at the boy. Her immediate thoughts were of Morgan. What in the world was Kent doing in Flatbush? And with whom?

Someone now thumped on her window. It made her jump. She turned her head to stare into the face of an officer. She rolled down her window.

"Oh, man . . ." she heard Kent whisper in alarm.

"Something wrong?" the officer asked her.

"I'm sorry," she stammered. "I thought there was an accident."

"No accident. It's a possible stolen vehicle. Please move along. You're holding up traffic here . . ."

The officer turned away to shout orders at another car, and Patricia turned her attention once again to Kent. He was watching her from beneath his lids, but squeezed his eyes closed against her silent scrutiny.

Patricia eased into traffic. They were on the road a full minute before Kent spoke in a thick, heavy tone.

"Sorry . . . I bothered you."

Patricia didn't respond right away. She was still putting all the bits of information together. It was one thing for Morgan to have business out of town. It was quite another for him to leave a fifteen-year-old boy alone for more than twenty-four hours unsupervised.

"What happened tonight?" she asked sharply. "I want to know what you're doing here."

"Nothing happened," Kent mumbled. "I . . . just got sick."

Patricia sighed impatiently. "The reason you don't feel well is because you've been mixing drugs with alcohol, Kent. What do you know about the Cherokee?" There was no response. "Look, you can either talk to me, or I'm turning around and we'll go back and talk to the officer. It's your call."

They drove another block in silence.

"I was with Pete Connors and Britt Harris," he said, without confessing to anything.

Patricia didn't push him. There was enough time to get the full story.

"Thanks for . . . for coming to get me."

"I'm glad I was able to." She sighed. "What would you have done if I hadn't been home?" He groaned and Patricia knew he hadn't considered that.

"I . . . don't know. Walk."

After that Kent kept his eyes closed and his arms hugged tightly around his middle. He moaned every time the car took a turn or braked at a light. She took pity when sweat broke out on his forehead. Patricia pulled a handkerchief from her purse and silently passed it to him. He wouldn't take it.

"I'm not trying to patronize you. But I don't really want you to be sick all over my car."

He took the handkerchief and wiped his face, momentarily holding the flowery fabric against his nose and mouth.

"Where do you want me to take you?" Patricia asked.

"Home," Kent murmured, giving directions.

Patricia began formulating in her mind exactly what she was going to say to Kent once they reached the brownstone, but her lecture was forgotten when Kent rushed past her and just made it to the bathroom where he was promptly sick to his stomach. The sounds made Patricia sorry for the boy. Her annoyance at his father for being unavailable grew in proportion to Kent's suffering.

She paced outside the bathroom door, knowing that if she entered now Kent would feel humiliated. Instead, Patricia found her way to the small neat kitchen where the only evidence that it was ever used was an empty cereal bowl and juice glass and a half-filled mug of cold coffee. She searched through the cabinets until she located tea bags, and she put water on to boil. It was suddenly quiet and the purging noises had stopped. She walked quickly to the bathroom, opened the door, and found Kent kneeling on the floor, his forehead resting against the cold porcelain of the sink.

"Feeling any better?" she asked softly.

"I'm going to die," Kent gasped out in a miserable voice.

"The good news is, you won't." She stood behind him and rested a hand on his shoulder. "Why don't you get into bed. I'll bring you something to calm down your stomach."

Kent struggled to his feet and headed slowly out of the bathroom. He stumbled to the staircase and up to his room. Patricia watched him go, squelching the sudden desire to fuss over him. She returned to the kitchen to finish the tea, and in five minutes was headed to the second floor. The door to Kent's room was partially opened, and when she looked in, she found him curled in a fetal position under the blankets. His jacket and outer clothing had been dropped to the floor.

Patricia carefully sat on the side of the bed. "I brought you some tea."

"I can't," he groaned.

"It will make you feel better. My grandmother always said so. She used to put mint in mine to sweeten it." Kent quietly moaned. "I'll just leave it on your nightstand in case you change your mind." Patricia set the cup down. "You'll be okay in the morning," she whispered, looking down on him.

"It . . . wasn't my fault," Kent muttered.

Patricia leaned closer. "What wasn't?"

"It wasn't my idea . . . to take the Jeep. I didn't know . . . Britt was going to do it."

"Why didn't you try to stop him? Why didn't you just walk away?" Patricia asked reasonably.

There was a long silence before Kent spoke. His shoulders shrugged under the blanket. "I don't know. He wasn't going to keep it or anything. He said we were just going to ride around for a while and . . . and . . ."

"What about the drinking and the

marijuana? Did he force you to take those, too?"

"Connors knew someone who was having this party. We were going to fill balloons with stuff and then go out . . ."

"What was in the balloons?" Patricia asked.

"Paint."

She grimaced and slowly shook her head. "What went wrong?"

"We . . . were just fooling around. We threw the balloons at each other and . . . and then in the Jeep we heard sirens . . ."

"And thought they were coming after you."

"Britt got crazy. He was going to try to outrun them. I got scared. I jumped out. Then Britt lost control and the Jeep went up on the curb. He got away . . . but I think somebody grabbed Connors."

"And you?"

"I . . . hid. I waited and then called you. I didn't know what else to do," he whispered, his voice weepy and tired.

Patricia sighed again. She was tired, too. She wanted to comfort Kent. And she wanted to shake him soundly as well, as if that would bring him to his senses. But it wasn't going to be that easy. She stood up.

"You got off lightly tonight, Kent. But don't think that it's over," she said quietly.

"Are you . . . going to leave now?"

The voice was low, soft . . . slow. It was the voice of a fifteen-year-old who'd used poor judgment, who was confused and needed reassurance.

"No, I won't leave you alone," she said softly. Kent settled down under the covers.

"You going to . . . tell my father?" he asked.

There was more curiosity than dread in the question and it made her smile. Yet she was careful in how she answered, not willing to betray father, son, or herself.

"It would be better if you told him yourself what happened. But I won't lie to him," she compromised.

Although he sighed deeply Kent said nothing more, and within the next minute was asleep.

Morgan automatically glanced at his watch as he stepped from the town car and turned to assist Beverly.

"God, I'm tired," she said with a deep dramatic sigh. "I still think we should have stayed longer and then flown home. All of this in and out of cars, cabs, and planes in twenty-four hours just wears me out," she said peevishly.

Morgan was noncommittal as he signed the voucher for the driver. He lifted the leather case that contained his computer notebook and all the business documents from the trip to Chicago. He silently took hold of Beverly's arm and steered her to the entrance of her building. The doorman nodded politely and held the door.

"I would think it's a small price to pay for sleeping in your own bed," Morgan finally said quietly as they waited for the elevator. "And you came away with a new client. The least you can do is thank me for taking you along."

"Thank you," Beverly recited obediently.

She brightened and seemed to catch her second breath once they entered the apartment. She hurried to put on a light and the familiarity of her own space made Beverly smile at Morgan.

But he stood thoughtfully, not noticing as a frown wrinkled his brow. She shrugged out of her light coat and hung it in the hall closet. She grabbed another hanger and held it out to Morgan. He stared at it.

"Can I use your phone?" he asked suddenly, already moving into the living room and reaching for the instrument.

"You know you don't have to ask," Beverly murmured as she stepped out of her high heels and pulled off the clip earrings she wore. She silently watched Morgan dial a number and after a brief wait begin to talk.

"Hi. Checking in to see how you're doing. I'll try again in a bit," he said succinctly but stared at the receiver before he hung up.

"Morgan?" Beverly began, gaining his attention. "You were right. It was a good idea to come back to New York. And we still have the rest of the night together." she said with soft allure.

Morgan again checked his watch. "It's getting very late . . ."

Beverly slowly approached and smiling into his face began maneuvering his suit jacket off. Morgan was unresisting, but he didn't help, either.

"I know. So why don't we just move

along to the next item on the agenda?"

Morgan put his arms around her and sighed at the way she pressed and fitted her hips against his. He immediately became hard. "Just how long is this list?" he teased.

She lightly kissed his mouth and shook her head as she loosened the knot of his tie. "Only one thing left."

He chuckled at the sly innuendo, aroused by the promise. Yet, when Beverly circled her arms around his neck and brushed her parted lips against his, Morgan found himself hesitating a split second. His mind turned swiftly to the phone call he'd just tried to make home but the moment won out. He returned the kiss, enjoying the way Beverly's mouth welcomed him. She rotated her hips against his arousal and he deepened the kiss. Beverly had never been afraid or hesitant to take from him what she wanted. Morgan liked not having to ask. Except that right now, he felt the need to slow down.

There was something he wanted to say to Beverly, about being there . . . and getting home. He *was* tired, Morgan realized, as he pulled his mouth free and groaned. "Bev . . ."

"Let's go to bed . . ."

He frowned. Shook his head in confusion and felt like he was on fire. "Beverly . . ."

"We can talk in the morning."

He shook his head again and this time gently pushed her away. "I'm sorry. You know I can't stay. Kent has been alone the whole day. I need to get home and see if he's okay."

Beverly pulled away, annoyed. "Oh, for Christ's sake, Morgan."

"I never said I would stay the night," Morgan said firmly.

"Of course you didn't. You've never had to. That's just the way it's always been."

Morgan pulled off the tie and slowly began to fold it. "I told you. Things have changed. And it's not just Kent. It's me as well." He frowned, trying to focus his thinking. "I haven't been much of a father . . ."

"Maybe that's your ex-wife's fault."

Morgan put the tie in his pocket. "Leave Melissa out of this."

Beverly sighed. "But he's changing your whole life. You have no time for yourself anymore, almost no time for me."

"Maybe that's true. But Kent has a right to it more than anyone. Look . . . I swore that when I had kids I wouldn't raise them the way my father raised me. With indifference. When it suited him. With bullying. I'm not going to fit that image of the black man not being responsible for taking care of his kids." He turned to retrieve his suit jacket and put it on. "From what you told me you don't even remember your father."

"He was a good-for-nothing," she bit out.

"I don't plan to be." He stood in front of her. Morgan put his hand on the side of her face and bent to kiss her firmly closed mouth. She was going to punish him. "Things between us don't have to change . . . if only you'd try to understand what I'm going through. You could even be a good influence."

Beverly looked skeptical. "How's that?"

"I want Kent to know black folks who are together, and have their own business and are making good money, and living good lives. Colorado is too . . ."

"White bread?" she asked with a laugh.

Morgan shook his head. "Just not New York."

She smiled tightly at him. "I don't know about influencing a fifteen-year-old. But I can see this is a point I'm not going to win."

"There's nothing to win or lose."

"Oh, yes, there is. Anyway, I give up. I'm not going up against a kid. And I'm not going to fight you, Morgan. But like I said . . . I'm not going to sit around and wait for you to have time for us."

Morgan flexed his jaw muscle tightly as he stared at her. "I hope that's not a threat," he said softly.

Beverly arched a brow and smiled at him. "No threat." She kissed him lightly. "Just the terms of my willingness to negotiate."

Chapter Four

Patricia hugged herself against the coolness of the rooms, and conflicting emotions as she made her way back to the first floor of the town house. It was a beautiful old structure, but for all its comfortable male furnishings it felt hollow. It was not obvious that a fifteen-year-old boy lived here as well. The surroundings lacked a certain spontaneity and coziness. It lacked the stuff that made a place a home, the lived-in disorderliness of occupants. It lacked warmth and identity.

Patricia stepped out of her shoes and flexed her tired feet against the smooth wood floors. She passed into the living room, glancing around as though in the furnishings and details of the room she would find out who Morgan Baxter was.

There was a small terrace at the back. Patricia opened the doors, and the late-night cold air refreshed her. She still had a little of her headache. She closed her eyes for a second, wondering how long she would have to wait for Kent's father to return home, or if she would have to consider staying the night. Patricia glanced doubtfully at the long leather sofa.

Then she heard a key in the door and turned around quickly as it opened. She stepped back into the living room as Morgan Baxter came through the entrance.

Patricia observed him silently as he closed the door. Morgan had struck her in their first meeting as being a man in control, but in this moment Patricia saw only a man who appeared bone-tired and very pensive. The contradiction was intriguing. It suggested a much more complex man than she would have credited. She was about to make her presence known when Morgan called out first.

"Kent?"

"Shhhh," Patricia ordered quietly, raising a hand as he turned, stunned, toward her. "He's asleep."

Morgan just stared at her. Then he began to frown. He looked toward the stairwell, apprehension making his heart race. He then glanced back to the slender woman whose face and hair stood out against the darkness of the room.

She cleared her throat. "You want to know what I'm doing here," Patricia began calmly enough.

"Obviously," he agreed with a nod of his head. Morgan shrugged out of his coat and tossed it carelessly over the banister. He put his hands in his pockets and slowly approached her.

Patricia watched his eyes take in her appearance, her presence, with skepticism.

"Kent . . ."

"He's fine," she rushed to reassure Morgan. "Well, actually, he's sick. Not sick, really, but just not feeling very well," Patricia explained awkwardly.

"Why isn't he feeling very well?" Morgan asked tightly.

Patricia braced herself. "It's Halloween."

Morgan's frown deepened. "What's that supposed to mean?"

"I think he ate something that didn't agree with him. Candy . . . and other junk. I drove him home."

"From where?"

Patricia pressed her hands together, thinking quickly. "I was asked to chaperone the Halloween party at the high school. You should go and check on him yourself."

Once more he looked toward the stairwell but delayed a moment longer. Instead, Morgan continued his slow approach to Patricia until he was standing intimidatingly close to her. He suddenly had a perverse desire to see her rattled and uncomfortable. He wanted to see if he could get past Patricia's control, make her lose her balance. He wanted to test where her buttons were . . . and how many of them he could press.

"What really happened?" Morgan said.

"I just told you."

"No you haven't. I believe you chaperoned a party at the high school. Everything else is suspect."

At first Patricia actually thought to challenge him, if only to show that she wasn't going to be browbeaten by him. Yet what Kent had done tonight, getting high and nearly arrested, couldn't be ignored. It was a warning that had to be taken seriously.

Morgan's jaw tightened and Patricia

got a glimpse of his annoyance. "I want to know exactly why you had to drive my son home."

His strong masculine face clearly showed exhaustion; after all, he'd been traveling all day. But it also indicated someone who was fully alert and not in the mood for games.

Patricia shook her head slightly. "He was with two other boys tonight. I think they got, er, a little creative in their Halloween mischief."

"How?"

His tone made her flinch involuntarily. "The usual thing."

"If you mean he did something he shouldn't have, then just say so," he said impatiently.

"I don't know that he did," she said with equal impatience. "I . . . I only know that Kent was . . . drinking. And he wasn't in any shape to come home alone. He called me."

Morgan could only stare at her, an expression of dread in his eyes. "What else?" he asked flatly.

Patricia knew there was no polite way to say it. "He'd been smoking." Morgan squeezed his eyes closed and murmured an oath. "We should be grateful

120

that it wasn't worse. No one got hurt
. . . but it was stupid."

"It doesn't matter!" Morgan gestured
angrily. He turned away and cursed
again in frustration.

Patricia flushed slightly. "You were
fifteen once. Do you remember the
things you used to do on Halloween?"

"It was dumb stuff."

"Do you regret any of it?"

"I suppose. I never thought much
about it, dammit!"

"Look, killing the messenger is not
going to help Kent. Why did you leave
him alone anyway?" Patricia asked
tartly.

Morgan moved restlessly and Patricia
was surprised to find him searching for
an answer.

"I thought I could trust him."

"Trust is not an issue. Don't you see
that Kent is trying to get your attention?
You give him a chance, and he's going
to push the envelope and grab that
attention any way he can."

"You and I should have a talk," Morgan said wearily.

"I've been trying," Patricia said
righteously.

"Where do you live?"

"In Park Slope. Why?"

"That's not so far away."

"This late at night, it is."

"I thought we could talk now . . ."

Her head was pounding again, and this was not the time to square off with Kent's father. "No, not now. I want to get home. You'll just have to make another appointment . . . and try to keep it this time." She tried to walk around him, conscious that he was watching her intently. She was in her stocking feet.

Morgan stepped aside. "They're by the end of the sofa." He watched as Patricia slipped the pumps back on. "I'm sorry if I yelled at you. I'm sorry you were inconvenienced tonight."

"I'm glad I could help," Patricia said with professional dignity. "But unless what you do for a living saves lives, I can't believe it's so important you can't find time to sit and talk about your son's future."

"A few hundred jobs are at stake and the welfare of as many families, but no, none of that is more important than Kent."

Morgan's gaze followed Patricia in open curiosity. Now that he'd gotten past his initial anxiety and anger, he could see that she hadn't been fazed by his reaction at all. She had the sort of self-assurance of someone who didn't give a damn what people thought of her. It was so different from how Beverly would have reacted, how she *had* reacted to his leaving because of Kent. But then, the two women were different.

"You're very interesting," he observed, following Patricia to the door. "You didn't even hesitate to come to Kent's aid tonight. Why not? When does school let out for you?"

Patricia waited before answering. She wasn't going to be baited into personal confessions. "You weren't available. I didn't think Kent should be left alone."

Morgan stiffened at the implied criticism. He narrowed his gaze on Patricia and walked past her to the telephone on the coffee table. He pushed a button, waited several seconds, and then pushed another. His voice came back, artificial but clear, in three different messages for his son. In each one Patricia could detect growing impatience and worry.

"I'm sorry. I don't think Kent realized

123

you tried to reach him."

"I had no idea where he was all evening. He didn't tell me about a party at school, or anything else he had planned," Morgan stated emphatically.

"Don't wait for him to tell you. He won't. Maybe Kent needs to know you care enough about him to ask."

Morgan stared at her, watched the stubborn tilt of her chin. He was still annoyed that Patricia in some ways understood his son better than he did. "You're right. I should have done things differently. Thank you," he said grudgingly.

"You're welcome," Patricia murmured. She didn't feel particularly vindicated by his concession. Then he caught her off guard again.

Morgan stared at her for a long moment. "So you think I'm a coward, eh?"

"I didn't mean it the way . . ."

"Sure you did. I've noticed you're not afraid to speak your mind."

"I try to be honest. Anyway, I was just annoyed. Mrs. Anderson shouldn't have told you what I said."

"She thought it was pretty funny," he said wryly.

"But you didn't," she murmured.

He shook his head. "Not at first. Then I realized you were probably right, just not for the reasons you imagined. Did you get the pumpkin?"

She blinked in astonishment and adjusted her glasses. "Pumpkin? That . . . that was from you?"

"Who did you think it was from?" he asked, again annoyed.

"I had no idea. Quite honestly I wouldn't have thought of you." Patricia looked at Morgan closely, wondering if she'd missed something. Suddenly she was pleased by his admission. Flowers would have been too personal . . .

Morgan regarded her. "I left a note for Kent to take it in with him this morning. You probably thought it was a letter bomb," he said tightly.

Patricia kept all traces of amusement from her face.

"I wanted to apologize, I guess, for last Thursday. I gave you a hard time." Morgan narrowed his gaze on her. "You have a poor opinion of me."

"That's not true . . ." she demurred.

"Don't try to get over on me now. I like your honesty better," he said, acknowledging to himself that there was nothing coy about Patricia Gilbert.

She adjusted her glasses to hide a momentary nervousness. "Well . . . it was a . . . thoughtful gesture. A little odd, but nice." She tilted her head a little and frowned at him. "Why did you agree when I called you a coward? I was being sarcastic, but . . ."

Morgan walked away from her, rattling the items in his trouser pocket like so many worry beads. When he turned to face Patricia again, his features were tight. Embarrassed.

"Because you're probably right. Kent scares the hell out of me. He's not a kid anymore and there's a lot about being fifteen that I've forgotten." He slowly walked back to her. "At his age I thought I knew everything, but I didn't know squat. I didn't know where the dividing line was all the time, and I didn't know how to admit that I didn't know. All lip and no way to back it up.

"When I was growing up being black was starting to have some advantages. But what Kent faces is different. Harder. Know what I'm saying?" She nodded. "I'm a little uncomfortable with trying to force my experiences on him. Things change. Sometimes it's hard to tell if they're better. On the other hand, there's a lot I could teach him. There's a lot he needs to know just to survive."

"I would say his survival instincts are pretty strong," Patricia observed.

Morgan shook his head. "Not the kind I'm talking about. I don't want his inexperience to hurt him but how can I be there for him, and *not* be there? I'm afraid of doing the wrong thing, saying the wrong thing."

Patricia stared at Morgan as he made this extraordinary confession. She continued to stare even after he'd stopped talking. "It sounds like you don't know each other very well."

"There's a pretty big gap," Morgan admitted truthfully. "I guess you know from the school records that he's only lived with me a short time. Kent was raised in Colorado by his mother, my ex-wife."

"Yes, I know that much," Patricia confirmed quietly.

Morgan paced a few steps, cracking the knuckles of his hands. "His mother has done a pretty good job so far." He stopped and faced her, his dark eyes tired and filled with uncomfortable reflections. "But there are other ways in which we've both failed him."

Patricia wondered how far she should go with her own observations. She decided to remain cautious. "I realize that Kent is not like most of the other kids. I think he's had a different kind of life in a lot of ways," she said.

Morgan looked more embarrassed. "Did you ask him about it?"

She shook her head. "Not yet. I need his trust first before he'll tell me how he feels. The fact that he's new to the East Coast and New York doesn't help. There's a lot he has to adjust to. I think he's having a hard time. Unfortunately, kids are clever at jumping all over someone who stands out."

Morgan's head turned sharply to her. "What's going on?"

Patricia recalled Kamil's vicious attack on Morgan's son. "Nothing Kent can't handle," she stated confidently.

Morgan looked closely at Patricia, trying to gauge and assess her. His mouth was grim and his eyes hard. He debated silently for several seconds before taking a chance. "Do you know what the trouble is?" he asked bluntly.

Patricia slowly nodded, keeping her attention focused on Morgan's face. She didn't attempt to play around the issue.

"I think so. Kent's biracial, isn't he?" she asked softly.

Morgan didn't respond directly. He turned away and sighed. "I should have gotten him sooner. It was a mistake not staying close to him. It's hurt him."

Patricia didn't ask why he hadn't. "That can be remedied. I think you'll both find you have a lot in common."

Morgan grew interested. "Such as?"

A few obvious attributes came to mind, but Patricia forced them out of her head. She would want to give a more substantial example than the fact that father and son had strong aggressive chins and thoughtful personalities. That they were both good-looking and very appealing.

She shook her head. "It's late. I'm going home. If you make an appointment to see me, we'll talk about it."

"How about next Tuesday. Ten? I'll clear my calendar."

"How about next Tuesday at two. And I'll believe it when you walk through the door," Patricia said tartly as she opened the door to leave.

Morgan tilted his head in agreement. "One thing . . ." he said, following her. Morgan's gaze was suddenly meticulous in its examination of her. "What did you go to the party as?" he asked.

Patricia stared at him and responded flippantly, "A black widow spider."

Morgan pursed his lips. "I'm sorry I asked."

Patricia stopped and turned halfway around. Morgan continued approaching her, but with a purpose that made her slightly suspicious of him.

"Your hair is amazing, you know."

"My hair?" she asked, dumbfounded. Then she recovered. "My hair has nothing to do with anything," she said tightly.

Morgan considered her closely. He was fascinated by the sudden rush of color to her cheeks. "I bet it does. I bet you have lots of issues."

"You have a lot of nerve," she whispered, opening the door.

Morgan nodded as the door closed. "So do you."

Morgan turned wearily from the door. In a way, he was glad that Patricia Gilbert had quickly grasped the circumstances of Kent's problem, and his. In another way, it annoyed the hell out of him. He didn't like having to air his personal business. So far Kent had not asked questions about his mixed racial heritage but Morgan was sure they would come eventually. He still didn't know how he was going to handle the questions about Melissa and himself. Their lives and their marriage . . . its failure. Morgan knew he couldn't just haul out the past some evening after dinner and explain to Kent in an hour and a half how he came to have a white mother and a black father.

He traveled across the floor to the stairwell that led to the upper level. He began climbing the stairs with a heavy sense of foreboding and impatience. Perhaps it had been foolish of him, overly hopeful, to think that he and Kent could become part of each other's lives and that the fit would be perfect. It hadn't been. Uneasy would be a good word to describe their relationship. Confusing would be another.

He sighed deeply, tired and tense. But there was no way, Morgan knew, that he could go to bed himself without first checking on Kent's condition. Patricia's careful telling of the facts notwithstanding, he was afraid of what he would find. The door to his son's room was partially open. Morgan had never been invited in . . . and he'd never asked to be. Once he'd given the room to Kent back in June, it had become absolutely and understandably his son's private domain, and he'd never given much thought to his right to access.

Kent was curled up in a fetal position in the center of the bed, lightly covered by a bedspread. Morgan quietly approached the bed and, thankful for the bedside lamp, stared intently at the boy. Kent was in a deep sleep, his breathing heavy but even. Morgan eased the chair out from the desk and sat down. Kent looked so young in sleep. More than just defenseless, rather innocent. It stroked Morgan's ego that Kent physically favored him despite the fair skin and slightly wavy hair. And it evoked strange feelings in him to recognize the traits and personalities that were from Melissa, his ex-wife. He quickly got off that thought, got up, and looked around the room.

It was surprisingly neat. There were schoolbooks and paraphernalia on the desk. Morgan spotted a Mont Blanc pen and was surprised. It seemed a very expensive item for a fifteen-year-old to have, and he wondered if it had been given to Kent by his mother or grandfather. At the foot of the bed was his knapsack. There was a black leather strap trailing out from under the bed. Morgan investigated and found a camera. He picked it up and placed it on the desk so that it wouldn't be stepped on. He'd never seen Kent use the camera before and wondered what he took pictures of. There was a football behind the door and a small stack of *Sports Illustrated* magazines. Morgan made a soundless self-deprecating chuckle. He had no idea that Kent liked either football or photography.

The only pile of clothing was what had been discarded as his son had undressed and gotten into bed. Morgan stared at them before bending to pick them up. Two distinct odors caught his attention. The smell of alcohol. And of vomit. There was also paint on the legs of Kent's jeans. Morgan's gut tightened at the thought that Kent was involved in something he wouldn't approve of.

His gaze quickly took in the rest of the room, trying to detect the most likely place for a teenage stash. Alcohol. Drugs. Grass. Weapons. Morgan wanted to search through every drawer and corner of the room until he found the signs of rebellion and independence . . . of trouble. But he knew that he couldn't. If he found anything he'd have to do something about it. And if he found nothing he'd feel ashamed at his lack of trust. When the flash of panic subsided, Morgan quietly left Kent's room and deposited the handful of clothing in the bathroom hamper.

With justifiable weariness Morgan headed to his own room. He stripped and climbed into bed, exhausted, with his mind in turmoil. For a moment he wished that he hadn't left Beverly's quite so quickly. He was so wound up that sexual release at least would have taken the edge from his tension. For a moment he also thought of Melissa, remembering how angry they both had been at the end when there didn't seem to be anything else to do but divorce in order for each of them, and their son, to survive. And the anger had never been at each other. It had been at feeling helpless at the odds against their marriage working.

Morgan tried to settle down but had two other coherent last-minute thoughts as he drifted off to a fitful sleep. One was that he wanted his son to love him. And the other was, he wanted Patricia Gilbert's respect.

" 'Lo?"

"Good morning."

"Morgan?"

The voice was alluring, husky. "You sure sound sexy when you wake up," he drawled.

"It's seven-thirty in the morning, for God's sake."

Morgan smiled. He sipped from his coffee half stretched out on the sofa with the cellular phone cushioned between his shoulder and ear. "Bad time to be calling?"

"You're fishing, Morgan. I didn't ask if there was someone in your bed." The feminine voice was lazy with indignation.

"There isn't," he assured her honestly.

"Is that why you're calling? Checking up on me?"

"How about I'm calling because I miss you. And to say I'm sorry again about last night." Morgan could hear her movements as she settled more comfortably in her bed. *Was* there someone with her?

"You could have done something about it last night."

There was a moment as Morgan listened to Beverly McGraw's soft yawn. The sexiness in her voice was slowly fading. "I thought you understood I had to come home." Morgan was a bit piqued that he couldn't tell if she was really alone. And she hadn't asked yet about himself.

"I do. But that doesn't give you the right to ask how I spent the night."

Morgan didn't see any point in pursuing the issue. Beverly was still punishing him. She quickly changed the subject.

"We've talked about everything except your latest project. What's happening with Sager? Has it gone to contract?"

Morgan took another sip of his coffee. He looked out the terrace doors to the few bare trees in the yard behind the house, dreary indicators of the season. It was still too early, too quiet. The mornings always made him feel lonely. "Not yet. The company managers are still suspicious. They think this is a takeover, pure and simple."

"Have you pointed out that their last director was running the operation into the ground? Another six months and they all would have been out of work."

"You can't approach them that way. It's a small company. It's like a family. Besides, it was the devil they knew versus me. I was suspect from the beginning because I wasn't from their community."

"But you're offering them a way to survive," Beverly said impatiently.

Morgan chuckled. He could afford patience to wait and get what he wanted, to change their minds. But he recognized that if she was in his place, Beverly, as a woman, would lose precious time first trying to prove she was capable of doing corporate negotiations. As a black woman she might not get the chance at all. Second, she was expected to prove she wasn't going to throw in the towel to get married. Worse still, that she wouldn't get pregnant and leave. Morgan grimaced. She had apparently decided against both.

"I think there's more than survival at stake here. There's a matter of tradition and identity . . ."

"Oh, please," she sighed dramatically.

Morgan could almost see her sliding down against the pillows, her short sable hair being fluffed by her long fingers.

"No wonder these people are in trouble. They're not treating the business as a business."

She was shifting again, and again Morgan knew she was lying on her side so that the weight of her full breasts created the roundness and cleavage that he'd found so provocative. When he didn't respond to her comments Beverly downshifted.

"I had to sleep with socks," her voice intoned quietly. "It got cold in my bed last night with no one to keep me warm. Does that answer your question?"

"What question?"

"The one you haven't asked, yet," she said softly.

Her honesty stabbed at him. They had no holds on each other, no commitments whatsoever. Neither of them had wanted one. Their relationship had always been clear and uncomplicated. Physical and companionable. But the distance between them imposed by Kent's arrival in New York definitely changed the rules.

"I'm a big boy. If you have someone in reserve just say so," he said evenly.

"I'll step aside anytime." She laughed, a rich seductive laugh. It was one of the first things Morgan had noticed and liked about Beverly McGraw.

"I don't believe you don't care and you'd give up without some play. Anyway, I was only teasing. I *was* annoyed last night. And how is the prodigal son?"

There was some amusement, but no ridicule in Beverly's question. But even so Morgan winced as if a sore spot had been touched. He swished the last of his coffee in the cup. "I shouldn't have stayed overnight in Chicago."

"Is he in trouble already?"

"It was Halloween," Morgan said dryly, recalling Patricia Gilbert's answer to him the night before.

"Uh-oh. Sounds like you came home to a surprise. Or don't you like being a father."

"It's just taking some time, that's all," Morgan commented evasively.

"I haven't heard that you're thrilled with the arrangement."

"You haven't heard that I'm not. Like I said, it's just difficult."

She sighed. "I can't decide if you're a fool or a martyr to have let this happen.

It's so late to play catch up. He's so big and there's so much you have to worry about. I'm glad I never had any kids."

Morgan put the cup down a little too hard. He felt a vague irritation, but didn't have time to explore it.

"Are you calling to say you're coming back soon?" Beverly asked in a silky voice, again changing moods.

The thought had crossed Morgan's mind. And then he remembered what was waiting for him here. He remembered Patricia Gilbert's righteous impatience with him. And guilt made Morgan aware of his own level of neglect. "Why don't you come here? You can meet Kent. We could spend the time together . . . How about next weekend?"

She chuckled softly. "The whole weekend? And where will I sleep? No thanks. I don't think that's such a hot idea."

"You'll like Kent," Morgan said automatically.

"Yeah, I'm sure he's cute and wonderful but . . . I think it would be too awkward. I'll take a rain check."

Morgan heard a door open and close on the second floor. Shortly the shower started in the bathroom. He trained his eyes on the top of the stairs, his ears to the sounds. "If I didn't know you better I'd say you were afraid to meet my son."

"Attacking my ego is not going to work, either. My maternal instincts are dormant and I'd like to keep it that way."

The unbroken rhythm of the water convinced Morgan that Kent was merely standing under the spray, letting the downpour pelt him into consciousness. "Don't you ever wonder if you're missing out on being a mother?"

"No," Beverly said succinctly. "Besides, I never found a man I wanted to have kids with. And I certainly didn't want to be raising a child by myself. I saw how my own mother struggled. You may not be father material, for all you know."

"Thank you," Morgan said dryly.

"I told you I'm out of my depth with kids. If you want some input on the Sager project I'd love to meet with you and David."

"I don't need you on the Sager negotiations."

"You need me in your bed, right?"

"I didn't say that."

"Am I wrong?"

". . . I hoped you still felt the same way."

Beverly drawled seductively. "I do, Morgan. I'm having some pretty hot thoughts at this moment. I remember what you do to my nipples . . . hmmmm . . ."

Morgan closed his eyes and cursed silently.

"But you're not free to give me what I want, and I don't think I can give you what you want."

"Are you sure you know what that is?"

"Is that a serious question? Of course I do. You want someone to curl around at night, someone to exchange intelligent and clever conversation with. Someone who'll take you as you are and not tamper with the parts. Not dump on you about the past."

"You used to do some of those things pretty well. Is there any reason for anything to be different?"

"You also expect me to act as some sort of surrogate to your son. I can't. *That* makes it different."

"So you're going to give up on what we have?"

"Morgan, I don't know. What do you want me to say? We have a lot of fun together but it's not the same anymore. You may not like to hear it but your son is a distraction. And you can't table your relationship with him the way you would problems in business. I want to see you and I want you to make love to me until the room steams over and we're completely drained . . . but not as an escape because you're having problems with your son."

The shower had stopped. Morgan's mild irritation had returned and was not so mild anymore. His attention drifted and he heard the bathroom door open. In another few seconds Kent appeared at the top of the stairs. His short hair was damp and flat and Morgan could see his scalp; his skin had a yellowish tinge and he looked very uneasy. Morgan slowly sat up and stared at the boy. He looked into those dark eyes and felt a sudden connection. He could see an uncertainty that he himself was feeling. He didn't hear much of Beverly's last few words.

"I'm sorry it can't work out next weekend," Morgan said into the phone. "I haven't given up."

"I'm glad, because neither have I. Another time, maybe."

"Maybe . . ." Morgan repeated. "I'll call you." He hung up the phone.

Morgan got up and walked to the foot of the stairs. Kent had on sweats and he was barefoot. For whatever reason it pleased Morgan that they were both dressed the same, as if that were an instinct that identified them as being alike. "Come on into the kitchen. I'll fix you something."

Morgan had poured a fresh cup of coffee and was pulling eggs, milk, and bread from the refrigerator when Kent made his appearance in the doorway, eyeing his father suspiciously. His hands were rolled together under the front edge of his sweat top, making it balloon out.

"Sit down." Morgan pulled out a stool from the large central counter and went back to his preparations. "I was going to make some French toast and bacon for breakfast."

Kent took the seat offered, but looked like he would bolt for the bathroom at the mere mention of food.

"How are you feeling this morning?"

Kent glanced at his father uneasily. "What do you mean?" he asked in an early morning croak.

Morgan broke three eggs into a small bowl. "I mean, how are you feeling? Miss Gilbert said you got sick last night."

"Oh, yeah," the boy said with a vague nod.

"How was it?"

"What?"

"The party." Morgan watched Kent and could see another confused thought forming.

"It was okay. I don't mean the thing at school. I didn't go to that," Kent admitted quietly.

"Where did you go?" Morgan asked, focusing on adding spices and milk to the eggs.

Kent licked his lips and kept his gaze down. "A . . . a couple of us just hung out. There was a . . . a party and . . ."

"I bet parties haven't changed much from when I was your age," Morgan commented quietly. "I hope nothing . . . illegal went on."

Kent suddenly began to blush. "Dad, I . . . I don't know."

Morgan glanced briefly at his son. "Do you want to tell me about it?"

Slowly Kent shook his head. "No," he answered. "Nothing happened. Except

I . . . got sick."

Morgan continued to look at him. "Are you sure?"

"Yeah, I'm sure. I asked Miss Gilbert if she would bring me home."

The wire whisk swirled through the eggs. "I didn't expect to come home last night and find her here," Morgan said, but could get no further information from his son. He was disappointed.

Kent watched his father's actions and his forehead broke out in a sweat. "I . . . I really don't think I could eat anything. My stomach . . ."

"I didn't think so. The French toast is for me. That's for you." He pointed to the mug of coffee and watched Kent's reaction.

"It's coffee," Kent said blankly.

Morgan heated a skillet and began dipping slices of bread into the mixture. "It's the best cure for a hangover. The alternative is raw egg in orange juice."

The skillet made bubbling sounds as the bread slices were placed into the pan. Morgan could sense his son's surprise in the silence behind him.

"I don't have a hangover. I wasn't drinking . . ."

Morgan turned around. "It doesn't

146

have to be liquor. Beer can do the same thing to you. A six-pack would do it. Especially mixed with grass." He wiped his hands on a towel and leaned back against the counter watching the boy.

At first Kent shrugged and refused to meet his father's gaze. "What did Miss Gilbert say? Did she . . ."

"This doesn't have anything to do with Miss Gilbert. I was hoping you would tell me what went on."

An array of emotions crossed Kent's features before he settled on just being stubbornly silent. The toast continued to bubble and overcook, but Morgan wasn't paying attention.

"There's nothing to tell. I mean . . . I did have a few beers but that's all."

Morgan felt a sweat of anxiety break out on his own skin. Kent's answer told him more than he was expecting and more than the boy intended.

"Kent, look. I know we really haven't spent any time together and maybe that's part of what's wrong between us. I've been busy lately and I probably should have said no to some of those meetings. But I didn't think you wanted me on top of you all the time watching everything you did. I thought you could be trusted on your own."

"And I thought you'd care," Kent suddenly blurted out.

Morgan was stunned. "Care about what?" The boy just stared at the countertop. "Come on, Kent. Talk to me," he urged impatiently.

"I didn't mean to say that."

"Yeah, you did. I'd like you to tell me what you *meant* by it." When Kent still said nothing Morgan threw the dish towel into the sink in frustration. "Maybe you'd be happy back with your mother. Maybe this isn't such a . . ."

"No!" Kent's expression became stubborn, his eyes narrowed. "I don't want to go back to Colorado."

Morgan frowned at the contradictions. "But you don't act like you're happy to be here."

"I am, it's just that . . ."

"What?" Morgan prompted.

Kent moved his head in a confused gesture. "I don't want to get in the way."

Morgan frowned. "You're not in the way."

"Don't send me back," he murmured.

Morgan retrieved the towel, and meticulously folded it. "Does your grandfather still talk to you about you going

148

to the academy?" he asked thoughtfully.

Kent seemed surprised by the question. "That's all he talks about," he
grumbled. "He says the academy builds
character and teaches respect and discipline."

Morgan shrugged. "He's probably
right. Being at the academy could open
a lot of doors for you, offer good opportunities. You'd do well there."

"I don't need the academy to give me
character," Kent said scathingly.

Morgan pursed his lips. "What does
your mother think?"

Kent shrugged. "She says it's up to
me to do what I want. She said, maybe
I should talk to you about it, but it's
pretty hard to argue with Granddad."

Morgan looked at his toes. "Yeah, I
remember he could draw a hard line.
So, do you think you want to take his
advice?"

Kent shifted uneasily on the stool and
looked furtively at his father. "No."

"Why?" Morgan forced himself to ask.

Kent finally glanced at him. "I have to
find out for myself if that's what I want."

"What about you and me?" Morgan
asked. He wasn't sure he was fully

prepared for the answer, but there wasn't going to be a time when it was easy. And unless he had some idea if a relationship between him and his son was possible, it didn't matter why Patricia Gilbert wanted to have a discussion with him.

"You and me?" Kent repeated, confused.

"That's right. Are we just going to live in the same space together, or is there a chance we'll get to know one another?"

Kent thoughtfully ran his finger along the edge of the counter. He used his fingernail to meticulously scratch a dried piece of food. He shrugged. "I thought . . . we could get to know each other." His voice was barely a whisper.

Morgan studied his son for a long moment. "Fair enough. I just don't want to know you're trying to escape the pressures from your grandfather by coming to me."

"I'm not running away. That's not why I came here."

"I hope not."

"I don't want to go back. I promise I won't drink any more beer."

Morgan shook his head. "That's a

promise I can't ask you to keep because you won't be able to. But I'm going to ask one thing of you, Kent. I don't want you to ever lie to me. If we can't try to be honest with each other, then there's no point."

Morgan was unable to mask the frustration and his tone of voice gained the boy's attention. Kent stared at him silently.

"I want you to be able to talk to me and ask questions. Tell me what's on your mind. I mean to keep in touch with what's going on with you in school. I want you to make friends." Morgan stared at the sullen boy. His inclination was to let it go at that, but he knew he couldn't. He had to make it clear what the boundaries were, and who was in charge.

"Another thing. You have to understand that you don't get away scot-free with what happened last night. You're old enough to take responsibility for your actions."

Kent looked at him, his eyes blinking rapidly as he gnawed at his lip. "What are you going to do?" he murmured fearfully.

Morgan slowly shook his head. "Not

me. You. If anything else went on last night, now is your chance to come clean about it."

Kent continued to stare. He swallowed and stuffed his hands into the pockets of the sweat top. "Nothing happened."

"Only because no one got hurt. You're under age and you were drinking. Marijuana is illegal and you can go to jail for possession. I won't put up with criminal behavior in my son. It won't happen again, right?"

"No, sir." Kent nodded meekly.

"You don't have to call me sir," Morgan murmured impatiently. Then he softened his tone and leaned toward his son. "I'm your father, Kent. Not a warden."

Kent nodded, not looking directly at his father. He silently lifted the mug of coffee and took a quick slurping sip. He made a face and looked at his father. "How did you know I was drinking beer?"

Morgan suddenly saw Patricia Gilbert as she stood stalwart and determined before him last night in defense of Kent. "Do all kids think adults are dumb? Let's just say I prefer to drink it, not wear it." Morgan turned back to the skillet and flipped the bread slices over. He stared at Kent for a long time. "We need to get out of here for a while. Why don't we do something together? Maybe check out a movie this afternoon?" His voice was smooth, almost indifferent. "Unless you have other plans."

"We can do that . . . if you want," Kent said with a shrug.

Morgan pursed his mouth and arched a brow. There was no great show of enthusiasm, but at least Kent hadn't said no. He was being cool. Morgan chuckled low to himself as he served the French toast on a plate and, despite Kent's earlier protest, pushed the breakfast toward him. He used to be cool once, Morgan considered.

But that was way before he realized that being an adult was not all it was cracked up to be.

Chapter Five

"What happened on Friday night?" Jerome asked as he dumped his olive drab shoulder satchel on his chair and entered Patricia's office. His anorak jacket was unzipped and hung open. His gloves were attached by hooks to the zipper tab.

"I don't know," Patricia murmured absently. "What happened on Friday night?"

She sat at her desk drinking tea. There was a thick textbook spread across her lap, and she occasionally jotted notes on a pad. Her glasses were perched on the top of her head.

Jerome opened a brown bag, reached in, and pulled out a wax paper-wrapped cinnamon raisin bagel. He noisily peeled back the paper and offered half of it to Patricia. She declined with a shake of her head.

"There's a rumor in the office that one

of our students got picked up by the police that night. In someone else's car."

Patricia gave Jerome only a brief glance as she shifted in her seat. "Did the rumor say who exactly?"

"Whom," he corrected, biting into the bagel and licking a glob of cream cheese from the corner of his mouth. "Britt Harris was mentioned. And Pete Connors. I know about him 'cause he's been bragging. It's like some sort of rite of passage for these guys to get booked at least once by the cops."

"Only until the indictment is handed down," Patricia commented dryly. "I bet Britt was the instigator and Pete just tagged along . . ."

"I'm not finished," Jerome interrupted.

Jerome's tone was so pointed that Patricia finally lifted her attention from her reading to stare at him.

"Connors is telling people that he and Harris suckered Kent Baxter into going along with them. I'm not sure I believe that."

"Why?"

Jerome chewed thoughtfully for a second. "Why, what? Why did they include

Baxter or why don't I believe it?"

"Pick one," Patricia said, shrugging.

"The kid's a loner. He's not the kind to pick Connors for a friend, or vice versa. Frankly, I think Baxter is too smart to do something dumb like steal a car and get arrested. He's different than the other boys."

Patricia accepted Jerome's observation with a nod. She turned a page in her book and hid her thoughtful expression. "Well, like you said, it's just a rumor."

"There's something else, Pat. I found out that the Baxter kid is getting jumped by some of the black boys. Didn't you tell me you broke up a fight between him and Kamil Johnson?"

"That's right."

"Well, Kamil and his posse have really been doggin' him."

"Because he's new. It'll settle down."

Patricia glanced at Jerome with the brief idea of confiding her information about Kent. But she couldn't. She recalled how stoically Kent had been abiding his persecution at the hands of the other boys, because he had no choice. He wasn't just being tested. He was being asked to justify himself because he *was* different. Patricia felt a sudden jolt of recognition and identification that she knew she couldn't say anything to Jerome. He wouldn't understand. It would have been too much like picking the scab from a still healing wound, revealing a nasty little secret that black people wouldn't acknowledge and wouldn't discuss. That they very harshly judged one another by skin color. What made someone black? How *black* was black? She remembered what being challenged was like. It still happened.

"Maybe I should have a talk with him after all," Jerome said thoughtfully.

"Don't," Patricia said firmly, sitting forward and looking earnestly at him. "He's not going to tell you anything. If you try to single him out you'll only make it worse."

"So what do we do? Wait until someone gets knifed in the hallway?"

Patricia shook her head. "It's not going to come to that."

"I don't know if I'd bet the ranch on that," Jerome said, finally slipping out of his coat. As he spoke, the phone began to ring.

"I'll get it . . ." they both called out,

but Jerome sprinted to his extension before Patricia could dig out her phone from beneath a pile of papers.

"Patty, it's for you anyway," Jerome called out.

Patricia sat straight and quickly stacked her notes and textbook. She pushed them aside as she reached for the phone. "Who is it?"

"Guess," Jerome said wryly.

Patricia hesitated for a fraction of a second, but she didn't have to guess. The unexpected tension in her stomach signaled an awareness that took her a little by surprise. But when she spoke she kept her tone formal and crisp.

"Patricia Gilbert. May I help you?" She quickly detected the quiet male chuckle.

"We'll get to that in a minute," Morgan Baxter drawled. "How are you wearing your hair today?"

"Excuse me?" Patricia asked, trying to sound as if she didn't know what he was talking about.

Morgan laughed. "I'm sorry. I guess I should apologize for what I said to you but you know I'm right. You're still self-conscious about it, aren't you?"

"Oh, Mr. Baxter. Good morning," Patricia said politely, feeling her face and neck grow warm. She looked up and found Jerome standing in open curiosity, watching her as she spoke to Morgan. She tried to ignore him.

"I also owe you a belated thanks for taking care of Kent on Friday night," Morgan said in a much more sober tone. "He and I had a long chat on Saturday morning."

"I'm very glad to hear that," Patricia said. She smiled vacantly at Jerome. He wouldn't budge.

"You're very formal all of a sudden. What? No sharp response? No open challenge?"

Patricia laughed nervously and swiveled in her chair away from her audience. Jerome settled in a slouch against the frame of the door. "I . . . I can't very well do that." There was a momentary pause.

"I get it. You're not alone."

"Yes, that's correct."

Morgan chuckled again. "You know, I could turn this into a very interesting conversation . . . but I won't. The next time I spar with you, *Miss* Gilbert, I want to do it face-to-face so I stand an even chance."

"Then, is there something in particular I can do for you?"

"Actually, there are a few things. Most important, I'm calling to confirm tomorrow. I'll be there this time."

"That sounds like a good idea," Patricia agreed, staying with her official tone, and searching for her appointment calendar. Jerome obligingly lifted it from a bookshelf above her head and handed it to her. "Thank you," she said to him, hoping he'd then return to his own business.

"I probably deserved that, but I hope you're not being sarcastic," Morgan said.

"No, I'm not. I mean, you don't understand . . ."

"You're surprised I called, aren't you?" Morgan asked abruptly.

Patricia thought she heard a certain inflection, like disappointment. It was the second time and it made her feel responsible. "Not that you *wouldn't*, Mr. Baxter. I just didn't know how long it would take," she said honestly.

"I think Friday was a pretty direct wake-up call. I'm a risk taker . . . but not with my son. He and I have a lot to make up between us."

"I'm so glad to hear you say that, Mr. Baxter," Patricia responded.

"Are you?" Morgan asked quietly. "You mean, me humbling myself?"

"That's not what you're doing. You're only recognizing that there is a problem."

"This is not going to be easy, you know."

"I know. But it's not going to be impossible, either."

There was another slight pause.

"I'd really like to know where you get your confidence," Morgan said with candor.

Patricia slowly began to smile. "The same place you get yours," she replied.

Kent fingered the handkerchief that was bunched up in the pocket of his hooded sweat top. Touching it made him feel a little nervous, and the moisture from his palms dampened the delicate fabric. The housekeeper had warned him not to get it dirty, but Kent found that he liked rubbing his fingers over the softness. He'd been walking around with the handkerchief for two days. It reminded him of Ms. Gilbert.

A whistle sounded and Kent glanced

up. He focused on the thirty or so boys around him, and the sound of basket-balls bouncing. The rubber soles of sneakers squeaked against the wooden floorboards. All around him were the profane comments and responses, grunts and laughter of the guys in his gym class as they goofed on each other, or tried to show one another up.

"Okay, I want to see the next group over here for the climb. Rashad, put that ball down like I told you . . ." Mr. Harper, the instructor, said in annoy-ance as he pointed his finger at the teen. "You, too, Baxter. And take off that top. It's not that cold in here."

"Yeah, Baxter. Let's see how much of a pussy you are," Shawn Bishop chal-lenged.

There was snickering agreement, but Kent ignored it. He was squatted down against the wall. With his feet braced against the floor, Kent pushed upward from his position and made his way across the room. He hated gym class. It was such dumb stuff they had to do. It wasn't any fun and almost everything was indoors. He missed the five-mile runs around the school track field of Colorado, and the swim meets in the seventy-five-foot pool. Duncan didn't even have a pool. Kent pushed the handkerchief deep into his pocket and pulled the sweat top, by the collar, over his head. He stopped thinking about Colorado Springs. He still didn't want to go back there.

"Why we gotta climb a rope for, man?" someone asked in disgust.

"I seen him climb the rope. He can do this, shit," one of the boys confided in those around him as Kent walked by.

"Yeah? Then let him climb my dick," Kamil muttered.

There were more guffaws, palm slapping, stomping of feet, as if Kamil had said something profound they'd never heard before.

Kent walked past his classmates with a slow controlled gait. He'd learned how to in the first week of school. He'd learned how to hold his head at an angle, like he didn't care. And how to look away from a person, like they didn't exist. He'd learned how to stare down some of the other guys, and they were the ones who didn't mess with him anymore.

They'd all made him a target right from the start, because he had light skin. That's what they'd said. He was a white nigger who didn't belong with them. A lot of them had sounded on his mother and called her all kinds of names. The third day of class a group of boys had scagged him on the school bus. They'd surrounded him in the back, slapped his head, and thrown the book he was reading out the window. One day his locker had been broken into and someone had pissed all over his gym clothes. After that he had learned how to be careful. And how not to complain. But they still called him nigger.

The whistle blew again.

"Come on, come on, move it on up, man," Mr. Harper said, waving the lagging group of boys over to the next exercise.

Kent tossed his top aside on the floor. Then he suddenly jerked forward from his chest as something pounded into the center of his back with a hard, stinging thud. Kent caught his footing and half turned as the volleyball bounced along the floor and eventually rolled to a stop. Someone scooped it up and casually bounced it, eyeing Kent.

"Hey, you got in the way, man," the

boy said, waiting for Kent to respond.

Kent stared at him for a long moment. The boy took a step closer. He drew in his chin and made a brief hand gesture with his pinkie and index fingers.

"You got something to say 'bout that?"

"Yeah. My grandmother can throw the ball better than that," Kent said quietly, and turned away. Behind him was only silence for a moment.

"Fuck you, man."

"You wish you could," Kent shot back. There was a smattering of uneasy laughter.

"Oh, shit. My man ranked on you. You gonna take that shit?"

Kent approached the suspended rope. He bent and slapped his hands in the tray of crushed rosin, coating them to cut the friction on the rope.

"There's no safety net and only one way down," Mr. Harper said as the next seven boys lined up. "Let's go . . ." He clapped his hands loudly and jerked his thumb skyward.

Kent took hold of the rope. He gritted his teeth and concentrated on the hand-over-hand pull. He raised his knees to grip the rope and wrapped his ankles around the trailer as he levered himself upward. All the while below him were catcalls and dares. But Kent quickly reached the top, rang the bell, and shimmied back down.

"Good, Baxter." Mr. Harper nodded as the boy stood catching his breath.

Kent dusted off his hands and looked around for the gray top. He couldn't find it. His glance swept around in a circle, trying to identify his sweater. To his left there was sudden riotous chortling, great outbursts of raw laughter.

"Oh, shit! My man here is a limp wrist fag. Ain't this some shit?"

Kent turned and saw Darryl Ash holding his sweat top. And the handkerchief. Someone snatched it from Shawn and began an exaggerated feminine sashay, waving the cloth in the air.

"Quiet over there," Mr. Harper called out.

Kent straightened his shoulders and took a deep breath. Crossing his arms he placed a hand flat under each armpit so they wouldn't shake. He sneered bravely at the boy, Darryl.

"I'd let you have it, but your mama's so dumb she uses her sleeve to wipe her nose."

The sweater and handkerchief were

abruptly dropped as Darryl tried to charge forward. Kent braced himself and kept his eyes on the boy. When he was within three feet Kent dropped to his knees and turned his shoulder into Darryl's stomach. Upon impact both Kent and Darryl crashed to the gym floor. But that's as far as it went. The teacher brutally grabbed Kent by the back of his tank and pulled him away from the other boy.

"Aw, come on. Let 'em fight, Mr. Harper," someone pleaded.

Kent knocked Mr. Harper's hand away, his adrenaline pumping. He kept his eye on Darryl, ready to go if he had to. Mr. Harper stepped between them. He grabbed Kent and Darryl none too gently by their shoulders. He glared at Darryl.

"To the locker, Ash. Go on, get outta here."

Darryl turned his wrath on the gym instructor. "Hey, don't be grabbing me like that, man."

Mr. Harper got in his face and pointed toward the gym door. "Did you hear me?"

"Just don't be touching me . . ." Darryl muttered, backing away.

Mr. Harper put the whistle in his mouth and blew sharply. Everyone got quiet.

"This period is *not* over yet. Any of you want to fight? Sign up for the wrestling team. Or take it off the premises. Got it? Back to what you were doing. Darryl . . ." he said warningly.

Cursing, Darryl snatched up his varsity top and made a grand exit, slamming his way through the door.

Kamil suddenly stepped in front of Kent. "You sorry motherfucker. You gonna wish you kept your ass on the farm, Jack. Think you hot shit 'cause your daddy's rich. You act like you white."

"Kamil!" Mr. Harper called out. "You're next."

Kent and Kamil continued to square off until finally Kamil bumped past him and headed for the rope. Kent watched him walk away. Then he retrieved his sweat top and the now dirtied handkerchief. He stood trying to smooth it out, then he realized that the instructor was approaching him.

"You're finished for the day, too, Baxter."

Kent nodded and headed for the

locker. The teacher stopped him.

"No. You go take a walk outside. I don't want you and Darryl in the locker room together. You wait until the end of the period before going in there, understand me?"

Kent nodded again. Mr. Harper returned to the routine being performed across the room. Kent turned away and, slipping the sweater back on, headed out the side door that led to the football field and the viewing stands. He almost collided with Eric Patton.

"Yo, my man K," Eric said in greeting. He lifted his hand to Kent for the proper response.

And Kent did so almost automatically. Even though he was surprised he tried not to show it. He'd never had a problem with Eric. But he was still careful. He took the hand and clutched it.

"Talk with you later, man," Eric said with a nod and entered the gym before the door closed.

Kent looked at the closing door briefly, feeling a sudden surge of relief. He had expected Eric to be just like the others, especially since he was tight with Darryl and Kamil. But outside school last week, Eric had caught up with him as he'd headed toward the local pizza place. Eric had started asking questions about Colorado. He wanted to know where it was. And it was Eric who talked about Kamil.

"Nigga's fucked up," Eric had said scathingly.

"He's your friend."

"Yeah, man, but Kamil don't know how to chill, know what I'm sayin'? His old man is in the joint, and his mama got somebody new in the house. He can't deal with that."

Kent shrugged. "Doesn't have anything to do with me."

"Don't matter. He just lookin' for someone's ass to whup. Don't let him play you, man. Kick his ass back. That's how you do." He looked at Kent. "You all right. You don't cut and run. Yeah . . . you be cool. Your mother white?"

Kent had felt defensive. "What about it?"

"Nothin', man. I went out with a Latino girl once. Her daddy tried to have me arrested." He laughed, shaking his head in disbelief. "My girl now, she black but she light skin. I got a little girl, lighter'n her. She real pretty." He grinned in obvious pride.

But Kent hadn't answered because he didn't know how to. He didn't know if that was so special, being so light. The color of his skin had only gotten him into trouble.

Kent walked to the field and climbed halfway up the wooden stands. He sat watching for several moments as some of the girls from the cheerleading squad worked on a movement. One of the girls' gym classes was playing soccer. He looked to his left and spotted Ms. Gilbert and a scattering of other students and faculty who were on free periods. Mr. Daly and Mrs. Teasdale, the principal's assistant, were there, too.

Kent felt for the handkerchief again. He knew he should just go over and give it to Ms. Gilbert, but he was suddenly afraid, like he might do something stupid in front of her and she would think he was a jerk. But he climbed down from his seat and made his way behind the bleachers to where the three faculty members sat chatting. Kent paced slowly back and forth behind them as they commented on the cheerleading routine.

"Why are they shaking their rear ends like that? That's so . . . suggestive. Don't you think so?" Mrs. Teasdale uttered.

"That's how they dance, Florence," Ms. Gilbert said.

" 'Cuse me."

The three adults turned around at his voice. Their expressions made Kent feel like he'd interrupted something private and important between them.

"What is it?" Mrs. Teasdale asked first, her tone official.

"You looking for me?" Mr. Daly added.

Patricia Gilbert was watching him closely. Kent shook his head and nodded in her direction. "I want to see Ms. Gilbert."

Mrs. Teasdale frowned. "What are you doing out here? Are you supposed to be in gym?"

"I'm finished. I was just waiting for the period to end. I saw Ms. Gilbert and I just wanted to . . ." He stopped.

Patricia stepped down to the ground from her seat. "I have to get back anyway. Come on, Kent. We'll walk together." She waved to her colleagues as she and Kent strolled away. But Patricia started around the perimeter of the stands, in the opposite direction from the entrance back into the school. A much longer route. "We can talk on the way." She smiled encouragingly.

Kent fell into step beside her, grateful that she hadn't started asking questions in front of the other two. But now that he was alone with her and had her attention, he felt awkward. He gave her a furtive sideways glance.

"I like your boots," Kent murmured.

Patricia raised her brows. "My boots? Thank you," she said with a light chuckle.

"I like your hair, too."

Patricia pursed her lips. "Why do you like my hair?"

Kent shrugged. "I don't know. I guess because it's sort of curly. And the color is nice."

"You've never seen this color before?" she asked in curiosity.

"Sure. But not on someone . . . like . . . like you."

"You mean, someone black, right?"

"Yeah." He shrugged again, embarrassed.

"Hmmm . . ."

"Ms. Gilbert? Is your mother white?" Kent blurted out. His face became flushed.

Patricia was stunned for a moment. It was an inappropriate question. It was nosy and personal. And it was not un-expected.

She remembered when she was about eight years old and one of her class-mates had continually touched and fin-gered her ponytail because, she'd said to Patricia, she had good hair. After school Patricia had asked her grand-mother, Gilly, "What is good hair?" A slight smile played around her mouth before answering.

"I . . . I'm sorry. I shouldn't have . . ."

"No, my mother wasn't white. Neither was my father. They were both black, Kent."

"Oh . . ." he finally murmured, looking puzzled. "Then how come . . ."

Patricia considered the boy's frowning expression for a moment. "Why did you ask me that?"

Kent stared down at the ground. "I don't know."

"Kent . . ." Patricia put her hand on his arm to get his attention and they stopped walking. "You *do* know."

He pouted. The crisp November air was starting to make his earlobes and cheeks turn pink. Kent gave Patricia a furtive glance. "Well . . . when I first saw you, I thought . . . you know," he started awkwardly. "I wasn't sure you were black."

"Is that what Kamil and the others thought about you?"

Kent got annoyed. "Kamil's an asshole." He winced and shook his head. "I'm sorry . . ."

Patricia arched a brow. "What made you decide I was black?"

He looked directly at Patricia now, his eyes openly scanning her features. "I don't know. It was something about the way you talked to me. The way you act, and stuff."

"The only thing I can say is that I identify black because I *am* black. I can't help how I look and I can't do much about it. But I can do something about how I feel and what I believe and how I behave. I define those things about myself. No one else."

"Yeah, but nobody sounds on your mother, and you don't have somebody like Kamil in your face all the time," Kent grumbled.

Patricia sighed. She had Gertrude Forrest. And some men she'd known briefly but would have liked to have known better. "You know, when I was your age . . . even younger . . . I went through the same thing you're going through."

"Yeah?" he asked skeptically.

"It's very complicated, Kent. I'm not sure I can explain that the way some people see you has nothing to do with you."

"You mean white people. I know about that. I just don't understand when . . . when blacks give me such a hard time. I'm black, too."

"Have you always felt that way?" she asked carefully.

"What?"

"That you're black?" She watched as Kent's entire body moved and flexed; first stiffly and then loosely, as if trying to settle just one way.

He looked away. "When I was a little kid, I thought I was white just like my mom. But then everybody started telling me that I wasn't. And then she told me herself that I was black. I asked her how come. She said because that's how everybody was going to see me and treat me because my father is black."

"How do you feel about her telling you that?"

He shrugged indifferently. "Okay. It was just that . . . that . . ." He looked poignantly at Patricia. "Like, I wasn't black enough. I don't talk like other kids. I don't know the same things they do."

"Would you like to be more like them?"

"Not like Kamil. Eric's cool but . . . I don't want to be like him, either. I just want to be the way I am and have people like me. You know?"

Patricia nodded and turned to begin walking again. "So what are you going to do about someone like Kamil?"

He squared his shoulders and made a sound of indifference. "Blow him off. I don't have to be his friend. I don't even like Kamil. But if he wants to take me on, that's cool. I can handle it."

Patricia smiled doubtfully at Kent's bravery. It wasn't quite that simple. He was only fifteen and had a long way to go. She didn't even bother suggesting that he didn't have to fight anybody . . . but that was an adult thought. Even at fifteen she'd had to defend herself.

"I had a great-grandfather, on my father's side, who sailed from America on a freighter. The story goes he stowed away and when he was caught the crew was going to throw him overboard . . ."

"Yeah?" Kent breathed, fascinated.

"But he talked his way into a job instead. He reached Europe and met a woman from Ireland. They eventually had to leave and come back to America to marry because she was condemned by her family and village for falling in love with a black man. They had four children. One of them was my grandfather Ian. Then he married a black woman from Virginia. That was my grandmother Gilly.

"On my mother's side, her grandfather was part Seminole Indian and part Spanish . . ."

"Wow," Kent whispered.

Patricia chuckled. "Talk about mixed blood . . ."

"That's *way* cool."

"That grandfather married a black woman from the Carolina sea islands who was a Gullah, a descendant of African slaves. I'm a product of all of that history. Just like you're the result of your mother's history and your father's history."

Kent stared at her and then narrowed his eyes thoughtfully. "You know what I really hate? When you fill out a form and they ask you to mark if you're white or black. What if you're both?"

"What do *you* do?"

"I'm going to start checking off other."

Patricia looked down at the ground. "I'm not sure that's an answer. No one should have to be an 'other.' You know what we should all do? Ignore the boxes. Make them irrelevant."

"Why do we need to mark boxes for anyway?" Kent asked in genuine curiosity.

Patricia took a deep breath and then chuckled helplessly. She looked at her watch. "We'll have to talk about it some other time. You should get inside . . ." she said as they neared the school entrance once more.

"Ms. Gilbert? Do you think my parents made a mistake having me?"

Patricia was thrown off guard. Mistake? She quickly looked over the tall, handsome teen, seeing the flicker of doubt in his dark eyes. "I think your parents are very lucky to have you for a son. And you're very lucky to have parents who love you so much. They each might show it in different ways, Kent, but you must know that they love you."

"Sure," he muttered dispiritedly.

She knew he was searching for another answer, but Patricia decided it would have to come from his parents. Or he'd have to work it out for himself. "I suppose you want to get your notebook," Patricia said, changing the subject smoothly.

Kent looked at her blankly. "Notebook?"

"Well, I guess the answer is no. I thought that's why you wanted to see me."

"Not really."

"Then, what is it?"

Slowly, he stopped walking and faced her. They were almost near the gym entrance again. He withdrew the now crumpled handkerchief from his pocket and held it out to her.

Patricia looked slightly surprised as she took the hankie. It was wrinkled and balled, with fuzz from the inside of Kent's pocket sticking to it.

"I didn't want you to think I was going to keep it or anything. I'm sorry it looks kind of messed up, but . . ."

"Don't worry about it. I can wash it," Patricia said.

"I . . . I also wanted to thank you. For helping me on Halloween."

"Did you tell your father what happened?"

"Yeah, sort of," Kent admitted uneasily.

"And what did he say?"

"He said I wasn't to lie to him." Kent glanced up quickly. "But I'm not going to say who I was with. I didn't mention Britt or Connors's names."

"That sounds fair. It could have been much worse, you know."

"I guess."

The end of the period bell rang inside the school, and a whistle was blown to signal the end of the squad practice and the soccer exercise on the field. The group of girls applauded themselves, and then began to make their way back to the building. They jogged past Kent and Patricia, calling out greetings as they went. One young girl trailed behind, not dressed for either activity. Patricia said hello to her.

Kent had never seen her before but couldn't help noticing her short dark hair and very red lips.

Patricia brought the girl over to him.

"Kent, I'd like you to meet Gabriella Villar. You two should get to be friends."

Kent reluctantly faced the girl. He was a little annoyed that he and Ms. Gilbert had to stop their conversation. And he didn't really want to meet anyone new. The girl didn't even look at him, as if she could care less. Well, so did he.

"Gabriella is a new student this year, too. She's from Spain."

"Hi," Kent responded. "You're a freshman, right?" he asked with a tone of superiority.

She nodded, but didn't look directly at him.

"Does she speak English?" Kent asked Patricia.

Gabriella raised her gaze to him, like he'd just said something stupid. "Of course I speak English."

Kent stared at her. She had a soft voice and pretty eyes.

"I think you two will certainly recognize each other from now on," Patricia said with a wry laugh.

The two young teens remained silent. Kent stared off into space, and Gabriella looked down at the ground. The second bell rang.

"You'd both better go, Kent." Patricia turned to the girl. "Why weren't you dressed for gym, Gabriella?"

She pouted. "The suit is too big, and it is ugly. I look silly."

Kent looked at her again. He didn't

think she'd look silly.

"You can't go through the whole year using that as an excuse," Patricia informed her sternly. "Ask the instructor if you can get an outfit that fits."

Gabriella shrugged. "Why do I take this gym? What is it for?"

Kent chortled. "You have to take it, so you won't get soft and fat."

Gabriella looked strangely at him. She blushed deeply and looked hurt. "I am not fat," she said and pushed past him to hurry into the school.

Kent looked disgusted. "I didn't say she was fat," he grumbled.

"I think she misunderstood."

"I thought you said she speaks English."

"Speaking and understanding is not the same thing. And I think it was the way you said it. Don't worry about it."

Patricia shook her head and looked at her watch. "I have to go, too. Someone is waiting for me upstairs . . ."

"Can I get my notebook tomorrow?"

"Sure. Come by anytime."

"Can I come at lunchtime?" Kent asked.

Patricia blinked at his eagerness. Suddenly she felt the need to be cautious. Nonetheless she smiled as she reached for the door. "Okay. I'll see you tomorrow, then. You better hurry or you're going to be late for your next class . . ." She rushed inside before she could be detained longer.

"Pickett and the rest of management think they can hang tough, but they're gonna go down. It's just a matter of time. They're stuck with inventory they can't move and no money to bring in new stuff."

Morgan finished scanning the columns of numbers, the statistics of Sager Electronics. He put down the page and picked up another. His company accountant had reworked the figures and projected another set of numbers. They would work if a different management style was implemented with different long-term goals, and if innovative marketing was employed for the products Sager currently distributed.

"Did you explain my plan? The idea is to give them a broader base for distribution."

"We've been over that. But they have no vision, Morgan. They're completely bush league and I don't understand why you want to prop them up. In a couple of months they'll beg for the offer you're making them now."

Morgan sat back and pushed the papers away from him. He glanced at his Northeast regional director, David Sullivan. He knew David was impatient with his plans for the Sager company and that his reasons for being impatient were not unjustified. An awful lot of time and energy — more than even Morgan had first thought would be necessary — was being spent on acquiring the company. It would have been quicker to just offer a buyout and take it over himself. But he wasn't interested in running an electronics distributor. And to have turned around and resold it would not have suited his purposes, either. What Morgan had been able to project was that Sager could be in a good position to be one of the top distributors to business, rather than to try to hold on to a consumer base that was actually declining . . . especially where computer software and hardware were concerned. He had a way of tapping into the changing health care industry, and Sager was going to be the conduit.

David was idly rotating his index fingers along the inside of a rubber band. He was self-confident and cocky, but Morgan had seen it backed by both an impressive résumé and demonstrated business acumen. David was right about Sager, but only if the consideration was the enormous profit that could be made by buying out the stockholders of the company and then putting up parts of the company for sale on the market. It would be easy and quick. And unnecessary.

"What would you do?" Morgan asked rhetorically.

David sat up straight, his lean body agile and quick and poised with impatient energy. "I'd take it over and put it in turnaround. Simple. Quick and dirty."

Morgan arched a brow. That's what he thought. He'd used the term himself the very first time he ever bought out a small business. The experience had been both exhilarating and enlightening. The results had made him a lot of money, but had displaced half the work force.

David Sullivan, with his virile Californian good looks and mentality, with his ability to charm and to quickly size up an opportunity and to go for it, reminded Morgan of his younger self as he tried to prove his self-worth. He appreciated David's zealousness. Yet at first he'd been very suspicious of David Sullivan's motives in wanting to work for him. When talented young white men talked about wanting to contribute to a black-owned company and its plans for the future, Morgan was always inclined to wonder about a hidden agenda.

Morgan stared thoughtfully at David Sullivan, knowing that David wanted to be a big fish in a lake, rather than a little fish in an ocean of sharks. A very smart idea. It was always best to know your limitations.

Morgan looked at his watch. He didn't want the Sager acquisition to be "quick and dirty," but he was running out of time and arguments to give the company.

"I've scheduled another meeting for this afternoon."

David shook his head. "Why waste your time? They don't understand we could take the ball and run with it if we wanted to . . . and win."

Morgan sat forward, frowning at David's assessment. He felt impatient. He picked up a bound report and chucked it over his desk toward his director.

David picked it up and leafed through the pages. Then he looked at Morgan. "You're not serious. Most of the managers at Sager are Neanderthals, Morgan. Why would you leave them in? Look what they've done to the company."

"Exactly. They've brought it along this far. It just expanded faster than they could handle. They could still do a good job with the right guidance. I'm trying to convince them to let us guide them. There's a lot of potential in Sager and I have plans for the company." Morgan stood up.

"If you say so. I can take care of this this afternoon," David said, thumbing through the report.

Morgan again looked at his watch. Prudence told him it was important for him to be there. David had pretty good judgment in client meetings, when he wasn't being flippant and tactless. But urgency of another nature won out. "I do have a conflict." Morgan adjusted his tie and walked to get his jacket from a narrow closet behind the door.

David sat back in his chair with no thought of leaving now that his meeting with Morgan was through. He viewed his employer casually as Morgan finished preparing to leave his office. "I'll take care of Sager. You know, this could go a lot smoother if you'd just let me take over."

Morgan hid his reaction to David's suggestion. "I don't see any need for that. What you're doing at this stage is fine."

David shook his head. "You could get called away again. Like now. Lack of continuity could become a problem."

"I don't see how," Morgan said smoothly. He turned to stand right in front of his manager. They were about the same height, maybe David had an inch or so over him. And he was younger, with the tautly framed body of a man in his prime and very conscious of his looks and appeal. But Morgan knew that he himself held another attribute granted him by instinct, history, and the need to survive. *Attitude.* "You want to explain what you're getting at?" he asked crisply.

David spread his hands. "Simple. Who's in charge if you're not here?"

"I am," Morgan said with a tight smile. "No decision comes out of this office that doesn't first come from me. I hope we understand that." David's smile was too casual, nearly patronizing, but Morgan was used to that in him.

"Loud and clear," David said good-naturedly, stepping aside so that Morgan could reach the door. "So . . . are you planning on coming to Sager later?"

"I don't think so. You're only making an offer. Don't press for a decision from them today, but make it clear that we expect a response sooner rather than later. Answer as many questions as you can without giving away all the details. You can fill me in tomorrow."

Chapter Six

Morgan peered through the hurricane fencing, his attention focused on the football and track field. Off to the left was the three-story contemporary building that was Duncan High School.

It was not like the high school he'd gone to in Los Angeles, which had been a post-World War II gray cement structure, institutional and devoid of character. His high school was a claustrophobic box compared to this environmental wonder. There had been no lawn at his high school and almost no trees. And what had passed for a track field had been rutted and cracked and had weeds growing in the crevices.

On the open track field an instructor blew his whistle and shouted orders. The team responded with a kind of swaggering arrogance and desultory movements that, Morgan saw with amusement, indicated the dozen or so boys were well aware of their physical prowess. The development of their bodies that was now settling into defined biceps, abdominal ridges, and tight hard muscles. For Morgan, it evoked the memory of never noticing that he was growing chest hair until he realized the girls all seemed to find it sexy. It was probably close to forty degrees outdoors but, of course, none of the guys seemed to care about the cold. They were invincible.

He had not liked school very much himself. At least, not until it was almost too late. School had been boring and structured. It wasn't until the start of his junior year in high school, when he'd thought of dropping out, that Morgan had begun to think about his future. He joined the basketball team only because it meant traveling regionally to play other schools, and he liked being away from home and the on-again off-again appearance of his father. Morgan found that playing basketball focused his mind and energies. It was a game of strategy, quick decisions, and movement. It was a game of team coordination that pulled him out of his personal isolation.

He was only allowed to play, however, in exchange for equal attention to academics. A black teacher, a crotchety old woman with a cane — who'd actually threatened to use it on him for wasting his mind — and iron determination, had seen to that. He began to excel in another subject, math. Suddenly, while listening to the repetitive drone of the teacher, Morgan found that the algebraic and geometric formulas were making sense. It was all very logical. It became a challenge to do the assigned problems because he knew that, no matter what, there was going to be a neat and precise answer. It was a turning point in his life.

He realized that with some effort and thought there was always an answer to be found to any question or problem. At least of the math kind. The people kind remained difficult. But by the time he'd graduated, he'd managed a partial athletic scholarship that took him away from L.A. and into another life. His one compelling thought, beyond thankfulness, had been to become important . . . and rich. Everything else that had happened had been unexpected.

Morgan pushed away from the car

and, thoughtfully considering his son, began walking toward the main entrance of the high school. On the stairs to the entrance, there were some students milling about. To Morgan they seemed both so young and so old.

The interior of the building was bright and seemed to vibrate with youth. Several students and teachers passed him and he was sensing how different the atmosphere of school felt from any other environment. It felt protected and safe, if a little sterile and unreal. It also made him feel old.

He stepped into the first open doorway he passed. There he was given the directions to Patricia's office and a visitor's pass. Morgan had almost reached the end of the hallway when he heard the voices just before he turned the corner. One was that of Patricia, the other a younger voice speaking quietly and with uncertainty. Both voices were talking in Spanish.

Morgan stood at the corridor junction and watched what was apparently the end of an interview. Patricia's hands gestured as she spoke. She lightly patted the girl's arm in reassurance. Her glasses were pushed to the top of her head, and without their interference Morgan could now see the delicate line of her cheek and her nose that had a slight hump on its bridge. Patricia's pre-Raphaelite hair was pulled back from her temples and forehead, giving her a youthful and guileless appearance.

"*Venga donde me cuando tenga que hablar. Intiendo?*"

"*Sí.*" The young girl nodded.

Patricia smiled at her and spoke gently. "*Yo erá tímida también. Entonces, hablaré Englés?*"

"*Trateré.*"

Patricia shook her head. "In English."

"I'll try," the girl said with a shrug.

"Good. Now don't worry. Everyone likes you fine. You get high marks from a lot of the boys, like Pete Connors." She chuckled lightly.

The girl rolled her eyes. "*Bruta,*" she muttered darkly and walked away from Patricia. She gave Morgan only a brief glance as she continued past him and on down the hall.

When Patricia spotted Morgan she stared blankly at him for a second. Then she hastily reached for her glasses and slid them to her nose. She stood straight, trying to ease the sudden tension in her stomach. She didn't know if she was preparing for a confrontation, or if he was simply affecting her usual good sense. It wasn't as if she didn't know they'd come face-to-face again. But still Patricia felt a sense of surprise.

She'd known he was expected today, but still Morgan could see he'd caught Patricia off guard and drew a perverse pleasure in the observation. She was dressed appropriate to the environment, wearing a crisp white blouse with the collar up at her nape and the sleeves rolled almost to her elbows. Her skirt was denim, an A-line shape that fitted to her slender hips, the hem ending just below her knees. His attention came slowly back to her face. There was a quick flash of awareness and annoyance in her eyes, but Patricia was just as impertinently studying him.

Patricia's tension persisted. It was odd seeing Morgan Baxter here, in her territory. He seemed out of place in his expensive business suit with his air of urbane sophistication.

"I'm here," Morgan announced.

"You're almost forty-five minutes late."

"So were you the first time we met. Now we're even."

Patricia grimaced good-naturedly. "Touché."

Morgan put his hands in his pockets, pinning his trench coat and suit jacket open. "I wasn't really keeping score," he said quietly. "But I guess we both like to be right."

She inclined her head. "Are you going to be difficult about this?"

Morgan frowned, wondering if she'd guessed his mood. If she had, then it only made things worse. "I hadn't come with a plan. It probably depends on what you have to say."

"This is not going to be an inquisition, Mr. Baxter."

He grinned. "If you stop calling me Mr. Baxter, I won't counterattack."

Patricia shook her head, her nose tilted slightly upward. "This is an official meeting. I'm the counselor and you're the parent. On school grounds those are the rules." With a small wave of her hand Patricia indicated the open office door before she turned to walk into the room and to her desk.

Morgan appeared in the cubicle entrance behind her and Patricia had the strange sensation of the room shrinking. He seemed taller than she remembered, and his presence had the effect of making her surroundings suddenly seem disorganized and cramped. His dark eyes held no particular expression as his attention swept quickly around the office. He thoughtfully read her laminated state-required certificate for counseling, behind which was stuck a very dusty and very dead white rose.

Morgan noticed the shelf of thick academic texts with esoteric titles on child development and psychology. And then he became particularly interested in the few framed photographs on the back edge of her desk. He leaned closer for a better look. One image was of an older woman who had to be a relative. The thick and short wavy hair on the woman standing next to a younger Patricia said heredity. And there were similarities in the shapes of the jaw, mouth, and eyes although the woman was darker in complexion. The photo of a young black couple with children was also intriguing. The toddler was a carrot top with fair skin and looked for the world like a little white girl. The only thing visible of the infant in the woman's arms was just a dark layer of fine baby hair. There was a last picture of Patricia that was the most interesting of all. She sat in a group of half a dozen young adults who were on some sort of outing on a beach or a lake. Judging from the appearance of the other men and women, Morgan would guess perhaps in a Latin country. He stared at the image of Patricia, however, whose startling hair was in dreadlocks. His perception of her shifted dramatically.

"You speak Spanish," he observed.

Patricia whirled around to face him. He'd heard her conversation in the hallway with Gabriella. "Not very well."

Morgan turned from the photographs to stare at her. He stood close enough to notice that her glasses neither magnified nor shrunk the brightness of her gray eyes. He wondered, absently, why she even wore glasses when she didn't appear to need them. "You make yourself understood," he finally replied.

"I studied in high school and college, and I worked one summer in Guadalajara, Mexico. I became fluent there."

"Mexico? Why not Spain?"

She looked squarely at him. "It costs less to travel to Mexico."

Morgan merely nodded. "So, what did you do in Mexico?"

Patricia leaned back against the edge of her desk. He was standing a little too close. *To forget* . . . she thought. She shook her head shortly. "I was a waitress at a small café that was popular with the university students. I lived with a Mexican family."

Morgan regarded her thoughtfully. "You worked. Everybody else partied."

She merely smiled. "I was probably the only one who had to work. But I had fun," Patricia admitted.

"Why didn't you stay stateside to work? It should have been a whole lot easier."

She stared warily at Morgan, suddenly realizing the personal nature of his questions. She couldn't help the blush that stained her cheeks. "I thought the experience would be good for me."

Morgan sensed the evasiveness of her answer and was intrigued. "And was it?"

She thought of the ways of how difficult that summer had been. She thought of Drew and the unbearable disappointment of his betrayal. Patricia pursed her lips, something she did unconsciously when considering a response. "Very . . ." she said quietly, and then abruptly ended the conversation by sitting down.

She indicated the chair next to her desk for Morgan, but he moved it so that he sat adjacent to her. They were still too close. Patricia crossed her legs at the knee as he stared at her, waiting for her to begin. It was suddenly difficult and she took safety behind an official speech.

"Well, let me start by saying that it's too bad you weren't able to attend the orientation at the start of the school year. It was a good opportunity for everyone to meet. Teachers, students, and parents."

Morgan arched a brow, without knowing if she intended criticism or not. "I thought I explained that."

"Yes, you have. I'm only saying how that meeting might have helped. Things might not have evolved so far. This meeting might not have been necessary at all."

"Why don't you tell me why it is now?"

She heard the authoritative voice of the executive speaking. Cut to the chase. She adjusted her glasses. "You know that Kent's homeroom teacher has reported him late to first-period class . . ."

He frowned. "No. I didn't know."

"Well . . . fifteen times so far."

"Fifteen . . ." Morgan repeated, clearly stunned.

"He's also cut several classes, and even when he's present he doesn't participate. His grades are okay, but definitely down from his last year in Colorado."

The expression on Morgan's face tightened, and he fixed Patricia with such a cold look that she felt he was somehow holding her to blame. She sat forward in her chair, feeling a need to make Morgan understand.

"There's been some warning. You and I both know that what's going on is not about Kent's schoolwork per se, or his classes."

"Go on," he ordered.

She opened her mouth to continue, but then just looked puzzled, at him. "Don't you have any clue as to what this is about?"

Patricia stopped again as Morgan's expression closed. She watched as he slid down in his chair. Just a little, with his knees apart. It was the way Patricia had always seen young black teens sit as she talked to them in her office. It was an attitude of challenge, yet she knew he wasn't aware of it.

Morgan braced his elbows on the arms of the chair. He cupped his hands together and rested them against his mouth. Not being able to see his mouth made it that much more difficult for Patricia to gauge his feelings. It seemed deliberate.

"Yes, I do," Morgan began to answer after a very long thoughtful pause. "You hinted at it the other night. He's having trouble with the other kids at school. I bet he's being pushed up against the wall to prove himself. To show that he's black and he's down with the program."

She was dumbfounded. "How does he do that?"

Morgan almost sprang forward, confrontationally. "First of all by not backing down. By being prepared. It means knowing what you're up against . . . and *still* getting over, despite everything thrown at you. Can Kent do that? Can he walk the walk *and* talk the talk?" Morgan drawled, slipping quite easily

into the tone and vernacular of someone with street smarts.

"You couldn't be more wrong about
Kent."

Morgan shook his head impatiently.
"Patricia, I'm not saying that's all of
it. I hope we're all much more than
that. But Kent is going to grow up to
be a black man in an America that
hasn't learned to get beyond the color
of a person's skin."

"Your definition leaves a lot to be
desired," she said tartly.

"So, what did I leave out?" He spread
his hands.

"Being proud of who you are, no matter what. Kent has all of that. You
shouldn't need anything about him to
be different. It makes me wonder if
you're speaking more for yourself."

If it was possible, Morgan's expression
became even harder. It was on the tip
of his tongue to hurl at Patricia that
she wouldn't know. "I would think that
some of the struggle is familiar to you.
I just don't know if pride is enough."

She shrugged. "Is it ever? That's not
our exclusive burden. I didn't mean to
suggest that somehow you . . ."

"I should have been around more to

teach him," Morgan said slowly, emphasizing each word.

"Don't lay your guilt on Kent," Patricia
said with a frown. "He's learning on his
own. In a way, that's better."

"That doesn't exactly absolve me, of
my responsibility as a black father, a
black man."

Patricia felt suddenly odd, staring into
the face of a man who hid his history
well when he had to, camouflaged by
experience and success. This was the
side of Morgan she didn't know. But the
past was still where he started from.
She realized now that there was a
chasm between father and son that was
not solely generational.

"Perhaps you and Kent . . ."

"Patty?"

The voice from the outer office caused
both Morgan and Patricia to draw apart.

"Patty, this ought to be worth at least
three future favors. I spoke to . . ."

Morgan and Patricia stood up when
Jerome appeared in the doorway. He
glanced quickly back and forth between
them.

"Sorry . . ." Jerome uttered, stopping
short of the threshold to Patricia's office. He closely scrutinized the tall black

man in the elegant navy-blue business suit and fashionable designer tie. And when the man and Patricia stood up, Jerome felt insulted by the glare he received from both of them. "I didn't know you had a late appointment today."

"This is Morgan Baxter. He's Kent's father." Patricia looked at Morgan. "This is my colleague, Jerome Daly."

Jerome held out his hand and put a tight cold smile on his face. "So, you're Kent's father. We wondered if we were ever going to meet you."

"Have you been staying awake nights thinking about it?" Morgan asked with smooth sarcasm.

"Jerome, Mr. Baxter and I are in the middle of discussing Kent," Patricia said broadly.

Jerome did not take the hint. He peered through his glasses at Morgan with a long and steady appraisal. His demeanor was both challenging and impertinent.

"Armani?"

Morgan lifted a brow. "No. Ferrantino."

Patricia became impatient with the sudden shift in topic. The two men ignored her and continued a conversation that made no sense to her. Jerome leaned in a relaxed manner in the door frame and crossed his arms over his chest, locking his hands under each armpit.

"I thought all capitalist CEOs wore Armani."

Morgan smiled thinly. He put his hands in his pockets. "I wouldn't know. I'm not a capitalist CEO."

"It's getting late and I would like to finish this meeting," Patricia interjected strongly. She finally gained Jerome's attention and glared, shocked at his goading of Morgan Baxter. "You'll have to excuse us."

"Right." Jerome nodded, not particularly repentant. "Well, at least you're finally taking this seriously."

A bell shrilled in the hall outside the door and the interruption caused a wave of relief to inexplicably sweep through Patricia. It didn't release the tension, but instead seemed to wind it tighter. She turned to Jerome. "Maybe you'd better do a quick check of the halls and make sure class change is going smoothly."

"It's the last class for the seniors, Pat.

I don't think I have to escort them to the exits."

"Taking what seriously, Mr. Daly?" Morgan asked quietly.

Jerome looked at Morgan carefully. "Your son. Kent could become a problem if he's not checked. His behavior so far this semester says the kid is in conflict. He needs someone to pay attention to what he's doing in and out of school."

"Jerome . . ." Patricia began in warning.

"And you don't think he's getting that from me."

Patricia glanced apprehensively to Morgan. She would not have put it in so careless a phrase, but she could see from the dangerous narrowing of his eyes that Jerome had hit a nerve.

"Frankly, I don't think so," Jerome answered.

"What Jerome means is . . ."

"I know what he means. You've been discussing a lot more than my son." Morgan glared at Patricia, his gaze sharp and furious. "I didn't expect to become a casual subject during lunch."

"That's not what happened . . ."

"We were thinking of Kent," Jerome cut in.

"You don't have the right to suggest that I don't care about my son!" Morgan said tensely, pointing a finger at Jerome.

"Morgan . . ." Patricia turned to him, slipping into familiarity so easily she never noticed. She only wanted to control the damage. "We're not trying to get in your personal business, but you must understand that our primary concern is for Kent."

"You got what you wanted," Jerome said suddenly.

"What?" Patricia asked, looking at him in confusion and annoyance.

Jerome had to raise his voice against the noise of the students in the hallway. No one thought to close the outer door. "Kent is back in practice for the next game." He turned to Morgan. "I hope he can run. The team could use a good free safety."

Morgan looked to Patricia. She could only return his gaze in helplessness. His eyes stayed focused on her face and she saw more than just anger and frustration. There was betrayal . . . and disappointment. She wondered if he meant it exclusively for her. She leaned forward. "This is not exactly what I had in mind."

"Isn't it? Well, it worked anyway. You've shown you understand more about my son than I do. He never mentioned he was interested in football. I admit I never asked. But a little more knowledge about Kent's history could have prevented what's happening now. I accept the blame for that, too. I didn't, as you implied, make myself available. But I don't like the feeling of having been tried, judged, and convicted by you and your colleague."

Morgan's anger was palpable and even Jerome stood silently fascinated as the tirade spewed forth. But Morgan's anger only served to raise Patricia's. She was mad at Jerome for his untimely and undiplomatic interruption. And Patricia was mad at herself because she'd read Morgan Baxter all wrong.

"If you and I could just sit down," Patricia tried calmly.

"I don't want to sit down," Morgan said harshly. "We've had our talk . . ."

"Don't yell at her!"

All three adults turned at the sound

of the young angry voice in the doorway. Kent stood tightly clutching the strap of his knapsack, which was slung over his shoulder. He strode forward to stand confronting his father and Patricia. Jerome moved, unnoticed, out of the range of fire.

"Kent," Morgan began sternly.

"Did you come back for your notebook?" Patricia asked, somewhat foolishly, she realized, but Kent was facing his father and ignored the question.

"Don't yell at her," he repeated.

"I wasn't yelling. We were discussing . . ."

"Me. Yeah, I know. Look, I'm sorry I'm so much trouble."

Morgan frowned. "Where did you get that idea?"

"Kent, I don't think you understand," Patricia tried.

"I'm just messing up my father's life."

"Stop it, Kent," Morgan warned again.

The boy took a step closer to his father. His voice was gravelly and strained with feeling. "Why don't you just say it? You don't really want me here. You wish I wasn't your son, right?"

Patricia's eyes shifted quickly to Morgan, feeling his shock and his hurt in the pit of her stomach.

"You're wrong," Morgan said quietly. "I wish we could have talked before this became public so you'd know how I feel."

"What about how *I* feel?" Kent asked tearfully. "Ms. Gilbert is the only one who listens to me."

"Kent, that's enough," Patricia said to him, hearing the buildup of rage within the youngster. "Try to calm down. Your father is here because he cares a great deal about what happens to you."

"Why didn't he ever want me to live with him before now? Why did he stay away from me for all those years?"

"Oh, Christ . . ." Jerome muttered uncomfortably from his corner.

Kent looked from a stunned Patricia back to his father, whose expression could no longer be read. "You don't get it, do you?"

The question hung in the air and no one seemed to have an answer for him. Kent stared at his father, his body rigid against the inclination to tremble. He waited for a response but could not see that the moment made it impossible for his father to say a word. And he could not tell that his father's silence had nothing to do with not having an answer. Kent turned abruptly and rushed out of the office. The silence hung between the three adults, buffeted oddly by the noise of the students in the hallway.

Jerome cleared his throat, making his presence known once more. "This isn't unusual," he said with a calm that grated against both Patricia's and Morgan's nerves. "Kids can get pretty unreasonable at times. I'll check on him."

Morgan took a step toward the door. "I'll go after him."

Patricia put a hand on his arm. "Let him go. Both of you," she commanded firmly. "He's angry now. In a while he'll be embarrassed and then sorry." She stared at Jerome. "He'll only feel worse if you try to talk with him."

Jerome slowly nodded. He looked at Morgan as though wanting to say something. Instead he merely shrugged, looked at Patricia, and backed out of the office. "I'll . . . er . . . check on the hall traffic," he finally conceded, walking away.

"So," Morgan began in the silence that

followed Jerome's departure, "what have we accomplished?"

Patricia suddenly felt great empathy for him. "Now we know exactly what's troubling Kent."

"Not *we. I* now know what the problem is. Me," he said ironically.

Patricia winced. It was a terrible admission for anyone to make. "Morgan, you're wrong. The same way you know that Kent is wrong. It's just . . ."

"Just what?"

Patricia sighed helplessly. "It's going to take a little time and patience."

Morgan shook his head. "I've already lost fifteen years. I know what has to be done." He turned to leave.

"Please don't do anything right away. At least not for a few days. And don't be angry with him."

"I'm not angry with Kent," he said impatiently. "I'm angry with myself. I don't see that any of this is really his fault."

"He doesn't get off scot-free. He has a responsibility, too."

"For what?" Morgan asked, puzzled.

"To try to be fair. To listen to your side, too. And you can't read his mind, Morgan. He has to tell you how he feels.

Encourage him to."

"How?"

Patricia slowly smiled. "That's part of *your* responsibility. You have to figure it out."

Morgan gestured with impatience. "That all sounds very clever but it's just a theory."

"It takes work, Morgan. You said you had no choice but to trust my judgment, but you do. Trust your own instincts. Remember, you're the parent. You're the one in charge. It's up to you to make Kent want to trust you."

"I don't think . . ."

"And don't think too much about this. Just do what feels right."

The muscle in Morgan's jaw flexed furiously as he stared at Patricia trying to get a sense if his trust was, in any way, going to be misplaced in her. It went against his self-respect and his need for control to rely on anyone else for anything. It rankled him that he was out of his depth.

"You won't lose your son," she said quietly. She suddenly held out a hand to him.

Surprise caused Morgan's brows to lift as he took her hand firmly in his own, noting the strength and warmth in it, even though it was so slender and fine-boned. He looked down at her hand momentarily, startled by the paleness of it against his. He held it while he studied the bright assurance and challenge in Patricia's eyes. "I could use all the friends I can get," he commented stiffly.

Patricia hadn't considered it quite that way. But still, she found herself being cautious. "That's a possibility," she hedged.

"I better go after him."

She hesitated. "All right. Just remember what I said. And also remember that this doesn't have to be a fight for Kent's soul."

He frowned. "That's a strange thing to say."

She shook her head, smiling slightly. "All you have to do is recall what it was like when you were with Kent's mother. Who got on you for that decision to marry outside your race . . . and why."

Morgan's expression grew a little caustic but he pursed his mouth. "I still don't believe it's as easy as you make it sound, Patricia."

"That's because you're goal-oriented,"

she said, using a term he was more likely to appreciate. "But your son's well-being is not negotiable. He *is* growing up black. He knows exactly who he is."

Morgan stared at her as if something had just been clarified for him. He finally admitted that he, too, had imposed a judgment on Patricia based on what he saw. What he saw now was someone who'd been there . . . done that. And survived.

He squeezed her hand. "We've finally gotten around to first names. Patricia . . ." he said in a quiet voice, staring at her.

She realized she made no attempt to withdraw her hand although her lack of movement was not meant to be provocative. And then Morgan surprised her completely when he slowly raised her hand and gently kissed the back of it. He waited for her to respond. When Patricia didn't . . . couldn't, Morgan released her. Since neither of them seemed to know what to say after that, he simply turned and walked out of the office without another word.

She *did* understand.

Morgan pulled his tie loose and sat wearily on the sofa. He felt tense and anxious as he picked up the phone and began to dial. He checked his watch again and then rubbed his hand over the back of his neck. Morgan was acutely aware of the silence in the town house. It was not the same as when he lived all alone here. Kent's presence had changed the rhythm of everything in his life. But he'd arrived home to find it empty, and he had no idea where his son was. The silence increased his anxiety.

"Ventura, Inc. Good afternoon."

"Connie, it's me."

"Yes, Mr. Baxter."

Morgan sighed as he lifted his feet and rested them across the edge of the coffee table. "I'm not going to make it back in this afternoon. I got tied up at the high school. Are there any messages?"

"A few. The Brooklyn Downtown Development Corp. wants you to meet with them next week. Mr. Tanner from Sager called as well as Ms. McGraw. Also a reminder from your accountant about your personal taxes."

"Is David there?"

"Yes, he is. Shall I put you through?"

"Please . . ."

While he waited, Morgan again checked the time. Maybe it wasn't so late, after all. The rest of the high school students would only have been dismissed an hour ago. Still, he couldn't help wondering if Kent would . . .

"Sullivan."

"David. What's going on?" Morgan inquired briskly.

"Sager's beginning to tilt, finally. In our direction. This took too damned long if you ask me. They'll go for your offer if they have a say in the new management."

"What will they give up in return?"

"They'll let us reorganize. We can do what we want about the new marketing. And they'll be open to restructuring their distribution channels."

"It's a start. But I'm not finished with them yet."

"I didn't tell them you're going to want your own hand-picked team to go in right at the beginning. Let's just get them to sign and get this show on the road."

"Sounds good, so far. We'll talk in the morning."

"Mañana . . ." David said irreverently, and hung up.

Morgan sat for a moment longer, unable to feel gratified that the negotiations were heading toward a closing of the deal. And for the moment he had no desire to return Beverly's call. He still had Kent's whereabouts on his mind.

Against Patricia's advice, Morgan had tried to search for Kent once he'd left the office. But it was impossible, since Kent could have disappeared almost anywhere in the building. Morgan had stood across the street from the school for a while. He had not seen Kent and had given up in frustration. He'd just have to wait it out now, until the boy came home. Then he hoped that the two of them could begin to straighten out the mess they were in.

Morgan got up from the sofa and paced the room restlessly. He hoped that what had happened in Patricia's office with Kent was a misunderstanding. But he'd been truly shocked by the amount of raw anger from his son. Morgan took notice. A pretense and veneer had been stripped away leaving him stunned and unprepared. He had looked into Patricia's eyes and seen not condemnation or judgment, but recognition and empathy. And a validation of his fears. In front of witnesses he had been struck nearly powerless by a fifteen-year-old. Morgan had a flashback to how his own father would have handled him had he been in Kent's place. With the back of his hand. With parental rage in his voice that would claim absolute power. Morgan wondered if Kent was expecting some sort of punishment to fit his crime. But it wasn't a crime to be fifteen and very, very angry. Besides, he figured with insight tiredly, *he* was the one in disgrace, not Kent.

Morgan heard a car door slam outside the town house. Curiosity sent him to the hall window just in time to watch Kent walking slowly up the entrance steps. He felt a wave of relief relax the muscles in his neck. Still, Morgan felt himself bracing for the confrontation. It was time. He opened the door and Kent, hesitating in surprise for a second, stepped inside.

"Come on in," Morgan said. "How'd you get home?"

"Ms. Gilbert gave me a ride."

Morgan was ambivalent about the information. Patricia coming to their rescue was becoming a habit.

"I . . . I didn't think you'd be here," Kent said gruffly, his voice husky.

Morgan closed the door and stood regarding his son. He fought against a very alien urge and thought it best not to touch Kent. "I came right home after the meeting with your counselors. I wanted to be here when you got in."

Kent advanced into the room, his features drawn, and his eyes suspiciously bright. "I guess you're mad at me."

"I was worried. You were pretty ticked off when you ran out of the office."

"Sorry . . ." Kent pouted.

Morgan nodded briefly. "You should be. Are you okay?"

"Sure," Kent said stiffly. He walked past his father and headed for the stairwell.

Morgan watched him go. He clenched his jaw and irritation deepened his voice. "Just hold it right there. I thought we were going to be honest with each other." Patricia's voice floated into his head with advice . . . *make him talk to you; and listen.* "You're not okay. *We're* not okay. I want you to tell me about it. Whatever it is."

Kent didn't respond. He kept walking slowly toward the staircase. His knapsack was dangling from one hand, a strap trailing along the floor behind him.

"Answer me," Morgan called out, his voice sounding thunderous in the uncomfortable silence between them.

Kent stopped at the foot of the stairs with his shoulders hunched forward. Suddenly he turned around and in the motion he flung the schoolbag aside. It slid a short distance, bumping into the legs of a chair in the entrance of the living room. The chair scraped on the wooden floor.

"Fuck!" Kent said in such an outburst of rage that his voice croaked.

He stood with his teeth bared and clamped tight, his chest heaving as he breathed in short, angry spurts. Morgan stared at his son before he began walking toward him. Strangely, he wasn't surprised. And he wasn't taken aback by Kent's outburst. If anything, Morgan accepted it as the first honest demonstration of his son's pent-up feelings since they'd been together.

There was a rapid flurry of emotions

that he could see take place on his son's face. Finally, Kent seemed to settle into pure anger and a horrifying display of pain and vulnerability.

"Fuck," Kent said again, but this time as if he were exhausted. "I waited for you to come and get me."

"Come and . . . get you?" Morgan asked blankly. Had he missed Kent after all, somewhere near the school this afternoon?

"I thought you would. I thought . . . you'd just show up and do it."

Morgan's stomach knotted so suddenly it produced a sharp cramp. Kent wasn't talking about this afternoon at all . . . "It's very complicated, Kent. I couldn't just come for you. The courts gave custody to your mother when she and I divorced. You have to understand that."

"Well, I don't. Why should I? What's the big deal about saying you want me to come and live with you, huh?"

Morgan felt all those years of wrestling with just that thought come crashing down on him. Why should he expect a fifteen-year-old to accept a decision he had no part in, but which had affected his life? Morgan made no attempt to excuse himself. He had no defense against the damage he and Melissa had inadvertently inflicted on their son.

Kent struggled against the continuing wave of his hurt. He kept swallowing to keep back the tears. "Granddad said you didn't want a half-black kid. He said you wouldn't want to have to tell people about me."

The muscle tightened again at the back of Morgan's neck. He had always known that the reason Melissa's father, Colonel Stowe, had readily accepted Kent as his grandson was precisely because he didn't look particularly black. But Kent didn't need to know that. "Your grandfather said a lot to you, I take it. He shouldn't have told you those things. There was your mother to consider, too. She didn't want to give you up because she loves you."

Kent shook his head. "But I thought that as soon as you could you were going to come and get me. You never did." His voice quavered.

"I tried to explain the best way I knew how in some of my letters."

"I didn't want letters!" Kent almost shouted. "I didn't even read a lot of them. I wanted *you.*"

Morgan put his hand out in supplication to his son. "Son, I hear you," Morgan said calmly.

Kent just stared at him, before a heart-wrenching sob broke loose from the boy and tears began to spill down his cheeks. Morgan watched, momentarily helpless. He was experiencing the most damning sense of regret and loss, and then outrage, and then . . . he didn't know what else. It all became a jumbled mess in his heart.

"Lots of my friends back home have divorced parents. Their fathers do stuff with them."

"Look, your mother and I decided not to live together anymore, but that had nothing to do with not caring about you." Morgan had almost touched the boy's shoulder when Kent pushed the hand away.

"I had to make up lies about you," he gritted tightly.

"Because you were too ashamed to tell your friends you didn't know anything about your own father. Didn't even know where he was most of the time. Right?" Morgan filled in flatly.

That insight seemed to do Kent in. He sat down heavily on a step. He was crying openly now. "I . . . hated you. I wished you weren't my father." He wiped his face with the heel of his hand. Sniffled back a runny nose. "Mom always told me the same thing. 'Of course your father loves you,' " Kent mimicked. "I asked, then how come you never came to see me, and she'd say, maybe someday. I got tired of hearing that shit. After a while, I didn't believe her."

Morgan came closer. "Then why did you call me last summer? If you hated me so much, why did you leave Colorado and come here?" Kent looked sullen and buried his face in his crossed arms, unable to answer. "Maybe it was to punish me, to tell me you hated me." He stared down at his son, and his voice dropped. "Maybe you just wanted to know about the black part of you. The part that comes from me. You're my flesh, man. We're blood." Now Morgan did rest a hand on Kent's shoulder and squeezed firmly. "You're my son, and I love you."

Morgan was astonished at how unfamiliar the words sounded. But nonetheless his throat seemed to close over them, hampering his ability to breathe. His vision began to blur. He squatted down until he was nearly at eye level with Kent.

"Why don't we just try to know each other. I missed out on a lot, too. I could learn a few things from you."

Kent lifted his face, and his eyes were red and watery. "Maybe I don't care anymore."

Morgan clenched his teeth to keep the unexpected jolt of hurt inside. "We'll have to find out, won't we? You made the first move and I admire you for that. It took guts to come to New York. Now it's my turn. I guess I have to prove myself to you." Kent glanced at him warily. "You're old enough to see for yourself whether I'm what your grand-dad says I am, or what you want me to be. But I warn you; you may not like everything you find out."

"It can't be worse than not knowing anything," Kent whispered reasonably.

Morgan's mouth twisted into an ironic grin. "Tough guy. I like that."

Kent again gave his father a furtive, suspicious glare. "Why should I believe you now?"

Morgan stood up. He made a gesture with his free hand, and then dropped it heavily again to his side. "I don't know. Why should you?"

Kent shrugged indifferently. He bent and reached for the strap of the knapsack and, standing up, swung it to his shoulder. He silently turned and started up the stairs.

Morgan forced himself not to follow, not to even say anything more. He also began to feel his hope dissolve. Maybe it *was* too late. But halfway up, Kent stopped. He stood for a moment in indecision with his back to his father, before he turned his head and glanced down at him standing at the foot of the stairs.

Morgan had no idea what had stopped Kent, and he could only just stare back. Suddenly Kent started back down. He dropped the sack. When he reached the foot of the stairs Morgan could see that the boy's expression had cleared, even though his face was still flushed and fresh tears were about to spill. Kent held on to the banister tightly, as if afraid to let go.

"Daddy . . ." he began with uncertainty.

Morgan stood perfectly still. He couldn't think of any other time since Kent had come to live with him that the boy had called him that.

"I'm sorry, son. I swear I never meant to hurt or disappoint you. Maybe I was just a little bit afraid, too."

"Why would you be afraid?" Kent asked suspiciously.

"I thought . . . maybe you wouldn't want me to be your father. What if you believed you really belonged in Colorado with your mother and grandfather? It might have been a lot easier for you," Morgan finished broadly. He could tell from Kent's expression that he understood what he meant.

Perhaps it was the drop in the tone of his father's voice, or even his comments, which Kent had never even thought of before, that propelled him forward. But he went, unashamed, right into his father's arms. It was an awkward, clumsy embrace. Kent started to cry again. And now . . . so did Morgan.

Just then he remembered the feel of Kent as a newborn, as a baby in his arms. Kent's inherent helplessness, his warm soft body had made Morgan feel as if this child was the only worthwhile thing he'd ever done in his life. Not until this instant, with his son growing swiftly into manhood, did Morgan regret deeply all the lost years.

"I couldn't stay there anymore," Kent mumbled. "Mom knows I love her, but . . . I want to be with you." The words were almost lost against the fabric of his father's shirt.

And still Morgan couldn't say a thing. He couldn't seem to hold his son close enough. He was never going to let Kent go again. And he was never going to stop being grateful that he'd been given, that his *son* had given him, a second chance.

Chapter Seven

The conversation and debate flowed into the corridor as the four men ended the afternoon of discussion about the Sager Electronics Company.

"It's looking good, so let's not do anything to spook them, now," Paul Banyon advised.

"No pun intended," Morgan murmured easily. The other men chuckled.

Paul turned to David Sullivan. "You had some good ideas. Mind if I cop a few for some of my other projects?"

David shrugged and nodded in Morgan's direction. "I don't if the boss doesn't."

Morgan stopped walking as they all reached the center reception area and Connie Anderson's desk. "As long as we get what we want. And if you make a killing in the future, you give us credit."

"I knew there was a string attached," Paul said dryly.

Morgan smiled. "That's why *you* work for *me.*"

Paul turned to Morgan's secretary. "Thanks, Connie, for letting us work uninterrupted. Can I make you an offer you can't refuse?" he teased.

Connie smiled graciously. "I don't think so, but thank you for the thought."

"You've done a first-rate job, Morgan," Brian Isaacs, the second lawyer, said. He put out his hand and Morgan took it to shake.

As they all stood saying their good-byes, Beverly McGraw entered. She smiled brightly at the gathered men, immediately drawing their attention.

"Hello, everyone. Looks like I just missed a summit meeting."

The two lawyers, professionally acquainted with Beverly, exchanged harmless banter with her. Morgan watched as her personality swept everyone around her into the circle of her charms. He reflected absently that she was at her best with an audience, and when she could be in control. He had to smile secretly to himself. Sometimes Beverly forgot herself and tried that same routine with him. Forgot that if anyone was going to appreciate the game she ran it would be himself.

The side of Beverly he knew best was more basic and earthy. More honestly herself, without the trappings of pretense. Not a professional, but a woman who was hot and sensual. Morgan had always enjoyed Beverly's facade precisely because of the contradictions.

As Beverly postured, flattered and flirted with the men, Morgan watched her, recalling the first time he'd seen her professionally in action. She had overwhelmed her legal opponents on one deal by introducing a pushy, bluffing attitude of intimidation she'd learned in her black neighborhood. She'd boldly thrown around terms like bias, politically correct and racism, to the discomfort of the other players. She'd won her point by figuratively beating them over the head with her presence as an African-American. She had never been above manipulating to get what she wanted.

For a quick moment Morgan had an image of Patricia Gilbert and found himself drawing an instant comparison to Beverly. Night and day, he thought quickly. He instantly regretted the analogy. It was too ironic and obvious. It was unfair.

Beverly nodded a hello to Connie before turning to the departing attorneys.

"Don't forget. I'm available to work with you on some of your more sensitive cases. I'm talking Affirmative Action, gentlemen."

The two men didn't answer directly, so much as laughed nervously and nodded as they headed toward the elevators. David chuckled in appreciation as Beverly air-kissed his cheek. She looped her arm through Morgan's as she stood next to him, grinning like a Cheshire cat.

"Man, you never let up. You go right for the jugular."

"I just want to make sure they notice me."

"A little more subtlety might have worked better," Morgan said. Behind him, Connie's phone began to ring.

Beverly shrugged. "Walter Kiernan heads that firm. He knows me. He'll get a good laugh at knowing I made two of his partners squirm."

David tisked and grinned at her. "You're a bad girl, Ms. McGraw."

"I just play the game better than they do."

"Maybe," Morgan began. "But I wouldn't count on always winning."

"Mr. Baxter. Telephone."

"Oh, no, Connie. No more today," Beverly said as she urged Morgan toward his office. "It's almost six and Morgan clocked out an hour ago. And he's taking me to dinner."

"Can you take a message, Connie? I'll return the call in the morning."

"It's your son," Connie said.

Morgan stopped in his tracks, pulling slightly away from Beverly as he turned to Connie. He could immediately detect Beverly's impatience in the way she let go of his arm and audibly sighed.

David exchanged a knowing glance with Beverly. "Family first," he said, touching her arm familiarly as he passed her on his way back to his own office.

Morgan pointed to the phone in Connie's hand. "I'll take it at my desk." He left Beverly and strode into his office.

"We have reservations . . ." she hinted quietly after him. Morgan didn't respond directly, and she sighed again as he closed the door. She turned to Connie with a frown. "Does that go on a lot?"

"What do you mean?" Connie asked politely, glancing over a number of papers on her desk.

"These personal interruptions during business hours. Does Kent call Morgan at work often?"

"First of all, Mr. Baxter would never consider his son's calls interruptions. Second of all, he has instructed his son to call whenever he needed to. And third . . . it's after business hours. You said so yourself," Connie finished with a pleasant smile, hoping to forestall Beverly's annoyance.

"Whatever," Beverly murmured, pacing the area outside Morgan's office.

"Have you ever met Kent?"

"No, can't say that I've met many fifteen-year-olds."

"Probably, you're right," Connie conceded. "But I would think you'd want to know this fifteen-year-old. He's Morgan's son, after all. It might make all the difference."

Beverly stood still long enough to look thoughtfully at Connie Anderson, not prepared to discuss her personal relationship to Morgan with his secretary.

"I don't want to confuse the issues," she said. "This shouldn't be a matter of Morgan having to take sides."

Connie raised her brows. "If you say so . . ."

"Do me a favor, Connie, and buzz Morgan. Just to remind him I'm still waiting."

But Connie had no time to comply as Morgan came out of his office.

"Oh, Morgan," Beverly said, relieved. "We'd better hurry. And we might still make the second show at Sweetwater's if . . ."

"Connie . . ." Morgan interrupted, distracted as he handed his secretary a note. "Kent went to a basketball game at the Garden with some of his friends. Could you call to see when they expect the game to let out?"

"Morgan . . ."

"Certainly, Mr. Baxter."

"Also, arrange a car to pick up Ms. McGraw at the restaurant and take her home after we have dinner. I'd say about nine o'clock."

"Morgan," Beverly tried again, this time showing some impatience.

"We're going to make dinner," he said, holding up his hand to her. "Then I'll

238

have to pass on the Sweetwater's show."

"Why? Do you suddenly have a curfew?"

"No, but Kent does. I can't expect him to obey it if I'm not home in time to see that he does."

"Oh, for God's sake, Morgan," Beverly sighed.

"The Garden said the game should be out by about ten or a little after," Connie informed Morgan as she hung up her phone.

"Fine. I told Kent I wanted him to head straight home after the game."

Beverly raised her brows. "You know he's not going to."

"Maybe," Morgan said smoothly as he prepared to leave his office for the night. "I know he'll push the envelope. I don't think I blame him."

Beverly shook her head. "When I was his age no one cared if I came home on time or not. Nobody bothered setting a time."

"I remember something similar," Morgan said earnestly. "There were nights I didn't even go home. I stayed over with a friend. I scared my mother more than I should have. She always thought something had happened to me out in the street. Or, at the very least, that the cops had picked me up just because."

Beverly finally gave Morgan a wry smile, regaining some of her humor. If not in sympathy at least in recognition. And she knew she was going to win this point.

"Things haven't changed, is that right?"

"Not much," Morgan said.

They walked the four blocks to the Hudson River Club.

"You look wonderful," Morgan murmured, trying to forget the bad start to their evening.

Beverly silently accepted the compliment as they waited and checked their coats. Then she leaned with familiarity against Morgan, her perfume and the smell of her skin causing Morgan's nostrils to flare with pleasant memories. But it felt awkward to touch when he sensed that a lot of the old intimacy was missing between them.

"It took you long enough to notice. And I was starting to feel really chilly back in your office. Right now, I'm starving," she said coyly as they headed toward the main dining room.

Morgan placed his arm around her

waist and guided her forward at the signal from the maître d'. "So am I, but we'll have to settle for Caesar salad and the entree."

Beverly laughed. "So, you're going to punish me. No dessert, either?"

"We'll see," Morgan answered cryptically.

He tried not to think about what they would have been doing at another time. Dinner would have come considerably later, and they would have split a bottle of champagne. Instead, after they had been seated he ordered Beverly's standard wine spritzer to his scotch on the rocks while they glanced over the menu. Morgan set aside his nocturnal fantasies about Beverly McGraw. For now the thoughts seemed surreal.

"We never seem to have enough time together anymore, Morgan." She tapped the rim of her glass lightly against the side of his.

"I'm getting used to it."

"Well, I'm not. There must be something we can do about that," she said suggestively, sipping and peering at him over the edge of the glass.

There was sincerity and longing in her voice, but Morgan saw no point in this kind of agonizing. He'd learned how to minimize his sexual discomfort in the absence of any satisfying opportunities. He just wanted to enjoy being with Beverly for the moment. And now, Morgan found he had a totally different impression. Suddenly, something about Beverly seemed changed. Or maybe nothing had changed at all and she'd always been this way . . . beautiful and seductive, but calculating and self-absorbed. Very smart and quick-witted, but impatient and sometimes insensitive.

Unlike Patricia Gilbert, who just worked hard at proving her point through logic and reason . . . and guileless persuasion. Who, despite her feistiness, had a soft femininity that was genuine and alluring in its very subtlety.

"If you'd made me another offer, I could have waited on dinner," Beverly now said to Morgan. She arched a brow. "I can *eat* anytime."

Morgan returned her smile even though he realized he felt no particular regret. "Now you tell me."

She shrugged lightly. "I thought you said you hadn't given up, yet."

Morgan ignored the question. "What was that all about in my office? Why did you make it so difficult for me?"

She pursed her lips. "I was anxious to get you away from there and have you to myself. I wanted to share some good news. I was asked by the governor to be part of a task force to encourage minority business contracts with the state. *And* Matthew Bogan wants to hire me back as a consultant. I think they're desperate for some 'faces.' You know. Ethnicity to flash around the office. They're getting more black-owned business dealings, and there's no one on board in his company who understands the subtleties of negotiating with black folks."

Morgan nodded. "Nice to be in demand."

She reached out to lay her hand gently on his arm, and stroked the fabric. "I'm not sure I want to bail Matthew out, but there are parts of the deal which have great possibilities. I'll do less traveling and we can see each other more. Our paths are going to cross more often now in business."

Morgan kept his eyes on her face. "It sounds interesting. Do you expect me to make a counteroffer?" he drawled.

"If you need me." Then her expression changed, grew immediately watchful. "What's up? I thought everything was under control on your Sager project. Do you want me to come in, after all?"

The abrupt shattering of the mood irritated Morgan. He frowned at her. "Why this interest in Sager? It's not the kind of company you'd want to handle. It can't offer you a thing. No one would notice you there."

Beverly grimaced and sipped at her drink. She turned her attention to the menu to hide her expression. "I always make myself noticed," she said firmly.

He believed her. She was very quick, very capable . . . and very persistent. But Morgan had misgivings now, about a longer relationship with her, realizing that Beverly also saw his son as someone in the way. She wasn't making it easy for him to be comfortable with her demands.

"Look, just relax. It's after five and I don't want to do any overtime. Let's talk about something else besides business and deals."

"I think you mentioned a counteroffer."

He hesitated. "I did. I may have things going on in London at the start of the year. I usually give over those trips to David but . . ."

"David hates London. You know, this would be so much easier tonight if your son wasn't living with you."

Morgan could feel a certain reserve tighten the smile that curved his mouth. His gaze swept over Beverly's face. He saw no malice or indifference . . . only a lack of compassion and patience.

"My son is not the problem. The problem is one of priorities. Yours is convenience, Bev. I choose to compromise."

Her pouty smile was one of easy concession. Beverly was not easily insulted. "So, we're playing catch-as-catch-can."

Morgan tried not to get annoyed with her. "You're the one who won't give an inch. I understand your point of view. I wish you'd do the same for me where my son is concerned."

She laughed lightly and shook her head, sensing the ire in Morgan's tone and attitude. "I got under your skin, didn't I? Sorry I baited you. I think you've changed, Morgan. You used to be more fun. I've missed going to bed with you these last few weeks."

Morgan blinked at her and started to laugh. He shook his head, bemused. "Now I know why you're such an effective lawyer."

"Tell me," she said, grinning demurely.

"Your ego is solid as a rock. You cut right to the chase. Don't you ever have any moments of doubt or introspection?"

She gave a brief tilt of her head. "No. The minute you start to second-guess yourself or to have doubts, someone is going to try to do you in. What's wrong with knowing what I want? Any smart black woman who doesn't is in deep trouble. A lot of my girlfriends ended up with kids at seventeen and eighteen and deadbeat boyfriends who can't do a thing for them. Not me. *No* one is going to control my life, and I don't need anyone to take care of me, thank you.

"If you don't ask or demand what you want, it's never going to happen. Nothing just drops into your lap from wishful thinking. You know that. You came from the same place I did, Morgan. Enough said," she finished wryly.

Morgan continued to stare at her reflectively. He couldn't fault Beverly's reasoning. It was right for her. And that was the problem, he suddenly realized. It was all about Beverly. Her forthrightness was what first drew him to her. No one got over on Bev. He'd hired her to negotiate a contract for Ventura, Inc., when he'd first opened offices in New York. She'd saved him hundreds of thousands of dollars on the deal. And Bev had also made him very comfortable in more than just a professional way. That had been both satisfying and challenging.

A week after that first deal, they'd become lovers. They'd spent three uninterrupted days in Beverly's co-op with the phone unplugged, fulfilling the anticipation that had built up during the business they'd conducted. It had been an interesting relationship of intellect . . . and lust. But there had been limits, not the least of which was Beverly's ambitions. Despite all the appropriate comments, it rubbed Morgan's ego the wrong way that she always put herself first. The company she was with now was global, and he knew that Beverly would eventually have her sights set on an overseas assignment. Doing a stint with the governor meant a certain amount of power. It was lucrative. A good business decision. But it fulfilled *her* needs . . . not *theirs.*

Patricia Gilbert came to mind once again, but this time Morgan didn't see differences between her and Beverly McGraw. Instead, he suddenly saw Beverly as a completely different woman than he'd known . . . than he'd imagined her to be.

It was Patricia Gilbert's fault.

"I'm sorry there wasn't time for something else tonight," Morgan reassured Beverly. It was easy to say it now. "Besides, as you keep reminding me, there is Kent."

She shrugged. "Too bad. It could have been great."

When they left the restaurant after dinner, Morgan escorted Beverly to the waiting town car that would take her home. With an authoritative signal from Morgan the driver discreetly walked twenty feet away from the car as he and Beverly climbed into the plush back seat.

Although they had long outgrown petting and necking in secret dark places, that is exactly what they resorted to. Beverly let out an uncharacteristic giggle as they settled back. Then she turned into Morgan's arms, encouraging a return of her embrace. The kiss was not very satisfying because of his sense of the place. And it was frustrating to hold his desire in check while discouraging Beverly's bold caresses. He shrank from the long, tapered finger that slipped into an opening of his shirt between button holes, to trail deliberately through the curled hair on his chest.

Morgan innocently brushed her hair with his hand, felt the weight of the curls, the sculpted stiffness from spray, and everything instantly changed. His image blurred. Morgan's need and knowledge of the person he was with shifted. He dropped his hand and abruptly broke the fusing of their lips. His desire ebbed and died. Just like that. He heard Beverly's impatient intake of breath.

"Morgan, not yet," she whispered softly, leaning into him.

He surprised even himself by holding her off.

"Morgan?" she questioned, annoyed and confused.

"We can't finish this, so let's not start. Besides, you'll blame me if your suit gets crushed." He tempered his withdrawal with a short kiss on her mouth.

Beverly gave in with a sigh and sat back. She drew her fur coat about her and casually fluffed her hair with a hand. Morgan watched the movement, his mind suddenly drifting and his imagination playing games. He turned to get out of the car.

"I'll give you a call," he said as he watched Beverly rearrange herself comfortably across the entire back seat.

"I hope you have a completely sleepless night," she said with a coy smile.

Morgan watched the car pull away, and he continued to watch for a long time. He felt relief. Relief that the evening had been nothing more than dinner and harmless sexual flirtation. Relief that he'd not engaged any more of himself in Beverly than the boundaries of their affair. Relief that he had not made a fool of himself.

But Morgan also had a sudden, vivid sense that the affair with Beverly McGraw had probably run its course. It could no longer work under the current set of circumstances. And those circumstances were not going to change. At least, not his.

Morgan also realized that from that night onward, nothing was going to be the same again. He felt neither happy nor sad about that, but rather an excitement that was based on nothing more than anticipation. Of what? Well, that was the thing. He wasn't quite sure. Except that now he could vividly recall that moment in Patricia's office when he'd kissed her hand. He hadn't meant anything by it, except maybe to say thank you. They'd both been taken aback. He'd seen her eyes brighten for a moment before they filled with caution. The whole event seemed to mark a space in time — like tonight — when things changed.

Morgan walked to the corner of West and Vesey streets and hailed a cab to take him home to Brooklyn. He heard again Beverly's parting comment about their aborted lovemaking. He was not going to have a night of wishful dreams or emotional nightmares. But it was a restless night, nonetheless.

Patricia surprised herself by being nervous and excited about going to the football game. Usually she didn't attend, but she also couldn't deny either her pleasure or excitement when Kent had asked her to be there. Other than to admit to a curiosity as to how Kent Baxter was working out on the team.

The game was at a high school farther south in Bensonhurst. She'd arrived twenty minutes before the start to sit alone in the visitors' stand, only half filled with girlfriends and parents of the players. She didn't see Morgan Baxter among the Duncan contingent.

The sun was bright and the air very clear and cold. Patricia was reminded of why she'd never gone to football games. It was an outdoor sport played in the worst weather of the year. A light breeze blew what remained of fall colors and sounds across the field, where both teams were warming up. Patricia could identify most of Duncan's players who were bulked up in their game uniforms. It made them different from the boys she was familiar with during the week. This was alien territory. This was part of their other life, where she really didn't have a place, either as a parent or a friend.

Gilly had once warned her about confusing the two, about projecting her own loss and needs on the students. About trying to make up for the void in her own life that had made her so angry and so lonely as a young girl. Gilly also reminded her that giving so much of herself was admirable, but it was also nice to sometimes be on the receiving end. Patricia squirmed restlessly on the cement seat, acknowledging the drift of her grandmother's advice.

Patricia watched the cheerleaders practicing on the sidelines. She saw Kyra Whitacre arrive in a car driven by her mother. From the sullen detachment of the girl Patricia sensed that they had had a fight. Kyra silently got her duffel from the back seat of the car and her pom-poms, and hurried to join the rest of her squad.

Mrs. Whitacre left quickly, but other cars arrived and soon the atmosphere was loud, cheerful, and festive. Patricia had no trouble spotting Morgan Baxter when he finally arrived. His car was a metallic gray BMW among the midrange models and minivans. When he climbed out he took his time to survey his surroundings.

He looked different. Most obvious was

the absence of a suit and tie, and the expression and carriage that went along with business attire. A muscle spasm rippled unexpectedly in Patricia's chest. Her earlier awareness of him, at meetings when she didn't have time to censor or examine her impressions, came to full alert attention. Patricia couldn't help staring at Morgan Baxter and feeling so much of her earlier resolve about him falter and die.

A gust of air prickled over her skin, even under her jacket and sweater. Loose strands of unruly hair, combed into a French braid, blew across her face. Patricia ignored them, her attention returning to Morgan Baxter as if she hoped that he had somehow changed in those few seconds to someone ordinary whom she could ignore.

Morgan was dressed in broken-in jeans where the fabric and casual design emphasized his long athletic legs, a trim supple body. There was a heavy cable-knit sweater of ecru wool worn over a burgundy cotton turtleneck. He wasn't wearing sneakers but a pair of dark leather boots. He stood with his hands stuffed into the back pockets of his jeans, his navy-blue ski jacket was unzipped and open. His stance made him seem watchful and appraising, as if trying to decide the outcome of the game and the afternoon. Mixed with Patricia's tension was relief and admiration. She was very glad that Morgan had come to watch his son play.

She saw Morgan scan the field, watching the boys for a moment. Then his attention turned to everything else around him. Before his gaze could reach the stands and their occupants, Patricia hastily dug out a pair of sunglasses from her great bag and hid herself behind them. She concentrated on the conference taking place between the game officials and team coaches as the two school players readied themselves for the start of the game.

A noisy group of fans was seated in the stands on the home side of the field. When Duncan played Seagate High School, there was always an edge to the games that went beyond mere competition. Bensonhurst and Midwood were also rival communities. Bensonhurst was still an insular neighborhood of old Italian families and smaller accepted pockets of Portuguese and Brazilian immigrants. But there were no blacks. The segregation, never thought about during most of the school year because the two groups were so far apart, became a point of contention during the school games.

Excitement and insults shouted because of school spirit was one thing. When racial differences and pride entered the picture, it became something else. Ugly, and potentially dangerous.

At kickoff Patricia looked for number 19 but Kent was sidelined in the first minutes. After the play was over she casually glanced to the parking lot, but Morgan was no longer there. Another quick scan and she found him halfway up the viewing stand, in conversation with the mother of one of Duncan's players. Patricia recognized her. She was an attractive, friendly woman, a single parent. She was available . . . and looking.

Patricia quickly turned her attention back to the game, pretending a concentration that was false. She began to feel out of place again, and wondered if she could possibly slip away unnoticed after a few moments. She felt her attention divided between the action of the charging bodies and blowing whistles on the field, and the imprint of Morgan Baxter somewhere out of her vision flirting with a woman who was not wary of him. And who, no doubt, found him attractive.

Duncan lost the ball early to Seagate, and the team played it safe by kicking a successful field goal to get on the scoreboard. Patricia still didn't see Kent in the play.

"Hello."

The muscle in Patricia's chest twisted a notch tighter. She looked up, feigning calm surprise. "Hi . . ."

Morgan looked around at the other Duncan supporters and families. "Why are you all the way over here in a corner by yourself?"

Patricia smiled. "I'm an observer."

He stood looking down at her, his dark eyes squinting against the sunlight, his smile easy and friendly. "It's Saturday. You should only be cheering them on to win, not dissecting their behavior."

She was glad for the sunglasses. Maybe he wouldn't sense her agitation. "Oh, I'm here as a fan, too. But I'll probably slip away after a while unnoticed."

Morgan surprised her by laughing outright. "Patricia, I can tell you for a fact you'll never go unnoticed."

He stood studying her in such a disconcerting way that she nervously adjusted the glasses, moved her bag from one side of her legs to the other, cleared her throat.

Morgan frowned and then was totally charmed by Patricia's wool gloves, each finger a different color, like a box of crayons. Only she would dare to challenge convention and get away with it, he thought. "Are you allowed visitors while you're in exile?" he asked, suppressing more laughter.

"If you like . . ." She indicated the empty space to her right, and Morgan lowered himself, his arm brushing and settling against her. Patricia thought him unnecessarily close but ignored the instinct to move. For long moments they silently watched the game.

"Thank you."

Patricia turned to stare at him. "What for?"

"For spurring Kent on. If he gets to play it'll mean a lot to him. I'm grateful."

Patricia shook her head. "I told you. I

don't think I have that kind of influence on people."

"Don't you?" he asked quietly, eyeing her.

She grimaced, ignoring the question, "We're already down by a few points, the quarter is almost over, and Kent hadn't been put in yet."

"It's early. Maybe the coach changed his mind about using him."

On that note Morgan fell silent, looking out onto the field. Patricia could tell, however, that he really wanted his boy to be given a chance. A whistle from the field drew her attention as well to the next play.

Kent's estimation of Duncan's weak backfield was suddenly proven when, on a short flare-out pass, the Seagate wide receiver broke several tackles and raced sixty yards for a touchdown. The Seagate bleachers went wild. On the sidelines Patricia and Morgan could hear the Duncan coach yelling his head off about the sloppy play of his team.

On the next Seagate advantage, they again drove steadily downfield, but had to settle for a field goal. Patricia glanced over at Morgan as Kent finally took up his position. She herself was too conscious of the man next to her to concentrate for the moment on the game. Suddenly Morgan wasn't just Kent's father, or any parent, he was a male of the species, and a noticeably attractive one.

She noticed the way his eyes narrowed as he squinted against the bright day and the breezy air. His brow furrowed. She saw the muscle flexing in his jaw indicating more than just casual interest in his son's performance in the game. Patricia felt the way the entire length of Morgan seated next to her was a wall keeping her warm against the crisp air.

"Come on, Kent. Heads up . . ." Morgan shouted, cupping his hands to his mouth.

Patricia looked back to the field and tried to pick up the action. There was another flare-out pass, but this time Kent charged across the field and slammed down the receiver with a jarring hit. Both players went down hard. She watched, stunned, as a rival team player took a furtive punch at Kent's head. Patricia gasped, grabbing at Morgan's arm and clutching tightly, but Kent rolled to his knees and spryly jumped to his feet to resume his position.

"All right, Baxter!" Patricia heard someone shout.

On the next play the Seagate quarterback went to the air with the ball. His wide receiver cut left to an open spot in the middle of the field and turned, looking for the ball. The Duncan cornerback was a few steps behind, but into the play came Kent, slipping in front of the receiver in a perfect position to intercept the ball. He jumped . . .

"Get it, get it!" Patricia urged excitedly.

The ball glanced out of Kent's outstretched fingertips and fell to the ground. A collective groan went up on both sides of the field.

"Rats," Patricia moaned in frustration. "He almost had it."

But Morgan was on his feet, shouting, "Way to go, son!"

Patricia looked perplexed. "Wasn't he supposed to catch it?"

Morgan's brow furrowed as he sat down and then he laughed. "How much do you actually know about this game?"

"Not much, except that the object is to win" — Morgan laughed again — "and don't let the other guys get the ball."

"I guess that's reasonably accurate. For someone who doesn't know a lot about the rules you certainly get very excited."

"I'm cheering. Besides, Mr. Baxter, I have a vested interest in this game," Patricia said, her attention momentarily diverted as Seagate lined up in punt formation. "Come on, *team!*" she urged.

Morgan's amusement sobered. "Two weeks ago you were calling me Morgan. What happened?"

"Did I? I shouldn't have," she said quietly.

"Why? I don't mind. I want you to."

She shook her head in doubt. "It's the setting, I guess. The children . . ." she floundered.

"They're not children," he reminded her dryly. "They're young adults in disguise."

"I can't forget who I am," Patricia said.

"Appearances?"

"More like propriety."

"I thought we'd agreed on friendly terms? For Kent's sake," Morgan said, his attention pointedly on her.

"Yes, I know, but . . ."

"You don't want to give the wrong impression?"

Patricia nodded her head.

Morgan leaned toward her.

"What would be the wrong impression?"

She silently studied him for a moment, the game and everything around them forgotten as she tried not to shy away from the implication of his question. It was wide open for interpretation and Patricia perfectly understood some of the innuendos.

"One that's inappropriate to the circumstances," she responded smoothly, meeting the intense speculation in his eyes.

Morgan didn't push the matter, but turned back to the game. In pure self-defense Patricia did the same. She thought, perhaps, that she was overreacting again, but Morgan's sudden playfulness had taken her by surprise. It had a personal tone that she was unprepared for and her defenses were still in place.

Duncan's offense finally started to roll, and as they drove downfield Patricia became more comfortable in Morgan's company. Together they cheered and applauded the Duncan team. It gave them both a neutral focus. She forgot about wanting to leave early. And she ignored the occasional glance in their direction from the pretty parent whom Morgan had spoken with earlier. When an unfair call was made, Patricia stood up, shouting her displeasure just as vigorously as any parent. Morgan laughed.

"What's so funny? What are you grinning at?" she asked.

"Why is it that women with red hair always have such tempers?" he drawled in amusement.

Patricia sat down and hugged herself, even though she wasn't feeling nearly as cold anymore. She wondered if his ex-wife had red hair. "Please, no stereotypes. Anyway, I don't have a temper," she said defensively.

"Passion, then," Morgan suggested softly.

She averted her gaze. "I'm strong on conviction, that's all."

"I'm not complaining." Morgan shook his head, still amused. "I'd rather have you on my side than against me. I bet you're a contender when you're mad."

Again, she made no response but only

stared at him. She knew she was probably being too guarded with Morgan Baxter, too sensitive to his teasing.

For his part, Morgan was surprised that Patricia could be teased. He was pushing her buttons again, he admitted to himself. But this time not in retaliation. Not because he wanted to score points against her ability to face off with him over his responsibilities, over his son. Morgan wanted to see what Patricia would be like when the teasing had the element of flirtation. He'd discovered almost at once with Beverly that she didn't waste time with that level of romance, unless she was initiating it.

The idea made Morgan suddenly stare at Patricia. She was deep in her own thoughts, momentarily distracted from the football game. Is that what he was engaging in? Romance, courting . . . flirtation. Although he gave his attention back to the action on the field the suggestion of getting next to Patricia Gilbert had been firmly planted . . . and had taken hold.

The score was 10–3 at the half, and although Duncan did score a touchdown midway through the third quarter, they missed the extra point. The score was 10–9 going into the final minutes of play. Worse still, Seagate had the ball. They didn't take any chances with their fragile lead, and kept the ball on the ground.

The quarterback handed off to the fullback, who plowed into the line. Hurtling forward came the Duncan middle linebacker, with Kent right behind. The linebacker laid on a brutal hit. The ball came loose.

Bodies dove, hands outstretched. The ball hopped a few times over the turf. Kent lunged forward and, swooping it up, gathered it to his chest. He sprinted toward the open field on the sidelines, shrugging off one attempt to tackle him.

"Good move! Go . . . go!" Morgan shouted amid a thunderous uproar from the crowds, coming to his feet. Patricia followed his example.

Kent dodged away from another tackle and ran for almost thirty yards, down to Seagate's nineteen-yard line, before someone made a running lunge for his ankles. Kent tripped and sprawled forward, crashing to the ground. But he still had possession of the ball. The Seagate players caught up and half a dozen bodies jumped on top of him, fighting to wrest the ball free.

"Oh, my God . . ." Patricia heard herself gasp.

"He's okay," Morgan said calmly, although his attention narrowed to the action on the field as a whistle blew to stop the play.

"Is he hurt?" she questioned, reaching out to find Morgan's arm. Fans were cheering wildly on the Duncan side.

"He's okay," Morgan reassured Patricia.

He lifted the arm she was holding on to and his hand briskly rubbed the back of her shoulders. Patricia wasn't sure who Morgan was really comforting. But it certainly worked for her. For a second her attention was split between concern for Kent and the strong reassurance she felt physically from Morgan.

The referee was separating arms and legs. When all the players were untangled, Duncan was still in possession of the ball. At the very bottom, Kent lay immobile with a referee standing over him. Patricia stole a glance at Morgan's face. It was calm and expressionless, except for the deep furrowing of his brows and the clenching of his jaw.

Kent slowly rolled onto his back,

gasping for air, and lay there with his knees up. A silence came over the field as the coach ran to Kent.

The coach and Eric Patton took Kent by the arms. Slowly they pulled him to his feet. He wobbled unsteadily when they released him, but then found his balance and stood more or less straight. He began walking off the field, releasing the chin strap on his helmet.

Fans on both sides of the field applauded.

The game continued but Duncan was unable to make a first down. Their field goal attempt went wide. They lost by one.

But the game wasn't over, yet. A dozen boys from both teams were squaring off on the field in a closing cluster. Before the coaches or fans knew what was happening, there was some pushing and jostling. Helmets came off and were tossed aside. Bodies collided and racial slurs and insults started flying.

Patricia was stunned. "Morgan, what's going on?"

"They're frustrated. They can't let the game go," he told her, but he carefully watched not only what the players were doing, but also the possible intent of everyone looking on. The rest of the players from both teams rushed back onto the field. The coaches blew whistles and waded into the crowd trying to separate the two teams.

"Oh, no," Patricia breathed anxiously as she and Morgan watched Kent join his teammates. Still wobbly, Kent literally threw himself into the middle to confront one of the Seagate players. They were right in each other's faces. The other boy was bigger than Kent, and Patricia felt her insides tense. He was still trying to prove himself.

She grabbed Morgan's arm yet again. He said nothing, his attention focused on his son. Patricia blinked at him, noting the satisfaction in Morgan's gaze. The pride.

"Aren't you concerned? Do you think this is okay, what's happening?"

He slowly shook his head as the melee on the field began to dissipate. "That's not what mattered. He backed up his teammates."

But Morgan saw much more than that. The Duncan team was made up almost entirely of black youngsters. He saw no hesitation in his son aligning himself. Kent watched Eric Patton's back. And the one called WeeGee stood with him.

"You sound pleased about it."

He glanced briefly at her. "Yeah. I guess I am. I don't think anything would have happened. Too many people. It was just a show. Don't you get it?"

She felt impatient and foolish. "No, I don't."

Morgan started to laugh easily. His hand dropped from her shoulder to rub slowly down her back, and then finally away. He put his hands into his jacket pockets.

"The boys were just trying to make a point, that's all. Don't mess with us." His smile was knowing. "They lost the game but not their pride."

Family and friends began emptying the stands, but neither Morgan nor Patricia made a move to leave. They silently watched the boys finally head into the school locker room. The field soon stood deserted. And then they silently turned to face each other.

He was looking at Patricia as if he could see past the dark glasses. She no longer felt protected by them. As she returned his attention Patricia accepted that there was an obvious interest in Morgan's regard of her that closed quite a bit of the distance between them. It was totally new, like he'd never really seen her before. Or perhaps, more accurately, had never given her a fair chance. It was not uncomfortable, no longer surprising, but caution bells pealed in her brain.

"Why don't you go make sure Kent's okay?" she suggested.

He shook his head. "He's not going to want me down there right now. He had the wind knocked out of him before, that's all. No real damage done."

"He played well, don't you think?"

Morgan smiled at her. "Yeah, he played very well. Kent is smart and he's quick. He could be a first-rate athlete if he wanted to. OJ Baxter," he suggested with a grin.

"Is he at all interested?"

Morgan's smile wavered. He pursed his mouth and crossed his arms over his chest. "I don't know what he wants to do. We haven't gotten around to talking about it, yet. I know, I know . . ." Morgan said, forestalling advice. "I could ask, right?"

The sun had shifted across the landscape and they stood in the encroaching dark of late afternoon. Patricia was forced to take off the dark glasses and reveal herself. They were the only ones left in the stands.

She didn't feel safe being alone with Morgan Baxter. She put away the sunglasses and took out her regular glasses instead, setting them on her nose. She glanced at Morgan as his hand reached out. A gust of wind twisted her loosened hair across her cheek. The back of his hand, strong and surprisingly warm, smoothed the strands away, brushing against her skin. Patricia watched his face and expression, afraid to guess what he was thinking.

Morgan was disconcerted, watching the distinct differences between them as his own hand seemed so heavy, dark, against Patricia's skin tone. For a brief instant Morgan experienced the ambivalence he'd first known touching Melissa, wondering if she would pull away from him, when actually she said she'd been waiting for him to not be afraid. *Is that what I've been,* Morgan silently asked himself, *afraid to see what would happen if we touched?*

"What happens after the games?"

Morgan asked, breaking the spell.

"Parents go home. The winning team gloats. Both teams go for something to eat somewhere. Not together, of course. The cheerleaders tag along."

"What do you do?"

"I go home, too. I have things to do. My Saturday chores still need to get done."

"What will happen to you if you wait until tomorrow to do them?"

"Nothing," she said, chuckling.

"Good," he responded without explanation. Then he began descending from the stands. Patricia slowly followed.

She watched Morgan's brief encounter with the interested parent again. Patricia sidestepped them and continued walking. The cheerleaders were gathering their equipment and discussing where everyone would meet. Kyra Whitacre was the only one silent on the subject.

"The new routine looks pretty good," Patricia complimented the girl. "The team should try out for the regional championships."

"Yeah, maybe," Kyra said indifferently.

Patricia watched as most of the girls

from the squad gathered and Kyra walked away from them. "Aren't you going, too?"

"I can't." Kyra spoke patiently. "I have to get home. My mother told me to 'cause I have to watch my sister and brother."

"Oh. I'm sorry. Maybe next time you can arrange for a sitter," Patricia offered.

Kyra grimaced in anger. "I *am* the sitter."

Patricia, unable to think of quick words of comfort, stood by silently. Suddenly a cheer went up as some of the football team members slowly exited the Seagate High School having changed into street clothes and carrying their gear.

Patricia stood silently next to Kyra as the girl pulled a jacket from her equipment duffel and pulled it on. Across the way, the other squad members called out her name. Kyra perked up noticeably when Eric called out for her to join the players and other cheerleaders.

She watched as Peter playfully looped his beefy arm around the girl's shoulder and whispered something into her ear that made everyone laugh. Kyra pushed him away and returned to where she'd left her things.

"How will you get home?" Patricia called out to the girl.

"I'll take the bus. Bye," Kyra said, turning to run after her classmates.

Patricia nodded absently, watching Kyra leave. She was somewhat uneasy as to whether Kyra would actually go home.

There were still small islands of people and conversation but Patricia was already separating herself from the afternoon event with stoic determination. She'd always hated being thc extra person in a group. It was time to leave.

"Hi, Ms. Gilbert. You made it. Thanks for coming."

Patricia stopped at the sound of Kent Baxter's voice. She stood watching him as he approached. His gait was uneven as he swung his thickly packed duffel against his leg.

"Thanks for inviting me."

"We lost . . ."

Patricia grinned at the disappointment in his tone. "Don't sound so down about it. You played a good game."

"We still lost," Kent said patiently, as if she didn't get it.

"You made some great plays. It showed quick thinking on your part," Morgan said, approaching them from the other side. He clamped a hand on Kent's shoulder. "You did good. How are the ribs?"

Kent shrugged off the concern airily. "Sore."

Morgan stood next to his son, and Patricia's gaze traveled back and forth between them. The early evening light hit both male faces in the same way, and she was struck with the startling similarities. Even their expressions were the same. Patricia felt a funny kinship between the three of them, a mutual attraction that for a second pulled them all together. It was quickly gone.

"Well, you gave me a scare. I was happy to see you stand up," Patricia voiced honestly.

"I wasn't really hurt," Kent said with a shrug.

"What was all that business about afterward?"

Kent dropped the duffel and straightened his shoulders. Both Morgan and Patricia noticed how his body movement settled into an ease that hadn't existed a month ago. He gestured with his arm and hand, the way the other black boys did. It was an affectation that made him the same.

"No big thing. Seagate tried to play us, that's all. Next time, we'll kick their . . ." he suddenly stopped.

Patricia kept her smile hidden and watched the flush creep into Kent's face. She had the suspicion that if she looked at Morgan he, too, would be covering his real reaction.

"My man . . ." Morgan said in amusement. "Yeah . . ." He tightened his hold on his son's shoulder.

Patricia watched them with a personal sense of satisfaction. Kent tried to hide his obvious pleasure in his father's praise. Morgan and his son had finally connected.

"Yo, Baxter!"

Eric Patton was signaling for Kent to come with him and the other team members. Kent looked from his father to Patricia.

"I'll see you at home later," Morgan said, releasing him.

"Where are you going now?" Kent asked.

Morgan put his hands in his pockets

and glanced at Patricia. "I thought Ms. Gilbert and I would stop and get something to eat. That seems to be the thing to do after a game."

Kent hesitated, staring at Patricia before he glanced at his waiting classmates. Patricia sensed he was more inclined to stay than to go, but not because he didn't want to be with the team.

"It's okay for you to go," Morgan encouraged. "I just want you home before midnight."

"Midnight . . ." Kent whined in complaint.

"And I'll see you on Monday in school," Patricia added when Kent turned his attention to her.

"Kent, come on!"

"Hey! You guys take it easy tonight, all right?" Morgan called out after him, taking Kent's duffel to load in his car.

"Come on, Dad . . ." Kent made to complain again but Morgan, with just a look, silently forestalled any more discussion. "Right," Kent sighed wryly before jogging off to the others.

Patricia turned to Morgan and found him staring off after the boy. "I'd better go myself," she said quietly, drawing

Morgan's attention. She felt envious and a little guilty, as if she had been eavesdropping.

"After we have dinner."

She shrugged but felt herself starting to blush. "You only invited me out so Kent wouldn't feel he had to stay with you."

"Or with you."

She frowned at him. "What do you mean?"

Morgan touched her arm, guiding her in the direction of the parking lot. "I told Kent we'd probably go to dinner because I want to go to dinner with you. Wouldn't you like to have dinner?"

"Yes, but I'm not so sure I should have it with you," she said tartly.

"Do you have a date, or would you rather eat alone?"

"That's not what I said," Patricia said impatiently.

"Then, how about some island food?"

Patricia ignored the question. She stopped to face Morgan, peering thoughtfully at him. "Why would you want to keep Kent from me? Have I done something wrong?"

Morgan's expression softened. "No. You've actually done more good, Patricia, than I can ever thank you for. But we need to be careful from now on."

Her stomach tensed and she adjusted her glasses. "Careful?" she repeated softly.

Morgan grinned at her expression. "I'll explain over dinner. Do you want to suggest someplace or will you follow me?"

Patricia's mouth dropped open, but Morgan had already headed to his car. "But we can't . . ." she called out.

Morgan opened his trunk and dropped Kent's duffel in. He headed for the car door. "Yes, we can. You asked a question that I want to answer. Since you seem safer with me in a public place we'll go to a restaurant. I'm hungry. I could cook something at my place, but I guarantee you wouldn't want to eat it. I don't think I can talk you into an evening with me at home anyway. Can you cook?"

Patricia marched over to him, her surprise fading. "Wait a minute. This sounds like outright blackmail."

His grin was seductive and pleased.

"Absolutely."

Chapter Eight

Patricia closed her menu and took a sip of water. Seated across from her Morgan was still considering the choices. She considered him. Patricia thought better of that and reopened the menu instead. And closed it again.

She would have to wing it. She'd have to feel her way through the evening with Morgan because she wasn't sure, yet, what it was going to be about. Patricia's caution made her feel childish, but it was hard to ignore her history with men. Contentious, painful . . . and disappointing. She'd made poor choices in the past for very odd reasons. Her instincts where men were concerned were not always to be trusted. And, unfortunately, the motives of some of the men she'd dated had been suspect.

Patricia looked covertly at Morgan as he considered his dinner choices. She wondered what his personal life was like. What kind of women he dated. She knew nothing of his ex-wife, except that she was white, but was that a factor in the kind of woman Morgan would be interested in? The thought made her uncomfortable. For the first time Patricia admitted to herself that Morgan Baxter was a very attractive man. To just say he was handsome, however, would trivialize many of his other attributes that she had come to know firsthand over the past month. It was enough for Patricia to believe that other women must find the same appeal. Yet, she knew that there were compelling reasons, beyond her own insecurity, for being careful of Morgan's motives.

Was he courting her? And was this going to be another case of mistaken identity?

The thought stung. It had happened before, as she recalled her senior year in college. Drew Connelly. The scholarship. The humiliation . . .

Drew, who'd thought she was white but dated her even after learning that she was black, Patricia had believed, given what he knew, she could trust. But in the end, he'd used her in a way she had yet to overcome. It had had little to do with her skin color at first. And then it had *everything* to do with it. It had been a betrayal that had cost her a dream, and changed her life. And set her straight forever. Patricia had learned the hard way that no matter what she might be inside or what made her what she was, people still only saw what they wanted to see.

What did Morgan Baxter see?

Was he capable of subterfuge? Of prying open her secret defenses, extracting her trust . . . and leaving her soul bare?

"Do you know what you want?" Morgan asked, looking up as he closed his menu.

Patricia was perplexed by the question. She wasn't sure she should take it at face value. "No, I don't."

"Surprise yourself. Order at random. Experiment."

She shook out her napkin and spread it over her lap. "I have the feeling that you're baiting me," she said warily.

Morgan's brows shot up. "Am I? Or are you just feeling defensive?"

"Why would I feel defensive?" Patricia asked shortly, irritated that he so often came close to the truth.

Morgan took his time answering, disconcerting her with his thorough gaze. "You're used to being in charge, having all the answers, being the expert. I'm the same way. But some situations don't call for diagnosis or forethought. They should just happen. You were the one that told me so, remember?" he finished quietly.

Patricia still felt cautious. Her whole body was tensed and poised and she didn't like the feeling. She knew that part of it was her attraction to and awareness of Morgan.

"I was talking about how you might respond to your son. That's different."

"So is this. Right now it's about us, not Kent."

Patricia felt the flush rising under her skin. His tone and voice were easy, self-assured, smooth. Somehow the tables had been turned. He knew exactly what he was doing.

"I told you, this is neutral territory. I'm not looking to compromise you. Relax."

"I'm not sure I understand," she murmured.

Morgan crossed his arms on the table and leaned slightly forward. The overhead lamp threw light across his dark hair, and shadows on the strongly de-fined features of his brown face. She could detect the vague outline of where his beard would grow and fill in, but his cheeks and jaw seemed perfectly smooth. Patricia realized that she was staring, and Morgan had been studying her, too.

"I can't think of any other way to get to know you, Patricia. Your job and mine almost preclude any chance to get together. Except for school events."

"That's as it should be," she said primly.

Morgan laughed. "Whose rule is that? Isn't it unfair?"

"To you, maybe. You don't seem to understand or appreciate my position. I am responsible for children's welfare, their trust, Mr." — he gave her a sharp look — "Morgan. I have to keep the boundaries clear."

"You're using school and children as an excuse. I thought you and I were going to be friends. But only during school hours and only when you say so, right?"

Patricia took another sip of water. "I'm sorry."

Morgan reached across the table and

took the glass from her and held her hand. "Don't be sorry. Just don't be afraid of me."

Patricia felt slightly hypnotized. Not threatened, but uncertain again. "What is it you want?" she asked quite seriously.

She could see Morgan thoughtfully considering the question. It made Patricia realize that she did have her own expectations. But she was afraid to face them squarely. His eyes seemed to look her over centimeter by centimeter. It was a serious look that slowly changed as the corner of his mouth twitched.

"I want to know where you got the red hair."

Patricia held her breath and swallowed. There it was. She knew it would come up sooner or later. She felt the painful constriction in her chest and a stifling heat rush to her face. Already she was cloaking herself in invisible armor. She gently twisted her hand free and put them together in her lap.

"Why are you so interested in the color of my hair?"

He kept his gaze steady on her. He knew he was venturing onto a sensitive topic. He knew he risked Patricia's withdrawal and the reinstatement of her uncertainty. Morgan also realized that unless he was willing to take that risk, his perceptions, and hers, would persist.

Nonetheless he felt embarrassment sneak up on him and he fought to hide it from Patricia, hoping it didn't show in his eyes, couldn't be heard in his voice or words. That once it was clear to him that Patricia was black he'd wished that she were not so light. It was only recently that it had occurred to Morgan that if a single thing about her were different she wouldn't be the Patricia Gilbert he'd come to know and respect. And there was the other thought as Beverly suddenly came to mind, and Jeanine before her, and a few other black women whom he'd partnered himself with after his divorce . . . that he'd never dated or been interested in another white woman since his wife.

Morgan tilted his head, but he wasn't particularly surprised by Patricia's question or response. He shrugged easily. "I'm curious about your background. You have a real understanding about Kent. I think it's a lot more than just good training as a high school counselor. I think you have personal experience.

"I want to know about you. That doesn't mean I'm judging you, Patricia," he ended quietly.

She gnawed on the inside of her bottom lip. "From my father's family. My great-grandmother had red hair. A great-uncle or aunt here and there."

He raised his brows. "Is that it?"

"That answers your question."

A waiter finally appeared to take their order and Patricia selected an appetizer and entree from the menu. When the waiter left the table, Morgan leaned across to talk to her.

He was frowning. "Why don't you like to talk about yourself?"

She looked straight at him. "It's not that. I don't like obvious questions. I just want people to deal with *me*, not my background or appearance. Especially since I can't do much about either."

"But all of that is what makes you, you. It's unavoidable."

Her smile was ironic. "I hope you remember that when your son has doubts." Morgan shifted his gaze and nodded. "You admitted that at the beginning even you wondered about me. What did you wonder?"

Morgan stared at her and shrugged.

Patricia watched him and shook her head. "See? You want me to open up but you won't be honest and confess that the minute I walked into your office that first time you thought I was some meddling, overbearing *white* school official who was going to get on your case."

Morgan stared back, his jaw flexing but his eyes sparkling once again with the kind of challenge he felt with her. He slowly nodded. "Okay. It's true."

Patricia wasn't sure she was relieved or furious with Morgan. She wasn't sure what it was she really wanted to hear him say. The truth was still unsettling.

Patricia murmured across the table. "I get pushed and tested. If I'm light, I must think I'm white. I can't begin to tell you how many times that was thrown at me. I never considered myself anything but black. When people don't believe me, it's hard. When black folks don't believe me . . . it hurts. For some men, I become a trophy, someone to show off. I guess if I threw a nigger-bitch-fit then that would prove I'm okay, right? It's crazy."

Morgan squirmed in his chair. He had a vivid image of Beverly during some of their disagreements, the way she could carry on. "That's not what I'm about."

"Then what about Kent's mother?"

Morgan's eyes became overly bright. He could still feel the stuff thrown at him because of Melissa. When he was with her. When she was pregnant. He said defensively, "I was in love with her. Melissa is a good person. I don't consider myself a member of the soul patrol. If I've learned anything, it's that there's more than one way to be black."

"Then you should understand what I'm talking about," she said quietly, listening to his clipped words.

"Are you angry with me?" he asked.

Patricia had to think about it. She realized, suddenly, that she wasn't, but she had been prepared. She'd been holding herself tightly, waiting for an attack or accusations, waiting to be disappointed by Morgan's answers.

"I don't want the color of my hair or how dark my skin is to matter. I don't want them used to try and figure out who I am. Or where I'm coming from. I don't want to have to prove I'm okay.

"I know you love your son, Morgan. I know you want a relationship with him. I also know you're very concerned that Kent accepts his black heritage and that he doesn't get caught thinking he's white. I don't see that in him. Kent's in a tough position at his age because someone is going to want him to pick a side. In a way even you're asking him to. My parents are black, but I've always had to justify myself." She shook her head. "I'm not going to do that for you or anyone else."

"I'd never ask that. I think you're a beautiful woman."

"Now you're trying to flatter me," she said softly, watching him.

Morgan's mouth twisted. "I meant what's inside, too. I like you, Pat. I like you a lot." His voice was urgent in his attempt to convince her.

His confession hit a nerve.

"Look," Morgan said earnestly. "I'm in no position to cast stones at you, or to dig too deeply. I've had my butt kicked, too. You've already said it. Over Kent's mother. Marrying a white woman. Let's just forget all that stuff for now. No past, no history."

She decided to let it be. And then was

unexpectedly tongue-tied. She was used to being self-protective, but Morgan had not argued with her, tried to score points, or tried to be right. His acceptance made her feel shy and awkward with him. Now what? This was the part she wasn't very good at.

"Did I seem disagreeable?" she asked.

"Careful, maybe. You got your back up a little. Maybe you were just feeling guilty."

"What on earth do I have to feel guilty about?"

He shrugged. "For spending time with me. For playing adult and not mother hen to a bunch of teenagers who need you less than you think."

"You sound like Jerome."

"Bite your tongue," he murmured dryly.

Patricia found herself chuckling. "Jerome has a different view than I do of the students and handles them differently."

"With the same results?"

"Pretty much."

"Then I guess I'm not so wrong. So relax."

The waiter returned with their appetizers. Patricia stared blankly at the steaming brown mixture that was aromatic with peppers and spices.

"What is this?" she asked when the waiter left.

"Don't you know what you ordered?"

"I took your advice and just picked something."

Morgan chuckled. "That's curried goat."

She stared expressionless. He laughed uproariously.

"If you don't like this I'll get you a sack of McDonald's to take home with you."

Patricia grimaced at him. She picked at the meat, moving it around her plate. "What if Kent doesn't get home by midnight?"

"First of all, he won't. The first time he came home later than I asked, I didn't know what to do. It never occurred to me that he wouldn't listen. The second time he was more than an hour late and I was ticked off with him. I was also worried," Morgan admitted.

Patricia listened carefully. "What did you do?"

"Not let him get away with it. The punishment was insignificant, I don't even remember what it was. I wanted Kent to know I make the rules."

"Does he listen to you?"

"Sometimes. It's that and the fact that his mother does things differently. She gives him a lot of leeway."

"And how do you respond to that manipulation?"

Morgan arched a brow. "I remind him that I'm not his mother. That backs him up."

"Good for you," Patricia applauded lightly. "You're getting the hang of this."

"Am I?" he asked with a vague smile. "I thought I was too late."

"You're gaining Kent's love and respect, even if it doesn't always seem so. You know what really makes kids grow? Love. My grandmother told me that.

"You have to be different than his mother. Stronger. That's probably one of the reasons Kent came to you. He needs reasonable boundaries. He needs the firmness and guidance of male authority. He also needs to know you want him and that you love him. But he'll never admit that." Morgan nodded thoughtfully, eating slowly from his dish. Patricia tilted her head and watched him. "Do you ever talk with Kent about his mother?"

"Not really. Only in the most superficial way."

"Do you mind if I ask why?"

Morgan looked uncomfortable. "I'm not sure how to get into that yet. I know he has a lot of questions and there are things I want him to know, but . . ."

"It's difficult?" she asked quietly.

"Very . . ."

Their mutual understanding was in the shared smile.

"Do you have bitter feelings toward your ex?"

He looked totally taken aback. "Christ, no."

"Sometimes it happens. You know Kent is going to feel an allegiance to his mother. She raised him. He'll defend her no matter what."

Morgan's gaze narrowed. "Of course he loves his mother. I just want to know that he has some feelings for me, too." He glanced at Patricia. "Or at least as much as he has for you."

Patricia swallowed. "Does he?"

"Ummm. I'm starting to wonder if I should be jealous," Morgan replied, watching her, but there was teasing in his regard.

"Oh."

"Kent says you're easy to talk to, and you listen."

"I was trained well," Patricia tried to joke.

"I don't think his feelings are so clinical."

"Oh . . ."

"You already said that. Kent's got a crush on you. Do you realize that?"

She looked at him and nodded.

"Does it bother you?"

Patricia thought a moment and in the openness of Morgan's question and curiosity, she was honest. "A little."

"What are you going to do?"

"I don't know yet. But please don't say anything to Kent. Don't even hint at what you're thinking."

"I won't."

"And you don't have to discourage Kent from seeing me, Morgan. That's the worst thing you could do right now. I think the reason that he feels . . . that he" — she gestured awkwardly — "likes me is because I'm the perfect ally. I can't tell him what to do and he doesn't have to obey me."

"But he does listen to you. I've told you. Don't underestimate your influence on either of us." Morgan reached out and rubbed the back of her hand. "Can I offer a suggestion? Don't blame yourself for whatever happens from now on."

"What's going to happen?" she asked innocently.

"Nothing, until after Thanksgiving."

That was too provocative a statement for Patricia to just let go. She opened her mouth to question Morgan further, but the rest of dinner was served.

Morgan comfortably switched gears and launched into a tour of the various dishes, suggesting that they share. She wanted to pursue his last comment, but the conversation swept on to the more immediate task of eating.

Everything was delicious, but spicy and pungent. Patricia's tongue tingled with the flavors and enhancements of the exotic dishes.

"You know a lot about island food. Do you eat here often?" Patricia asked.

"Not often. But I gained my appreciation right here in Brooklyn. That and a couple of short trips to St. Lucia."

"Are you from New York?"

He shook his head. "L.A."

"California. I never would have thought."

"I'm almost afraid to ask what you thought. I remember the pumpkin episode."

Patricia's eyes were bright with amusement. "The pumpkin episode?"

"Did you throw it out?"

"No. As a matter of fact I baked it and used the meat to make muffins and a bread."

"How come I didn't get any?"

"You don't strike me as the sort to like muffins." Patricia looked at Morgan thoughtfully. "I thought you were from somewhere like Chicago, or D.C., or Baltimore."

"Why those cities?"

"Well, they're all big cities."

"So's L.A."

"Yeah, but I don't believe that anyone does anything in California."

Morgan laughed as he boldly speared a piece of yam from her plate. "Airheads and sunshine? Boyz from the 'hood?"

"Well, not everyone."

"Thanks . . ." Morgan murmured.

"Did you inherit the family business?"

He finished the rice and beans and started on the vegetables. "The only thing I inherited from my father was a lot of IOUs from his cronies. He actually had a pretty decent position as a security supervisor at Metro-Goldwyn-Mayer studios when it was still called that. He drank himself out of that job when I was about twelve, and did odd jobs for a while until he just walked away one day. What I have I built up on my own.

"My mother worked as a cashier in a pharmacy. For some reason it made her think that I might become a doctor. There was a minor problem of not having any money for medical school, and I didn't want to be a doctor."

"What did you want to be?"

He smiled wryly. "Not much. I hung out with the guys in the neighborhood. Didn't get into anything serious, but I never thought of doing anything with my life."

"When did you change your mind?"

"You mean, *who* changed my mind. This old lady teacher in school. Mrs. Conklin. We used to call her the Bad Black Witch of the West. She cornered me one day and really lit into me, waving her cane in the air. Gave me the whole deal about making something of my life, and not embarrassing the race . . . she was from *that* generation. I have to admit I thought she was bugged." Morgan shook his head in amusement. "But something happened and I started to believe her. I was seventeen and I was really angry at my father for walking out on the family. I think I wanted to get back at him, show him I wasn't going to be like him."

Patricia listened quietly. She patted her mouth with her napkin and wondered if he could see any correlation between his anger at his father and Kent's toward himself. "Did you ever see him again?"

"Yeah, now and then. Then I got a scholarship to go to Michigan. In the second semester my father had a stroke and died. He was living in a boarding-house."

Patricia remained quiet, knowing that to say she was sorry would be meaningless. But when he glanced at her there was an empathetic smile on her lips.

"And then there's my sister. Annette."

"You have a sister?" Patricia said in some surprise. It occurred to her then that she'd previously only connected Morgan to Kent. And in a more nebulous way to someone who'd been his wife, and who was white. But of course he was part of a larger family community.

"An older sister. I think Annette always felt cheated by the sort of family and environment she'd been born into. In other words, there must have been a switch at the hospital and she should really have been the daughter of a very wealthy, very cultured family. She rectified the earlier mistake by marrying well. She lives in Arlington, Virginia. My mother still lives in L.A."

The history was told with both humor and understanding, and with an ease that made Patricia envious. And nervous. She wondered if Morgan would expect a similar sharing of confidence. Patricia looked at her plate, unable to finish the rest of the meal. She put down her fork.

"Why are you a counselor?" Morgan suddenly asked.

"Pardon?"

"Why not a teacher or an actress? Or even a doctor? That one passes through every parent's mind."

The question was so unpredictable. No one had ever asked her before. The memories it evoked rushed through her and stirred up unfinished business. Drew, again. And all she'd lost just because of him.

Patricia recovered and her expression became wistful. "I was in a play once in fourth grade. I played a tree . . ." Morgan chuckled. "I did teach for a while, but I found I spent a lot of time talking with students about their problems instead of English Lit. I found the kids more interesting and challenging." She became reflective as Morgan waited silently for her to go on. "I did want to be a doctor. That was at the top of my list," she confided quietly.

"What happened? Too expensive? Didn't pass the entrance tests?"

Color crept up Patricia's neck to her face, and she didn't look directly at Morgan. A part of her past loomed over her that remained unresolved. "I was accepted to medical school. I wanted to be a pediatrician. But . . . well . . . it just didn't work out."

"So, you went into counseling instead? That's pretty far short of your goal."

"Not really. I'm finishing up my dissertation paper. I take my orals next spring."

He whistled softly. "I'm impressed. Were your folks disappointed when you changed your mind?" Her expression seemed frozen and her gaze dropped to her plate. "Did I say something wrong?"

"My parents were killed in a highway accident when I was quite small. I don't really remember them very well. Gilly raised me. My grandmother."

Morgan nodded silently. "How about brothers and sisters?"

"I had a baby brother. He died with my parents."

Morgan closed his eyes and groaned softly. When he opened them they sought forgiveness and he took hold of her hand again. "Jesus. Maybe I better stop asking questions and let you talk."

"Maybe some other time," Patricia said, quietly putting an end to the opportunity.

She tried to pull her hand free. She suddenly realized that he was caressing it, massaging the skin until little eddies of ticklish delight moved up her arm. He wouldn't let the hand go. It wasn't so much that he was touching her that Patricia keyed into as it was the response of her whole body to the contact. It was so immediate, absolute.

They stared at one another, like they had in the stands of the football game. Only now she felt mesmerized, thrown into slow motion and a dawning acceptance of Morgan's interest. Patricia didn't feel shocked. She might have guessed a long time ago if she hadn't been fighting her awareness so hard. But that didn't mean she was ready to give in. If anything, she dug her heels in.

"Morgan . . . why are you doing this?" Patricia asked, her breath seemed thin and breathless.

"I told you. I want to get to know you. Maybe I'm asking something you have no interest in giving. We won't know until we take Kent out of the middle of our acquaintance and just see what happens."

She couldn't turn away, couldn't ignore him. Morgan's mere presence, let alone his declaration, demanded not only an answer but acquiescence. She fully understood that. Patricia eased her hand from under his, but with a slight reluctance, as if she didn't really want to. Slowly she shook her head, moistening her lower lip.

"I can't get involved with you. I just can't," she whispered.

Morgan remained easy. "Are you still afraid people will talk?"

"Why me?"

"Why not?"

"Morgan, that's not an answer."

"Then we're back to why not just wait and see what happens, aren't we?"

The waiter came to clear the remains of their meal. A nosy foursome was seated at the next table; the check came and had to be paid. And Patricia escaped to the ladies' room to confront the wide-eyed excited woman in the mirror. She was trying to decide if the look was one of fear or expectation. Afterward she and Morgan met in the parking lot of the restaurant. She thanked him for dinner.

"Patricia . . ." Morgan got her attention as she was about to open her car door.

The way he looked at her made her curious, and she stood still as he approached closer. Morgan suddenly removed her glasses and in the same motion bent forward to kiss her. It just missed being full on the mouth. Her move to avoid the touch of his lips was too slow, and she had to contend with the feel of his mouth on hers. It was a mixture of firm intent and gentle pursuit. His mouth had the faint aroma of spices from dinner. Morgan allowed several inches of space between them, his eyes sparkling and fixed on her features. She never moved, although her heart had suddenly begun a painful pounding.

Morgan folded her red-framed glasses and handed them to her.

"It will be interesting to find out some-day why you wear these. You don't really need them."

Patricia silently took them and made no pretense of putting them back on. She fumbled with the snap opening on her purse to drop the glasses inside. Morgan hadn't moved and there was no place for her to go. Her back was almost against the car. Morgan's hand reached for her arm and firmly pulled her for-ward. Her head snapped up to stare at him. She felt awkward and helpless as she watched his handsome face, en-thralled by the gentle look of purpose and interest in his eyes.

"Patricia . . ." he whispered again.

She should have been prepared . . . but wasn't. Patricia thought her heart was going to push clear through her chest.

Her eyes drifted closed of their own accord as Morgan lowered his head to kiss her again. Only this time formality and politeness, the propriety that she was so concerned about, disappeared. Pretense shattered as Morgan's mobile mouth pressed firmly, forcing her lips apart. His tongue slipped slowly inside causing Patricia to catch her breath with the sensual invasion.

For a second she wondered if they looked odd together. A black man kissing what would appear to be a white woman. She wondered what was going through Morgan's mind, given his first feelings about her. But there was no hesitation on his part. Having committed himself to the moment Morgan kissed her with a kind of confidence that was assertive, but not aggressive.

Patricia stood, unable to move, as a sudden delicious wash of longing flooded her system. Her stomach twisted and fluttered like butterflies of temptation. Morgan possessed her mouth, controlled the kiss, and kept on with the tender but electrifying assault until Patricia felt dazed. Her legs began to feel numb.

Slowly Morgan tightened the embrace,

his hands splayed across her back, around her waist, the bulkiness of their outer clothing thwarting any closer intimacy. His mouth moved over hers with a kind of knowing expertise, but didn't seem calculated. She could hear his breathing, feel his growing desire in the slow kneading actions of his hands and fingers. She began to feel overheated, but remained transfixed by the power of Morgan's kiss and the blissful exploration of his tongue in her mouth. Patricia gave in completely, forgetting about coherent thought and just falling into the euphoric abyss.

She was embarrassed to find she wasn't prepared for Morgan to end the kiss. He wasn't abrupt, but it was too soon. Her lips remained parted, her breath a gentle rush when their lips separated. She kept her eyes closed, trying desperately to gather her wits. She was disoriented . . . and bewildered by the overwhelming effect of Morgan's kiss and touch.

Patricia lowered her chin, and drew her bottom lip in between her teeth. She was afraid Morgan would see it tremble. She heard his soft sigh of satisfaction. Felt a light kiss on her nose, and then her forehead. He squeezed her waist.

"Well . . ." he drawled.

There was surprise in the quietly uttered word.

"Well, what?" Patricia asked.

Morgan reluctantly released her, sliding his hands down her arms to grab her hands. When he looked into her eyes, his held pleasure and knowledge. His face was shadowed by the night, but she could see the sparkle of his eyes, the pleased smile on his mouth.

"I think I owe my son, big time."

She was confused. "Kent? For what?"

Morgan's smile was indulgent. "For you, of course," he whispered.

Chapter Nine

Kent dragged the knapsack from beneath the edge of his bed where it had been indifferently kicked the night before.

"Shit," he cursed mildly when it swung wide and knocked a pile of things off the edge of his desk to the floor. The sound of something landing with a thud caught Kent's attention. He bent to retrieve it. It was an Olympus 35mm single lens automatic camera. He stared blankly at it for a moment before awareness and memory clenched at his insides.

Kent sat on the side of his bed and dropped the sack but continued to hold the camera, turning it over and over in his hands, as if he didn't know what to make of it. He felt something akin to panic surge up through his body. He was trying to remember where the camera came from. And why. Then it came back in mortifying details. That sensation of thrill and fear mixed together, when he'd walked past the art studio last September, seen the camera sitting unattended on a chair, and taken it, now turned to dread and embarrassment. At the time it had seemed so easy. But then he didn't know why he'd wanted the camera, or what to do with it. Except to bring it home and hide it.

He got up and rushed to his desk. He shoved aside things and searched with his hands until he found the two CDs taken from the school library. But that still wasn't all he was looking for.

"Shit!" Kent said this time in frustration.

"Kent?"

He started, his heartbeat thumping in alarm. Kent turned to stare at the half-opened doorway. His father was in the hall, headed toward his room.

"You almost ready? It's time to get out of here."

Kent looked around his room quickly. He then crouched and shoved the camera under the bed, wrapped in a discarded T-shirt. He turned and plunked down on his bed as his father tapped quietly on the door and walked in. He bent over, covertly pulled a boot lace loose, and slowly retied it. He glanced up at his father.

"I . . . I'm coming."

Morgan watched him silently for a moment, nodding when he saw that his son was dressed and ready.

"Want me to drop you off at the train station?"

"That's . . . cool," Kent murmured, finally standing up.

"I'll see you downstairs . . ." Morgan said, glancing over the desk at its messy surface. He reached out and knocked on the end of the desk . . . next to the CDs. "In one minute, right?"

Kent held his breath until his father left the room. Then he tossed the CDs into a drawer already containing cassettes and computer discs. He grabbed the knapsack and rushed out the bedroom door with a final look behind him to make sure nothing else was out of place.

But he had no idea where he'd left the pen from Mrs. Lechter's desk.

Morgan walked past Connie Anderson's desk and headed down the hallway toward David Sullivan's office. He missed the casual greeting of a passing clerk, not out of rudeness but distraction. He'd called Patricia Gilbert to ask her out, to find a place and time and event that had nothing to do with Duncan High School or his son. Someplace conducive to adult conversation and privacy. Patricia had said no. In mild annoyance Morgan admitted that he hadn't expected that. Not after that open talk they'd had. Especially not after that kiss . . .

"Mr. Baxter, the conference room is set up for your meeting tomorrow morning. Is there anything else I can do?"

Morgan frowned, forcing his attention to the immediate details of his business and the administrative assistant waiting for further instructions.

"Just make sure a light buffet breakfast is arranged for eight people. And lots of coffee."

"No problem." The woman nodded and walked away.

But Morgan continued to stand there, slipping back into reflection. His mouth lifted at one corner in irony and frustration. Patricia had fooled him. Or rather, he'd fooled himself.

He hadn't arrived at Kent's game that

313

Saturday with any set plan, because he hadn't expected Patricia to be there. But outside of the arena of school, and the camouflage of the students' welfare, Morgan had seen an opportunity to find out what else lay behind the cautious gray eyes and professional manners. And the moment he'd begun to get too personal, she'd seen right through him. She'd called him on it. And yet, that kiss had been something. It changed everything.

Morgan realized that he hadn't counted on that, either. In Patricia's response he could still feel her control. But underneath, when he wouldn't let up, Morgan felt a glimmer of agitation, the essence of passion. The movement of her lips and the electrifying dance of their tongues had given her away. And he'd been thinking about that kiss ever since.

Morgan started down the corridor again, still pensive and still dissatisfied. He wanted to know what more there was behind Patricia's response to him. But there was also Beverly.

He could hear David's voice even before he reached the office. It wasn't so much talking as murmuring, leading

Morgan to believe the call was personal. His door was partially open, however, so Morgan walked in unannounced.

David was bent intently over a full page of text and numbers, a spread sheet with projections. The phone was squeezed between his ear and shoulder, and he was making margin notes and checking items as he talked. He was conducting Ventura business, but whoever he was talking to had the full force of his charm. Then his body language changed, his tone became all business, as if realizing he was no longer alone.

"Sounds good to me. We have a few more things to get settled, signed, and sealed, but I think we've got this thing licked. And . . . ah . . . I really appreciate your help."

David finally looked up, spotted Morgan in front of his desk, and silently beckoned him to sit in any of the available chairs. Morgan didn't move, standing with his hands in his pockets as his gaze briefly swept around the office. He never knew whether to be irritated or amused by David's open display of self-admiration, the metaphors that so described his personality. Framed photographs of himself from ski trips, rock climbing, and beach vacations. A picture of him with Michelle Pfeiffer, autographed. An expensive pair of lizard-skin cowboy boots were in a corner. Several unopened bottles of Evian water were lined up on a book unit next to the Standard and Poors.

"Hey, they were tough, but we were tougher. But what difference does it make? Everyone comes away a winner, right?"

Morgan decided not to sit down, forcing the younger man to sit back in his chair and look up at him. But his presence did not hurry David through his conversation so as not to keep his boss waiting. David stared up at him in a manner that almost anyone would consider insolent. It made Morgan grimace. He didn't play those kinds of games. His ego didn't require it. Besides . . . he was in charge.

Their gazes met and locked, like a challenge. David suddenly laughed.

"That sounds like an offer I can't refuse," he drawled. "I'm going to hold you to it . . . Great . . . Talk to you soon." He hung up the phone and spread his hands in a gesture of apology, a benign grin on his handsome face. "Sorry. That's a call I had to finish."

"What's going on?" Morgan asked.

"What do you mean? Something wrong?"

"I want to know where we stand with Sager. You assured me you only needed another week or so to bring them into line."

David slowly leaned forward again, never losing the calm smile. He lifted the spread sheet in front of him, turned it upside down, and presented it to Morgan. "Done."

Morgan felt mollified. He also felt vaguely unsettled. He'd been reluctant to turn over most of the Sager negotiations to David, but in all honesty, David had steadily moved things along. He conceded that the decision to devote more time and attention to Kent meant relinquishing total control over some of his plans. About that, David had been right. But David had reported back on most of the meetings. Morgan had little to find wrong, other than not always having direct contact with the Sager reps himself and being two months past schedule on signing an agreement. David had guaranteed it would happen before Thanksgiving. The page of terms and points checked off showed that David had been as good as his word.

"How does it look?" David asked.

Morgan arched a brow and pursed his lips. "Excellent. They've given you just about all we've asked for."

David shrugged. "We haven't done likewise, of course. It would have been counterproductive. But we gave enough to keep them happy. Most of the management team has been scaled back, but no one's out of work. I know that was important to you."

Morgan was thoughtful for a moment as he quickly glanced over the page again. It all looked and sounded good. "What else do they want?"

David's brows rose. "If there's anything else they haven't said so. I'm sure there are more surprises coming, but I don't think I'd worry about it. If you can get them to sign off on the items you're holding, you'd still be in control of the company. Like I said, everyone wins."

Morgan wanted to ask more questions, but he had a meeting with a visiting European economist over another project, another negotiation. He gave David a brief smile. "Good work,

David. Set up the meeting to sign the contracts." He turned to leave the office.

"Sure thing. They'll want us to come over before . . ."

"No. The meeting will be here."

David looked confused. "What difference does it make?"

"To use one of your terms, 'home court advantage.' We made them feel safe and unthreatened by letting their management call some of the shots, but this is still my game, my rules. This is still business."

David was silent, his expression blank and still. Then he again shrugged, as if it didn't matter to him. His smile was pleasant. "Hey, I thought it was over once we got what we wanted."

Morgan gave a cryptic smile in return as he finally departed. "It is. But the ball stays in our court."

Morgan walked out of David's office and almost immediately his attention drifted back to Patricia. She was like a magnet drawing his sensibilities. He wanted to get next to her, and she wasn't making it easy. And, Morgan recognized with irony, it was a unique experience to not have a woman openly welcome his interest and advances. So, why had she turned him down? Probably he'd moved too fast. But what if Patricia Gilbert just wasn't interested? Morgan cursed softly under his breath. That wasn't the answer he was looking for.

It was after four when he finished the conference call with several people, and the economist who'd come to his office. Morgan had been uncommonly impatient all afternoon until Connie told him he had a call. For a heartbeat Morgan hoped it might be Patricia changing her mind. But it was Beverly on the line.

"I forgive you," she opened.

Morgan pursed his mouth. "That's nice. For what?"

"For not calling and apologizing. We haven't seen each other in a week. Connie said you've been very busy and had a lot on your mind. Including me, I suppose."

Morgan couldn't deny that, but still felt put off by her presumption. "I'm trying to cover a lot of bases before Thanksgiving."

"I have a case to review with a client at the World Trade Center this week. Why don't we plan on getting together?"

Morgan was quick to note that Beverly

had left the question somewhat open-ended. She didn't say to get together for what. Oddly, he wondered what Patricia Gilbert was doing just then. The significance escaped Morgan as he and Beverly set a place and time to meet.

Patricia lifted the wooden box from the bookshelf and looked inside. It was empty. She turned back to the desk surface, afraid to touch the mess of papers and folders for fear of disrupting some organizational system known only to Jerome. She looked into his pencil caddy, under the edge of the blotter, but only found a duplicate set of Jerome's car keys.

With a murmur of frustration Patricia pulled open the top desk drawer and began riffling through. She and Jerome had always had an open-door policy when it came to the use of materials and books in the office, and they'd sometimes had to invade each other's office space, such as it was. Which was why it came as a real shock to Patricia to find the box of condoms.

She dismissed the thought that Jerome was being secretive. After all, there they were as soon as you opened the drawer. But the very presence of the contraceptives sent a queasy flood of speculation into Patricia's head. She stared at the foil packages.

"What are you looking for, Patty?"

Startled, Patricia turned to face Jerome, using her body to block the desk drawer. "I'm looking for the keys to the file cabinet in the outer office. Someone pushed in all the locks."

Her voice was admirably calm, but Patricia knew that Jerome was watching her with curiosity, watching the blush that stained her cheeks. Yet he merely pulled open the center drawer and, without taking his gaze from her, extracted a key ring. Patricia took the keys and smiled her thanks. Jerome silently continued to regard her.

"What's the matter? Did you find love letters from Mrs. Forrest?"

Patricia smiled hesitantly at Jerome's humor. "I'm sorry. What you see is surprise."

Jerome turned and sat on the edge of his desk. He folded his arms across his chest. "So what are you surprised about?"

She faced him squarely. "You have condoms in your desk."

He slowly nodded his head. "Yeah? So?"

"I just . . . Jerome, you're not distributing them, are you?"

His look was expressionless, and he continued to stare at her until she felt like she was on the spot. "Why didn't you ask if they belong to me?"

"Because either way I don't think they should be here. What if someone found them?"

"Someone has. You. You're not happy about it. Why?"

"Because we have no authority to give out condoms. The school board, let alone the parents, would have your license in a minute."

Jerome abruptly stood up and walked to the entrance of his office. He turned around to stare at Patricia intently. He appeared calm, but Patricia knew he was angry.

"The condoms belong to me."

"Look, I'm sorry if I've gotten personal, but . . ."

Jerome shrugged. "I suppose you had to ask. But what would you do if one of the students, a girl, let's say, asked you how to get birth control pills or a diaphragm?"

Patricia frowned. "I . . . I don't know. No one's ever asked."

"Well, one day someone's going to."

"Jerome, I'm not sure we should be playing parent."

"But isn't that what we're asked to do all the time? We get personal. We get into family business, into students' faces asking questions, giving advice. We dig into their psyche and preach responsibility and patience. They're just words, Patty. What do you do when a kid comes to you because he or she needs more than words? And when they come to us instead of their folks, what do you think that means?"

"We don't have all the answers."

"You're right. But sometimes we have the ones the kids need the most."

Jerome became agitated as he talked. He returned to the desk and stood directly in front of her.

"The one thing we never talk about with the students happens to be the single most important thing on their minds right now. Sex. Forget not getting along with parents or hating a brother or sister. Forget grades and college and future careers. It's 'Will *she* like me, will *he* ask me out? Can I score?' " He carefully enunciated the last three words. Then he reached past Patricia and closed the drawer containing the condoms. "It's safe sex versus a harder decision later on."

Patricia looked at him. "I know you're right, but I'm just concerned about overstepping the bounds of our authority."

"No you're not. You're concerned about the presence of the condoms. You have to trust me on this one, Patricia, because I'm not saying any more."

"I have to tell you I'm very uncomfortable with this. What are you going to do about that box in your drawer?"

"Leave them there, and lock the drawer," Jerome said airily.

Patricia sighed impatiently. "Just be careful. Please," she cautioned quietly.

He leaned toward her, his eyes bright and mischievous. "I'm always careful. Was there something else?"

Patricia moved to a nearby chair and sat down. Jerome again sat on the edge of the desk. "I'm worried about Kyra Whitacre."

Jerome looked down at his sneakers. "Still? Why?"

"I think she's getting too close to Eric

Patton. Her grades are slipping . . ."

"I told you not to worry about Eric. Kyra's too young for him."

"She doesn't seem to think so. When I see them together . . ."

"It's not what you think. Believe me. Look, Eric is just a friend. She's like a kid sister to him. It's a good relationship for both of them."

Patricia frowned. "Are you sure? I'm not convinced he's an ideal big brother, either."

"Yeah, that's what you said when I told you a friendship was developing between Eric and Kent. They're an odd couple, but it works. They each have a little of what the other wants and needs. I'm telling you, Kyra's okay. You need to worry what you're going to do about Kent Baxter and that crush he's got on you."

Patricia turned her head away. There was a sound at the door. In another half second Kent Baxter himself appeared.

"Hey. We were just talking about you," Jerome piped up.

"You were?" He glanced back and forth between the two adults.

Patricia stared pointedly at Jerome,

wondering if he would really be so indiscreet.

"Yeah. I hear you're doing real well on the football team. Congratulations."

"Thanks. Uh, Miss Gilbert, I was just wondering if I could see you during your lunch break?"

Patricia glanced at Jerome, openly pleading for help.

"I'm afraid I beat you to it, Kent. Miss Gilbert and I have some official stuff to talk over. Lunch is the only available time today." He waited for Patricia to confirm his story.

"If it's really important, Kent, I have a few moments free after the last period this afternoon." She could see that he was momentarily flustered. She'd always been available to him before.

Kent took a step back out of the doorway. "No, that's okay. It was no big deal."

"Well, maybe we'll try to arrange something for tomorrow. Come by in the morning."

"Sure." Kent nodded, but with an awkward turn he left the office.

Jerome was watching Patricia. She glanced briefly at him, her expression troubled. "I know, you don't have to say it. I owe you one."

His smile was understanding. "Don't think I'll forget."

She laughed lightly at the oft-repeated line between them.

"So, what do you want to do for lunch?" Jerome asked, jumping to his feet.

"This is Thursday."

"What about it?"

"Well, you sometimes take off and go to your secret rendezvous with person or persons who have remained nameless for months. Won't they-he-she be disappointed if you don't show?"

"Oh . . ." Jerome responded blankly. Then he recovered and motioned for Patricia to precede him out the door. "I won't be missed."

Kent left the building feeling very stupid. Why hadn't he told Miss Gilbert he'd come back later in the afternoon, like she suggested? It had never occurred to him that she wouldn't be free at lunchtime. Kent knew that she sometimes had lunch with Mr. Daly, but that was probably only because nobody else would eat with him. Kent still felt dumb. Now he didn't know what to do, and he didn't have any lunch. For a moment he thought of just cutting the rest of the afternoon, but he knew that not only would his father find out about it, he'd be really mad.

He began to walk around the side of the building toward the front where most of the students hung out during the breaks. He saw Pete Connors acting like a goon over some girl. He saw Eric and Britt and some of the other guys, but he didn't really want to be with them right now. Kyra Whitacre ran past him as she crossed his path on her way to catch up with the other group.

"Hi, Kent," Kyra called out, but didn't wait for an answer.

She hung around the team a lot, but he didn't really know her that well. She was just a kid. He turned and continued to walk.

"Yo . . . Baxter. I hear your mama's so white she cries milk."

A burst of raucous laughter started from behind Kent. He continued to walk, but glanced casually over his shoulder at Kamil and three or four other boys sitting on the hood of a parked car. He hunched up his shoulders and braced himself. He turned to face the quartet as he walked back-ward.

"Yeah? Your mama's so dumb she thinks a quarterback is a refund."

There was just the barest pause before those same boys, Kamil's friends, fell out in loud laughter.

"Oh, shit! My man ranked all over you, Kamil. You gonna take that?"

"I'm gonna kick your ass, you white motherfucker . . ." Kamil spewed out.

Kent faced forward and continued walking. He was alert, but was too far away and didn't think Kamil would try anything right then.

From the corner of his eye Kent saw Mrs. Forrest from the office. She was trying to ask questions of that new girl, Gabriella. Gabriella kept shaking her head and murmuring, ". . . *no intiendo. Lo siento mucho.*" Kent walked on by.

The guys on the team complained that none of them could get next to Gabriella because she didn't know English. Kent had heard her called a stuck-up Latino bitch; weird. He saw her lots of times around the school but they never talked. Maybe she was still mad at him from when they'd first met. Miss Gilbert had asked him to be friends with her but Gabriella didn't seem all that friendly. Besides, he had enough stuff to deal with.

Kent finally stopped and sat on the steps to the front of the building. He pulled his Walkman from his jacket pocket and set the phones in his ears. The music rocked him, pulled him into a rhythmic beat until he forgot his disappointment at not seeing Miss Gilbert. Instead, Kent recalled the details of the dream he'd had about her.

He was running a race. There was a giant stopwatch around Coach's neck that showed fifteen seconds left to the race. He still had a long way to go to get around the track. Miss Gilbert was waiting at the finish line. Her red hair was like a flag, and she stood out clearly from all the onlookers. She cheered him on, yelling to Kent that he was going to win. But his legs felt like lead weights, and he was so out of breath. Suddenly there was his father wearing the stopwatch, clocking his speed, and telling him not to give up.

Kent ran on until Miss Gilbert appeared closer and closer and he could see her smiling at him, clapping her hands.

"You've won, you've won!" she was shouting.

But Kent couldn't stop running. He was past the finish line, going around the track again. It was like the momentum just moved him along. There, suddenly, was his grandfather looking stern, and his mother looking hurt and disappointed.

"You should have run faster," Granddad said.

"Now you can come back home," his mother said.

He ran right on past them, too . . .

Then there had been the second dream. Kent hunched his shoulders and closed his eyes tight, willing the second dream into visualization. It was at a football game. He was lying on the field holding the ball, and couldn't seem to get up. Miss Gilbert knelt beside him, her hair was spread out like a red curtain that surrounded him. She was bending over to stroke his face. "Kent . . ." She was smiling. She was going to kiss him . . .

Kent's eyes opened sharply. He looked around to see if anyone had noticed. He felt strange in his body. Hot and hard. He stood up quickly and started back around the side of the building the way he'd first come. He took a couple of deep breaths and turned up the volume on the Walkman.

When he looked up he saw Gabriella again. Connors was with her now. Kent could tell right away that something was up between them. Connors was standing too close to her, but instead of walking away Gabriella was standing her ground against him. Kent hesitated, and then walked over to join them.

"Leave her alone, man."

Connors, turning mean with the interruption, pointed a threatening finger at Kent. "Fuck off, Baxter. Who asked you?"

Kent pulled the earphones out and turned to Gabriella. "Why don't you just walk away?"

" 'Cause she don't understand you, man," Connors said.

Kent ignored him and started toward the side entrance to the school. "Come on," he said to Gabriella over his shoulder. "The break is almost over anyway."

Kent saw Connors's arm shoot out suddenly. His palm connected with Kent's shoulder, pushing him slightly off balance.

"Bruta! Gordita!" Gabriella hissed at Connors.

"See, I told you. She just talks Spanish," Connors smirked.

"How do you know she's not cursing you out?" Kent asked.

"Eat my squirrel," Connors said in annoyance and walked away to the laughter and whistles of his waiting cohorts.

"I don't need your help," Gabriella said with a pout at Kent.

"Fine," Kent said indifferently. "Next time I'll just let him hit on you and you can handle him yourself." He walked away.

"He didn't hit me," Gabriella said.

Kent ignored her. He heard her hurrying after him.

"All right. I am sorry. I thank you for trying to help me."

"Look, it doesn't matter to me. Most of the girls would tell him to go get a grip, but you don't know any better. He was trying to scope you out."

Gabriella looked at him strangely. *"Como?"*

Kent was exasperated. "Didn't you understand what I said?"

"What does it mean, to scope? Why

do you say he hit on me?"

Kent sighed. "Connors was just trying to check you out. You know, trying to get your attention. He wants you to like him."

Gabriella stretched her eyes open and shook her head. "Never."

"You mean, not in this lifetime."

She understood that and giggled. "Oh, *sí.* Yes. Not in this lifetime."

Kent smiled at her. She learned fast. "What did you call him?"

"*Bruta?* It means stupid. And *gordita,* like this . . ." She demonstrated by puffing out her cheeks and making a large circle in front of her chest with her arms.

Kent cackled. "Naw, Pete's not fat. He's huge!" Kent laughed and Gabriella joined in. He repeated the words to himself. "That's cool. I gotta remember that." He looked more closely at Gabriella. She was sort of little and cute. She had pretty eyes, and you really noticed her mouth with all that red lipstick. "I heard you before with Mrs. Forrest. How come you pretend you speak no English?"

Gabriella seemed annoyed. "She takes me to this group or that club. I don't want to go. The girls are all childish."

"But you'll make a lot of friends."

"This is what Miss Gilbert say to me."

Kent nodded. "Well, maybe she was right. I didn't have any friends at first either."

She shrugged and pouted. "It doesn't matter. I will leave in another year and my family will move somewhere else. Maybe I will go at the end of June. There is no point in making friends because I will only lose them again."

"Okay, so what if you do? You're saying you're not going to have any friends at all for a whole year? Sounds dumb to me."

Gabriella glanced furtively at him. "But they all laugh at me because I am different."

"How do you know? If you keep pretending you don't speak English everyone is going to give up caring."

"Kent . . ."

He stared at her. It was the first time she had ever said his name and it sounded weird, like the word "can't" with a soft "a."

"What is Homecoming?"

"It's the weekend of Thanksgiving. All the former students come back to Duncan. There's a football game, and dances, parties. They see old teachers and stuff."

"Miss Gilbert, she says I should come to Homecoming."

"I'm playing in the game," Kent boasted. Not that he really cared if she knew. She probably didn't even know what football was.

Kent turned his head as Connors and several of his friends strolled past him and Gabriella. Connors suddenly turned, doing a lumbering dance step backward, mimicking a woman with her hands on her hips.

"I'm Chiquita Banana . . ." Connors sang crudely in a falsetto. But he was the only one who thought it funny.

Kent looked at Gabriella to see if she was hurt or angry. She looked at him and Kent could see that she wasn't. But she was beginning to smile and so was he.

"*Bruta.*" They both nodded, and laughed.

Chapter Ten

"I appreciate your calling, Mrs. Anderson."

"As I said, I'm sorry it has to be on such short notice, but Mr. Baxter said it couldn't wait."

Patricia waited for Mrs. Anderson to give her more information, or a hint as to why Morgan wanted so urgently to see her. Of course she had her own speculations. The sudden knot in her stomach, the rush of tension that made her feel so hot, made Patricia wonder if Morgan was still going to pursue a relationship beyond the one she'd established. Yet, Patricia seriously doubted that Morgan would have used his secretary as a go-between for anything personal, no matter how long she'd worked for him. Which only left the possibility of Kent as being the subject in question.

"I can leave soon but I can't get there

much before three-thirty, I'm afraid."

"That's fine. Anyway, Mr. Baxter is holding a contracts meeting at the moment. I'm sure I can guarantee that he'll be free when you get here."

"Then I'll see you about three-thirty."

Patricia hung up the phone with mixed feelings. On the one hand she was certain that this call from Morgan at the eleventh hour before Thanksgiving was about Kent. She hoped it was nothing serious, but she was secretly pleased that Morgan continued to seek her advice and guidance. But the more complicated question remained at the back of her mind of whether the request to see her was personal.

And yet, when Morgan had called her earlier to ask her out it sounded to Patricia too much like a date. A date meant them being alone. A date would end at her apartment, at the door. In another kiss. She'd already asked herself why she hadn't stopped him the first time. Quite simply, it was because she'd never thought to.

In the spontaneity of that moment she was curious about how Morgan would kiss her, and how it would feel. It had been, in her mind, unbelievably erotic in its thoroughness because it hadn't been just to satisfy himself. Morgan wanted her to respond, to feel something, too. She had. Even now her insides curled with the memory of how nice it felt to be kissed by him.

Since there was absolutely no point in torturing herself this way, Patricia shook off the questions with no answers, and got up from her desk. She lifted an armful of textbooks and left her office, encountering Jerome in the outer room.

"Where are you off to?" he asked absently as he looked quickly through a sheaf of notes and messages.

"Down to my car with these books. I have some reading to do."

"Over the holiday weekend? Why don't you give it a rest?"

"Because I'm almost finished with my paper. I'm just starting to see the light at the end of the tunnel. I have my orals scheduled for the spring."

"Don't worry. All the work is going to pay off for you. If I decide to go for a post graduate degree, can I use your notes?"

Patricia grimaced. "You say you hated

school. I'm surprised you got this far," she teased.

"Poverty is not an attractive option. I'm kind of used to the idea of regular meals and a decent place to live," he said dryly.

"I have to admit you'd make an interesting therapist. Radical, at least."

Jerome shrugged off the idea.

"So, when are you leaving this afternoon?"

"About two or so. I have a meeting with Kent Baxter's father before I get on the road."

Jerome pursed his lips and adjusted his glasses. "Is this a professional meeting?"

Patricia stared at him. "What's that supposed to mean?"

Jerome winced. "I'm sorry. It's my motor mouth."

Patricia didn't let up. "I want to know what you meant by that, Jerome," she pressed.

"Look, Patty, I didn't mean anything. Don't go off on me."

"Don't call me Patty," she said tightly.

He frowned at her. "Man, are you touchy lately."

Patricia sighed and briefly closed her

eyes, trying to control her annoyance. "I didn't mean to snap at you. I just don't appreciate your teasing right now."

"I wasn't teasing," Jerome said earnestly. "I think Baxter could go for you, given one ounce of encouragement."

"I haven't encouraged him," she said tightly.

"Fine. Then you have nothing to worry about and you can tell me to shut up."

"Shut up. What are you doing for Thanksgiving?" she asked as they walked down another hallway.

"I've been invited to dinner by a friend," Jerome answered indifferently.

Patricia glanced at him. "Is she pretty?"

"*He* is not bad-looking," Jerome corrected dryly. He stopped in the middle of the hallway. "More to the point, his wife thinks he's pretty cute. I suspect I was invited because they have someone they want me to meet. Good intentions. Bad idea."

"Sounds like fun," she responded absently.

"Hey, I'm always grateful for a free home-cooked meal," he said flippantly, heading off now toward a stairwell. He stopped and looked back on her. "Have a good one. Say hi to Gilly."

"I will. Take care, Jerome," Patricia murmured.

"Oh . . . Pat?"

She looked at him askance, as she held open the exit.

"Don't fight it."

Jerome then walked away before she could even think of an answer.

There wasn't much traffic in downtown Manhattan. All the smart folks had already left for the long weekend. And when Patricia walked into the lobby of Morgan's building, she found it quiet, almost deserted, and the only sounds were the mechanics of the elevator as it moved. The same officious receptionist was on duty but this time he merely acknowledged her politely and rang through to Mrs. Anderson when Patricia gave her name.

"I'm glad you could make it." Mrs. Anderson smiled as she met Patricia.

"And I'm on time."

"I wasn't going to hold that against you."

"Well, I still feel I need to make up for

my first visit and to get on your good side."

Mrs. Anderson laughed lightly. "You already have."

"I have? How?"

"By being someone that Mr. Baxter has a very high opinion of." She gave Patricia a knowing smile. "And I think he likes you."

Patricia kept a smile fixed on her lips, but couldn't think of anything to say to Mrs. Anderson's announcement. She wondered how Morgan's assistant would know all of that.

"Mr. Baxter is waiting for you. I don't want to be the cause of your being late this time. I'm sure you have plans for the weekend."

"Just a drive to Virginia."

Mrs. Anderson, halfway to the door, stopped and turned. "I hope you're not going to drive that distance all alone?"

"I'll stop midway to rest and have dinner."

Mrs. Anderson nodded her approval, as only someone who'd raised children would. "Good. Have a happy Thanksgiving . . ."

"Thank you. Same to you."

Patricia turned at the sound of a door

opening behind her. There stood Morgan. She stared at him, aware of every aspect of him. The gears in her body started churning, but Patricia maintained her control, remembering that there was no need for her to believe that this meeting was anything other than official. Judging from the tight, stern look on Morgan's face, she would also say the matter was serious.

"Hi," she said, and then regretted sounding so sophomoric.

Morgan merely pushed the office door open. "Come on in."

His apparent preoccupation was unsettling to her. Particularly after their brief encounter recently that had held intimacy and promise. Patricia walked hesitantly past him to the conference table, still littered with pencils and pads, documents and water glasses from Morgan's earlier meeting. She glanced at him thinking that maybe his demeanor had nothing to do with her. Maybe it was because of some business problem.

"Take a seat over here," Morgan instructed, indicating a comfortable leather chair in front of his desk. "I'm sorry you had to delay the start of your weekend. I appreciate you coming in."

She frowned. His excruciatingly polite tone put distance between them. In a way she was grateful. But in another . . . "I assumed it was important." She sat and calmly crossed her legs.

Morgan swiveled in his chair to face her. "It's about Kent." He picked up a letter.

She became perfectly alert, even a little frightened. "Kent? Is he okay?"

"Physically, he's fine. Emotionally, I'm not always sure. Psychologically? You tell me." Morgan handed her the letter.

The top sheet was a letter from a law firm representing one Bernard R. Kahn, resident of Brooklyn and owner of a 1995 Jeep Cherokee Sport 4x4. The said vehicle, stolen on the evening of October 31 but subsequently returned, had sustained damage. The letter was in the form of an invoice requesting payment in the amount of $750.00 to be used toward the repairs and legal fees. The letter also indicated the names of two other implicated subjects, Britt Harris and Peter Connors.

Patricia felt herself grow hot with embarrassment. Morgan was deceptively calm, waiting for her to finish reading, but his jaw was tensing reflexively.

"Were you hoping that I wouldn't find out?"

Patricia slowly shook her head and gave him back the pages. "No. I was hoping that Kent would have the courage to tell you himself about that night."

"Why did you lie to me? Why did you cover for him?"

He was angry. In self-defense Patricia's own anger began to rise. "Because I knew that *he* knew he'd done something stupid. I didn't lie, Morgan. I told Kent I wouldn't."

"But you left out most of the facts," he accused impatiently.

"Look, I wasn't sure what actually happened. When I went to pick up Kent that night, he was alone. He was not in custody, and there was no suggestion that the police or anyone else was looking for him. Kent felt bad enough about being stoned and drunk . . ."

"What about how I'd feel?" Morgan cut in.

"I guess I didn't count on you being patient and understanding. Maybe that night Kent wasn't sure he could either."

"One of you should have given me the benefit of the doubt. You, at least."

Patricia sighed, trying to maintain her calm. "Look, I told Kent I wasn't going to lie for him. I didn't. I told you what I knew. And I really thought that Kent would confess everything. I trusted that eventually he would."

'If I remember correctly you wanted me to trust you. *This* is what I got in return," Morgan said, tossing the pages on his desk.

"I thought the police would simply return the car to the owner and . . ."

"Dammit!" Morgan cried, slapping his palm on the desk.

"Morgan . . ." Patricia began, only to be brusquely interrupted.

"My son almost got caught for stealing a car, for Christ's sake. What next?"

"You should have been home that night," Patricia retaliated. He narrowed his eyes and glared at her. "It wasn't a very serious prank and fortunately no one got hurt."

"Serious enough. That whole scene could have gone wrong. Black boys out for a joy ride, the police come along . . . with *guns!*"

"Pete Connors is white," Patricia murmured, although it was hardly a significant fact under the circumstances. "I'm certain at least Kent won't do anything like that again."

Morgan tilted his head. "Are you? Then I guess as a black man my imagination is a bit more fertile than yours."

"Don't start that," she said impatiently.

"I know there are all kinds of things he could get involved with, and you can't guarantee that Kent won't."

"No one can make that kind of guarantee. I'm not always right, but mostly I am. I'm trained to be sure. This is what I do."

"Don't you think it's a bit risky to be so sure with someone else's kid?"

Her eyes blinked rapidly and Patricia was glad she'd worn the glasses after all. A surprising stab of pain shot through her chest. She bit back her sharp retort. It would do no good to be self-righteous, because she was partly in the wrong. But it actually hurt to have Morgan criticize her. She stood up, clutching her tote to her stomach, feeling her integrity challenged.

"You've made your point," she responded softly.

For just a moment she imagined that he looked sorry. She thought that he might say so, that his voice might change to that husky teasing one that made him easy to like and trust. That made her feel she could take a chance with him.

"I don't think I have," he answered grimly.

Morgan pushed his chair back, reaching for a small black nylon duffel under his desk. He opened the bag and unceremoniously dumped the contents onto the desktop. The clatter made Patricia jump.

"What do you suggest I do with these things? Pretend that he hasn't stolen them?"

She stared at the items. The heat grew more intense within her. She gave Morgan another glance, long enough to notice that the anger also held genuine worry. Patricia picked up the pen. Mrs. Lechter had mentioned missing a very expensive pen. The camera was not new, but it had an identifying number painted on the bottom. All of Duncan's sports and club equipment was marked this way.

"I found these in his room. They don't belong to Kent. So how are you going to cover for him this time?"

She looked at him. "I'm not going to even try. But I think you can help more than I can."

"How?"

"By putting all of this back and not saying anything."

"What?" Morgan's face registered shock.

"How long have you known about these things?"

"I suspected something in October when I first saw the pen, but I wasn't sure."

"Have any more items turned up in the last three weeks?"

Morgan looked confused. "I don't think so. But so what?"

She took a deep breath. "I think it means that Kent's not taking any more things. It means he feels he no longer has to. He may even be trying to figure out a way to give it all back. He may have secretly hoped that you'd find everything. It doesn't seem like he made much of an effort to hide them from you in the first place."

"What are you getting at? Are you suggesting that Kent deliberately took things that didn't belong to him and then left them for me to find?"

Patricia considered the question, gnawing her lip. "Well . . . sort of." Morgan made an impatient gesture and got up to pace behind the desk. "Morgan, listen to me . . ."

"Dammit, Patricia! I *did* listen to you. I didn't have much choice since I didn't know what the hell *I* was doing. I still don't."

"Morgan, you're shouting . . ."

"Is this what being a father is all about? Is this what I can expect from my son? When do we get to relax?" he asked in anger.

"Maybe never," Patricia said with equal force.

That got Morgan's attention. He stood staring at her.

"You have a choice. You can either throw your hands up and surrender, or grope in the dark to understand and grow with your son. One way requires a lot of work *and there are no guarantees,* Morgan. But it's up to you."

Patricia had pushed a button, and could see by his stiff expression that he had immediately not chosen to give up. They stood silently glaring at one another before Morgan finally made a visible effort to calm down. His brows were like arching storm clouds, his eyes intense and piercing. His jaw worked furiously until finally he stopped the spasmodic clenching. His nostrils flared as he took a deep breath. He sat down again and pulled his tie loose wearily.

Patricia sat, too, but stiffly on the edge of the chair. She played with the collar of her turtleneck sweater, with a lock of her hair. The electric charge stayed in the air, generating an odd heat between them. It suddenly struck Patricia as strange that so much feeling existed between them in that moment that was not the least bit sexual.

"I didn't just give up Kent when he was a child. I didn't just ignore him. But I had no say in his rearing because I wasn't there. A lot of that's my fault. I'm trying to make up for too much lost time, Patricia. It's hard."

"I know," she whispered. Her empathy returned. She sat back in the chair and cleared her throat. "What I was going to say is that Kent was probably acting out his own fears at first. He was aggressively trying to get your attention any way he could. I think he was also testing you, Morgan. How forgiving could you be? Would you not care at all? Would you send him back to his mother?"

Morgan listened silently but intently as Patricia talked. When she finished he sat for a moment, closed his eyes wearily, and sighed.

"We had a talk about that. I thought it was all settled. I want Kent to stay. I'm just getting to know him, and I actually enjoy his company. But I also told him there were to be no lies between us. I won't put up with that."

"Have there been?"

He frowned and thought. "No, I don't think so. Except for this little surprise."

"Kent didn't *lie* to you about those items. He just hasn't told you about them."

"That's subtle hairsplitting," he commented.

"Well, we have to give Kent a chance to correct this one on his own. Put these things back where you found them."

Morgan pursed his lips and frowned, his gaze skeptical. "What if he doesn't?"

Patricia chewed her lip, a wave of uncertainty shooting through her at her own presumption. "If he doesn't, then there's a real problem. But I'll bet almost anything that Kent won't disappoint us."

"You know him so well?" Morgan asked quizzically.

"No. But I understand the behavior."

"What will you bet?"

She blinked at him. "Excuse me?"

"What are you willing to bet?"

Patricia shrugged. "I don't know. It was just a figure of speech."

"For you, maybe. But I'm going to hold you to it."

Patricia nodded. She moistened her lips and seemed hesitant. "I don't mean to be a know-it-all. But I really do remember what it was like to be his age. A teenager. It was awful." Her voice dropped off to a whisper.

Patricia's face softened and she seemed so vulnerable. Funny, he suddenly had no trouble imagining what it must have been like for her. Morgan's gaze wandered over her pale features, the wavy red hair. There was an incongruity but he saw Patricia for what she was and not what he'd first believed her to be. Morgan began to feel that he understood quite a lot about her. He absently rolled a pencil across his desk blotter, frowning at the movement. "I'm sorry for what I said. About him not being your child."

She felt the blush creep up her neck to her cheeks. "I understand. You were upset."

"I know you understand, Patricia. But I want you to forgive me. It was uncalled for."

She looked at Morgan because his tone, his voice, had changed. "All right. I forgive you," she said softly.

Morgan shook his head with regret. "And I had no right yelling at you."

Patricia smiled, but stood up and turned toward the door. She heard Morgan get up behind her. "Don't worry about it. I've been yelled at by other parents, too."

Morgan stood in front of her. She had a strong sense of being shielded by him, a stronger sense of his masculinity. She looked up into his face, more relaxed now and with a different brightness in his eyes.

"Do you want to punch me out?" he asked sheepishly.

Patricia started laughing. "I don't think so. Thanks for the offer."

"You might want to consider a rain check," Morgan continued, relieved that she wasn't going to hold his temper against him. "I didn't mean to get angry at you, Patricia, but I'm terrified of what's going on with my son. I'm not sure what to do."

Patricia smiled warmly at him, finding his admission endearing. "Believe it or not, you're doing fine. Stick with it."

He shook his head wearily. "I don't know if I can handle any more surprises."

"I hope you can," she said earnestly. " 'Cause there's more where that came from." She casually indicated the things on Morgan's desk.

Morgan's gaze became gentle and an enigmatic smile curved his mouth. "You are a good friend. I don't think I've ever had one before."

Patricia grimaced. She was surprised at the disappointment that sank deep within her. She turned to leave the office. Morgan reached out to grab her arm. He firmly pulled her back to face him as they now stood behind the partially closed office door.

"Why wouldn't you agree to go out with me?" he asked quietly.

She hesitated. "I had some important reading to finish for my dissertation."

She kept her eyes focused on the loosened knot of his tie.

Morgan pulled her closer. "Are you sure that's all it was? What about the last football game?"

She didn't answer directly. He pulled her tote from her hands and dropped it carelessly on the chair next to her. Patricia laid her hands flat on his chest. She had no particular thought at the moment of resisting. There was a certain relief, which she didn't want to get into, at Morgan's not being angry with her. "The team won without me there."

"Kent wondered where you were. I missed you . . ." he confessed.

"I'm sorry . . ." her voice trailed off. She lifted her gaze to his, mesmerized by the intensity in his eyes.

Morgan took off her glasses. Then he slowly bent toward her. His image blurred until finally Patricia felt the warm pressure of his mouth, and her eyes drifted closed.

She tilted her head back, liking the feel of Morgan's lips. Their mouths settled right where they were supposed to in perfect contact. Just like that last time. There was a gentle, fluid movement of his mouth against hers. She felt a relaxing of her limbs as Morgan manipulated her mouth with slow expertise, and something ignited at her core. She felt suspended, light. The kiss was not yet deeply intimate. Just gently teasing. She kept her reaction tentative, waiting for Morgan to lead her into that enticing buildup of desire. But then he slowly ended the kiss.

He leaned closer to see right into her eyes. "You didn't expect that, did you?"

She took a deep breath to clear her head. "Men make passes. I know that."

Morgan chuckled. He stroked her hair, brushed her cheek with his thumb. "That was not a pass. That was on my agenda. I wanted to kiss you real bad before you got out of my office. I was mad, but not *that* mad." He kissed her temple and squeezed her gently against him. He dropped his hands slowly and stood back. His expression was regretful. "It's too soon. And today . . . I didn't want to confuse the issue. I still don't want Kent to be in the middle. Do you understand?"

Patricia nodded. And she didn't disagree. She took the glasses Morgan held out to her without comment and put them in her coat pocket.

"You're going to your grandmother's for Thanksgiving? Gilly, if I remember."

"Yes. And you?"

"Kent and I are going to be guests at Mrs. Anderson's. And I got some tickets for the Giants game at the Meadowlands on Sunday." Morgan sighed. "And Kent's going to something with that Eric kid and a crew of boys on Saturday. I haven't asked what."

She grinned. "I don't think you should. The temptation to make him stay home might overwhelm you. It'll be okay."

"So you keep saying."

She nodded briefly and turned to walk through the office to the outer door. There she turned once more to see Morgan framed in his office doorway. He had the most smoldering, seductive gleam in his eyes. She felt a funny little catch in her throat watching him. She wondered suddenly why she ever thought she had doubts about Morgan Baxter.

"Why are you looking at me like that?" Patricia asked self-consciously.

He shook his head. "You'll figure it out on your own," Morgan said in a husky tone.

"How do you know I will?"

"Like you, there are some things I'm very sure about," Morgan answered smoothly.

"Hello?"

"Hi, sweetie. Happy Thanksgiving."

"Mom . . ." Kent said blankly.

On the other end of the line there was a bright but nervous laugh. "Why are you so surprised?"

"I'm not. It's just . . . Happy Thanksgiving," Kent said awkwardly.

"I know we talked about a week ago but I wanted to hear your voice. Am I calling at a bad time? I didn't have any idea what you and your father had planned for today or anything."

"We're going over to Mrs. Anderson's for dinner."

"Mrs. Anderson?"

"Dad's secretary. She invited us."

"That's nice. So, how are you doing?"

"Everything's cool," he murmured.

"I'm glad to hear that. I guess that means you and your father are managing together."

It wasn't really a question, but the slow flush that heated Kent's face and neck made him realize that he hadn't told his mother very much about how things had been going with his father. He slumped back heavily against the wall next to the phone table, and slid down until his butt hit the floor and his knees bent upward in the air.

"Yeah," he finally answered softly but hesitantly. He didn't want to say anything that would make her feel bad. Something stupid. "We're doing okay."

"How did your last ball game go? I have to keep your grandfather informed."

"We won."

His mother laughed lightly. "Your father must have been so proud. He loves sports, too. Anyway . . . I hope he's glad to have you there."

Kent couldn't answer that. He hoped so, too.

"What are you and Brad doing for Thanksgiving?" he asked quickly.

"Oh . . . we're cooking. Brad's parents are flying in from Seattle. They're sorry you won't be here. They still talk about the wedding last spring, and what a handsome boy you are," she said, chuckling. "I agree, of course."

"Mom . . ." Kent whined.

"Am I embarrassing you? It's true. As

a matter of fact you resemble your father a lot."

Kent blinked. "I do?"

"Yes. You do."

There was a moment's pause. Kent was thinking. "So . . . you like being married to Brad?"

"Yes. He's a good man. A good person. I love him, Kent. You know, he'd really like a chance to get to know you. You may not believe this but I think he's a little afraid that you don't like him."

"It's not that . . ."

"I hope not. He understands how things are with you right now."

Kent got hot all over again. "Does he? How would he know?" he challenged quietly.

"Because I've told him. You have to understand something, honey. No one comes before you in my life. If Brad couldn't accept the fact that I married your father, and we had you together, then I wouldn't have married him. It couldn't work. You're my son, I love you."

He thought about that. "Oh."

Kent heard his father starting down the stairs. He scrambled quickly to his feet. "Mom, Dad is coming. We gotta go."

"Yes, I know. I just wanted to wish you a happy Thanksgiving and to make sure everything was okay."

"It is." He glanced around the partition of the wall. His father was opening the hall closet and switching on the inside light.

"Kent? Are you ready?"

"Yeah. Almost," he called out.

"Who's on the phone?"

He didn't answer right away, frowning over what to answer. He spoke softly into the mouthpiece.

"Mom? Dad is right here. He wants to talk to you."

"He does?" his mother said skeptically. "Well . . . fine. Put him on."

"Okay," Kent said eagerly. "Hey, Dad?" Kent stood with his palm over the speaker end of the telephone. "Dad, it's for you."

Morgan came from the hallway with his and Kent's jackets. He tossed a heavy varsity jacket to Kent who deftly caught it in midair. Kent held out the phone to his father.

"Is it Mrs. Anderson? Did you tell her we're on our way?"

Kent shook his head. "It's Mom," he said quietly, and walked away.

Morgan couldn't help feeling immediately cautious and suspicious of the call. There had never been hostility between him and Melissa. They had not parted disliking one another. If anything, there had been a sense of bewildering confusion and pain that so much had worked against them that they couldn't seem to control. Morgan took the phone from his son, sparing Kent a glance of both sadness and encouragement. He spoke calmly into the receiver.

"Melissa. Hey . . ."

Kent did the polite thing and left the living room. The short conversation he'd had with his mother made him feel a little guilty. He wondered if his father ever felt the same way. The hardest thing to deal with was her asking him if he wanted to come home.

He didn't want to hurt his mother's feelings by admitting he liked living in New York with his father. He was finding out that unlike his grandfather his father talked to him instead of lecturing, and he tried to listen. He didn't want to go back to Colorado, but he couldn't tell his mother that.

He walked into the kitchen. It wasn't easy to hear anything from here, so he stood perfectly still leaning against the wall. He rocked a foot nervously back and forth, chewed on the cuticle around his thumb, and listened to half of the conversation between his mother and father.

"Hello, Morgan. Happy Thanksgiving."

"Thanks. Same to you . . . and Brad."

"Kent said you got invited out to eat," Melissa probed.

"My secretary invited us."

"Oh. Are you, ah, dating your secretary?"

Morgan laughed to himself.

"Mrs. Anderson's daughters and grandchildren live out of state. She's alone for the weekend, and I'm not much of a cook."

Melissa gave a short laugh. Like her voice, it had a light, playful quality to it. "Sorry. I didn't mean to suggest anything."

"Don't worry about it. So, how's everything going?"

"I'm pregnant."

Morgan felt a sensation like all the warmth draining out of his body. He recalled quite clearly the time Melissa had told him she was pregnant with

Kent. She had said it the same way. Quickly, with no preamble or coy hints. And he'd been just as stunned. He also remembered how they'd boldly declared that their child was going to be a real twenty-first-century kid. Multicultural, like the world would be. It seemed so hopeful.

Morgan shouldn't have been surprised. Melissa was thirty-seven. Plenty of time to have more children. She and Brad had been married for close to a year. He'd want his own kids. Not someone else's son. Especially not . . .

"I haven't told Kent yet."

"Why not?" he asked, still feeling a bit peculiar.

She chuckled nervously. "I guess I'm a little afraid to. I don't know how he'll react. Whether he won't mind or he'll hate the idea."

"I think you should just tell him. You can't keep that from him."

She sighed deeply. "I know, I know . . . So much happened so quickly. And I hadn't counted on Kent wanting to go to New York when he did. It was a real surprise."

"I bet it was," he said in sympathy.

"Oh, don't worry about me, Morgan. I

appreciate the thought, but this is really important for Kent. For all of us, I suppose. I don't think either one of us anticipated . . ."

"No, I didn't."

"Life's full of surprises, isn't it?"

"That's an understatement," he murmured wryly. He cleared his throat. "How's your father? Still in the military?"

After a moment there was a soft laugh. "Morgan, I know you don't care how my father is. You don't have to pretend with me. Enough damage has been done. I only want my son . . . our son . . . to grow up feeling good about himself, and not hating either of us for having loved each other once."

Morgan clenched his jaw tightly. "You've done a hell of a job, Melissa. He's great. I feel like I should be thanking you or . . ."

"Please don't," she said quickly. "Then it's going to be okay with you two?"

He looked over his shoulder suddenly, but he was alone and it was quiet. Morgan turned back and spoke more softly into the phone.

"I'm proud of him. There's still a lot of stuff to work out but I'm glad he's here with me. But it must have been tough for you."

"Very," she barely whispered. "This new baby will never replace him, Morgan. You have to believe that."

"I hear you. Tell Kent."

"Yes. Soon."

Morgan shifted from one foot to another. He checked his watch. "Listen, we're going to be late."

"Oh, of course. Well . . . it's good to talk to you."

"Same here. I mean it. All the best to you and Brad. When are you due?"

"May tenth, or thereabouts."

He didn't feel there was much more to be said. "Happy Thanksgiving again."

"Same to you. Kisses and hugs to Kent. Tell him to keep in touch."

Morgan grinned. "Right." He put the phone down and stared at it for a moment. Their past seemed so long ago. Almost unreal, except for Kent. He looked at his watch.

"Kent? Come on, we gotta go."

Kent appeared quietly, slowly shrugging into his jacket. He was pensive and subdued. "I'm ready," he mumbled. He didn't look directly at his father.

Morgan glanced at him, noting the

closed expression, the pale face. "Are you okay?"

Kent looked squarely at his father. "What else did Mom want?"

Morgan put a hand on Kent's shoulder, as if to make his words easier to hear. "She's hoping to hear from you a little more often in the future. Don't worry about the phone bill. Your mother misses you."

Kent blushed. "I know. I will, I promise."

"You'll get two weeks during Christmas to see her."

Kent stared at his father. "Are you sending me back?"

Morgan smiled. It made him feel better to hear the question and doubt in Kent's voice, but that was not his purpose. He wanted to rub the boy's hair, the way his father used to do when he was a kid. Except that Kent had recently cut it and it was still militantly short. Morgan was beginning to like it.

"No, I'm not sending you back. But don't you think it would be a good idea to go to see your mother over the holidays? At least for part of it. Don't forget, you haven't seen her or your grandfather in almost six months."

Kent nodded silently, still uncertain.

"For Christmas, Kent. You can always come back."

The boy relaxed. "What about you?"

"I might go to L.A. for a few days."

"To see Grandmother Rachel?"

Morgan nodded and gave Kent a little push. "Come on, let's go or Mrs. Anderson will think we don't know how to act." Morgan headed for the door.

"Dad? I . . . I just want to say . . . well . . . I'm sorry for the way I acted. You know, when I first came. I promise not to cause any more trouble. I'll be good. You won't be sorry you let me stay."

Morgan felt a welling of emotion, of love and gratitude and pride. One of his first thoughts was of wanting to tell Patricia. That could wait. He smiled at his son.

"I could never be sorry. You're one of the best things that's ever happened in my life."

"Yeah?" Kent asked.

"Yeah," Morgan confirmed with a confident smile. He realized with all his heart that it was absolutely true.

Gilly leaned around the edge of her high-backed chair and, pulling the curtain back, glanced out the window. Finally, after more than an hour of anticipation, she could see her granddaughter coming down the path to the house. Patricia was taking her time, contemplating each step she took. She walked absently, in the way of someone familiar with their surroundings and feeling safe. But that had taken a very long time to achieve. During all those years growing up her granddaughter had been the brunt of cruel speculation, hateful bias, and outright alienation. She had sat or stood at her window many times watching out for Patricia as she left the house or was returning home. It still made her burn with rage and helplessness when she remembered the first time Patricia had been harassed, literally chased home by classmates who'd acted in unison to bully her.

From a distance Patricia looked like she'd wandered into the wrong neighborhood, with her high yellow complexion and red hair among the darker-toned black community. *Lord, Lord . . .* Gilly had lamented more times than she could count, *do you know what you have done to this child?* And who, Gilly questioned as she took off her reading glasses, her eyes filling with concern, had hurt her child now?

Gilly watched as Patricia suddenly stooped to pick up something in front of her on the ground. Her face was a study in wistfulness and concentration as she examined her find. She was gnawing on her lip. Gilly rightfully prided herself that she knew her granddaughter well. She had a pretty good idea what Patricia's thoughtfulness was all about.

Patricia resumed her slow approach to the house. Gilly let the curtain fall back into place and rose slowly from her chair, mindful of her arthritic joints. She went into the kitchen and lit a fire under a kettle of water. Then she removed the last two slices of pumpkin pie from the covered cake plate.

Patricia came in the door with a rush of cold air. Her cheeks were red and her eyes were shimmering bright, even if she did still seem distracted.

"You're just in time. I thought some hot tea would be nice with the last of the pie."

Patricia chuckled as she shrugged out

of a heavy down jacket and pulled off the colorful knit hat. "I'm going to be fat by the time the weekend is over."

"You look fine, sweetie. Hopefully you'll never have to worry about that again."

"Yeah, but I don't want to start an old habit either."

Nonetheless Patricia got plates and silverware from a cabinet. Gilly put a teabag in one mug, two generous scoops of cocoa in another.

"How was your walk?"

"Oh . . . good," Patricia sighed.

"What did you find on the street?"

Patricia arched her brow, her expression wry. "Keeping an eye on me?"

"Always."

"I found a penny. It's supposed to bring good luck, isn't it?"

"Did it help?"

Patricia was puzzled. "The penny?"

"No, child. The walk."

"Help with what?"

"Whatever's on your mind."

Patricia glanced at her grandmother and smiled. "I guess there's no point in telling you everything's fine. I'm not good company this weekend."

"Do you want to talk about it?" Gilly

asked casually.

Patricia did not answer immediately as she set the table. She put a slice of pie on each plate, got napkins, took a seat as Gilly poured the hot water. Gilly sat down and the two women looked at one another. Patricia smiled to herself. She recalled that while growing up Gilly hadn't used words, threats, or raised voices to get her to do the right thing. Gilly had "looks." Right now she only saw her grandmother's concern.

Patricia lifted her fork and stabbed off a piece of the pie. "I'm scared," she whispered unexpectedly.

Surprised, Gilly raised her brows. She watched Patricia closely. "Of what? Or maybe the question is, of whom?"

Patricia flushed and avoided Gilly's direct gaze. She shrugged. "A fifteen-year-old kid. He reminds me a lot of me. I think maybe I'm getting too close to him."

Gilly dunked her tea bag up and down in her cup. "Is it because he reminds you of being a teenager, or of certain things you went through?"

Patricia frowned. "Yes," she responded succinctly.

"Well, that covers just about everything."

"Actually, he's probably handling things a lot better than I ever did."

"I remember when you were about that age, you were very unhappy and very difficult at times."

"I remember being overweight and wearing glasses. I remember kids making fun of me."

"Well, I also remember that you were smart and funny and had a temper that wouldn't quit."

Passionate, Morgan had said, Patricia recalled to herself.

"So this child you're working with at school . . ."

"It's like history repeating itself. With a small difference."

"Which is?"

"Kent is biracial. So there's the whole color identity thing."

"Humph! And I bet he's having the hardest time with the black kids. Lord, when are we going to get *over* that?"

Patricia merely shook her head. She wasn't sure there would ever be an answer. She turned the penny over and over in her fingers, mentally making a childish wish.

"He's living with his father now, in New York, but Kent was raised by his mother. She's white. They're struggling a little with the father/son relationship."

"What's he like?" Gilly asked.

"Oh, he's terrific. Very bright. Sweet. He's on the football . . ."

"No. I mean his father."

Patricia felt her cheeks get warm. She gathered her wits as she finished the pie. "He's a businessman. Runs his own company . . . divorced from Kent's mother."

Gilly began to grin in an infuriatingly knowing way. "What else?"

"What do you mean, what else? Morgan's very concerned about Kent, and he's really making an effort to connect." She blinked rapidly. "He's . . . interesting. He . . . he gave me a pumpkin," she mentioned, although making it sound irrelevant.

"Really?"

"It was Halloween."

Gilly chuckled. "I see."

"I know what you're thinking, and . . ."

"The way you're talking about this man sounds to me like you like him. Morgan. Good name."

Her grandmother said nothing more as she meticulously squeezed the excess liquid from her tea bag and placed the bag on her empty pie plate. The pause was beginning to drive Patricia crazy until she recalled that this was Gilly's way. She took in information and processed it slowly. But then she was sure to make an observation guaranteed to punch holes in even the most logical straightforward thought.

Patricia unconsciously braced herself and gazed steadily at her grandmother, who nodded silently and pursed her lips. There was not a wrinkle on her brown face, but the scattering of freckles on Gilly's cheeks and nose made her seem younger. But she was getting on, and Patricia was aware that her stiff and knobby limbs pained her more than she would ever admit.

"What? What are you thinking?"

"So are things better between father and son?"

"Oh, yes," Patricia said in relief. "They're going to be fine."

Gilly now stared at her. "And what about you?"

Patricia looked at Gilly, opened her mouth to speak . . . and closed it again.

She lifted her cup and saw that it was empty. She put it down, shaking her head. "I . . . I don't know."

Gilly leaned toward her. "Stop beating around the bush, girl. What's on your mind? What's in your heart?"

Patricia was evasive. "My heart has told me some pretty dumb things. It's led me into troubled waters. It got broken."

"It *healed*," Gilly enunciated firmly.

"Every now and then it still hurts," Patricia whispered in a thin voice.

"I know, sweetie, but I want you to stop thinking that everything that hurt you was your fault. Let's talk about the father of your student. Why are you afraid of him?"

Patricia looked at her grandmother for all the world like a seventeen-year-old with her first serious crush. "I think he likes me."

"Sounds good to me."

"No, I mean . . . he *likes* me."

"Oh. You mean like you think he wants to take you to bed."

"Gilly!"

"Don't Gilly me. You know what this is all about. Why are you acting so foolish about it?"

Patricia lifted her shoulders help-lessly. "I'm counseling his son. That's more than a conflict of interest. It could be unethical. I'm trying to convince my-self that Morgan and I are just . . . friendly."

"Good place to start." Gilly got up and headed to the stove to heat up the water again. "But if you ask me you already have plenty of friends. Time to move on to something more serious."

There was a long silence. Gilly glanced over her shoulder and found Patricia sitting with her chin propped on her clasped fists.

"That's what I'm afraid of." Patricia's voice was barely audible.

"Do you like him, too?"

Patricia silently nodded.

"And you can't figure out why he gave you the pumpkin?" Gilly chuckled. "You definitely have been hanging around teenagers too long. The poor man is trying to get next to you, sweetie. You've forgotten how to flirt and be a grownup woman."

"No. I don't think I ever got that down right to begin with," Patricia said dryly.

'And this Morgan doesn't sound like an adolescent classmate with too much ego and smarts for his own good. He's a man."

"I know that." Patricia frowned.

"Well, sooner or later the man is going to make a move on you." She suddenly pried the penny out of Patricia's hand. "And wishing on pennies isn't going to help one bit."

Patricia laughed, shaking her head. "You're unbelievable."

"You know I'm right. The question is, hon . . ." Gilly took her seat again. Grinning, she tilted her head toward Patricia. Her eyebrows raised on her lineless, wise face in an expression of challenge. "What are you going to do about it?"

Chapter Eleven

Kent took the steps two at a time in his stocking feet. He hadn't bothered with shoes. He didn't have time. He *had* to find that damned pen. He scanned quickly around the living room, hoping that something would jog his memory and help him remember where he'd put it.

He looked in the nut dish on the coffee table. In the magazine basket on the floor next to the sofa. Under all the chairs. He pulled away the cushions and searched with his hands along the seams and crevices. Nothing. Kent began to sweat and his palms grew damp.

He'd forgotten all about that stuff, until he'd seen the camera again on his bookcase. Kent was sure it had been moved. Immediately he'd thought of the housekeeper. But she wasn't due for another two days. So . . . it had to be his father. The CDs were still in the drawer.

But he couldn't find the pen.

Kent stood breathing hard. With his hands on his hips he turned in a slow circle, glancing around the living room once more.

"What are you looking for?"

The sound of his father's voice sent a swift spasm of dread through Kent's body. He jerked around to face him.

Morgan had heard Kent running down the stairs, and thought he would seek him out from the tiny den behind the kitchen, at the back of the house. But then Morgan had heard the sounds coming from the living room.

"N-nothing. I mean . . . I thought I left something down here."

He gestured with his hands and shoulders and headed back to the staircase. His heart was thudding in his chest.

"What is it?"

"That's okay. It's not important."

"Maybe I've seen it."

Kent slowly stopped, turned, and faced his father. He stared at him helplessly, remembering the promise he'd made and his word given. Remembering everything he stood to lose. "It was a pen."

Morgan looked steadily at his son, reading all the signs clear enough to know how careful he had to be. Mindful of Patricia's warning, he smiled easily as he approached Kent. He slapped him playfully on the shoulder.

"I think I saw a pen." He walked to the large-screen TV and picked up something from the top. He turned with it in his outstretched hand. "Is this it?"

Kent couldn't think of a thing to say. He had no excuses, and to lie seemed . . . dangerous. So he stared at the pen in his father's hand and nodded.

Morgan returned to Kent's side. "I found it last week and knew it wasn't mine. I meant to ask you about it. Aren't you going to take it?"

Kent looked like that was the last thing he wanted to do. But he wiped his palms down the legs of his jeans and took the pen quickly.

"Thanks," he whispered.

"You should be careful with it," Morgan said quietly, watching his son. "You wouldn't want to lose something like that. It looks expensive."

He didn't wait for Kent to answer. And

he no longer wanted to stand and watch his response. Morgan walked out of the living room and left his son standing in the middle of the room.

It was the first snowfall of the season.

As Patricia pulled into her parking space and turned off the engine she stared out her windshield. She was caught between delight at the first real sign of winter and apprehension about hazardous driving conditions. She was remembering, too, that snow was a harbinger of the Christmas holidays. A reminder of the time of year when her parents and brother had been killed. Her initial pleasure quickly faded. The love and support of her grandmother notwithstanding, the holidays always made her feel sad. She wondered abstractedly, as she got out of her car, if Morgan had felt the same way all the years he spent Christmas without his son. Had he visited his mother or sister? Had he celebrated with other women?

Patricia retrieved her school papers from the passenger seat. Behind her she heard someone call out her name.

"Patricia . . ."

She recognized Morgan's voice and the intimate way he had of saying her name. She turned to find him standing next to his own car halfway down the block. Patricia felt nervous anticipation twist her insides. She clutched the tote and seemed unable to move as the stern expression on Morgan's face captured her attention. But she was also thinking in exact detail of that moment when he'd kissed her at Kent's first football game. And even just before Thanksgiving in his office. Everything had changed between them.

"What are you doing here?"

Morgan was now at her side, staring enigmatically at Patricia. His camel-colored overcoat was open to the winter air. He didn't seem in the least affected by the temperatures, but she was beginning to feel cold.

Morgan held her door open. "Get in," he said.

Confused, Patricia obeyed. She released the lock on the passenger door as Morgan got in and locked them into the cocooned silence of her car. He swiveled around in the seat to face her.

"What's going on?" she asked as calmly as she could. But she knew.

Morgan was looking steadily at her, his gaze roaming over her features as he pursed his lips. But he didn't look particularly pleased.

"Why don't *you* tell me what's going on. You've said no to any chance for us to see each other alone. Why did you hang up on me yesterday?"

"I . . . I didn't hang up. I said I had to go. I . . ."

"You hung up. Ask Mrs. Anderson. I started laughing so hard she came into my office to find out what was happening."

"You laughed?"

"It was the only thing I could think to do at the time. I couldn't confront you since you wouldn't see me. I couldn't rip my phone out of the wall."

Patricia guiltily averted her gaze. "Morgan . . ."

"It's not going to go away, Pat." He cupped her chin and forced her to face him. "I'm not going to disappear."

She could say nothing. She just stared at him, hating that she'd done something so childish because she was afraid to allow herself the other feelings. She faced forward and frowned through the windshield at the falling snow.

"Someone will see us together . . ."

"Right now, I don't give a damn. The last time we were together I thought, I *sensed* that you were feeling the same way I was."

"Which was?"

"Very attracted. Very interested. Surprised for sure. Wanting to take it further and see where it leads. There isn't any commitment except to give ourselves a chance. What are you afraid of?" Morgan asked seriously.

"I'm not afraid, I'm . . ."

"You've got yourself so protected behind your role as champion of children that I can't get at the woman inside." He took hold of her chin again and made her face him. "I want to know her, Pat. I want to get next to that woman, I admit it. Is there something wrong with that?"

Patricia's mouth parted and she stared poignantly at him, unable to hide her own vulnerability when Morgan looked at her so honestly. She sighed deeply. "I can't get involved with you. I just can't."

His frown deepened. "Is this about Melissa again?" he whispered tightly.

She shook her head. "No. This is

about me. I don't want to complicate my life right now. I don't want to confuse my responsibilities, and I don't want to . . ."

"Feel what you're feeling?" Morgan offered carefully.

Patricia felt her insides roil. She decided to be honest, too. "I don't know what I'm feeling. I can't sort anything out right now. That's why I thought I should . . ."

Morgan slowly began to smile at her and she watched as his expression changed from annoyance to curiosity, to insight. His look of revelation made Patricia feel like she'd said the wrong thing. Or revealed too much.

"I don't think that means we should deny what's happening between us."

"You're being presumptuous."

"But I don't think I'm wrong."

After a moment Patricia shook her head, her resolve slowly cracking. She was ambivalent, both furious and confused, that Morgan was forcing a confrontation with her . . . demanding acknowledgment. But if she acquiesced and put it out there, then it would be true. "I shouldn't have let you . . ."

"Us. Your reaction to me wasn't a lie.

What makes you think you can control every aspect of your life? Or decide exactly how you're going to feel?"

"I don't want you to lecture me, Morgan," she said in agitation. "I don't need you to orchestrate something between us."

Morgan looked at Patricia for a moment, fascinated. He'd never known anyone who blushed the way she did so readily. Even Melissa never looked flushed and pink. "I'm not making this up. I'll tell you what's really bothering you. You weren't prepared. This is totally out of left field. It wasn't in the cards, right? So what?"

Patricia felt a tug of war between her curiosity and attraction to Morgan Baxter and a prudent desire to protect herself. She was pretty sure she couldn't have it both ways. And as if reading her mind Morgan leaned solicitously toward her.

"We don't sweep what's happening under the carpet. We try to be careful. But we take charge of our own affairs."

His choice of words caused a tightening sensation of fear inside of Patricia and a breathless awareness that Morgan was right. She looked at him. His face was close to hers and she could feel the warmth of his body, smell the clean scents of his skin, his clothing, the wool of his expensive coat. Morgan bent his head and let his lips pull erotically at hers, encouraging a response. He captured just her bottom lip and there was something so titillating and suggestive in the way he took his time.

"I was pretty ticked when you tried to put me off. But I'm feeling better already," Morgan whispered.

This time when he kissed her Patricia just accepted it. In truth, she'd been wondering if that same sensation would come over her if Morgan kissed her again. It did. And she indulged in the wonderful magic on her senses, closing her eyes to concentrate on the feel of Morgan's tongue thrusting gently into her mouth. The way he pressed to open her mouth wider; the way her heartbeat quickened as she returned Morgan's kisses. Patricia gave in to her desire to know this man. And she tried to push back the persistent reminder that she and Morgan were walking a tightrope. And she had terrible balance.

Morgan's hand held her head tilted to

him so that their mouths fit and fused perfectly. It was a long dizzying moment before he lightened the intensity, satisfied with Patricia's response. He sat back gazing at her. He realized that it had been worth the risk he'd taken to just show up and catch Patricia off guard. He'd gotten the answer he'd wanted.

"If you want me to leave you alone, just say so."

Patricia curled her hands into fists. She shook her head. Morgan stroked the side of her neck gently.

"And if you're not attracted to me, you can tell me that, too. My ego can take it."

She found herself smiling. "Now you're fishing."

"Damned straight. I want to know where I stand."

Patricia licked her lips and took a deep breath. "I don't deny that you're . . . nice. A good man, and . . ."

Morgan chuckled. He pecked her on the mouth again. "You're making me sound like your family doctor. Okay. I'll find out on my own. Fair enough?"

"I guess."

"I warn you, Pat. You may be sur-

prised at the result . . . we both could."
He glanced at his watch and sighed.
"I've got to get going. I'm keeping a
bunch of bankers waiting on me. And
you're going to be late for school," he
said playfully. Then he sobered and
reached out to squeeze her hand. "I
won't push. Believe me, I hear your
doubts."

"Do you?"

"Oh, yeah. I just have to prove you
wrong, don't I?" Morgan opened the car.
Cold winter air and snowflakes fluttered
in at them. Patricia shivered as she
watched him prepare to leave her.

"I'm giving a party for my staff and
business associates just before Christmas. I'd like you to come."

"Are you inviting any of Kent's other
teachers?"

"No, why?"

"I'm going to be out of place. I won't
know anyone."

"But you'll come? I want you to."

"I'll think about it."

Morgan nodded. "We'll talk. Maybe
you'll let me take you to dinner."

When he kissed her one final time
Patricia welcomed him. She knew, then,
there was no turning back.

And she wondered what she was going to wear.

It was only the second week of December and already the sights and sounds of Christmas were starting to appear all over the city. Red ribbons and festive lighting adorned windows and doors, lobbies and shop aisles. The sound of bells and music, the rush of traffic and pedestrians, seemed to promote more excitement and expectations than seemed warranted to Morgan.

Only three times in almost sixteen years had he ever spent Christmas with Kent. The first time the boy hadn't actually been born yet. Melissa was five months pregnant and they'd spent the first Christmas of their marriage in Denver. Instead of peace and joy there was the constant tension of warding off the slings and arrows of disapproval because of their interracial marriage. Because a white woman was having a black man's child. Kent had been three the second time, Morgan reflected, and he and Melissa had already divorced. Kent had cried most of that visit with him because he wanted his mother. It had been an emotionally and physically draining Christmas for both of them.

The third time, Morgan had flown with Kent to southern California to his mother's. All of her friends and neighbors had carried on over what a beautiful child Kent was. Morgan was uncomfortable with their apparent approval because of his son's light complexion and curly hair.

"Aspen is going to be a circus."

Morgan found David's interruption jarring.

"They're getting good powder these days so the skiing should be smooth and fast. Gets me away from all of *this*. You ski?" David asked Morgan. They hurried across the street against the light and turned down the block.

Morgan brought his attention back from the past. "Not recently," he answered, remembering how he'd learned. With whom. "I've been too busy with the company. My last vacation was three years ago."

"You need to kick back and relax."

David's comment had all the sensitivity of someone without any major responsibilities. Morgan responded automatically as David continued talking, following the casual conversation about his holiday plans, but not really interested in the details. They walked past a clothing boutique on their way to the restaurant for lunch, and Morgan spotted a bright yellow sweater that he thought Kent would like. And a sturdy leather knapsack. He made a mental note to get them as gifts for Christmas.

He wasn't used to planning for Christmas. For many years, especially after his divorce, it had become just another day. Often it was spent with his mother in southern California, where the holiday was a surreal kind of celebration under heat, sunshine, and palm tree fronds.

"With Sager squared away, now's a good time for a break. Grab your favorite lady and get away somewhere together. Someone like Beverly McGraw," David hinted with an irritating grin.

Morgan smiled briefly. "I'll give it some thought," he commented dryly.

The two men entered a trendy Italian restaurant that had a fully decorated Christmas tree in the foyer, complete with a running model train around the base. The maître d', recognizing Morgan, nodded and wordlessly headed off across the nearly full dining room to a small corner of tables that allowed for more privacy.

Morgan was surprised to see two other men already seated at the table. They stood as he and David neared. He had no idea that lunch was to be a foursome, and he gave David a curious look as everyone shook hands and sat down.

He didn't like surprises.

Morgan recognized George Tanner and Robert Frisk, two of the management negotiators from Sager. George was a middle-aged black man who'd worked his way up through the ranks of the company, from drafting intern to engineer designer to management. Robert was an MBA graduate from Brown. Smart, personable . . . and young. The contracts between Sager and Ventura, Inc., had been signed. The deal was considered done, except for one or two areas that Morgan had not thought of as major . . . until this moment.

He smoothly engaged in the chitchat as everyone ordered cocktails. Morgan had Pellegrino with lime. And waited.

"We're glad you could make it for lunch," George Tanner said hesitantly.

Morgan watched the man's apparent discomfort. But he also detected something else, a hint of skepticism and caution. Morgan understood it. Just then he and George were two black men trying to figure out where they both stood, and what was going on. "Thanks," he finally responded.

David shook his head, chuckling. "I owe Morgan an apology. He didn't know until this moment that you were both joining us for lunch." He turned to his boss with an expression of contrite regret. "I'm sorry, Morgan. The slip-up was entirely my fault."

"No problem," Bob Frisk said expansively, taking everything at face value. "It's always good to see Morgan."

"I guess I got caught up in my holiday plans," David said easily. "The negotiations took a long time. I don't know about all of you, but I could use a break."

"Sounds good to me." Bob nodded, downing half his drink and ordering another.

Morgan remained quiet, taking his time to glance over the menu while trying to assess just what the lunch meeting was all about. The thought that

David might have somehow engineered the whole scenario caused Morgan's gut to tighten.

George Tanner glanced pointedly at Morgan. "So . . . how does it feel to be adding another company to your stock-pile?"

Morgan put his menu down and sat back in the chair. The sarcasm did not escape him. "It's not a stockpile, George. Sager isn't a weapon. I don't intend to use the company against any-one. It's a good company, with strong potential, that has several weak spots. In another year or so, without some new ideas and controls, someone would have tried a hostile takeover, disbanded the corporation, fired the employees, and then sold the company shell to someone else. I'm not planning on doing that."

"I'm sure glad to hear that," Bob joked nervously.

"A lot of people are still concerned about their jobs," George said. "Every-body thinks you have your own people in mind for key positions, no matter what the contract says."

Morgan narrowed his gaze. "I intend to hold to the contract, no matter what everybody thinks. I don't gain anything by firing workers with good experience and knowledge of the company. Your people can run the day-to-day operations. I'll manage it."

George pursed his mouth, his thick black mustache bobbing over his lips. He started to say something, but then only nodded and drank from his water goblet.

Morgan looked sideways at David. "I'm sure David has already explained all of this to you."

"Oh, sure," Bob said with a chuckle. "Lots of times. David's an okay guy. You're lucky to have him."

David made a low discounting comment.

"There's obviously still something on your mind. Which one of you is going to tell me?" Morgan asked smoothly.

There was a long silence at the table, while the sounds of other people eating could be heard off in the distance. George and Bob exchanged brief glances. David turned half in his seat toward Morgan.

"I think the staff at Sager just needs a little stroking."

"I thought that's what you were doing

when I let you conduct the negotiations," Morgan said, a hint of impatience creeping into his tone that could not be ignored.

David laced his long fingers together. "Absolutely. George and Bob will tell you that I really hammered everything home. There's just one more small thing."

"I thought I'd made some pretty generous concessions," Morgan said as he looked quickly around at the three men.

"You have. That's why you should be pleased by the suggestion Sager has made to deal with lingering doubts from the employees."

"Should I?" Morgan asked. He turned to George, the only other person at the table who he believed might give him an indication of what was going on, but who now seemed unsure himself about why they were all together.

George spoke directly to Morgan. "A lot of the managers have been giving this serious thought. They know you can't be named director. You're already CEO. But we need someone at the top."

Bob Frisk cleared his throat. "What George is getting at . . . what the employees want, that is, is for David here to be named director at Sager."

Patricia came into the office to find Jerome in conversation with several students. The group was gathered outside of Jerome's office, making the tiny reception area seem crowded with tall, husky young males. All conversation stopped when she walked in.

"Hi, guys. What's going on?" Patricia asked.

There was no direct answer, just a short awkward silence until one of the boys backed his way to the door past her.

"Hey . . . I gotta go. I got practice."

"Yeah, me, too," said another, until in less than twenty seconds she stood alone with Jerome.

Patricia was amused, and she glanced at her colleague. "Was it something I said?"

Jerome turned and walked into his cubicle. She quietly followed. Patricia folded her arms across her chest when she saw the open drawer, the open box of contraceptives. "Jerome . . ." she began warily.

He put his hand up to stop her. "Before you start, Patty, let me just say this. The boys came to me."

"That's not the point."

"You're right. The point is they're thinking for once with their heads and not their Johnson."

"Wrong. The point is this is still not our area of responsibility."

Jerome got testy. "Bullshit."

Patricia pressed on. "We're supposed to work with the students *and* their parents. It's a cooperative effort."

"Great theory. So is it okay to assume that if the kids come to us it's because, for whatever reasons, they don't feel they can go to their folks?"

"Maybe," she hedged nervously.

"And if we're not the second-best choice, what do you think the third is going to be? At least give them some credit for coming up with an alternative. After all, we're always trying to ram that concept down their throats. Are we now going to be hypocrites about it ourselves?"

Patricia narrowed her gaze. She didn't have her glasses on but she didn't need them to see Jerome's face and every detail clearly. He passionately believed he was right. And Patricia knew he was.

"Well . . ."

Jerome suddenly turned to reach into the open drawer. When he turned back he held out his hand. "Here."

Patricia reluctantly put out an open palm. Jerome dropped a half-dozen glittering little packages into it.

"We all know what these are for. Unless you're dead from the neck up or the waist down, we should all be doing the smart thing, right?"

Patricia looked at the wrapped condoms. She didn't disagree. She'd always insisted that her partners be prepared. Or she was. She glanced at Jerome.

"The packaging is barely discreet."

He shrugged. "The results of unsafe sex are not discreet. The possibilities are not only staggering, they're deadly."

She started to give them back to Jerome.

"No, keep them," Jerome said, closing the drawer. "You never know."

The comment was both telling and wry, and made Patricia blush as if Jerome was reading her mind.

"The manufacturers have a sure thing, and they're getting clever with marketing. Those little suckers now come in flavors, scents . . ." He chuckled at her expression. "Colors . . . you name it."

She made a fist around the ones in her hand. "I'm not sure I should thank you."

Jerome stood looking at Patricia with a peculiar expression in his eyes, on his face. "You've stopped wearing your glasses. Your vision suddenly improve?"

"I don't really need them much anymore."

He nodded, still staring at her. "Men are going to make passes at you."

She knew he was teasing, but Patricia found she didn't know what to say. She could only see Morgan, hear his voice as he'd told her, she shouldn't hide her eyes. Jerome relented under her continued silence.

"Look, I'm sorry about snapping at you before Thanksgiving. And I've been impatient and a crab all this week. It's that time of the month."

Patricia laughed lightly. "I guess I can forgive you if you have lunch with me today. We haven't done that in a while." She was somewhat surprised when Jerome didn't immediately agree. He shrugged and turned to his desk.

Kent Baxter had no such hesitation. So when he said he needed to talk to her, Patricia suggested lunchtime. It took place in her office because it was raining.

At first she held some hope that Kent might want to talk about the small thefts she'd discussed with Morgan. Patricia hoped that sooner or later the objects would turn up in their rightful place.

"Hi, Kent," she began easily enough as he entered the office with a comfortable gait. So unlike the first time, when he'd nearly run out the door. As he headed automatically for her office, Patricia touched his arm and took a seat in one of two chairs in the reception area. "Ahh . . . let's sit out here." She began to unwrap her lunch.

Kent sat slowly in the next chair, clearly disappointed in the change of routine.

"I haven't gotten any reports from your teachers so far this month. I'm really glad that things are finally settling down," Patricia said formally, withholding a smile and trying to forestall any questions not directly related to Kent's six hours spent at Duncan.

Kent sat uncomfortably on the edge of his seat. He watched as Patricia began her lunch, and then he opened his knapsack to dig around for his. "How come we're sitting out here?" he finally asked.

Patricia swallowed and blinked rapidly. "I'm working on the city evaluations, and there are papers all over the place. It would have been too much trouble to move everything," she improvised. Kent nodded, accepting her answer. "What's up? What did you want to see me about?"

Kent slouched in his seat, his knees spread. He frowned over the task of peeling a navel orange. "I was thinking of maybe going on that ski trip in January that Duncan is sponsoring."

"Sounds like fun. Do you ski?"

Kent grimaced. "Yeah, but I was wondering. You know . . . who else was going."

Patricia looked at him carefully. She pulled the plastic top from her container of vanilla yogurt. "You mean, if you're going to be the only black student there? Probably."

"I thought so," he pouted.

"That doesn't mean you shouldn't go."

"I know, but . . . I get tired of always being the only black kid."

"Why don't you ask Eric or one of the other guys to come along?"

"Yeah, right," Kent scoffed. "I like them, and everything, but they always get on my case 'cause I do things they can't. They always say, that's what white people do. It's so stupid."

"Well, I agree. So you have to decide if it's more important to be able to ski or swim or whatever it is you enjoy doing, or doing what everyone else is doing so that they'll like you."

"Why can't I do both?"

"I don't see any reason why you can't. It's neat that you know how to ski. Maybe you can teach some of your new friends."

He shrugged. "I don't know. It makes me different from everybody else."

Patricia looked at him briefly and considered the spoonful of yogurt before eating it. "There's nothing wrong with being different, either. If you go skiing, you'll probably have a lot of fun. If you don't go, and just stay home, no one's going to care that you did."

"Well . . . I probably can't go anyway.

I don't have any money for the trip."

"Don't you get an allowance or some-thing?"

"It's gone," Kent mumbled uncomfort-ably. "My father made me give it all to that guy who owns the Cherokee. You know."

"Oh yes. Halloween. What are you going to do, then?"

"I don't know."

"Well, you still have a month to save up again. Maybe you could ask for the trip as a Christmas present." Another thought occurred to her. "What are you doing for Christmas?"

He sighed. "I'm going to visit my mom in Colorado."

"That's nice. You'll have a lot to tell her about New York and Duncan. You'll get to see some friends."

"Yeah. But I'm coming back," he added firmly.

Patricia smiled at him. "Good. Your dad will be glad to know that, I'm sure."

Kent, in eating his sandwich, was squeezing it until the mayonnaise and ham squished out the sides. He started nibbling at the edges. "Are you glad I'm coming back?"

Patricia kept her gaze steady and

open. "Of course I am. Otherwise you'll miss the ski trip."

"Oh . . ." he murmured.

She started to stand up.

"Miss Gilbert? Ah . . . do you . . . have a boyfriend?"

Patricia faltered for an indiscernible moment. She threw her lunch remains in the garbage bin and sat back to regard the teenager. In him she saw mostly Morgan, and the image flustered her. "Kent, don't you think that's a personal question?"

He only seemed mildly embarrassed. "Yeah, I guess."

Patricia played with her earring. "Why do you want to know?"

"It's just that you're . . . you're so nice. Everyone here likes you a lot. I thought that . . . maybe there's someone else you like, too." His glance was bold, and oddly innocent.

Patricia raised a brow at him. "Your question is out of line," she accused quietly. But Kent was not to be put off. She realized that his presumption was all her fault. After all, she encouraged the students to be open and honest with her. It had never gotten so personal until now.

"Do you like older or . . . younger men?" Kent asked curiously.

She stood up. "That's it. Lunchtime is over. No more questions." Kent reluctantly finished eating, and threw his lunch bag out. "I hear you're interested in Gabriella Villar," Patricia countered.

Kent was embarrassed and annoyed. "Who told you that?"

"I've seen you together. You squared off with Peter over her."

"It was dumb."

"Is Gabriella your girlfriend now?" Patricia asked shamelessly. Kent looked confused. "You seem to spend a lot of time together."

"We just talk. She's always asking me questions. She told me she's glad I don't have my ears pierced like all the other guys . . ." Patricia chuckled. "She's okay."

"She's cute."

"Yeah." Kent reluctantly nodded.

"Are you taking her to the Christmas party?"

Kent bounced out of his chair as if he'd been sitting on hot coals. His face was red. "I don't know. I probably won't go."

Patricia touched his arm. The look he

gave her twisted at her heart. She smiled gently. "You should. Gabriella is a little more sophisticated than a lot of Duncan girls. You two have a lot in common."

He looked at her helplessly. "I don't have a girlfriend, yet. But . . . do you have someone you really like a lot?"

Patricia was trapped. She thought of all the clever ways she could dodge the question, which would only have hurt Kent more . . . and fooled herself not at all. She felt uneasy with an outright lie. She thought of the long Thanksgiving weekend and the horrible restlessness . . . and loneliness. She thought of sitting with Morgan in the front of her car, warm and giddy from his kisses as snow fell outside around them.

"Yes," Patricia said softly. Hope made her answer easy.

Chapter Twelve

Morgan was edgy. He had no idea how he was going to say good-bye.

He began to pace the small waiting area, crowded with holiday travelers, bulky baggage, and wrapped gifts. Children, baby strollers, noise, excitement. Those departing on flights out of the city were kissed and waved off. Those arriving were kissed and welcomed with hugs. What would he and Kent do?

"Thank you for waiting, ladies and gentlemen. We are now ready for boarding on flight 819 to Colorado Springs. Will all passengers with . . ."

Morgan searched the departure wing corridor and caught sight of Kent ambling back to the waiting area. He'd gone to the men's room and the candy counter. Morgan raised a hand over his head and let out a short whistle. Kent picked up on the signal and began jogging toward his father.

"It's time," Morgan said, putting a hand on his son's shoulder. He led Kent back to the seat where he'd left a packed duffel, a shopping bag with Christmas gifts, his Walkman, a few magazines, and his varsity jacket. "Where is your boarding pass?" Kent tapped his shirt pocket. "And your ticket?" He slapped his back pocket and popped the last of his candy bar into his mouth. As his son gathered his belongings, Morgan put his hands in his pockets and stood watching.

"Thanks for the lift to the airport," Kent said.

Morgan shrugged lightly. "No problem. You have a good flight. Wish your mom and grandfather a Merry Christmas for me."

"I will."

Morgan touched the fading bruise on Kent's right cheekbone. "What are you going to tell her about this?"

"The truth. I took a sucker punch from a sore loser in a pickup football game."

"That's not going to make her feel better."

"I can handle Mom," Kent said confidently.

"I bet," Morgan conceded with a crooked smile.

They joined the end of the line inching toward the attendant checking tickets.

"Are you sure you have everything?" Morgan asked. He looked around.

"Yep."

They moved a few more feet. Kent dropped a magazine. Morgan quickly retrieved it for him.

"What are you gonna do for Christmas?" Kent asked.

Morgan took a deep breath. "Sleep late. Visit your grandmother in L.A. for a few days. Hit the slopes somewhere. Learn how to make lasagna so we can eat it."

Kent laughed shortly. "I don't think I'm going to like lasagna."

They were nearing the departure gate.

"Is it okay if I bring my skis back with me? Maybe we can go skiing together. What do you think?"

Morgan thought it was a great idea, but for the moment found it hard to respond. It was the first time that his son had suggested that the two of them do something together. Morgan nodded and kept his voice smooth.

"That's cool. You can probably teach

me a few things. I'm pretty rusty."

"Sure," Kent said, clearly pleased at the thought.

There was only one other person ahead of them now. Morgan stepped back and watched the final boarding procedures. He was well aware of the contrast between this moment and the one six months ago when he'd picked Kent up after his flight to New York. At first there had been almost total silence between them. Strained conversation, what there was of it. Awkward awareness of each other. They'd been virtual strangers. Yes and no responses until they'd arrived home. Those first few weeks had been some of the toughest hours of Morgan's life.

As he watched his son struggle with all of his things, Morgan knew this was the right thing to do. Kent needed to see his mother and stepfather, his grandfather and old friends. He now knew that Kent, by his own expressed wishes, would return, but Morgan was having real difficulties watching his son board the plane. He couldn't help feeling like he was losing Kent again, even for a few days.

"You're all set. Have a good flight," the

attendant said, smiling.

Kent faced his father. Each seemed to be waiting for the other to say the words first. The good-bye. A blush crept over Kent's face and he averted his gaze in the pretense of rolling the magazine into a tube. Morgan finally realized that he had to be the one to make the first move. He forced a smile to his lips, made a brief wave.

"You have a good time."

Kent blinked, suddenly dropped the duffel, and took three quick steps toward his father. They each had one arm to give to the embrace, but it was close and warm. A huge relief. Magazines and jacket got squashed between their bodies. The hug was quick, but a moment was all they needed. When Kent stepped back, his eyes were bright and he seemed more self-assured. He picked up the duffel again.

"See you." He disappeared through the gate opening.

Morgan stared at the now empty doorway until its lines and dimensions, even the color of the carpeting, began to blur.

At the sight of so many people at Morgan's party, Patricia didn't know whether to be relieved or frightened out of her wits. There were nearly two hundred guests in the large open room. Had there been only a few dozen people she could have met them all right away and been done with it. But in such a crowd Patricia knew she would either be lost or be forced to introduce herself all evening long. The only person she was likely to know in any case was Morgan, and she didn't immediately see him anywhere as she stood gazing into the bright room.

" 'Cuse me," a woman said as she brushed past Patricia. She was dressed in a tux and expertly balanced an hors d'oeuvres tray in one hand.

Patricia continued to stand peeking in the door, daunted by the number of men and women. She had to go in, or leave. She was pushed in.

"Umph! I'm sorry. Did I hurt you?"

"No, no. I'm okay." She smiled, straightening the neckline of her black off-the-shoulder dress, but resisting the urge to tug the skirt down toward her knees. The middle-aged man smiled apologetically, touching her elbow.

"I took the corner way too fast."

She laughed, shaking her head. Her

hair was pulled back in a twisted knot, controlled with two pearl-studded combs. "It's my fault for standing in the doorway."

The man looked her over. His smile was kind but mischievous. "Scared to go in?" Patricia nodded shyly. The man held out a beefy brown hand to her. His voice was deep and pleasant. "I'm George Tanner. Now you know at least one person. Come on in. My wife's right over here."

"I'm Patricia Gilbert," she responded, accepting the invitation gratefully.

Mrs. Anderson was in a safe little cluster of support staff from Ventura, Inc. Secretaries, clerks, accountants, and their various spouses or companions. Neither she nor the others felt particularly comfortable socializing with the executives and directors.

From where she stood, Mrs. Anderson saw when Beverly McGraw arrived. The attractive female attorney was dressed in a striking raspberry silk suit. The jacket formed a V neckline that was discreet but showed off noticeable cleavage. She watched Beverly play the crowd perfectly. She flattered the women, bantered with the men. She networked. Mrs. Anderson watched in amusement and admiration.

Mrs. Anderson was also in perfect position to see Patricia Gilbert come in, and she was pleasantly surprised. Patricia was simply but stunningly dressed for the occasion. Several men turned to stare. Several females tried not to. Of course, she could hardly be ignored with her abundant red hair. She was wearing an off-the-shoulder sheath that stopped two inches above her knees. A single strand of pearls. Patricia's black suede pumps had little satin bows on the front. She looked surprisingly sophisticated and reserved. Connie quickly looked around for Morgan, wondering if he'd seen Patricia yet.

He had.

As a matter of fact, Morgan couldn't help staring at Patricia as she stood with George Tanner and several other people. He had had no idea how he imagined Patricia would come dressed for the party. The glittering lights from the overhead chandeliers set her hair afire, burnished it with colors of a sunset. Her light skin offset by the black dress were perfect foils. And watching

420

her briefly in that moment, Morgan felt a pang of appreciation for what she had to endure. The ambiguity created by her outer appearance.

Patricia laughed lightly at a comment from Mrs. Tanner. She sipped from her wine. Gilly had been right. She spent too much time around adolescents. She was finding it awkward to be in a social situation with people her own age.

She hadn't seen Morgan yet. Of course, he might not even know she was here. The party seemed to have spread through several rooms. The conversation was lively and sophisticated, but Patricia couldn't stop her gaze from wandering off, looking in the crowd for just one person . . .

Beverly left the group of men laughing at her departing remark. Her eyes quickly roamed over the crowd to see if there was anyone she had missed that she should say hello to. She didn't know all of the players, but she certainly could tell who were the leaders and who were not. Knowing that saved time that might otherwise be wasted on people she didn't need to know.

She could tell the CEOs and executives. They were mostly white and all male. They paid little attention to most of the people around them and formed their own inner circle. The middle managers were also men, black and white. She recognized a vice president of American Express standing with his wife. Beverly smiled. She'd never met the wife before, but she remembered *him* very well. She decided against creating a situation for him, and turned to wander away.

She'd seen Morgan once, but it was clear that he couldn't get away to come to her. She had also noticed that he seemed to be staring at a rather pretty white woman with red hair. She wasn't one of Morgan's employees, and she certainly didn't seem like any other kind of business associate. Beverly wondered who she was, and was about to find out when her attention was caught by the head legal counsel of the Citibank Corporation. She'd met him a year ago at another function and remembered that he knew a lot of people in Europe . . .

George Tanner caught Morgan's eye across the buffet table. They nodded a greeting and George, after hesitating, came around to where Morgan stood with a drink in hand.

"Nice party, Morgan. Very generous of you."

"I'm glad you and your wife could make it tonight."

George took a glass of wine from a passing waiter. "She's enjoying herself."

Morgan looked closely at the man. "And you're not?"

George shrugged. "This is great. I'm glad I'm not paying for it," he joked easily. He glanced around the room. "Smart idea, inviting our group."

"I repeat, but not for you."

George frowned into his glass. "You were very fair with Sager. I know we gave you a hard time when the negotiations began, but you were okay about it. Did everything you said you were going to do."

Morgan sipped from his drink and watched Tanner over the rim of his glass.

"This is probably way out of line, but I'd really hoped to get a shot at being named director myself. I think I can do the job."

Morgan stiffened alertly. He watched the ambivalence in George between accepting a professional decision that went against him and pleading a case for himself. Morgan watched him thoughtfully, recognizing that the other man wasn't afraid to take a risk. He was a straight shooter.

"I'm sorry you're disappointed," Morgan said neutrally.

"I know Sullivan is your man. He's smart, he's capable. Did a good job for you and Ventura. We liked working with him. But if you had it in mind to give him the top job, I wish you'd have been straight with us about it. Sullivan didn't have to . . ."

"I haven't agreed to giving the position of executive director to anyone yet," Morgan said.

George straightened up. "But at lunch the other day . . ."

"I listened to what you and Bob had to say. That was all. I never agreed to anything."

George looked mildly annoyed. "You're right, of course. Didn't see that one coming." Then he looked skeptical. "On the other hand, I've probably lost any chance I might have had at that job."

Morgan's smile was mysterious. "I like to know what people expect of me. You were honest. I appreciate that. I haven't made any decision yet, George." He put his half-finished drink down and steered George away from the table and several other people. "David said something the other day that I fully agree with."

"He did?"

"He said the negotiations were long and hard, and he could use a break. We could all do with just leaving this alone until after the holidays. Just hang tight."

George slowly relaxed, nodding agreement. Then he raised his brow, and a lopsided grin appeared. "Hang tight? You sound like my kid."

Morgan nodded and pursed his mouth. "About fifteen years old? Thinks he knows everything?"

George laughed. "About sixteen. And *she* probably knows more than I'd ever want her to . . ."

Patricia stood in yet another group of people but she'd already lost the train of the conversation. Her fingers were cold and wet from holding glasses filled with ice. She'd still not seen Morgan, and was becoming disappointed and anxious. She didn't do well at these functions, and she was beginning to feel it.

"I will be happy to get you another drink if you wish."

Patricia looked to the smiling man standing next to her. He was slightly shorter than she was, and he spoke with an accent. "Pardon?"

"You were frowning so hard into your glass, I thought perhaps you did not care for your drink. Would you prefer wine?"

She smiled. "No, thank you. I've already had wine. Besides, I'm driving."

The man looked momentarily confused, and then his expression cleared. "Ahh. *Bueño.* It is good to be careful, no?" He shuddered. "How brave to drive around this confusing city." He took her hand, ignoring the cold dampness, and bowed over it. "Allow me. I am Señor Estéfano Miguel Villar."

Patricia brightened. He was slightly built with a Mediterranean handsomeness. "Mr. Villar. Patricia Gilbert."

"A pleasure."

"Do you happen to have a daughter named Gabriella?"

His eyes brightened in surprise. "Yes, yes. Do you know my daughter?"

"I'm a counselor at her school."

"I did not expect to meet anyone to-night from her school. Are there other teachers here as well?"

"I don't think so. Our host, Mr. Baxter, has a son at Duncan. He's also new to the school."

Further recognition showed on Mr. Villar's face. "Ah, yes. My daughter did say there was a woman with red hair who spoke Spanish very well."

Patricia laughed quietly. "I don't think so."

Mr. Villar leaned closer and spoke softly. "If you will permit me. My daughter, Gabriella, she has a little thing that she does. Harmless, you understand . . ."

Patricia nodded briefly. "I know. She pretends not to know any English. There's no need to worry. Actually, I thought it was a clever defense on her part."

Mr. Villar looked puzzled. "Defense?"

"Yes. Against being the new student in a strange city and school. I think Gabriella was afraid she might not fit in with the other students. She was afraid to try. If no one was friendly to her, she could always use the language barrier as an excuse."

Mr. Villar shook his head. "I'm afraid that my family has to move frequently because of my work. I am an economist. I teach, but frequently I am hired as a consultant. I will be working with Señor Baxter through the next year, possibly the year after that. My family has generously been subleased a house on Prospect Park South. I know it is very hard on my children."

"Gabriella is doing just fine. She has friends, she comes to the school events, she does very well in class. And she's mature at fourteen."

Mr. Villar pursed his lips. "It is difficult. We wanted to put our Gabriella in the international school. She would have none of it. She wanted to be like real American teenagers, she said." He shook his head. "And I am convinced, Señorita Gilbert, that I have you to thank for this transformation in my daughter. You are a beautiful woman of great understanding and patience."

Patricia started to demure, but someone spoke from behind her.

"I want to meet anyone who's that special," the voice said boldly.

Patricia absolutely froze. The male insinuation of the tone drew her attention.

Mr. Villar, with a slight incline of his head, bowed away to the other guests. Patricia slowly turned around. The tall blond man was good-looking and athletically built. His gaze narrowed and swept over every detail of her, quickly coming back to her startled gray eyes. His smile was ironic; he was calm and in control.

"Pretty, too . . ." he murmured in soft wonder.

For a moment Patricia was tempted to simply turn and walk away. She wasn't interested in a come-on. But she calmed her expression and removed the look of hesitation from her face. *I can handle this,* she thought playfully.

"I don't believe you said that. No one uses bad lines like that anymore."

David shrugged good-naturedly and grinned. "Why not, if it works? You *are* very pretty. Are you going to tell me that men haven't told you that before?"

Patricia felt herself flushing in momentary confusion. She took a deep breath and moistened her lips. "I didn't say that. I said it wasn't very original."

"Okay. Then let's move on. I'm David

Sullivan." He tilted his head, waiting.

"Patricia Gilbert."

"Do people call you Pat or Patty for short?"

"Only *very* close friends. And I hate being called Patty," Patricia said clearly, arching a brow.

"As in cake?" he ventured. David's attention wandered suggestively over her again, his gaze admiring and bold. "I certainly hope we can become friends. You're not with Sager, are you? I thought I knew everyone at the headquarters."

"No, I'm not."

"Wife or girlfriend of someone at Sager?" he persisted.

"I was invited by Morgan Baxter."

"Where has he been hiding you?"

Patricia chuckled. "You're something else. Not subtle, are you?"

"When it's called for. I thought I knew everyone who was anyone. Suddenly there's you."

"You don't need to know me. I'm just another guest. Here for now . . . gone in an hour."

Patricia smiled pleasantly and made to walk around David. He lightly grabbed her arm and held it, forcing her to face him.

"Okay, so I was too flip, too quick. Give me another chance."

"I don't think so," Patricia said, extracting her arm.

"Don't say no, yet. Once you get to know me, you'll probably like me," David said.

Again despite herself Patricia had to laugh. He was charming. "The thing is, I'm not interested." Again she tried to leave. Again he blocked her path.

"Okay, here's my last shot. I'm thirty-four years old. Gainfully employed at Ventura . . ."

She blinked at him. "Really?"

Sensing her interest David forged on. "I come from a solid West Coast family. No one's ever been declared crazy, and I don't have a criminal record. I have an MBA, type B positive blood. I hate broccoli, and I'd *love* to see you again."

She smiled uncomfortably. He was likable. "You pass, but I'm sorry."

"If there's someone else, I'll duel him. His weapon of choice. The pen, a knife, or a gun."

She frowned. "The pen?"

David winked and leaned in closer. "I write great love letters."

"Down, boy."

Both David and Patricia turned at the teasing voice entering their conversation. Patricia turned her attention to the other woman who was about her own height, but with more sensual curves, and feminine presence, dressed in a noticeable raspberry silk suit.

"Beverly," David drawled smoothly, giving the woman a long considering look.

Beverly didn't deign to acknowledge David's presence. Instead, she focused her attention on Patricia, examining her with a thoroughness that bordered on being rude.

Patricia returned the assessing stare, but smiled pleasantly. She was a bit startled by the black woman's open curiosity, but she also knew what the close scrutiny was all about.

"I'm Beverly McGraw," Beverly introduced herself with a forthright firmness. She didn't extend her hand.

"I'm Patricia Gilbert."

"I don't recall meeting you before."

"She doesn't work for Sager or Ventura," David supplied.

"Oh," Beverly murmured.

"Actually, I'm a little out of place here."

Beverly smiled graciously, her eyes once more taking inventory. "Not at all. I'd say you add an extra touch of class."

"And then some," David said.

Beverly only gave him the briefest glance. "Watch out for David. He's brilliant and cute, but a little full of himself."

"Thank you," David said good-naturedly.

Patricia, uncomfortable with the banter between David and Beverly, tried to smile. "That is a really beautiful suit. I love the color, but I couldn't wear it."

Beverly ran her hand lightly down a lapel. "Why, thank you. I thought it was a good color for my skin tone, don't you think?" she hinted broadly.

Patricia nodded. "Perfect."

Beverly then glanced thoroughly once more over Patricia. "You might be able to get away with it, but your hair would clash."

Patricia's smile became strained. She wished she'd never mentioned the suit.

"Well, if you're not one of the company contingent, what is your connection to all of these people?" Beverly went on.

"Not people. Morgan," David said with a raised brow.

"Is that right?" Beverly murmured, a slight edge of suspicion in her tone.

"My connection is with Morgan's son. I'm a high school counselor."

"Oh," Beverly said, clearly not liking what she was hearing. "How interesting . . ."

"Beverly! Someone told me you were here. Looking fabulous as always . . ."

A fourth person commanded their attention as he gave Beverly a cheek air-kiss and light hug.

"Winston, how nice to see you." She turned to David and Patricia. "You two go on. I've been looking for Winston all evening." She looked sharply at Patricia. "Nice to meet you . . . *girlfriend.* Maybe we'll talk later."

David and Patricia watched as Beverly linked her arm with the man and walked away, laughing over his whispered words.

Patricia processed the brief encounter, and wished she'd asked the attractive woman what *her* connection was to all these people, to Morgan, as well. She decided that chances were she and Beverly McGraw definitely would not have a talk later. Which was just as well.

"Attractive, isn't she? Sharp, too. But I'm partial to redheads."

Patricia frowned at David. Over his shoulder she saw Morgan across the room. Their gaze caught and Morgan gave a slight nod of acknowledgment, turning back to a guest. Patricia glanced back to David and found him studying her intently.

"You've made a mistake."

David looked puzzled. "What?"

She braced herself and took a deep breath. "You've mistaken me for someone white." She watched for his reaction. It was still confused. He shook his head.

"I don't get it," David murmured, staring at her.

Patricia felt foolish. "I'm not white. I'm African-American." She forestalled David's comment by holding up a hand. "Please don't say I don't look it." Her voice was calm but clipped.

"So what?" David asked smoothly.

"What do you mean, so what?"

"I mean, to me you don't look black. You just look beautiful. I don't particularly care that you're black. Hey, I'm not biased. I'm an equal-opportunity date.

If I like you and I'm interested, that's all that matters to me."

"You mean, just for sex?" Patricia asked bluntly.

David drew back a little. "That's part of it. But not necessarily."

"I still think you've made a mistake."

David took a moment to smile charmingly at her. "I don't think so. I'm still interested in getting to know you. If you ask me, Patricia Gilbert, you're more hung up about that race business than I am. Too bad. You really are attractive. If you change your mind . . ." He let it hang.

Patricia suddenly felt gooseflesh on her arms and bare shoulder. David waved at her and walked away. She stood staring after him thinking what a fool she'd made of herself. And feeling miserable. She resolutely walked away, blindly headed for anyplace that would give her quick sanctuary . . .

Morgan was finally working his way toward Patricia. He'd waited a half hour, until she'd settled in with the other guests. He didn't want to appear too obviously interested and have others take notice.

He began walking around the perimeter

of the crowd. He could see Patricia talking to David who, no doubt, was coming on to her. For an unexpected moment it bothered Morgan to see them together, but Patricia didn't appear to be either impressed or amused by David.

"Well . . . I finally caught up to you. Avoiding me, Morgan?" Beverly asked beguilingly.

Morgan reluctantly stopped and turned to look at Beverly. She looked gorgeous. "Good evening," Morgan murmured pleasantly.

"Is that all? Just good evening?"

"You look wonderful."

"Not wonderful enough. You don't seem particularly pleased to see me. Shall we go somewhere and talk about it?"

"I can't. I don't want to leave my guests."

The complacent smile on Beverly's lips vanished. She touched Morgan's arm and peered up at him earnestly. "Morgan, what's going on? What's wrong with you?"

Morgan arched a brow as he looked into Beverly's genuinely puzzled gaze. He realized the strong attraction she'd held for him, but he now also saw the limitations. Morgan could see that she was automatically assuming that if there was a problem at all, it was with him.

"The only thing that's wrong right now is that this is not the time for this conversation. I'm hosting a party. Just relax and have a good time. We'll talk later."

"When?" Beverly persisted.

"Beverly . . ." Morgan began patiently, but he also smiled absently to soften his aloofness. He wanted to avoid her quickly building irritation with him. And a possible unpleasant scene.

"Or is there someone else you'd rather be with."

Morgan gestured with his hand and glanced briefly around the room. "As you can see the guests are all business friends and colleagues. There's nothing personal going on here tonight."

Beverly smiled knowingly. "Funny. I just met someone a moment ago who doesn't fall into either of those two categories. What is your son's coun- selor, of all people, doing here tonight?"

Morgan's jaw tightened and he faced Beverly squarely. He didn't like her tone of interrogation. But he also had nothing to hide. "Because I invited her to come."

Not expecting so succinct a response, Beverly was silent as she tried to assess Morgan's words, his mood. "Is something going on that I should know about?" she asked bluntly.

"Other than that Patricia Gilbert has worked miracles with my son and been patient with my shortcomings as a parent, no, I don't think so."

A very slow, nearly patronizing smile shaped Beverly's mouth. "She's damned near white," she murmured quietly. "Is that what's got your attention? Suddenly I'm not what you want?"

Morgan was stunned by Beverly's comment, but controlled his expression and kept his voice calm and low. "As long as you mentioned it, you haven't been very understanding about my problems with Kent. For whatever reason, you chose to see him as some sort of competition. As you so often remind me, Beverly, he's fifteen years old. I thought you'd be able to deal with his acting like one. As to your other remark," Morgan said, his voice dangerously taut, "it wasn't worthy of you. It's not worthy of a response."

"I tried to be honest with you. I wasn't interested in being a mother substitute for your son," Beverly said righteously.

Morgan raised his brows in surprise. "I don't remember asking you to," he said. "I hope that answers your questions. Enjoy the party, Bev. Excuse me . . ."

He walked away. Beverly was instantly out of his mind.

And then he couldn't find Patricia.

She seemed to have vanished in just the few minutes he'd spent with Beverly. Morgan grew worried. Had Patricia left? Some of the other guests were beginning to. Was she still with David? He walked through the large reception room, methodically scanning the crowd for her. He couldn't see her anywhere.

"Good night, Mr. Baxter. Merry Christmas."

Morgan turned to Mrs. Anderson. She was dressed to leave. He smiled at her and bent to kiss her cheek. "Have a wonderful holiday, Connie. Don't let your grandchildren wear you out."

"If they start getting on my nerves, I'm getting on the next plane and coming back home."

"Connie . . ." Morgan hesitated. "Have you seen Patricia Gilbert?"

Connie smiled as if she knew a secret. "As a matter of fact, yes. I saw her head into the next room. At that end." She pointed to the opening at the end of the reception hall. "I'll see you at the office next week." She smiled and left.

Morgan quickly maneuvered his way through the remaining guests, politely putting off any attempts to delay him. He walked into the room Connie had indicated and found Patricia. There were only a few people here, sitting in comfortable chairs in quiet conversations. Patricia stood inside the entrance, looking for all the world as if she were trapped and had hoped this would be a way out. Morgan lightly touched her shoulder.

"Patricia?"

She whirled around. Her eyes were huge in her face. As a matter of fact Morgan realized that they were dilated. She looked disoriented. Morgan took hold of her hand tightly, acting decisively.

"Let's get out of here." He pulled her after him as he avoided the rest of the party and found an exit onto a corridor of the hotel lobby.

Morgan walked with purpose through the empty space, the party sounds and music fading behind them. They passed a bank of elevators and public telephones. They passed the newsstand and a gift store, closed for the night. They came to a set of double doors. Morgan opened one and stepped inside, bringing the still silent Patricia with him. It was a banquet room, empty except for stacked chairs and tables. It was dark. Morgan made his way into the room along a wall. He stopped and turned around, pulling Patricia into his arms.

There was no resistance in her. Patricia let herself lean into Morgan's chest. She pressed her nose into the front of his shirt inhaling the scent of starch, smoke, a mixture of feminine perfumes absorbed from the air . . . and himself. Patricia still felt completely dazed. Her heart was pounding in her chest and she hoped that Morgan could not feel it. She was just so glad that somehow he knew she needed to get away.

Morgan couldn't begin to guess what was wrong. He didn't know for sure if Patricia wanted to be held, but he needed to hold her. He hadn't expected to have a confrontation with Beverly McGraw. It didn't have to happen in this arena with so many witnesses. But it had been coming.

He'd realized only after that urgency to see Patricia a week and a half ago, after cornering her in her car that snowy morning, that he'd managed to uncomfortably position himself between Patricia and Beverly. But even then he'd known which way his interest really lay. Morgan knew that *this* feeling with Patricia he could trust. Her breasts, stomach, and thighs were pressed firmly against him. She was slender and light. She felt warm and soft. Her breathing was quiet, but ragged and hurried.

"Patricia . . ." he whispered her name, in that way that made her feel special. She pressed closer. He rubbed the back of her neck, rubbed his cheek against her temple, and felt her breath through the fabric of his shirt in one hot little spot.

Morgan closed his eyes and experienced such an unexpected sense of peace and safety and he didn't know why. Perhaps because she was just letting him hold her. He was glad for the moment that they couldn't see each other's expressions, couldn't interpret movements or sounds. Morgan liked the way she seemed to need him and accepted him now, without question.

His executive demeanor slipped away, and he became a man who only wanted to be with this woman. It was as if they'd kept the reality of the world as a buffer between them just a little too long, and whatever doubts he had or she had now evaporated.

At some point Patricia recognized that Morgan was doing more than just comforting her. She put her arms around his waist and returned the gentle gesture. There was a rekindling of hope and tenderness between them. Something had happened to Morgan, too, this evening. She sighed, turning her cheek to his chest. She reveled in the firm, long solidness of his body. She wanted Morgan to be the one to vanquish the past. She wanted to forget those moments with David Sullivan. And what he'd said.

"Everything is so complicated," Patricia observed in a murmur.

"Is it?" Morgan asked quietly. He

stroked her back.

"Don't you think so? Don't you worry about . . . you know, where things are headed?"

"It depends on what 'things' you mean. But no. I don't worry." Morgan settled his arm around her waist and brushed a kiss on her bare shoulder. "It's only complicated when you're unsure."

"That's an answer my grandmother would give."

"Okay then . . . blame it on cheese."

"This isn't funny, Morgan."

"I'm serious. Listen, when I was growing up there were only three kinds of cheese to buy at the local store. Swiss, American, and Velveeta." She giggled. "That was it. Now when you buy cheese there's almost two hundred different kinds to choose from. It's not so easy anymore. Low salt or low fat. Semisoft or sharp." Morgan drew back and his hands cupped her face. He could barely make out her features, yet he regarded her closely. "It could be simple if you just stayed with Swiss, American, or Velveeta, but it wouldn't be very exciting. And in your whole life if you never tasted brie or boursin or goat or feta, think about what you'd miss."

Patricia strained to see Morgan's face, too. But her heart started beating fast again because she could hear the texture of his voice, the teasing of his words. She could feel the gentle caressing of his hands on her face. Morgan was not talking about cheese.

"So you're saying that cheese is the reason life is so difficult?"

Morgan bent closer, looking at her mouth. His thumbs brushed the sides of her face. He shook his head slowly. "Not difficult, just complicated. Difficult is another story. Life is about taking chances. Otherwise, why bother."

When Morgan's mouth pressed on hers Patricia knew she was ready for something different. She stood with her eyes closed, letting the intimate darkness and the persuasive movements of Morgan's lips move over her. She stopped thinking and just opened herself to the tantalizing sensation Morgan was offering in his kiss.

He didn't hesitate and he held nothing back. He used desire and demand to manipulate her mouth open so that the kiss was seriously intense as his tongue gained entry and staked a claim. Immediately he got a response.

The taste of Morgan, the slow dance with their tongues, was intoxicating, and pure pleasure began to warm Patricia outward to her fingertips, and inward to her heart. She knew the effect on Morgan as well. Where their bodies met, his changed. A part of him grew obviously hard. The idea that she was responsible was very pleasing to Patricia, and the kiss was all the more sweet . . . all the more promising. Morgan could have pushed his advantage then, or Patricia might have encouraged him. But Morgan slowly and deliberately ended the kiss, his lips teasing her. She sighed.

"Oh, Morgan . . ."

"I've been trying to reach you all night," he growled in frustration. "Did David get fresh with you?"

She shook her head, liking that tone in his voice. "No, but there was a cast of thousands, and everyone wanted your attention."

"Bad time to get serious?"

"I think so," she breathed raggedly.

"I'm sorry."

"I knew it was a business party."

"I want to see you . . ."

447

She allowed a little space to separate their torsos. "And I want to go home."

"This will be over soon."

"You'll be here another few hours," Patricia said positively. She stepped out of his embrace, but let her hand delicately slide along Morgan's jaw and mouth.

Morgan didn't object. He took her hand once more, kissed the back of the knuckles. "Are you ready to go back through the hall and all those people?"

She nodded silently.

Morgan led them back the way they'd come. She said nothing. He didn't feel the need to. Something new had begun for them in the last ten minutes, but there was not going to be any time right now to explore it. And as yet it had no closure. He felt keyed up and excited.

As they once more heard the music and the noise of the party, Patricia pulled her hand free and composed herself. A polite space developed between them. She touched her mouth and wondered if she looked kissed. Were her eyes dazed-looking, like she felt?

She stopped outside the ballroom. "I can go on from here by myself. Your guests are probably . . ."

He put a hand firmly on the small of her back. "I'll walk you to the valet desk."

They continued past the entrance to the hall where the party was continuing. Just inside, Beverly stood staring, silent and disconcerted as she watched Morgan escort Patricia Gilbert away from his other guests.

Morgan got Patricia's coat from the checkroom and held it as she put it on. They waited together, Morgan holding her hand, as her car was driven up from the hotel garage. He leaned to whisper in her ear.

"That dress is a knockout."

Patricia smiled at the compliment. "This old thing?" she said with a mocking rise of her brow. Morgan laughed.

He put his arm around her shoulder and drew Patricia to his side as he opened her car door. "I'm going to have to teach you how to accept a compliment gracefully."

Morgan watched her settle in her car and start the engine. She glanced out the window at him, feeling vulnerable under his frowning stare, wondering what he was thinking.

"Thank you for inviting me."

"I'm glad you came. I'll call you to make sure you got home all right."

"You don't have to do that. I'll be okay."

"Humor me," Morgan said in a deep quiet tone.

When Patricia got home exhaustion quickly overcame her. Yet she didn't immediately want to go to bed. She kicked off her shoes, peeled off the panty hose. She pulled out the pearl combs and tried to finger-comb her hair loose. It was nearly one in the morning, but she felt lethargic and dreamy. Patricia could still hear the voices and laughter of the party, the background music. The excitement of the night vibrated in her head. She could still experience that moment when David had given back to her her own suspicions and fears.

Patricia poured herself a glass of wine and curled up in the corner of her sofa. She hugged a pillow and covered her legs with an afghan. She hoped the wine would do what her body was not yet inclined to.

Relax, Patricia admonished herself.

When she heard the buzzer sometime later, she didn't fully realize it was for her apartment. Curious, she put the wineglass down and climbed out of the afghan.

She padded barefoot to the door and the panel of buttons next to it.

"Who is it?" No one responded when she spoke through the intercom system.

But after a few minutes Patricia heard footsteps in the hallway as someone exited the elevator. She used the peephole to peer into the corridor. Still, she could see no one, although a key was turned in a lock several apartment doors away. Patricia stepped back from the door, hugged herself, and returned to the sofa.

The doorbell sounded next, startling her. Not bothering with the peephole, she unbolted and unlocked her door. Morgan stood on the threshold when she pulled it open.

"Why didn't you ask who it was?" he asked without preamble.

"How did you get into the building?"

"Your neighbor."

"Oh . . ."

The obvious having been dealt with,

they now stood regarding one another. But Patricia's heartbeat was like a triphammer in her chest. All of her anticipation came rushing back at her. Somehow, Morgan's appearance didn't seem like a surprise.

A familiar feeling went through her, changing her body rhythms. The tension in her stomach was coupled with rising desire, the desire that had begun earlier in the evening.

"I guess I didn't wake you up," he said, seeing that she was still dressed. Morgan walked into the apartment, forcing Patricia to step back.

"You didn't call," she said absently.

"I decided to come instead." Morgan's voice was very low. "Is that okay?"

"I couldn't sleep. I was waiting . . ."

Morgan closed the door and locked it. Patricia said nothing more. Impulsively she moved forward, closing the distance between them. His name was barely out of her mouth before they were locked together, mouths fused and hungry. Morgan cupped his hand to the back of her head, tilting it to just the right angle.

Patricia slipped easily, quickly into the delicious sensations that Morgan had evoked earlier in the empty banquet room at the hotel. They picked up right where they'd left off. There was a chilled aura surrounding Morgan. The winter air still clung to his overcoat. His hands and cheeks were cold, but his mouth, his tongue, stoked a slow heat in Patricia that warmed her.

She was overwhelmed. She didn't want him to stop kissing her as if his life depended on it. But he did stop, apparently satisfied for the moment, as he sighed deeply, and kissed his way to her cheek and then her ear. He held her tightly to his body. She knew that she'd been practically holding her breath waiting for this moment, wanting Morgan to take charge and make it easier for her to give in.

Morgan's fingers found the zipper on the back of her dress. He pulled it down until the dress sagged and Patricia found herself with nothing on but panties, and his stroking hands.

His chuckle was rich and seductive. "I'm sorry I took so long," he whispered.

Patricia supposed that the clear proof that she wanted Morgan Baxter was in her total acquiescence to him from the moment he came into her apartment. He released her long enough to take off his topcoat and discard it on the sofa. Then he stood before her, commanding and confident. She frowned slightly at him.

"What's wrong?" he asked, his voice raspy and seductive. He took her hands and pulled them down from where they'd crossed to cover her naked breasts. It was still a shock to see how white her skin was.

"You look like you're getting ready for a business meeting. I feel like . . . like . . ."

"I can take care of that."

The suit jacket came off. The tie. He began to unbutton the white shirt. Quickly the brown hair sprinkled over the expanse of his chest was exposed. The sight of his bare flesh did interesting things to the nerve ends in Patricia's body. She felt charged, and her senses heightened. As Morgan began to strip off his clothing, the man who was president of a company vanished into just a man who was much more primal, and who wanted to connect to her in a much simpler and purer way than what they had known so far.

Patricia experienced Morgan's masculinity and appeal in full force. She willingly surrendered to the rising passion, the heat of his hands on her naked back, as he drew her back into his arms. He pressed her close so that her chest was against his through the shirt, which now hung open. The feel of him, firm and warm, made her feel momentarily dizzy. She almost melted under the erotic eloquence of his kisses. Her knees began to weaken and she broke away from Morgan. Patricia looked deeply into his eyes and saw only desire, and a gentle tender smile. She led the way to her bedroom.

They didn't need the light but Morgan turned it on anyway. Neither could deny the curiosity. Morgan finished disrobing with Patricia's help. It took forever. They kept stopping to kiss and touch. When they were both naked, the meshing of their skin, the intertwining of their limbs, was like a Kente cloth pattern of brown and tan and white, of abstract shapes and movement. Suddenly they both stopped, their urgent kissing separating on a moist little sound. Morgan had his hands on her hips. He was fully erect. He suddenly began to look over her body. Thoroughly. She tried to stand perfectly still as he took his time over every detail.

For a long moment, Morgan could actually only stare. Patricia's skin was like cream. Her nipples were a dusty rose. The hair between her legs, red. For another startling moment Morgan thought of Melissa, and he briefly squeezed his eyes closed to make the image disappear. Patricia's pale skin confused him, made him scared. He wanted to make love to *this* woman. But did he want her for reasons other than who she was?

"Morgan?" Patricia questioned, stepping back from the intense scrutiny.

He reached for her, quieted her with a soft sound. Morgan put his arms around her again and moaned deep in his throat. He closed his eyes, holding her tight.

"Pat, I . . . didn't come with anything," Morgan said in a voice thick with desire.

Her mind was a pleasant euphoric fog. Of course it mattered. And then she remembered. She left Morgan and went to a bureau. Opening it she looked through the folded items. When she turned around she held out her hand to him.

"I have these," she said quietly.

Morgan stared at the glittery little packages. He took one from her palm and looked at her. She felt the need to say something.

"I don't want you to think . . ."

Morgan took her hand and kissed it. He pulled her closer. "Come here . . ."

She boldly watched as he prepared himself, but he kept touching her so the moment wouldn't be lost in a necessary detail.

Morgan sat on the side of the bed with Patricia standing between his knees. He kissed her breasts finding that her nipples were large and puckered. She massaged his shoulders and neck, ran her fingertips through his scalp. Morgan's hands stroked up the back of her legs to her buttocks.

Slowly he leaned back until he lay flat. He pulled Patricia on top of him. And as he kissed her, the sensual tension rose quickly in his body and made his breathing labored. He rhythmically massaged her buttocks, his erection insinuating itself forcefully between their bodies, pulsating and urgent. Patricia felt herself ready and undulated her hips against Morgan. Morgan groaned, lifted her hips slightly, pressing her against his rigid shaft. He shifted her to guide his organ into her, at the same time kissing her. He possessed Patricia from one end to the other. There was a moment of awkward heaving together until they found the rhythm and settled into it. But the tension began to build very quickly. Morgan held them coupled together and rolled, reversing their positions. It couldn't last long. Anticipation as well as foreplay had done its job. The sounds in the room were of satisfaction, bliss, joy — pleasure given and received.

He rode her body carefully, thrusting and retreating, nearly mindless with the exquisite friction that held him captive. Patricia clung to him and a mewling sound whispered through her parted lips. Embarrassed, Patricia gnawed her lips to keep silent. But Morgan would have none of that. He wanted to hear her. He wanted to see her response as they approached satisfaction. He wanted to feel every nuance of her body as it moved against his, unrestrained, open to him, as eager and needy as he was. He needed to know that he was responsible. Morgan chuckled deeply and kissed her, using the force of his tongue to ease her lips open until, against her will, the little sounds came forth once more.

"That's it . . ." he encouraged in a growl. He didn't want her to hold a thing back.

She grabbed at his back, her hands moving restlessly along his spine. She arched her back, affording Morgan the perfect position to be able to suck at her breast. "Ohhhhhoo . . ." she let out in a wrenching moan. Morgan thrust slowly again, finally releasing in Patricia the sharp agonizing little spasms of joy.

Morgan held her tightly as Patricia surrendered. He waited until her body muscles clenched into climax and pulsated her pleasure around him. Then he let himself go, driving with long, hard strokes until he, too, collapsed against her. They were both limp and sated.

Patricia tried to say Morgan's name. She gave up and simply sighed and stroked his back. She felt soft and sensitive under her belly and between her thighs. The explosion that had taken place in her loins had sent messages to the tips of her breasts, which Morgan was now gently caressing with his thumb. She couldn't even open her eyes. He was still sheathed within her. His hands held her face as he lifted his head to kiss her softly.

Patricia had to give Morgan credit for such strength of purpose. She couldn't move if her life depended on it. Luckily she didn't have to find out. She heard Morgan chuckle in a sound that spoke only of contentment with what had happened between them. They dozed for a while and then lay holding each other, gently exploring with their hands in the dark. She let her fingers roam over his chest. She followed the narrow groove the hair line made that ran to Morgan's navel.

"Morgan?" Patricia mumbled lazily against his skin. She could tell by his breathing that he wasn't immune to what her hand was doing.

"Hummmmm?"

The fingers trailed lower and she felt him surge and grow hard against her touch. The muscles in his groin contracted as her hand closed delicately around him. Patricia stroked the skin.

"Could we . . ."

His body stiffened completely. Morgan lifted himself to settle once more between Patricia's legs. He was both amused and pleased.

"I was right," he whispered. He pulled at her lips with his own.

"About what?" She put her arms around his neck.

He drew her legs up, searching for and quickly finding his true destination. He started to tell her that he'd always thought she was passionate. But this was not the time for analysis. "Let me show you . . ."

When Patricia opened her eyes again it was almost three-thirty in the morning. She lay curled against Morgan's side, using his biceps as a pillow. She sighed. "Are you awake?" she asked in a lazy croak.

"Mmmmmmm." Morgan turned his head on the pillow enough to be able to plant a kiss on her forehead.

"Are you going to stay the night?" she asked.

"There's not much left to the night. Why? Do you want me to go?" He wasn't shocked, just curious.

It took Patricia a long time to answer. "I look terrible in the mornings," she whispered.

Morgan tightened his arm around her and drew her head to rest on his chest. "Do you also snore?" he teased.

"I don't know. But I'm not sure I want you to find out."

Morgan laughed. "It's not going to matter. Sooner or later you're going to find out the worst about me. I hog the covers. I sleep all over the bed. And I look like a criminal before I shave. I really don't like to shave."

"I guess I'm just used to having my bed to myself."

"But you know it's going to change now."

"Will it?" she asked, her sense of independence immediately threatened. She forced herself up onto an elbow and tried to gaze into Morgan's face. "We made love together. That doesn't mean that . . ."

Morgan gently clamped a hand over her mouth to stop her. "I haven't asked for anything."

She blinked at him and pulled his hand away. "I didn't mean that. I just thought that . . ."

"Don't think," he advised in under-standing. "That's what you once told me. That's not what tonight was all about, Pat." He kissed her briefly and threw the covers aside, swinging his legs out of the warm bed.

"What are you doing?" she asked, con-fused.

"Reassuring you," he said, standing up and searching for his shorts.

Patricia bounded up in the bed, reaching for his hand. "Morgan, don't . . ."

He stopped, gazed at her, sat on the bed again. "You don't seem to be sure about what you want."

"Of course I'm not sure. I'm . . . nervous. I feel different."

Morgan got back under the covers and gathered Patricia once more in his arms. "That's fine. So do I. I also feel pretty good, Pat. And very tired."

She settled down. "Morgan?"

"Change your mind again?"

She didn't answer right away.

"It was . . . wonderful," she confessed almost shyly.

He said nothing either . . . right away. Morgan turned on his side to face her, their heads close together on the pillow.

He touched her mouth with his fingertips, recalling vividly the taste of her,
the darting playfulness of her tongue.
He replaced his fingers with a kiss. "I
was thinking the same thing. And I
don't give a damn if you snore."

Chapter Thirteen

The sun felt warm, like early summer. Against her cheeks and forehead the heat tingled, fooling Patricia into thinking it was actually hot, until she opened her eyes and saw snow on the mountains.

The ski lift was doing a brisk business. It stretched long and steep along the slope and through the pine trees, passing brightly dressed skiers who glided recklessly down the snow-covered ground for the sheer thrill of speed. Patricia squinted through her sunglasses into the distance at the double diamond run called Big Dipper. She could not see the turquoise jacket that would identify Morgan, but she knew that he was somewhere either on the mountain or on the lift.

Patricia grinned to herself as she took a drink of the hot apple cider with cinnamon. She kept her focus on the minute figures until she finally spotted Morgan zigzagging his way with ease and expertise down the slope. She couldn't believe Morgan's energy, his vitality, and his sense of adventure. This side of him had all come as a complete surprise to her.

They'd spent two days together after his holiday party. And then he'd flown to the West Coast to visit with his mother. Patricia had used the time working herself up into a state of total anxiety. She missed him. Everything between them was ruined. She couldn't concentrate on her work. There was no turning back from what they'd begun. She didn't know where it was headed. Doomed, probably. He'd made her feel happy . . . And yet a premonition of disaster infiltrated her waking hours.

When Morgan returned from California he suggested they go skiing. Patricia tried to convince him that she had never been on skis in her life. The confession had been a mistake. Teaching her to ski became his weekend project.

It wasn't a very cold day in the Poconos. Morgan had decided they could ski in jeans. They rented equipment for

Patricia and Morgan had loaned her one of Kent's lightweight ski jackets. It was bright yellow with a red stripe down each sleeve. Patricia had accepted the jacket with the comment that at least the ski patrol could easily find her body when she rolled off the mountain. Morgan had laughed but assured her he wasn't going to let anything terrible happen to her. She believed him, and nothing had.

Morgan had painstakingly led her through the rudiments on the bunny slopes, where all the other occupants were skiers under five feet tall. After an hour Patricia made the mistake of saying it seemed so easy. Morgan decided she was ready for the intermediate slopes. He'd taken her on the ski lift, and getting off, Patricia promptly fell. She fell a half-dozen more times trying to get down the mountain. Her jeans began to get wet. They made it down in just under an hour.

"Let's do it again," Morgan encouraged her. "Don't forget to plow. When you feel you're going too fast, you bail out by falling over. That's not the way to do it."

"Works for me," Patricia responded flippantly. "It's a lot safer than going into a tree at twenty miles an hour."

Patricia had never heard Morgan laugh so much as when he watched her progress on the skis. After the third run she fell only once, and she blamed that on Morgan for distracting her. She had begun a mantra in her head. Left ankle in to turn right, right ankle in to go left; plow to slow down. But in a bold attempt to go straight her skis didn't spread enough in the rear for control. She picked up speed.

"Plow! Plow! Don't you dare fall down!" Morgan yelled behind her.

Patricia keeled over on her side into the snow.

She lay still. She could hear Morgan skiing swiftly to catch up to her. He swished to a stop and quickly released his skis to kneel next to her.

"Pat?"

She could hear the anxiety in his tone. She couldn't respond. Morgan grabbed her arms and pulled her into a sitting position. When he looked into her face he found it was contorted in silent laughter.

"I'm . . . I'm sorry," she breathed weakly, laughter overtaking her.

"I thought you were hurt. I just lost

three years off my life," Morgan said dryly. He helped her stand up, brushed the snow from her clothes, and put his skis back on. He glanced at her. She was wiping laugh tears from her face. "What's so funny?"

Patricia felt like an idiot. What, indeed, was so funny? She looked at Morgan and considered the concern still on his face. She thought of how tender he could be, how strong. She thought of the bold erotic intensity he brought to their lovemaking. She considered the long quiet talks in the dark, Morgan's acceptance of everything about her.

"Nothing's funny," she finally answered. "I was just thinking that I'm having such a good time."

Patricia closed her eyes at the recollection, and took off the dark glasses. She tilted her face up toward the sun. She was risking skin cancer for her current happiness. She laughed silently at the thought. For the moment she'd take the trade-off.

A shadow blocked the sun.

"I hope that smile means you're thinking about me," Morgan said.

Patricia opened her eyes and found

him bending over her. He pecked a kiss on her lips without waiting for an answer and sat down.

"How was it?"

"I had a couple of good runs, but it was pretty crowded up there. Besides, I missed you."

"It's going to be years before I'm ready for that hill."

Morgan grinned at her and linked his fingers with hers. "By the end of the season I'll have you doing the advanced runs."

Patricia grinned back. "As my students would say, not in this lifetime."

He laughed. He opened his jacket and propped his feet with their massive ski boots onto the extra chair. He took her mug of cider and drank from it. "You are a lot of fun, Patricia."

She was genuinely surprised. "Really? No one's ever told me I was fun before," she said dryly.

He winked at her. "You've been hanging out with the wrong crowd."

"Probably . . ."

Then she stared at him for a long time. His dark glasses had mirrors on the front. They made him look intimidating and powerful. A space-age hero.

A new kind of black man whose ego was intact, and who was sensitive and kind. She wondered where it all came from. What had first been in its place before Morgan became a man who was sure of himself?

"How did you meet Melissa?" Patricia asked quietly. She never took her eyes from Morgan's face, although his expression and his reaction was partially hidden by the reflective lenses. He was very still for a moment, not saying anything. She wondered if he was looking at her. Was he angry, and trying to think of a way to tell her that he didn't want to talk about it?

Morgan took another swallow from the mug and gave it back to her. He slowly took off the glasses and squinted thoughtfully at her. "Pat, you don't remind me of Melissa. I don't have those kinds of fantasies."

"What kind of fantasies do you have?" she asked.

His smile was ironic. "That you'll trust me to know the difference between a fantasy and the real thing. But that's not what you asked, is it?"

She shook her head.

The muscles in his jaw flexed. "I met

her while I was going to Michigan State. Through my college roommate. Indirectly, that is. He didn't actually know her."

"Why did you choose Michigan to go to school?"

"I didn't. It was the only college that offered me a scholarship. Michigan . . ." He shook his head in wonder. "It was a far cry from L.A. I was lost there my first year. Almost gave up.

"People in Michigan ski. I didn't. My roommate, Dwayne, knew somebody who knew somebody who'd let a bunch of us stay at a ski lodge in Denver in exchange for working the weekend around the resort. I didn't want to go."

"Ego?"

He nodded ruefully. "That's right. But they kept jazzing me and then I felt I had to prove myself. Show them I could do anything."

"Men . . ." Patricia murmured.

"Hey, I didn't make up the rules. I just learned how to survive them. One thing I wouldn't do was take the beginner's lesson. There were all these little kids showing me up. I just couldn't do it. So I snuck off and tried it on my own. Spent most of the day on my butt."

"Sounds familiar," she said with a grin.

"Then this . . . white girl showed up. I was flat on my back in the snow trying to get up on those damned skis. I was mad as hell, and ready to wrap them around Dwayne's neck. She looked at me with this really friendly smile and asked if I was in trouble. When I said no, she called me a liar. And offered to give me some pointers. That's it. That's how we met. That was the beginning."

Patricia smiled briefly. She was taken off guard by the warmth with which Morgan had related the history. It seemed evident to her that no matter how things had ended up for Morgan and his wife, the beginning had been romantic. And genuine.

"She promised not to tell my friends. She was patient and knew what she was doing. She didn't laugh at me . . . and she wasn't afraid of me. But I was terrified of her. I wasn't looking for an adventure. I wasn't looking to buck the system or show I could have a white woman. It was just Melissa. She was very smart, very nice, very together. But I used to wish she wasn't white." He shrugged, looked pensive. "After a while it didn't matter. It was still very hard. Nobody liked it. I mean . . . I got warned, threatened, and jumped once . . ."

"Oh, my God . . ."

"Her father went ballistic. We never had a moment's peace. We never had a chance."

"I'm sorry," Patricia said awkwardly.

"Why?" he questioned. "Because you think it was a mistake, too. Or because it didn't work out."

"Because it hurt so much," Patricia said with feeling. Morgan reached for her hand and held it.

"I don't regret it, Pat," Morgan said firmly. "But the timing was all wrong."

She shook her head. "Not completely. You have Kent." She looked at their joined hands, reminding her of piano keys and zebras, ying and yang. "And then I came along . . ." she glanced at him cautiously.

He shrugged. "It was confusing, yeah. But not your problem. You're more understanding than most women I've met."

She blushed. "Have there been so many?"

Morgan shook his head. "A few. I'm quitting while I'm ahead," he said cryptically. He stood up, pulling her to her feet.

She didn't know exactly what Morgan meant, but in a way was sorry she'd ever asked about Melissa. Morgan's story raised more questions than it answered, although they had little to do with Melissa. Like what were his expectations of her? For them? "Do you want to go up again? I'm very happy just sitting in the sun."

Morgan was already shaking his head. "No. I've had it for today." He arched a brow and looked her over. "Are you dried out yet?"

"Almost."

Morgan's gaze became soft and seductive. He pulled her into a loose embrace and covertly ran his hands over her limbs. "I was thinking we ought to get you home and out of those things."

"Do you?" she smiled in return.

"I don't want you to catch a chill."

"You're so thoughtful . . ."

"And I'm getting hungry." He grinned seductively.

"What do you have in mind?"

"What do you think?"

Patricia smiled up into his handsome face, trying to believe that Morgan hadn't confused her with anyone else. Hoping that her trust of his present motives and his history with Melissa wasn't going to come back to haunt them.

"How long will it take to get back home?"

Patricia fell asleep on the two-hour drive back to New York. Morgan didn't mind. There was something very peaceful about being with her, and something comforting in the way she now relaxed and let herself go. Whenever Morgan thought of the night of his party and everything that had happened since, it seemed like their entire lives had been reinvented. It was as if in a heartbeat they had moved from a relationship that was uncertain to one that was familiar. In just under a week they had gone from cautious flirtation to a full-blown affair, to a level of intimacy and companionship that was a surprise. Not because it had happened, but because it felt so good.

Morgan smiled to himself, thinking for the moment of when they made love. His pleasure was intense. Sex didn't just happen and then they were done.

There was all the time afterward when they managed to stay connected. It meant more, had more depth . . . was more than satisfying.

Morgan glanced at Patricia briefly. She was a quiet, still sleeper. Her hands lay limp in her lap. As a matter of fact, he realized, everything about Patricia was quiet. She was a private person, self-protective. But not afraid to speak her mind when there was a real need. To encourage him. To guide his son.

The Patricia he knew he liked very much. But he recalled the question she'd asked about Melissa. It was more than polite curiosity. Morgan sighed in frustration. Yeah, he had been accused before about having a thing for white women. When he was with Melissa it was thrown at him all the time, especially by the black students at school. It had gotten very nasty. Maybe he was as fascinated as he was scared of her at first. Maybe he was just surprised that Melissa hadn't bought into the media myths about black men and had just dealt with him as a man. Wasn't that all Patricia had asked of him? Morgan thought he was trying to be honest. And he didn't want to hurt her but . . . was he getting her confused with his ex-wife?

Patricia was more passionate, more expressive than he would have imagined, but in many ways she was still surprisingly inexperienced. Yet, as giving and as caring — as a friend and lover — as Patricia was, Morgan could feel that she had not given herself totally to him. He wondered what was holding her back. Was there someone from her past still important to her? Or was he himself less so?

Patricia sighed and her body twisted to a new position. Her eyes fluttered open and she blinked at Morgan. She shook her head, embarrassed.

"Did I fall asleep? I'm sorry."

He grinned. "I didn't mind. You got a real workout on those skis and you're probably beat."

"Oh . . . I am," she murmured, stretching her shoulders. "Where are we?"

"Just approaching the Verrazano Bridge. You'll be home in half an hour. I was going to suggest going out for dinner, but I think we'll call it a day," he said, glancing thoughtfully at her tired expression. "I just want to drop off my ski gear first . . ."

She looked at him. "You don't have to."

"What? Drop off my things?"

"No. Take me home." A slow smile transformed his profile and he reached to take hold of her hand. "Tomorrow is soon enough."

Morgan suddenly sat forward, reaching for the telephone. He punched Patricia's number; she answered on the fourth ring.

"Hello?"

"You sound distracted. Did I interrupt something?"

"Hi," she said again. Brighter this time. "I've been reading Piaget all evening."

"Interesting plot? Any hot scenes?" He heard her laugh lightly. "Is this for your paper?"

"Yes," she sighed. "I have to prove I know more about this subject than my dissertation committee. It's a lot of work."

"So what will you do with a doctorate besides frame it for your wall?"

"Do some clinic work. It will help my certification with the state licensing board. Add weight to my credibility."

"I'll be glad to give expert testimony as to your credibility, Patricia."

She laughed. "I'll include that in my reference notes."

"You've spent almost your entire Christmas break working. When are you coming out to play again?" Morgan teased, trying to keep his tone light and understanding.

"Soon." She paused. "Morgan, why don't you come here. I'll cook something."

Morgan relaxed back in his chair. His mouth was fixed now with a pleased smile. "That sounds nice."

"This is going to be very simple," she warned.

"As long as it's not peanut butter and jelly."

On the way Morgan stopped for wine. He remembered she liked Chardonnay. Patricia had the door open before Morgan had even gotten off the elevator. There was something about the gesture of her standing in the door, her hair bright and shiny under the hall light, that made Morgan feel like he was being welcomed home. He removed Patricia's glasses, kissed her briefly, and held up his package.

"Bribery," she scoffed, nonetheless accepting the kiss and the wine.

"Gifts," Morgan corrected, closing the door behind him.

He followed slowly behind Patricia, watching as she walked barefoot to the kitchen. Her lithe slender legs were covered in black leggings, worn with a bright yellow tunic sweater that came past her hips. A tape played quietly from the living room. She poured a glass of red wine for him and began preparations for dinner.

When Morgan asked if he could help, Patricia was surprised but delighted. She set him to slicing mushrooms and making the salad. He pulled out the cuff links and rolled up his shirtsleeves. When she playfully tucked a clean dish towel around his waist to protect his suit pants, Morgan didn't object. It occurred to Patricia that Morgan had the most intact and healthy self-image of any man she'd ever known, black or white.

They ate in the living room at the coffee table, sitting cross-legged on the rug. For a while the conversation was desultory and Patricia fielded Morgan's questions about her doctorate program.

But Morgan sensed a certain evasiveness in Patricia's answers, as if what she was doing held no significance, or was a matter of course. He could hear no pride over her own accomplishment. For a while Morgan wondered if he should probe deeper, ask more questions, when Patricia mentioned the possibility of setting up her own private practice to work with adolescents. She talked of the seriously troubled kids at school who could use the intervention, but she also assured Morgan that Kent wasn't a candidate.

He told Patricia of Mr. Villar's high praise of her and how helpful she'd been with his daughter.

"Gabriella didn't really need any help. Just a little time and some nudging."

"That's what you said about Kent. You were right."

"He and Gabriella have a lot in common. She kind of looks up to him. I'm not sure Kent's really comfortable with that."

"Why wouldn't he be?"

Patricia frowned thoughtfully and hesitated. She shook her head. "I'm not really sure. I have to keep watching and see what happens next between them."

Morgan finished eating and picked up his wineglass. He looked at her. "Is he still friendly toward you?" he asked softly.

Patricia knew what he meant. "I think so. I'm doing my best not to let the relationship go beyond what it is without . . ."

"Without embarrassing Kent," Morgan supplied. She nodded. Morgan reached for her hand. "He'll be okay. You said so."

"He asked me if I had a boyfriend," she said, staring at Morgan.

"What did you tell him?"

Patricia looked at him, her eyes large and considering. "I told him that was a personal question."

Morgan stared back. "But did you answer it?"

"I said, there was someone . . ."

He didn't even blink. He didn't want to risk even a second of possibly misunderstanding her. He wrapped his hand around her fingers. "Anyone I know?"

"You should."

Morgan slowly grinned at her. "So there's no need to ask about the competition?"

Patricia was startled by the question and she did have an instantaneous flashback to another time, another man. But it was irrational to compare Morgan in any way to Drew Connelly. Except that Drew was the only other person who'd had the potential to break her heart. She shrugged lightly as Morgan waited for her response.

"None." Patricia tilted her head. "I guess I gave you a hard time, but I try not to play games. What's happened with you . . . it was so fast."

"Not to me it wasn't," he murmured.

"Maybe because you haven't looked at how much there is to lose. Anyway, here we are. Without Kent between us. I'm hoping Kent likes Gabriella Villar more than he's willing to admit. He'll soon forget his feelings for me."

"Maybe not. Kent thinks a lot of you."

She didn't want to think at all about what she was to Morgan. Patricia had not forgotten the stunning woman from the Christmas party in her raspberry suit. Beverly. She was more Morgan's type. She had more . . . of everything.

"He needs to focus on someone else. He'll be dating soon."

Morgan looked stricken. "He's too young yet. I didn't start taking out girls until . . ."

"But when did you have your first sexual experience?" Patricia gently interrupted.

Morgan groaned. "Jesus . . ." he whispered. He rubbed the back of his neck. "I was pretty young, but . . ."

"Kent's age? Younger? Nothing's changed, except that now what he doesn't know could hurt him. Have you had a talk with him about contraceptives?"

Morgan looked very uncomfortable.

Patricia was not surprised and she tried tactfully to help him. "I can talk to Kent about a lot of things, Morgan, but not about sex."

Morgan frowned at her. "Why is this coming up now?"

"You and I together made me think of it. Kent's feelings for me tell me if he hasn't had any experience yet, he's on the brink. He's not so much a boy anymore. His sexual awareness is part of his growing up . . ."

"I don't think I want to talk about this," he scowled. "I want to talk about you and me."

"We are. When does he return from Colorado?"

"Next Sunday. It won't make any difference between us."

"It will. We should have thought . . ."

"We did what was right and I'm not sorry. It's been good, Pat."

Patricia was thrilled to hear him say so, but she still felt cautious. She looked sharply at Morgan. "Kent doesn't have to know about us, Morgan."

He frowned. "We're not doing anything wrong."

"That's not the point. If he finds out he may not like it."

"He's old enough to understand that adults have intimate relationships . . ."

"We're not just any adults," Patricia insisted. "You're his father. I'm his counselor."

Morgan didn't look happy, but he didn't argue. "Does that mean you won't see me?"

Patricia's look of determination and good sense quickly dissolved into confusion. "I don't know. I don't see how." She appealed to him. "Morgan, I'm just afraid that . . ."

Morgan leaned forward to cup the back of her head and pull Patricia to him. He kissed her, removing the doubts and questions from her lips with gentle manipulation and caresses. "As long as we can keep seeing each other we can be careful. It will work out." Morgan stroked her cheek. "I thought we were going to keep Kent out of the middle of our relationship."

She shook her head. "I never said that. I'm still not convinced it's even possible."

"Let's not try to find an answer tonight." Morgan brushed his lips across hers again. "I have a better idea."

But Patricia felt uncomfortable with the compromise she'd made so that she and Morgan could be together. She sighed and pulled away from his seductive touch and reasoning. "I . . . I want to finish my reading. Just this chapter."

Morgan didn't argue. He helped clean up their dinner things, then he returned to slouch on the sofa with a newspaper, letting the cozy warmth of being with Patricia in her apartment relax him. He stayed away from any comparisons with the past, but Beverly came to mind. There was the uncomfortable thought that their relationship still hung out there, unresolved and with no closure. Morgan knew his ardor for Beverly had cooled off even before he seriously turned his thoughts to Patricia. The whole thing with Patricia felt different from anything he'd known before. Melissa had been an earnest attempt to love someone who *was* different. The feelings had been real in a surreal environment. It had been the wrong time and the wrong place. It had been painful.

Morgan let his attention drift from the newspaper in his hand to Patricia, who sat in a chair, her legs curled to the side. She read from her text quietly, occasionally making a note. The whole scenario struck Morgan as unique. This was not a momentary thing. Hit-and-run. He felt like taking his time.

There had been brief attractions, sexual dalliances. Long-term casual dating, short-term affairs. Until now, his heart had stayed out of it all.

Patricia frowned as she tried to concentrate on her reading. She should have kept to her resolve with Morgan about safeguarding their relationship because of Kent. She had known pretty much the moment Morgan's interest in her had gone beyond friendship and their mutual concern for his son. She wasn't so sure when the change had come in herself. But it *had* happened. And she couldn't be as sanguine as Morgan.

It was suddenly quiet in the room. When she finally glanced up at Morgan his head was resting against the back of the sofa and his eyes were closed. She thought he might be asleep. And in that unguarded moment Patricia felt as if anything was possible with Morgan Baxter. This was a man who was possible to believe in.

"Patricia?" Morgan called out in a drowsy voice, as if sensing her gaze on him.

Patricia got up from her chair. She walked to the back of the sofa and gently began to massage his shoulders. Morgan reached to cover her hands with his own.

"Do you want to stay?" she asked softly, taking the initiative.

"Can I?" he asked in return.

Patricia smiled. "Yes." It pleased her that he hadn't taken it for granted.

Morgan stood up and came around the sofa to meet her. She came readily into his embrace. His lips were gentle and slow, his tongue caressing. The kiss was peaceful, warm. The heat built very slowly. There was no rush. Then they let some space develop between them as they gazed at one another. Nothing else really mattered just then. Because the present always superseded the past.

Patricia silently took Morgan's hand and led the way to the bedroom.

Morgan's hand glided slowly along her hip and waist. Patricia's skin was smooth and soft. There was something very sensual about touching her as she slept. He had the freedom to enjoy her without it being cloaked in a desire for sexual gratification. He just enjoyed being with her this intimately. He rested his hand for a second before moving on to a breast. He slid his hand beneath it and let her breast fill his palm. The nipple was soft and puckered. Patricia moaned quietly and turned over, burrowing her back into his chest and stomach, but she didn't awaken.

Morgan smiled as he remembered the way she'd faced off with him in his office, that very first time. Who would have thought that moment would come to this?

And just what was *this?*

He tried to think of a concrete answer. It kept evading Morgan, slipping from his tongue and into the back recesses of his mind . . . because he was unsure. It was more than a momentary thing, *this* thing between him and Patricia.

He'd already awakened her once in the night because he just needed her. Now he felt he could wait until Patricia was up. Morgan carefully pushed aside her hair and touched his lips to the side of Patricia's neck. Then he got out of bed.

In the bathroom Morgan showered leisurely. Sticking his head under the shower spray, he let the force of the hot water slosh off the soap, wash away sleep, and stimulate him into alertness. The steam cocooned him as he stepped from the stall. He was briskly drying his hair, feeling cleansed and happy. He wished he could have a few more days with Patricia, but knew she needed this time to work on her paper, and he had one quick trip to make to Toronto for a meeting. He was aware that she was right and that their time and opportunities together would be limited once Kent returned from his holiday with his mother. Morgan heard the bathroom door open.

"Morning," he murmured.

Patricia stumbled in and plowed right into him. Morgan looked up quickly through the folds of the towel.

"Where's the sink?" Patricia mumbled.

"What's the matter?" She had her eyes squeezed closed, and she was groping blindly with her hands. Her hair was wild, hiding much of her face. There was suddenly something primal about seeing her this way, an element of her helplessness that sparked in Morgan an undefined need to protect. Patricia had always been so much in control of herself, always totally independent. Even when they were together. To catch her so totally off guard gave Morgan a window of opportunity that he wanted to take.

The steam in the bathroom was moistening Patricia's skin, releasing the sleep-sweetened scent of her skin. Morgan felt himself getting aroused. He took hold of her arm.

"What's the matter? Are you crying?"

"I've got something . . . in my eye. It hurts."

"Let me see." Morgan tilted her head back. He dropped the towel as he gently tried to get Patricia to open the afflicted eye. It was watery and red. "I think it's an eyelash. No . . . it's two. Just hang on."

They were both naked. For Morgan it suddenly seemed intensely erotic. The heat of the bathroom, the morning scent of Patricia. He woke up wanting to make love to her. Now his desire escalated as Patricia stood before him, helpless.

Patricia tried to stand still, but it was obvious she was uncomfortable and in pain and impatient with his attempts. There was the sound of stress in her breathing, but Morgan was only aware of the pert bouncing of her breasts.

"I'll do it," Patricia said impatiently, trying to pull her head away.

Morgan wouldn't let her move. "Keep still," he ordered firmly.

She did. It was a command Patricia found she couldn't refuse. Beyond the insistence was gentle concern. Such a little thing. Morgan was going to make it better. Her hands braced on his damp chest, the fingers restless. His skin was taut and firm, the knotty sprinkle of hair softened by the shower water. The bathroom smelled of soap and steam, and of Morgan. Patricia felt stifling hot. So did Morgan.

He used a tissue to gently dab the two lashes from her eye. When Patricia let herself relax, the lower parts of their bodies touched. Morgan pushed her hair back from her face, wiped the tears of the irritation away with his thumbs.

"Better?" he asked with concern.

Patricia blinked and stared at him. His hair was damp and glistening. Steam and moisture left a sheen to his chest and arms, emphasizing bone, muscles, and sinew. Morgan hadn't shaved yet, but Patricia felt an incredible awareness of Morgan that simply had to do with him being a man. She felt a quick rise of desire so strong she caught her breath sharply.

Morgan's concern vanished, and he suddenly concentrated on the look in her wide gray eyes. A trickle of moisture ran down Patricia's neck into the hollow of her throat. The pulse there was rapid.

Patricia glanced down. Morgan was completely erect. Her gaze met his again. She could hardly breathe and her lips parted for air. Morgan slowly crushed his mouth to hers. The kiss was hungry, pushing them quickly over the edge of a precipice neither had been aware they stood on the edge of. Morgan's tongue plunged into her mouth, exploring. The reaction was mutual, and overwhelming.

His hands tangled in Patricia's hair and their bodies touched and moved together in damp friction. His hands slid to her buttocks, cupping beneath them to pull her against his hardened penis. Patricia moaned as he lifted her. Morgan knew he didn't have time to move anywhere else. He sat Patricia on the counter. Her hip pushed a tissue box into the sink. His hand toppled a lotion dispenser. Morgan pulled her hips to the edge of the counter and forced her knees to part.

Patricia was mindless, delirious, holding on to Morgan tightly, afraid that if she let go she'd fall foolishly to the floor. She felt him search for and find her, pushing quickly into her. Patricia shuddered as Morgan thrust against her. She could say or utter nothing; he didn't let her mouth go.

She didn't know what was happening except she felt like she was spiraling out of control. She couldn't stop, she didn't want Morgan to. Patricia let Morgan rock them together, generating an instant pleasure that was so raw she clung even tighter to him, wanting him deeper. Morgan guided her to a climax that stripped all the air from her lungs, made her heart thunder, made her thighs quiver. Patricia buried her face in his neck trying to catch her breath, grateful to have him to lean upon. Rivulets of water ran between her breasts, down her spine. "My . . . God . . ." she moaned. Even her hair was damp now.

"All right. It's . . . all right," Morgan crooned, feeling her trembling and hearing her rushed breathing. He held her tight and continued to thrust into her soft body.

Morgan grunted and reached his own peak, clenching his teeth as his satisfaction soared, hovered for exquisite moments, and twisted back to ground level. He held her still, with her thighs locked around him. Steam held the scent of both of them. She moaned again and began to tremble.

He kissed her neck. "Am I hurting

you?" Morgan asked in a husky voice slumberous with repletion. He squeezed her bottom with his hands, a gentle caress.

Patricia couldn't find her voice. She swallowed and shook her head against him. But a sudden bewildering wave of emotion came over her. *Am I hurting you . . .*

A shock of painful memories seemed to split her chest, tear at her heart. In that instant Patricia felt totally vulnerable and she couldn't protect herself. But there was the overwhelming gratefulness of not having to. Morgan was going to catch her, break the fall. And set her down safely.

Patricia quietly began to cry.

Chapter Fourteen

When Patricia heard the intercom she didn't even bother asking who it was. She automatically assumed it was Morgan and rushed to push the release button for the downstairs door. He hadn't made any promises about seeing her tonight. In fact, he'd indicated that the business dinner he'd been invited to could run late. Patricia glanced at her watch. It was only nine o'clock. Had the dinner finished so early, or was it perhaps canceled?

While she waited for the elevator to arrive Patricia was aware that she was ambivalent and in a state of high anxiety over her relationship with Morgan Baxter. She couldn't deny the pleasure she felt now, being with him. She had discovered Morgan's quick sense of humor, playful teasing, and his own grounded self-confidence. But it was precisely those traits that made Patricia so nervous, because she was sure that something so good wouldn't — *couldn't* — last.

Patricia stood at her door ready to open it and thought of that early morning encounter with Morgan in her bathroom. The sensual details were still vivid and even now she could evoke the breathlessness and excitement that made her feel so vulnerable and scared all over again.

That was the word. Scared.

It came to her, in the intense mindless moment of release, that no one else had ever made her feel the way she had with Morgan. It had changed everything about her awareness of herself and of him, and Patricia was terrified that not only did he have the power to make her feel that way, but that she had no power to resist. If he could claim her so completely, then what would be left of herself? She wondered if Morgan himself had any idea how . . . *dangerous* he was?

Patricia heard the footsteps in the hall, but even as she opened her door she frowned. That was not the way Morgan walked. It wasn't him. It was the attractive woman from Morgan's

Christmas party. She felt immediate protective caution, and a curiosity as to how this woman had gotten her address and why she'd even need to. Patricia couldn't speak at first, so stunned, so suspicious was she of this sudden appearance of someone she hardly knew. But all the tension in her stomach warned Patricia to beware.

"Hello," Beverly said comfortably. "Do you remember me? We met at the Christmas party."

"Yes," Patricia said. "Beverly . . ."

"McGraw," she supplied with a smile. She stood on the threshold of the doorway. She gave Patricia a look, raising her brows and tilting her head, as if surprised that Patricia didn't have the good sense to know what to do next. "Can I come in?"

Patricia hesitated, every instinct telling her to make up some excuse not to have anything to do with this woman. But curiosity overrode her warning signals. Without waiting for permission, Beverly stepped into the apartment.

"What do you want?" Patricia stayed by the open door. She didn't want to encourage a long visit.

Beverly quickly glanced around the

hallway and living room, peering around the corner into the kitchen. "Very cute. Neat. Suits you." She faced Patricia again, pleasant and relaxed, her sharp gaze taking in every detail. "I just came to talk. I've been meaning to ever since I saw you at the Christmas party."

Patricia gestured in bewilderment. "I don't see what there is to talk about. We don't know each other."

Beverly stood right in front of her, to gaze into her face with a kind of calm and arrogance that Patricia found fascinating. The woman had nerve.

"Oh, lots of things. You and Morgan. *Me* and Morgan."

The remark had just enough of an edge for Patricia to realize that Beverly McGraw did not intend this to be a friendly chat as if they were potential girlfriends. She made an impatient sound, sucking her teeth. She had attitude as well, when she needed it. "Look, I'm not going to trade confidences with you. I have nothing to say about Morgan Baxter."

Beverly grinned slyly. "I didn't think you would. That's okay. I already know the answers."

"I think you'd better leave," Patricia said quietly. "I don't think you and I have anything to say."

"Why? Because I'm direct? Or because you're afraid of what you'll hear? Or because you've never met anyone like me?"

"Oh, yes. I know your kind," Patricia murmured.

Beverly chortled rudely. "*My* kind? And I *sure* know all about you."

Patricia stiffened and dropped her hand from the doorknob. "All right. Go on and say it."

Beverly's gaze narrowed. "Morgan won't get involved with another white woman."

There was no way Patricia could control the hot flush that quickly burned over her face. "You know I'm not white, *girlfriend*," she said sarcastically.

"Every time he looks at you he's going to think of his ex-wife and what a mistake that was. Morgan's going to remember he already has one kid that's so messed up and doesn't know who he is, he'll never have another half-black baby by someone who looks like you."

Patricia felt rage make her heart thud in her chest. "What does Morgan see when he looks at you? The real thing? A sister who can get down *and* dirty? If you're what Morgan wants, you have nothing to worry about. And you wouldn't be here trying to show how much blacker you are than I am unless you weren't sure."

Beverly's mouth tightened and pouted at Patricia. "Another high yellow bitch who plays it at both ends. I saw you with David Sullivan. I wonder if Morgan knows. I bet you've drunk from *that* cup, too."

Drew came instantly to Patricia's mind and her blush deepened. She could have avoided that whole episode, if she'd listened to her instincts; if she'd used all the information she already had about him from the very beginning. She crossed her arms over her chest, and narrowed her gaze on Beverly. "Is this a test to see who can out bitch who? Morgan knows who and what I am. We've already had that discussion."

"Well, he didn't have to fuck you to find out," Beverly said, her anger and frustration forcing her into common language. She regretted the slip when she saw the arched brow of her adversary.

"He obviously learned all he wanted to know about you . . . and changed his mind," Patricia murmured slyly.

"Bitch . . ." Beverly hissed.

Her nostrils were flaring and her fist was balanced on her hip in a confrontational pose that Patricia had faced more than a few times in her life. "You've already called me that. What's next? *Nigger* bitch? Better be careful or you'll prove yourself wrong about me."

Beverly gained control of herself. "You're only going to last for a fast minute. Morgan's going to drop you so hard you'll have black and blue marks that will show. So don't mess with me. I know enough to make your life miserable very quickly."

"Just say it," Patricia ordered impatiently.

"Okay. It could get back to your school that you're having an affair with the father of one of your students."

Patricia lost count of the number of emotions that swept through her. She experienced a moment of utter defeat.

"And Morgan will figure out soon enough for himself that being seen around with you could ruin his image and his business."

Patricia continued to stare at Beverly McGraw, astounded by the amount of unwarranted bile and vindictiveness spewing forth. Appalled at the no-holds-barred virulence of this woman who was a stranger to her.

"You could be right," she responded calmly, determined now to have the last word. "But one thing you can be sure of. If Morgan has rolled you over, then you no longer have anything he values."

Beverly only stared back, inadvertently ceding the moment to Patricia when she didn't answer. She opened the door and let herself out of the apartment.

Patricia stood in the ensuing silence, every part of her body trembling.

The office seemed to be empty when Kent arrived. He stood for a moment in indecision, wondering if he'd misunderstood his father and the instructions of that morning. Had he been told six o'clock? Was he supposed to meet his father in the lobby and not the office? The clock on the wall over Mrs. Anderson's desk said five forty-five.

"Hello, Kent."

Kent turned to see Mrs. Anderson

approaching. She was in a hurry and didn't stop to talk or ask him questions about school like she sometimes did. She rushed to her desk, searching through the papers and folders.

"Are you looking for your father?"

"Yeah. He told me to meet him. I think I'm a little early."

Mrs. Anderson found what she was looking for, but only nodded in the direction of his father's office. "He's in there. At least, he was a half hour ago. You can go on in. I'm sorry I can't talk right now. I'm faxing a document to London and I don't want to lose the open line."

"Thanks," Kent called out as Mrs. Anderson left him. Kent looked at the closed office door. He was reluctant to open it. He still wasn't exactly sure what kind of business his father ran, but it seemed important. And he still felt like he was intruding whenever he came here. Not that his father didn't want him to come, or made him feel unwelcome.

Kent looked down the corridor, hoping that Mrs. Anderson would come back and open the door for him. But when that didn't happen, he finally took a deep breath and approached his father's office. He turned the knob and pushed the door open slowly. His father was not alone.

Kent heard a woman's voice. He peeked around the door edge. His father was seated at his desk, but Kent couldn't clearly see him because there was a woman standing with her back to the door on his father's side of the desk.

"Morgan, why can't we sit down and discuss this like adults."

"Beverly, there's no point in this. I believe you, all right? But I think we both know it's too late for repairs. Just leave it alone."

Kent watched the woman lean forward and touch his father's face, but Morgan quickly caught her hand.

"Beverly, don't."

"Can't we try to . . ."

"Go on in," Kent heard Mrs. Anderson's voice behind him.

He jumped. The other woman quickly turned around. His father quickly stood up as well.

"I . . . I'm sorry. I didn't . . . I shouldn't have . . ." Kent stumbled over his words.

Mrs. Anderson appeared next to him.

"Oh, Mr. Baxter. Forgive me. I didn't know you were with anyone. I told Kent it was okay to come in. Hello, Miss McGraw."

Beverly merely smiled in response.

"There's no harm done," Morgan said. "Come on in, Kent."

Mrs. Anderson gave Kent a kind smile of encouragement and retreated. Kent reluctantly stepped into the office. Morgan came around the desk to meet him, putting a hand on his son's shoulder.

"Dad, I'm real sorry. I . . ."

"Don't worry about it."

Morgan was smiling. He turned to beckon to the woman behind him. She was a real knockout, Kent thought. She was dressed like pictures you see in magazines of important, rich women. Her smile seemed friendly, but the way she looked at him made Kent blush.

"Kent, this is Beverly McGraw. Beverly is an attorney. She's done legal work for my company. Beverly, this is my son, Kent."

Kent finally realized that his father wasn't angry at him for barging into the office without knocking. The woman held out her hand and Kent took it.

"Hello, Kent. I'm pleased to finally meet you."

Kent couldn't say anything. He had no idea why she'd been wanting to meet him. His father had never even mentioned her before. She was staring at him, making him feel uncomfortable.

"He's a handsome boy, Morgan. He came by it honestly."

Kent didn't know what the woman meant by that, and he could tell that his father was uncomfortable, too. His father looked at him.

"I'm sorry I kept you waiting," Morgan said.

"That's okay. I was early. Want me to wait outside?"

Beverly let go of Kent's hand and sighed. "No need. I'm leaving. My business here is over," she said dryly. "Boys' night out?" she asked Kent.

"We have tickets for a Knicks game."

"The tickets were my Christmas present from Kent," Morgan said, squeezing his son's shoulder.

"And what did Santa bring you?" Beverly asked Kent.

"I'm advancing him some allowance so he can go on a ski trip with his school. They leave next Friday after classes." The phone in Morgan's office began to ring. "I'll be right back. Take care, Beverly. I'm sure we'll see each other around. Good luck."

Kent sat in a chair outside the office door and picked up a business magazine to read while he waited.

"Do you like it here in New York?" Beverly McGraw asked him as his father returned to his office.

"Yeah, sure," Kent said politely, glancing at her very briefly. He was a little afraid to talk to her.

"Morgan has told me a lot about you."

Kent shrugged. "Yeah? I don't remember him telling me about you. Do you work for him?"

Beverly's smile was ironic, and completely lost on the teen. "You could say so," she said dryly. "Actually, your father and I . . . are good friends."

"Oh . . ."

Beverly realized she wasn't going to get information or an impression from the boy and lost interest. "Well, enjoy the game with your father."

"Thanks," Kent said as she headed for the door. He was still thinking about the way she had been talking to his father. The way she was touching him.

She stopped at the exit as David Sullivan came to meet her.

Beverly smiled at David, confronting him squarely.

"You weren't going to say hello?" he asked.

"Hello."

David glanced in the direction of Morgan's office. His kid was in a chair outside the door, waiting. "Trying to protect your ass?" he asked Beverly in a smooth drawl.

Beverly never blinked. Her smile remained fixed. "Don't start with me, David. You haven't won, yet. It's a good thing I never expected very much from you. You certainly haven't disappointed me."

"There speaks a woman shunned." David grinned. "Your plans backfired?"

"I take full responsibilities for my mistakes with Morgan," Beverly said calmly. "I didn't expect things to get complicated because of some other woman. Especially someone like Patricia Gilbert . . ."

Kent looked up briefly when he thought he'd heard Ms. Gilbert's name, but then he went back to his magazine.

David's eyes narrowed. "You better be

511

careful. Your past relationship with Morgan won't protect you if you screw around in his business."

She lifted a shoulder indifferently. "I can take care of myself. Unlike you, I have a fallback plan. The only thing I did wrong was to foolishly let my glands get the upper hand over my good sense and turn to you. It was a moment of weakness, David, so don't think too much about it. You like black women? Was that the turn-on?"

David chuckled softly. "You can't say you didn't enjoy it, when we were together."

Her smile became ironic. "Probably your one true gift, David. At least you're consistent."

"I'm a survivor . . ."

She smirked. "So are rats."

"Morgan will never know about our little toss in the hay, but he certainly is not going to trade off his own best interest for sex with you."

Beverly's eyes were filled with carefully contained rage. "Morgan and I were finished long before you called me, David, trying to find out what else I knew about Sager. Morgan never discussed that deal with me."

"So what was the meeting with him all about?"

She raised her brows. "I thought you weren't worried?"

"I'm not."

"Good. Then when everything *back-fires* in your face you won't be surprised."

Beverly turned and walked out of the office and never looked back.

David watched her leave with a curious speculative glance. He turned and looked at Kent, slowly ambling over to where the boy sat. David smiled, putting on his persuasive good-buddy face. "How's it going, Sport?"

Kent looked up slowly from his reading. "My name is not Sport. It's Kent Baxter," he said clearly.

The horrible feeling was back.

The one where she didn't know who she was. The one where no one else did, either. But Patricia tried to stay balanced. Positive. She tried not to sink into the defensive mode as she dealt with censure directed at her. The misconceptions that were really there, and the ones she only imagined. She was tired of justifying herself.

She kept her gaze focused on the screen, and the larger-than-life colors and movements that filled her vision. But the only voices and sounds Patricia heard were the ones in her head. They had started with the teenagers who'd passed the ticket line as she and Morgan waited to enter the movie theater.

The sudden audience laughter jarred Patricia out of her reverie. She had no idea what was going on in the movie. She felt Morgan grab her hand and tuck it in his.

"Hey. Are you paying attention?"

She smiled at him in the dark.

"I'm going to test you later," he teased. And then he sobered and leaned to whisper to her. "Don't think about it. It was stupid."

But Patricia couldn't help it. She'd been caught unaware because she'd dared to let herself go and not be cautious, because she was with Morgan. Overconfidence always did her in, put her in her place.

"Whatcha doin' with that white bitch?" one of the boys had said scathingly, making faces and gesturing to them.

At first no one standing on the movie

line seemed to pay any attention to the remark. Vulgar comments were uttered all the time on the streets of the city. But an immediate tension had grabbed at Patricia. Déjà vu. She and Morgan had swung their attention to the young men. She knew that they had no other agenda but to cause trouble.

One of the boys took offense at the way she stared at them. "What you lookin' at?"

Morgan squeezed her hand. "Don't answer." He turned to them. "Just back it up, my man. Keep moving."

They continued to shout obscenities. "*You* back the fuck up . . . my broth-*a*." But they finally were gone, trailing insults and curses.

The noise on the screen became irritating. And Patricia was annoyed that Morgan had so quickly put the incident behind him. But why shouldn't he? She pulled her hand free and leaned to whisper. "I'll be right back."

"Going for popcorn?" he asked, taking her coat and hat.

"No. The ladies' room."

Patricia didn't realize how long she'd been gone until she'd exited the facilities and found Morgan waiting patiently outside the door. She stared at him, trying to read his expression, wondering if he could read hers. His handsome face was void of any indication of his reaction to her, or the incident. Except for his eyes, which were curious and intent. Slowly, Morgan held up her coat.

"Let's go," he said smoothly.

Patricia slipped her arms into the sleeves, feeling guilty but grateful. "But the movie. You really wanted to see this."

"I'll catch it on video. I don't think you're much in the mood for car crashes and explosions."

The feeling stuck to her. Made her stiff and cautious. It got in between her and Morgan and prevented them from reaching one another. Patricia couldn't try. Morgan's attempts failed. It was more than the encounter with those boys, which was like a recurring nightmare. It was also that visit from Beverly McGraw. She'd been afraid to mention it to Morgan, uncertain as to his response. And it was a torment to feel that she was running very fast in the same place.

They stopped for dinner on Third Avenue in Manhattan and left most of the meal uneaten. They took a cab back to the Heights. In the quiet town house not a word was spoken as they left their outer clothing on the sofa and climbed the stairs to Morgan's room. For no reason, Patricia felt a wave of shame, anger and guilt as they walked past Kent's empty room. Too much all at once.

In Morgan's bedroom, he drew her into his arms and gently began to kiss her. She wished he'd say something. Reassure her. Make the other thing that had happened disappear. She wanted to get rid of the awful sensation of suspension. His strong hands massaged and caressed her, bringing her against his lean body.

"Relax, Pat . . ." Morgan whispered.

And the gentleness of his lovemaking, his persistence, began to do just that. Patricia's arms came up to circle loosely around his neck. She let him kiss her, wanting it to send the afternoon into oblivion. She wanted Morgan to convince her that he desired her for who she was, the person she'd shown him she was. Patricia let him squeeze her breast, let him rub the material of her blouse as her nipples became stimulated beneath. His mouth played at hers, manipulating with his lips and tongue. Not aggressively, but coaxingly. Gradually, he eased Patricia out of her insecurity, letting his strength wrap around her.

Morgan wasn't really sure what had happened. Except that he too had been thrown back to his past this evening with those boys. Almost seventeen years ago with Melissa. And his need to defend himself warred with the absurdity of the battle. It didn't matter, but then again it did. Morgan felt differently than Patricia. He *knew* how to fight it and not take it seriously. He could no longer be hurt with it. Patricia could.

Morgan began to strip their clothing off, urgently needing to get close to Patricia, hoping that the melding of their flesh and senses would dilute the sting of the verbal attack.

Under the covers the hard play of his body against Patricia's succeeded in assuaging the tension. Her attention turned to other things. The combination of searing kisses and the caressing boldness of Morgan's hands wiped Patricia's mind clean of doubt and filled her with urgency. She wanted Morgan inside her. She needed to feel the full power and possession of his body, as if he could purify her. She wanted the very act of climaxing to somehow give her peace. Wash away the ambiguity that held her prisoner.

Morgan climaxed, his hands under her buttocks, holding Patricia to him as he gently ground his hips against her. But Patricia never shared in the ultimate moment. When Morgan rolled away he put his arm under her head, and curled her into his heaving damp chest. He waited for her to say something, or to fall asleep. She did neither. And he knew she had not gotten relief. He sighed and stroked her face.

"If this was our first time together I'd feel real insecure."

"It's not your fault."

"What happened tonight didn't help. You shouldn't take those guys seriously."

"Those guys. Other people. It never ends."

"What are you talking about?"

"The past, Morgan. We never get very far away from the past."

"Just the past? Or someone in particular?"

"Please . . ." she whispered, turning flat on her back to stare at the ceiling.

"Okay, what are we talking about? *Who* are we talking about?"

Patricia started almost imperceptibly.

"Was there some guy who used you or didn't know how to treat you right . . . or didn't care enough?"

She turned her head to stare at him. "I don't know what you mean."

Morgan sighed patiently. "Pat, it isn't just what happened at the movie. It isn't just me. Sometimes we are great together. Other times I feel like . . . you still don't trust me. Like you're waiting for me to do something that's going to disappoint you. Or hurt you. I know you have to protect yourself against people like those fools today, but you do it with me, too. I feel it sometimes."

He came up on an elbow to gaze into her face, but Patricia sat up, hunching forward to hug her knees into her chest. Morgan tilted forward and kissed the side of her arm. There was no reaction. He plopped back to the pillows.

"Pat, you overreact to things . . . to people. Like tonight with those punks. What do you care what they think? Why did you get so upset because they showed their ignorance? I know it's not the first time it's happened . . ."

"*It's always there,*" Patricia said tightly. "Whether it's those boys, or David Sullivan, or Beverly, or you, Morgan. I *can't* get away from it."

"What do you mean, Beverly? What do you know about her?"

"Nothing."

"Don't tell me that. You found out that we had a thing going on once. That was before your time. You could have figured that out."

"You don't understand . . ."

"Maybe I don't. But unless we can talk about what it is *I've* done, don't put me in the same basket as all the other rotten eggs."

"I don't," she said, throwing the bed linens aside. "But people believe what they want to believe, no matter what they see. Isn't that right?"

"What are you getting at?"

"I'm only half of any relationship. The other half is still someone I need to trust will care about *me.* Instead, all the men I've ever known, black *or* white, have always had their own interest at heart. I'm a novelty. People forget I'm a woman with deep feelings, and a *soul.*"

Morgan made it worse. "Have you been involved with someone white?"

Patricia gasped. "For God's sake, Morgan!"

"I didn't mean it like it sounded . . ."

"What difference does it make? I'm here with you, not some white man. But okay . . . yes, there was once a white guy. His name was Drew and I knew him at Stanford. You probably want the sordid details, but I'll get to the point."

"Patricia . . ." Morgan began, trying to get her attention, trying to salvage something.

"He thought I was white, I let it pass for a while. Oh, 'cuse me. Poor choice of words, isn't it?" She stood naked, her body rigid but her chest heaving in anger. "I'm so *sick* of it! But Drew definitely had biases, so I told him the truth. It could have ended right there if he'd just walked away from me and let me the hell alone. But when he did that he made sure I'd never forget him."

"Pat, stop it . . ."

"You started this," Patricia nearly screamed at him.

"I don't need to know all of this. It was a long time ago."

"There's no such place as a long time ago." She began to search for her clothing among the pile on the floor.

Morgan sat on the side of the bed, unable to reverse the course they were on. "Pat, if you calm down, we can talk this through."

She began getting into her underwear. "This afternoon was difficult. I let those boys push all my buttons. I wasn't even thinking about anything special. Now I wonder what was really going through your mind while we were making love. What woman was in bed with *you?* Someone black . . . or white? Me or Beverly?" She looked openly at Morgan, disappointment clouding her gaze and anger making her eyes bright. "I never asked you if I was replacing Beverly."

Morgan's focus narrowed. "But you thought it? Dammit!" Morgan exploded. He got out of bed and stood naked, confronting Patricia. She stuffed the belt from her skirt into her purse, and looked around for anything else she'd missed.

"This is crazy. We're fighting because you've been hurt and feel insecure. I've been there . . ." Morgan reached for a pair of black sweatpants and pulled them on.

Patricia didn't soften toward him. Irrationally Morgan's attempts to explain only seemed to make it worse, because there was no explanation. It was gut-level stuff. And she'd started on a course she didn't know how to reverse. She only wanted to leave.

She pulled on her sweater. Her hair was disheveled and in her face. She glanced around for the comb that had held it in place earlier. She quickly gave up the search.

"Your question was out of line," she said formally. "Sleeping together doesn't give you the right to make judgments."

Morgan stared angrily at her. "Is that what we've been doing? Sleeping together, just having sex? I hadn't made any judgments. But there are things going on with you that maybe have nothing to do with me. Or is it *us?*"

"Look, everybody has a past. Most won't stand up to much scrutiny."

"That's a bullshit answer, Pat," he said impatiently.

She stopped her frenetic movements and stared at him. Her face was flushed with anger. "Okay. I really wanted to believe it was me you were interested in. But I don't know. I don't *know* what you see when you look at me, Morgan. Maybe you're no different from anyone else."

He felt tired. Morgan shook his head. "If you can't tell the difference, this isn't going to work."

"I don't *know* how to tell the difference," her voice quavered.

"Or maybe you're just afraid to find out. That's not my fault, Pat. I'm here now. You're the only one who can deal with the past. *I* did."

She couldn't answer right away, and Patricia felt much of her indignation already begin to burn itself out. She was exhausted and wired at the same time.

"I know this afternoon got next to you. The thing is, what are *we* going to do about it?"

The answer was suddenly very clear to Patricia. It was clear every time Morgan called her and she heard his deep voice teasing her. It was obvious when they talked about Kent, or whenever they touched. Certainly it was clear when they made love. The problem wasn't Morgan. It wasn't Melissa or Beverly McGraw, or those boys earlier. It *was* her.

She picked up her bag and turned to Morgan. He began walking toward her. She shook her head. "No, don't. I have to go. I can't see you for a while."

He looked like someone had kicked him in the stomach. "That's it? I don't get to have a say?"

"What do you want to say?"

Morgan sighed deeply. He stared down at the carpeted floor, and then finally into her face. "I don't know yet. But I don't think walking out is the answer."

"It's the only one I have for now. I need some time to myself, okay?" Patricia whispered, feeling the tears gather and threatening to close her throat. "I can let myself out." She hurried through the bedroom door.

When she heard Morgan call out to her, it tore at Patricia's heart. But he didn't come after her.

And she didn't stop.

Chapter Fifteen

"Are you all set for the ski trip?" Patricia asked Gabriella. She'd encountered the young girl outside the high school just at the end of a lunch period the first week of the new year.

Gabriella shrugged, but her eyes were bright with excitement that couldn't be disguised. "I think so. I would not be going at all if you had not talked to my father."

"Well, you know how fathers are," Patricia said rhetorically.

"I know how Spanish fathers are," Gabriella said with a roll of her eyes. "In my country a girl from a good family still sometimes travels with a companion. It's such a drag."

Patricia smiled at her use of the local slang. "I told your father that there will be several female chaperones on the trip."

"Yes, but you are not going. My father

trusts you, Miss Gilbert. I wish you would come."

Patricia averted her gaze with a guilty jerk of her head. She thought quickly not only of that incredible day with Morgan teaching her how to ski, but the painful chasm that now existed between them. It was her fault. "Me, too, but something came up at the last moment," she murmured, uncomfortable with the half truth.

Off in the distance Patricia heard the short blips of an emergency vehicle horn as it wound its way through traffic. Both she and Gabriella looked in the direction of the sounds, somewhere behind them.

"Kent Baxter will be going, too."

Patricia could hear the shyness in the statement, the near confession of gladness that Kent would also be on the school trip. "I hear he's a very good skier."

"I am not very good. I am afraid of breaking my leg or something . . ." Gabriella laughed. "Kent said he would show me some tricks so I won't fall down."

Patricia wondered if Kent felt the same admiration for Gabriella that she obviously had developed for him. The one thing she had noticed was that Kent had changed in some ways since the holiday break. He seemed to have grown a full inch or so over Christmas. Now when she stood facing him, he was taller. A certain shy quality he'd had at the beginning of the school year was gone. Patricia still realized that Kent had a strong regard for her that had to be monitored. But she could handle that. Morgan was altogether different. They hadn't seen each other in almost two weeks. That had been her decision, and she refused to admit to regret.

Patricia heard the siren again, louder this time. The emergency vehicle drove past them, its amber and red lights blinking like crystals. She returned her attention to Gabriella, but was only half listening as Gabriella talked about who she was rooming with on the trip, and the new ski outfit her mother had taken her to buy.

The siren suddenly stopped. The school buzzer sounded the next class.

"I better go. I'll miss my class," Gabriella said, waving quickly as she rushed toward the building.

Patricia called after her, "I'll see you before you leave."

Patricia turned the corner of the school and saw the emergency vehicle pull up to the side door. It was the exit nearest the girls' gym. There was a gathering of girls outfitted for class, huddled inside the doorway. Mrs. Forrest was there, trying to push them all back inside so she could close the door. The gym teacher stood at the back of the ambulance talking to a paramedic. The door to the school opened again and Jerome backed out directing, with his hands, the progress of a gurney. Patricia hurried over.

Jerome saw her coming and took a few steps to meet her.

"What is it? Did one of the girls get hurt?"

Jerome shook his head. His face was pale. They turned to watch the paramedics quickly wheel the gurney out of the building, a young girl huddled under the gray blankets.

"It's Kyra," Patricia gasped. She looked to Jerome. "What happened?"

He gestured helplessly. "She's hemorrhaging."

* * *

"I can't believe this. I just don't know what to say."

"You've been saying that for an hour, Patty. Will you please sit down? I'm getting dizzy watching you walk up and down like that."

"How can you just sit there and calmly discuss this when we have a major crisis on our hands?"

Jerome shrugged. He was slouched in his chair with his feet propped on his desk. He was not as comfortable as he looked, Patricia realized. His expression was tight and closed, hard to read. Very unlike the Jerome who was easygoing and irreverent about almost everything.

"We've had girls pregnant here before. There are at least half a dozen girls who had kids last year. The world didn't come to an end. They weren't sent out into the mountains alone. Many of them return to finish school and it's no big deal. Maybe it should be, but that's a different crisis."

Patricia stopped next to his chair and stared down at him. "I take it back. You're not really calm. You know this time it's different."

Jerome stared up at her. "And I

should feel just as guilty as you do?"

"Of what?" she asked, astounded.

Jerome was silent for a time as he stared speculatively at his colleague. "We both know why we're upset. Kyra is only fourteen years old. She gets pregnant and then she tries abortion. She apparently never considered coming to either one of us for help. She probably never said a thing to her mother. Why did she think she was all alone and had to handle it by herself?

"I'm guilty because I knew there was a problem. Kyra was very vulnerable. I tried to talk to her last September but I didn't want to come across like the heavy. Her mother was getting on her case all the time and I was afraid of pushing her too hard."

Patricia watched Jerome as he talked. She began to sense the deeper tension under his explanations that might cause him to blame himself.

"Why are you angry at me?" Patricia asked.

Again for a long moment Jerome stared at her as if he wasn't sure he wanted to answer. Finally he brought his feet to the floor. He sat forward, bracing his elbows on his knees and peering steadily at Patricia.

"Well?" she prompted too sharply.

"You think I'm involved somehow with what happened, don't you?" Jerome's tone was deadly clear and precise.

Patricia couldn't pretend that the idea had not crossed her mind. It was brief and irrational, but it had occurred to her. And she was desperately ashamed that she had not thoroughly considered benefit of doubt. Her entire body shivered. She and Jerome continued to stare at each other, and the longer the silence went on the more the chasm between them widened and hardened.

Jerome lost his patience.

"Say something, dammit!"

Patricia jumped. "I . . . I'm sorry."

"I don't want you to be sorry."

"I know you wouldn't do anything to hurt a student. You wouldn't give them bad advice."

"You mean like suggesting an abortion or arranging for one? I didn't know she was pregnant, Pat."

"When I saw you with her I . . ."

Jerome suddenly uttered an oath and sprang up from his chair. He stormed over to the file cabinet and brought his fist down violently on top of it. The resulting noise sounded like a small explosion. Patricia averted her eyes and waited.

"What kind of a jerk do you think I am, for God's sake? She's fourteen years old and . . ."

"Cut it out, Jerome. You're getting carried away with your indignation. I haven't accused you of anything. Believe me, if I thought you had, I would have said something . . . or had the police in here. That's the truth."

He blinked at her, his eyes looking small and furtive behind his glasses. Jerome sighed and slumped against the side of the cabinet. "Okay, I'm sorry. Maybe we're all overreacting right now." He glanced at Patricia. "We blew it with that kid."

Patricia stared poignantly at him. "I know."

The realization of how her own attention had been diverted since before Christmas grabbed at her and throttled Patricia with an awareness of how she'd failed the young girl.

"But didn't you think my instincts could be trusted? I knew Kyra needed to be treated carefully. And I knew that right now she doesn't seem to trust a woman to tell her what to do." Patricia looked surprised. "You hadn't thought of that, right?"

"That doesn't mean I ignored the fact that she was in crisis," Patricia said defensively.

"Go on, I'm listening."

"I've been watching her, but nothing obvious seemed to be happening besides her grades slipping and her relationship to Eric. You told me —"

"What I told you still goes." Jerome interrupted. "Aren't you going to be surprised to hear that I encouraged her to talk to you. I even told Kyra you'd be happy to give her information on how to protect herself if she got pressured to have sex."

"Jerome . . ." Patricia groaned, briefly closing her eyes in despair.

"Forget her mother for a minute. Forget the damned school policies or community opinion or state law. Why couldn't we just respond directly to what's good for the student?"

"Are we always so sure we know what that is?"

Jerome raised his brows. For the first time all morning he smiled, although it was entirely sardonic. "You mean, you're admitting you don't always have the answers?"

"I never said or implied that I did," Patricia answered stiffly.

"I didn't either. I'm the cynic, remember? But at least I was willing to take my best shot, Patty. I put *my* ass on the line," he spat out, jabbing his finger at her.

Patricia stared at him. Jerome began pacing. She was never going to be able to close the gap between them.

"I called the hospital this morning," Patricia announced quietly. "Yesterday when they brought Kyra in she was almost in shock. They told me that she's going to be okay."

Jerome chuckled silently in disbelief. "Physically, yeah. But that kid is going to need a lot of support and understanding. Much more than we can give her."

Patricia shook her head. Her mind began to unclog and to function. "I disagree. We don't just hand her over to someone else. She's still going to need us, but I'll make an appointment to see her mother. I think there needs to be family counseling as well."

Jerome gave her a wry smile. "You're

a little late, you know."

"She's not lost, yet. Besides, placing blame is pointless. Like you said, Kyra needs support right now."

Jerome sighed and returned to his desk chair to sitdown. "Hell of a way to be a teenager," he muttered. "I thought these were supposed to be the fun years."

Patricia rubbed her arms and pursed her mouth thoughtfully. "Any clues as to what boy might be responsible?"

Jerome shook his head. "I'm not sure. Someone here at Duncan. Probably on the football team. Kyra's a cheerleader this year and she hung around the team a lot."

Patricia looked hard at Jerome. He stared back, waiting. "Eric Patton?" she ventured.

Jerome emphatically shook his head again. "Absolutely not. I told you, Eric gets credit for seeing Kyra was too young and inexperienced for him. He did play on that. If anything I believe he tried to protect her, like she was a little sister or something."

"You know quite a bit about the two of them," Patricia observed.

"Yeah, well. I was paying attention,"

Jerome shot back dryly. Patricia blushed and retreated. "I'm sorry. That was a cheap shot. Anyway, it might not seem like it, but Eric could turn out to be the unsuspecting hero in all this. Sort of."

"Why?"

"He tried to talk her into going to a clinic for the abortion instead of some storefront doctor."

"Are you sure?"

"Last night her mother gave me permission to see Kyra, and she told me herself."

If Patricia had any thought that what had happened to Kyra would stay within the confines of Duncan gossip, it was destroyed with Mrs. Whitacre's nasty confrontation in the principal's office at the end of the day.

Patricia had been fielding questions from curious students all afternoon. She supposed it was hopeless to think Kyra's classmates wouldn't have heard about her being in the hospital, and several of them made it very clear that they knew exactly why. No one was shocked. It was very matter-of-fact talk around the school. Except that no one suggested outright what boy might have been involved. The students quickly developed a case of ignorance and innocence, closing ranks to protect one of their own.

Patricia learned of Mrs. Whitacre's attack on the front office from Peter Connors, a willing carrier of bad news. Jerome ran to the office, heading off the mother's tirade by assuming the role of intermediary. Patricia tried to contain the damage that threatened to spread out of control, and beyond the confines of the school.

Patricia was on the phone with a social worker from a city agency when Mrs. Forrest walked into her office. Patricia wearily finished her call and faced her colleague.

"Yes, Mrs. Forrest?"

Gertrude Forrest whipped off her glasses with a stern expression on her face. "How could you let that happen to that child? Don't you realize we have to pay more attention to *our* children than to the other kids here?"

Patricia narrowed her gaze. "Don't use that tone of voice with me, Gertrude. We do the best we can with *all* the children. You know they're still going to do what they want to, more often than not, no matter what we try to tell them."

"That child is only fourteen years old."

"I know. That child also made an adult decision she wasn't prepared to handle. It's not just Kyra, it's all of them. I want them to learn from those mistakes and not repeat them."

Gertrude grimaced with displeasure. "You're a fine one to talk. Acting like it's all her own fault."

"It's not a question of fault. But you don't help anyone by making Kyra Whitacre a victim. Don't teach her to believe somebody else is to blame when something doesn't go the way she wants, or if she doesn't get what she wants. That kind of belief system is not going to serve her well."

"But it's only the black girls who are getting themselves in trouble. Our children need our help."

Patricia blinked at the other woman, wondering why she, or anyone else, would assume that a girl getting pregnant was somehow connected to her race. "I agree that they need help, Gertrude. The question is not how could this happen, but what are we going to do about it? Are you and the other black teachers willing to participate in a program to teach these girls how to protect themselves and use contraceptives and why they have to? Can you think of ways to encourage them to say no, because they can have other options for their lives?"

Gertrude Forrest stood straight and shook her glasses at Patricia. "Don't try to put the responsibility on me. You're the one who's the high and mighty counselor. Think you know so much more than anyone else here. You should have been keeping an eye on Kyra Whitacre instead of some little foreign girl."

Patricia felt her face get hot. "If you really believe that, then you're part of the problem, Gertrude. You point your finger but won't intervene or participate in any meaningful dialogue with me or the parents. The pot calling the kettle black, as my grandmother would say."

Gertrude cut her eyes at Patricia, put her glasses on, and walked silently out of the office. Patricia felt drained when the encounter was over. And she was numb with a terrible sense of isolation.

By the time the last class of the day was finally over, Duncan High School was like a stew that had cooked too long and was bubbling over the sides of the pot. It was not going to simmer down. Kyra's mother was threatening a lawsuit. Mrs. Teasdale had calmed Mrs. Whitacre by promising a meeting where all questions and accusations could be answered. Patricia and Jerome were expected to attend. When Patricia thought the worst was over and she could catch her breath, deal with a terrible headache, and sit quietly for five minutes, she looked up from her desk to find Kent standing in her office doorway.

"Hi," she greeted him with a weary smile. "I haven't seen very much of you lately."

Kent didn't return the greeting. Instead he slowly pulled his hand out of his pocket and held it out to her.

Patricia glanced at Kent's face and then to what he had in his hand. Her smile wavered when she saw the hair clip. The one she couldn't find the last time she and Morgan had been together. Patricia took it, but stared at it as her mind went blank of any response.

"The housekeeper gave it to me. She

thought it belonged to one of my girl-friends. She said she was going to tell my father, but I think she was just joking."

When she looked at Kent, Patricia's heart sank at the disappointment and betrayal that seemed to cloud his eyes. Kent's mouth took on a firm line, exactly like his father's.

"It was in my father's room."

She turned the clip over and over in her hand. She instantly recalled that Morgan's mouth had been fastened to hers in delicious passion as he sought to release her hair from the pearl-covered hair clip. At the time Patricia was hardly aware of her hair being freed, and she certainly gave no thought to the discarded fastener. Not until later when she couldn't find it. It had never occurred to her . . .

Patricia glanced up at the young teen, so stiff and proud. So accusing. "What made you bring it to me?"

Kent shrugged. "It couldn't belong to that other lady. Her hair is too short."

Patricia didn't move, didn't change her expression. She did feel her skin grow cold for the second time that day. "What woman?"

"Beverly something," he said innocently.

Patricia thought quickly. She couldn't confess everything. She tried not to complicate matters with excuses. Half truths would have to do.

"How come it was at my house?" Kent asked.

Patricia shrugged. "I guess it came off while I was visiting." A simple truth.

Kent seemed surprised by the admission. "You were there? At my house with my father?"

"Your father and I had lunch last week. We went back to the town house to talk."

Kent squared back his shoulders. "Did you talk about me?" he asked accusingly.

She nodded. "Some of it was about you, but I gave no secrets away, Kent. I wouldn't have your trust or your friendship very long if I did that," Patricia said truthfully.

"Are you and my father friends?"

Patricia tried to gauge his feelings. And she kept her own current doubts about the state of affairs between her and Kent's father in check. Again she nodded. "Yes, we are."

"When Mrs. Torres gave me that clip, I thought . . . I . . ."

Patricia did nothing to help him out. She waited for Kent to find his own words. He shook his head impatiently.

"Nothing. Forget it," he mumbled.

"Thank you for returning it. I'd like to ask you a favor," Patricia said, trying to sweep quickly over the awkward moment.

"What?" he asked sharply.

"I persuaded Gabriella's father to let her go on the trip. I wonder if you'd mind keeping an eye on her? You're older and you know how to keep your head," Patricia skillfully worded the request.

Kent's reluctance lasted about ten seconds and then his ego kicked in. "If you want."

About a dozen of the students going on the trip had their own ski equipment, including Kent. He indicated his bagged gear as it was loaded onto the bus by the driver. Kamil and his gang passed idly by on the other side of the street, but kept their comments to themselves in front of the seven adult chaperons, parents, and teachers.

The students were in good spirits for the start of the trip. Patricia now felt sorry that she would not be one of them this year. She'd been asked just after Christmas, but had said no. That was when she had anticipated spending much of her free time with Morgan Baxter.

The students divided and filed onto the two waiting buses. In answer to questions as to whether there was beer or smoke on board either of the buses, the resounding chorus of "we're clean" rang a little false. Gabriella hurried over to Patricia and surprised her by flinging her arms around the startled counselor's neck.

"*Grácias. Muchos grácias, Señorita Gilbert, para su ayuda.*"

Patricia hugged the girl briefly. "*De nada, Querida. Tenga un buen tiempo.*" Gabriella climbed onto the bus. "*Y tenga quidado.*"

"Don't worry. I won't let her get zoned or anything," Kent promised gruffly. He pulled a piece of paper from his pocket. "I forgot to give this to my dad. It's about the hotel and stuff where we're staying. Could you get this to him?"

Patricia looked at Kent suspiciously,

but she took the paper and smiled. "All right. No problem." She watched the final good-byes as the two buses with cheering teens headed out.

For the past two weeks Patricia had thought about Morgan Baxter constantly.

She wondered if what she and Morgan had shared so briefly would have gotten any deeper if she hadn't backed off from important issues.

She looked at the folded paper in her hand. She had been trying to get up her nerve all day to contact Morgan with the note from his son. She already knew there was only one viable solution, which was why her stomach had been churning all afternoon, why she felt so cold as she stood outside the door to Ventura, Inc. It was six-thirty and she had waited, unseen, until Mrs. Anderson and most of the support staff of the company had left for the day. She felt like a silly adolescent, skulking the hallways so that no one would see her. Just in case she was about to make a fool of herself, or if she was going to be humiliated.

Patricia knew Morgan was still in his

office. She could see the desk light from within the open doorway. She could see Morgan was standing just inside the door in front of the oval conference table. His back was to her, and he was reading from a document while also wearily massaging the back of his neck. A jolt of unexpected awareness shot straight through Patricia as she watched him. She hadn't realized how much she'd wanted to see Morgan again until this moment. She rapped lightly on the door.

"Hi . . . may I come in?"

Morgan turned his head sharply. Patricia was disconcerted to see no surprise register on his face.

"Please do." Morgan nodded.

He turned to face her fully, his eyes perusing her. He acknowledged the instant sense of relief that stirred within himself. Morgan could detect from the look in Patricia's eyes, in her drawn mouth, that this visit was costing her.

Patricia glanced at the papers in his hand. "Am I interrupting?"

Morgan put the papers down. He never took his eyes from her. "It's nothing that can't wait."

Patricia nodded. She looked away.

Then back to him in nervous silence.

"How have you been?" Morgan finally asked. He crossed his arms and sat on the edge of the conference table facing her.

"Fine. Well . . . busy. Very busy, as a matter of fact." She had an eerie sensation of reliving that very first meeting in Morgan's office back in October.

"That doesn't surprise me," he murmured.

"And yourself?"

Morgan arched a brow. "Confused."

The one-word response made Patricia wince as he continued to stare at her. She couldn't say that Morgan seemed disinterested. Guarded, perhaps. But she found this nervous formality between them disheartening.

"Kent said he forgot to give this to you . . ." She passed Morgan the folded paper. "It's the information about where the students will be staying this weekend and a list of all the chaperons. There shouldn't be any problems, but just in case."

Morgan gave the page a brief indifferent glance. "Thank you."

That was it. End of conversation. She stared at Morgan, willing herself to say something agreeable and safe. She shook her head in frustration. Her mind was a blank.

"Well, I guess . . ."

"Why didn't you call?" Morgan asked, frowning.

Patricia's stomach somersaulted. "Why . . . why didn't I call?" Morgan held up the paper. "I guess I could have. Actually, I should have, but I . . . I . . ." Patricia took a deep breath and closed her eyes briefly. Her voice was trembling. Her hand gestured helplessly in the air. "No, actually I had to come. I needed to tell you that . . . that I was really off base and . . . I . . . I had this perfectly ugly confrontation with Beverly McGraw . . ."

"Why didn't you tell me that before? I could have set you straight about us."

"I couldn't. Whatever went on before you and I met wasn't my business. What was said between Beverly and myself doesn't concern you."

"Except if you believed I was playing you wrong."

Patricia blushed and couldn't answer, but she met Morgan's gaze squarely, knowing that they had to deal with this, or risk irrevocable damage to their relationship. "I felt I owed you an apology, Morgan. I wanted to be here in person and just say how sorry I am about . . . what happened."

"You could have done that by phone, too," Morgan said. "Left a message on the answering machine."

"I could also have faxed you, but I didn't. I wanted to face up to what had happened. A lot of that night was my fault." She knew she sounded a bit testy.

"What if there'd been no need to give me this information from Kent?" he asked, curious.

Patricia blinked at him. "I don't know."

Morgan carefully folded the paper and stood up. "I'll make it easy for you. I'm glad you came, Patricia. I appreciate that you're here. But I don't need any apology from you."

Her spirits nose-dived at his politeness. "Well, I guess I can't blame you."

"I don't want an explanation, either. I think it's pretty obvious that there are things that happened in our past lives we'd rather not talk about. Maybe we're both a bit sensitive about how black we are, how black we think we have to be.

But I don't believe in the 'Black Police,' and I'm pretty tired of living up to someone else's expectations, black or white. I'm damn sure not going to explain about Melissa, or my son, or which one of us he identifies with."

"I've always said you don't have to."

"Neither do you. But you still get angry. There was no purpose served by trying to dig into what went before us."

"I got too angry."

"Maybe not. But I want you to believe that after you and I got together I wasn't ever comparing you to my ex-wife."

She nodded. "I believe you."

Morgan walked a few feet toward her and then stopped. He stood with his hands in his pockets.

"You know, a bunch of us guys used to sit around the student union and describe the sisters by their skin color. But I knew it wasn't just a description. It was a rating system." Patricia moved restlessly, and Morgan put up a hand. "Now, hear me out. I was young and stupid, you know? Once I got involved with Melissa, of course, it was social suicide. The fact that I loved her made it worse." He shook his head thoughtfully and watched Patricia closely. "But

552

now . . . I don't know how to convince you it's really you I want, Patricia. The woman who knows how to back me up when I need it, set me straight when I get impatient, but who also knows how to be kind and caring. The one who understands and won't let me slip up on my responsibility to my son. None of those things come in color."

Patricia listened quietly and uncomfortably. But once again, as she had before, she felt only the honesty and integrity of Morgan Baxter. "It's hard ducking the attacks all the time."

"So let's not do it to each other."

He spoke quietly and his jaw tensed as if he wanted so much for her to believe him without forcing the point.

"So . . ." Patricia breathed out.

Morgan approached her slowly until he was standing directly in front of Patricia. "So . . ." Morgan repeated in a drawl. "Where do we go from here?"

She stared up at him, shaking her head. "I don't know."

Morgan reached out and touched her cheek with his fingertips. "You took the first step. I guess the next move is mine. Would you like to get away together?

We can spend a day or two apologizing to each other."

"Where?"

"Not far. The Plaza?"

It was the most romantic thing Patricia had ever heard of. To just check into a hotel right where she lived for the luxury of being waited on, the coziness of the room, and the chance for uninterrupted time alone with Morgan.

Everything they did was fairly pedestrian, but they were together and that was all Patricia really cared about. As she and Morgan walked aimlessly around midtown Manhattan, window-shopping and sipping cocoa at Rockefeller Center while watching the ice-skaters, she felt like she could breathe again. She felt like her life had been saved. She felt that Morgan Baxter was the most heroic man she'd ever met in her life.

Patricia got cold and didn't even mind. They warmed up by getting last-minute tickets to a Broadway play, finally returning to the hotel late in the evening.

There had been no intimacy between them beyond just holding hands, and it still didn't seem uncomfortable. In their roomy suite they faced each other. There was a tension, but it seemed filled more with anticipation than nervousness. It was as if the buildup of steam in a pressure valve had been released, and the flow was more natural and easy. Quiet.

"I could use something to eat. Do you want to go down to the lounge or should we order room service?" Morgan asked as he hung up their coats.

"Could we just stay here?"

"Sure. We'll see what we can have sent up."

"Good," she sighed. "Right now I just want a hot bath."

Morgan motioned behind her. "The bathroom's all yours. You're going to love the tub."

It was a huge modern jacuzzi and deep enough to get lost in. Patricia began filling it, and poured into it bath oil supplied by the hotel.

"I'll be back soon," Morgan called out.

Feeling cozy and safe and languid, Patricia began to peel off her things. She felt oddly light-headed. She didn't have any questions or guesses about the evening, or the next day, or next week. Just the moment seemed an extraordinary gift that she was willing to enjoy for what it was. She climbed into the tub and slid down blissfully into the perfumed soapy depths. She loved the vast roominess and closed her eyes. Patricia's body softened in the water and her spine curved against the back of the tub. She waited for Morgan to return, and the night to begin.

When Morgan came back it was very quiet in the room. He crossed to the bathroom and stepped into the half-opened doorway. Patricia's hair stood out against the sterile whiteness of the room, twisted into a knob. A slender pale arm hung loosely over the side of the tub, and her knees were drawn up, protruding like rounded twin islands out of the water.

"They're going to send dinner up later," Morgan said.

"Ummmm," Patricia murmured.

She kept her eyes closed and heard his sounds and movements in the other room. Morgan returned to her moments later. When Patricia opened her eyes Morgan was squatting next to the tub. He had placed two glasses of wine on the edge of the sink. He had taken off all his clothes and was stark naked. The smile he gave her was one Patricia liked and trusted, like when the two of them talked about Kent or things they felt good about. She felt such a sudden surge of warm pleasure, of trust and companionship, that for a split second Patricia wondered if maybe she was hallucinating. She was loving every startling moment.

"You look comfortable," Morgan said, kissing her exposed arm.

Patricia bent her arm so that her hand could stroke the side of his face. "I am. I think I'll stay here all night."

"Know what I'd like to do?" Morgan said seductively.

She smiled dreamily. "Why don't you?"

Morgan stood and stepped into the tub behind her. He straddled his long hairy legs on either side of her body. There was very little room to spare. He laid back in the tub and urged Patricia to recline against his chest. The hot water rose almost to their necks. Morgan's large hands soothingly stroked her arms and shoulders. Patricia sighed and melted under the titillating caresses. Beneath the surface, her fingers rubbed and worried the hair on his legs, massaged the rigid muscles of his calves and thighs. Felt the tickling of his flaccid bobbing penis against her back.

"Are you still feeling cold?" Morgan asked over the top of her head.

"Not so much. This is heavenly." She dropped her head back against his chest.

He massaged her upper limbs. "We should come back again."

Patricia felt his lips in her hair. She felt every nuance of his body. She was floating away in the pure sensation of gentle sensual touching, and the peacefulness of the two of them together. This felt much more intimate than if they were engaging in sex, and it was a noticeably different experience from any other relationship she'd ever had. Patricia wondered if Morgan had any idea that this was one of the most important moments of her life.

"Morgan . . . I want to tell you about Drew," Patricia suddenly said.

Morgan remembered the name from the night of their argument. He didn't want to go into that again. "I don't need to know. I believe that it was hard and that you probably got hurt, but . . ."

"It was more than just Drew thinking I was white. He did something much worse."

Now Morgan was curious. "God . . . he didn't beat you or anything like that, did he?"

She moved her head against his chest. "No," Pat murmured slowly. "What he did was to lie, cheat, and steal. He lied about caring for me at all. The summer I went to Mexico was to get away from Drew . . . and what he had done to me. I was trying to forget, and trying to figure out what to do with my life."

"So he broke your heart. I'd say you survived okay."

Patricia sighed. "I wish it was that simple. Drew was a graduate student in the business administration program the year I graduated. He cheated on a number of the important state exams. A bunch of other students were implicated, including me. But the thing was, the school couldn't actually prove how Drew or the other students had cheated. But I'd heard gossip. You know how news spreads through the grapevine on campuses. But, he got away with it and graduated. The school couldn't touch him."

Morgan became less sanguine and alert. This was leading to something, and he sensed now that it had nothing to do with Patricia having had an affair with a white student. "How did he get you involved?"

"By the very fact that he and I had been sexually involved. Lots of people, even professors, knew about us. Drew was real smart, but he also had a reputation for being a smart*ass*. At your Christmas party, when I met David Sullivan, he reminded me a little of Drew."

Morgan frowned. "David *did* try something with you, then?"

"Nothing really out of line. But it was his attitude."

Morgan sighed and gently hugged Patricia. The water rippled around them. "Yeah, he has lots of that," he drawled.

"Anyway, the administration questioned a lot of people about the cheating. I couldn't tell them anything because I didn't know anything. They didn't believe me."

"So what? They couldn't do anything to you."

"But they did. They took away my scholarship, Morgan."

He groaned, "Pat . . ."

"I couldn't go to medical school. Drew was responsible — directly or indirectly — for me losing my dream to become a doctor."

"Christ, Pat. I'm sorry . . ."

She sighed and chuckled very quietly in a self-deprecating manner. "I guess I'm still very sensitive about it and Drew. It took me so many years to stop feeling like a victim . . . and to stop hating him. And I shouldn't have thrown him up in your face like I did —"

"I understand."

"I don't even think that was about Drew, but about Beverly McGraw. I let her get to me. She seemed so much more the kind of woman you would want, that you'd be attracted to."

Morgan smiled and boldly rubbed his wet hands over her breasts. He gently undulated his hips under her buttocks. "I think I'm the best judge of who I'm attracted to. I've already decided, Pat, that it's you. I was so glad when you came to my office yesterday."

"I was afraid to. I thought that maybe you wouldn't be interested again."

Morgan smiled to himself at her admission. He slid his butt along the bottom of the tub and rested his head against the back edge. Patricia let her body ride with his and felt the water rise up to her hair and ears. Morgan let his arm circle around to her rib cage.

"Funny. I was feeling the same way."

Patricia could feel his heart beat under her head. She glanced down at the two of them spooned together, beneath the clear water. She felt extraordinarily female, her frame so much smaller than his, smoother and softer. She loved the sense of being cradled into his firm lean body, and feeling safe and secure. She lifted a wet hand and thoughtfully let the water drip along Morgan's exposed leg.

Patricia took another risk.

"Morgan, I'm not very good at this," she whispered.

Morgan picked up immediately on the strain of fear in the declaration. One hand stroked her arm, the other brushed over her stomach, the weight of his hand holding her securely against him.

"I don't suppose you're talking about taking a bath with a man."

Her head shook against his chest. "I have a terrible track record with men.

Many of them have gotten very weird with me. Or maybe it was me. I get defensive. I'm always worried that . . ."

Morgan kissed the top of her head again. It silenced her. "Pat, I don't have a track record at all. I have lots of experience and it's not worth a damn right now. There hasn't been a book written yet that's gotten it right about the man and woman thing."

She sighed deeply at his words. Unconsciously Morgan's hand rose to gently stroke his thumb against the underside of her breast. The tips of his fingers brushed over the extended rosy nipple. Her weight sank into him. "I think I'm just as uncertain as you are."

She held her breath. Her body began to burn under his stimulating touch. "Why?"

"I guess because this means so much more than I expected. I don't want to make any more mistakes."

"Then you'll understand if I sometimes get . . ."

"A little scared? I hope I'm important enough to you that it really matters."

She merely nodded.

The water grew tepid. Morgan took a washcloth, lathered it with soap, and began to wash Patricia's arms and shoulders. He was clumsy at first but she sat still, loving the gentleness of his long strong fingers. Loving the thorough attention Morgan gave to her. The water sloshed around them, changing their movement in the tub, rocking them against one another. The contact of the water, of their bodies together, made them hot and agitated.

After long moments of stroking and caressing her, the steamy sensuality had the desired effect and he could hear the change in her breathing, the hardening of his own body in intoxicating arousal. Morgan lifted himself from the tub, the water rushing from him. He helped Patricia out and toweled her dry. At least Morgan tried to. He kissed her neck and shoulder, inhaling the scent of soap and bath oil on her skin. He bent to dry her legs, stopping to kiss a hip and her stomach, deliberately missing the fascinating thatch of red hair curling just below. He didn't bother drying himself. He didn't want to waste the time or energy. They left the wet towels on the bathroom floor and went into the bedroom. Morgan pulled Patricia into his arms. The low immediate sounds of desire were mutual.

Her body became damp all over again as Morgan held her close. He boldly held her hips against his taut thighs and rocked his rigid penis against her. Patricia moaned, lifting her leg around him and balancing on the ball of her other foot.

The kiss was a trembling hungry possession of each other's mouths. The two-week abstinence had only whetted their appetites, revived a memory of desire. Standing awkwardly in the dim room had a tremendous drugging effect on both of them. Her hands slid down his moist back to his flanks, spreading over the flexing muscles. Patricia broke the kiss for want of air. Her forehead dropped forward against his shoulder.

"Morgan . . ." she moaned again with growing urgency.

Morgan maneuvered them next to the great bed. He jerked back the bed linens and they climbed onto the cool, taut sheets. Morgan positioned himself half on top of Patricia's body. His mouth sought out and began to suck on a breast, his tongue tormenting the turgid peak. His hand stroked her damp but hot skin, feeling her chest heave with her breathing. His hand roamed over the smoothness of her stomach and thighs, cupping languidly between her legs and stroking the wet center. Patricia uttered a helpless sound, rolling her hips upward toward the exploring hand, delirious with Morgan's boldness and wanting more of him. She stroked the back of his head and his neck, encouraging the erotic torture. The knock came fifteen minutes later announcing the arrival of their dinner.

They never bothered to answer the door.

Chapter Sixteen

"Miss Gilbert, I don't want to go in here."

"It's going to be okay. Your friends are going to be happy you're back, Kyra. You'll see."

"But everybody's gonna stare at me," the young girl cried and pouted.

"Maybe some of them will. But you're not the only girl who's ever had a difficult problem to deal with. You don't have to tell anyone anything. What happened is not a disease. They won't catch it. Just remember that they have little secrets, too. Okay?"

Kyra could only nod. She'd lost weight in the week she'd been out of school, and word had gotten out about why she was absent.

Patricia felt deeply for the young girl, but knew that it was going to be impossible for Kyra to avoid the talk and stares. And it wasn't because Kyra had gotten pregnant, that still remained a status thing with the girls, but because she didn't want to have the baby. Patricia knew that, fortunately, the judgment wouldn't last for long. The attention span at Duncan for scandal was pretty short because there was always something new going on to grab the moment.

"They better not say *anything* to me," Kyra said defiantly, her face smudged with tears.

"If it gets too hard for you, leave the classroom and come to me or Mr. Daly. You understand?"

Again Kyra nodded. Patricia opened the door to the class, which was already in progress. There was a sudden silence and all eyes turned to the young girl. But Kyra quietly slid into a vacant seat near the back of the room and opened her notebook. The teacher's voice picked up her train of thought, and the lesson for the day continued.

Patricia turned away from the classroom. Today was going to be the worst, but she knew that Kyra was going to be okay. She walked slowly past the library and an empty classroom. She passed the study hall and caught a glimpse of Kent Baxter slouched low in a chair and brooding intently over an open book. His leg was bouncing in nervous energy and Patricia wondered if he was really so enthralled with the text.

She watched him as she smiled to herself, feeling not only a sense of genuine pride and affection but also relief that just recently Kent had handled another difficult episode very well on his own — the matter of the stolen items.

It had quickly spread among the staff and teachers, one afternoon, that someone, very likely a student, had covertly left a brown bag on the desk of the principal's secretary. Inside she'd found CDs, a camera, and a Mont Blanc pen with a strip of paper tape to the barrel with Mrs. Lechter's name on it. Everyone was less surprised that the things had been stolen in the first place, than that everything had now quietly been returned. When the gossip had reached Patricia, she'd experienced enormous relief. And during her lunch break that day, she had called Morgan with the news.

She wondered if she should stop and

talk to Kent now or just leave him alone. Lately, there had been fewer occasions when he'd manipulated being in her company, when he'd asked her personal questions. On the one hand Patricia was relieved that he had somehow become distracted with something or someone else. But the growing indifference also made her worry. She had not forgotten that Kent had found her hair clip and had begun to draw his own conclusions as to how it came to be found.

She wondered nervously if Kent had found out for sure about her and his father. Had Morgan let something slip? Had she been careless? Patricia finally decided against talking to Kent, simply not prepared to field questions that might indeed concern her and his father. She walked quickly away from the room. Her heart was beating so fast and loud she thought she could hear it.

Still feeling unsettled and bewildered, Patricia made her way to the stairwell that would take her back to her office on the ground level. When she pushed open the stairwell fire doors and heard the loud male voices, she didn't immediately register the tensions of conflict.

Several students rushed past her, up to the next level.

"Don't run," she instructed automatically.

It was only when Patricia heard a thud and grunt, muttered profanities, and a girl's voice raised in alarm that she snapped out of her introspection. She stopped, listened, and raced up the stairs. Patricia rounded a banister and saw two young males locked in a struggle that rocked them back and forth on the landing above. She stared speechless as one of them slugged and punched with all his strength, with a force fully intended to do damage. The other combatant could only try to deflect the fists and protect his head from the blows. He was no match for his opponent.

"Okay, that's enough. Stop it!" Patricia heard her own voice raised. She was hardly aware of the five or six other students who stood and watched but made no effort to stop the fight. She flew up the stairs two at a time. She grabbed a hold of the body nearest her, feeling the sinewy twist and pull of muscles, the loosened oversize shirt slid through her fingers. "Stop it," Patricia yelled again.

"Miss G., you gonna get hurt!" a young girl yelled in alarm.

A fist arced over Patricia's arms with full force and landed on something that gave under the impact. Patricia reached blindly to grab whatever she could. She closed her eyes as another fist went alarmingly close to her face. Her whole body was jerked and pulled with the momentum of the fight. "I said stop it, now!" she practically screamed.

They didn't. There was grunting and cursing and other sounds on the stairs. The hall smelled of sweat and anger and Patricia realized too late that her presence hadn't even registered, that she was totally ineffectual against the fury of the two boys.

A kind of chorus of confused and excited chatter suddenly went up around her, along with shouts of concern for her safety. But then she couldn't disengage herself. Fear replaced her foolish attempts at peace, and Patricia knew she'd made a big mistake by trying to intervene.

She took an uncomfortable jab in her ribs. She lost her footing and twisted an ankle. Her foot slipped out of a shoe and when her foot came down she was too close to the edge of the top step.

The girl's voice screamed, "Miss Gilbert! Watch out . . . oh, shit!"

"Hey! *Hey!* Are you crazy? Knock it off. Now!"

Patricia heard Jerome's voice and relief made her release her hold on the still struggling bodies.

"I said, knock it off." Jerome's voice gritted as he pushed himself into the middle of the fracas.

A last punch was thrown. It caught Patricia just above the left temple, knocking her clear off her feet. She landed dazed on the floor. The crowd gasped audibly.

"Dammit! The next punch comes from me, get it? Now *back off!*" Jerome bellowed.

The fighting stopped and the two boys swayed, exhausted and disheveled, one bloodied and the other still in a rage.

"Eric, I told you to let me handle this."

Eric was trying to catch his breath, but he got right in Jerome's face. Eric was bigger.

"You ain't gonna do shit. That motherfucker . . ."

Jerome pointed a finger in Eric's face.

Eric cursed again and pushed his hand away. Jerome didn't move. "You are not in charge here. It's none of your business."

Eric sucked his teeth. Sweat beaded across his dark face from the exertion of the fight. He tried to back Jerome up, but Jerome never moved. "I'm makin' it my business."

"Not here you won't." Jerome stared him down.

Patricia was being helped to her feet, but she was more intent on whether Eric was going to take out the rest of his physical hostility on her colleague. "Eric, listen," she said.

Eric gestured to the other boy. Britt Harris. Britt was slumped on the stairs where he sat with his head bowed on his folded arms. "Okay, what you gonna do about it, heh? He fuckin' got . . ."

"Shut up, Eric," Jerome said firmly.

The conversation didn't make much sense to Patricia in that moment. Her head was throbbing. She held a hand to her side where a dull ache persisted. She reached out blindly as someone else awkwardly tried to help get her shoe back on. The papers she'd held earlier were given back to her, crushed and torn.

"I'm okay. I'm fine," she murmured.

"Okay, that's it. Show's over. Get out of here and back to your own business," Jerome ordered, clapping his hands for attention. As Britt was about to slip down the stairwell, in the opposite direction, Jerome grabbed the tail of his shirt. "Hold on a minute . . ." he whispered in the boy's ear. "In my office in ten minutes. Don't make me come looking for you, Britt."

Britt pulled away roughly and continued down the stairs. Eric silently grabbed his things and pushed through the nearest exit door.

"I'll get to you in the morning," Jerome shouted after him.

There was continued muttering as the students filed out of the stairwell. Jerome turned to Patricia and grabbed her arm to support her. He stared into her face with concern.

"I thought you were afraid of Eric," she said in an attempt at humor.

Jerome gave her a dark look and ignored the comment. "That was a dumb thing to do, Pat," he said with little apparent sympathy. "You *never* try to break up a fight like that." His hand turned her face and he cursed softly at the developing red mark on her jaw. "Jesus, Patty. You could have gotten hurt."

"You mean, I'm not?" She chuckled in a very shaky voice. Every part of her was shaking. She lifted her chin out of Jerome's hand. "What were they fighting about?"

Jerome only shook his head silently in disgust. But already Patricia was beginning to figure it out for herself. She tried to straighten her clothing, feeling as though someone had been beating her with a stick; she ached all over. Jerome turned to face her, his anger suddenly replaced by another kind of anger and concern as his gaze swept over her.

"I'm sorry."

"What for? This wasn't your fault."

Jerome sighed and shook his head, noting her bruises and pale face. "I think it is. I didn't handle this right from the very beginning."

Patricia let Jerome keep hold of her arm as they headed back to their office. She took a few steps and then stopped, looking at Jerome pointedly.

"Was that about Kyra?"

Jerome only stared at her and pursed his mouth. "You need some ice on that bruise," was all he'd say.

"I'm going," Kent muttered, nearly to the door and still shrugging into his jacket. He hurried past the living-room entrance.

Morgan looked up from a thick contract he was reading. He was half reclined on the sofa, his sneakered feet braced against the edge of the coffee table. A mostly cold mug of coffee was in one hand, and he was surrounded by supporting documentation, papers and reports scattered on the table and floor. Morgan's expression was blank and then turned puzzled as he looked at his watch, and then back to Kent.

"Hold it a minute. Going where?"

Kent barely contained his impatience. "Just out."

"It's eight o'clock at night, Kent. Where are you going?"

Kent hesitated before he turned to the living room and stood with his hands in his jeans pockets. "Some of the guys are getting together, that's all." His father waited. "We're going to hang out."

Morgan stared thoughtfully at his son. "At a friend's house?" He put the contract papers in his lap and clicked his pen closed.

Kent shrugged. "No."

"Then it sounds like trouble waiting to happen. Why didn't you tell me earlier?"

"I guess I forgot," Kent responded, somewhat rudely.

Morgan's jaw tightened as he stared at his son. "Are we back to that again?"

"What do you mean?"

Morgan put his feet down and sat forward. "What time are you supposed to meet your friends?"

"About nine," Kent answered suspiciously. "Why?"

"Good." Morgan put the report and pen aside and stood up. "Then we have time for a talk."

"Dad . . ." Kent began to object.

"Come in here."

Kent thought better of protesting. He walked into the living room to stand in front of his father.

Morgan stared at his son. Kent sometimes reminded Morgan of himself, but the problems that had ruled his life at fifteen had changed and the new ones had a whole new spin on them. When he was a teenager he could expect neither help nor sounding board from his father. Morgan didn't want that to be the case between him and Kent.

"I think you and I are overdue for a talk." He sat back and indicated a chair across from himself.

"Dad, can't it wait?"

"No. I don't think so." Morgan waited patiently, hiding his apprehension, and watched as Kent reluctantly sat down. "Is something up at school? Are you having trouble with classes or teachers again?"

"No."

Morgan nodded. "Okay. Is it something I've done?" His grin was self-deprecating. "I can be a little dim sometimes." Kent didn't answer. He didn't look up. Morgan became alert. "Then it is me."

Kent rolled his eyes and sighed dramatically. "Dad, it's nothing."

"I thought you understood that you could talk to me about anything. Have I ever given you reason to think you couldn't? You know I'm more than willing to listen to . . ."

"This is different." Kent clamped his mouth shut.

"Kent, this is like pulling teeth. How can you expect me to believe it's not anything when you've been walking around here with an attitude and your lower lip dragging? Look, maybe what you really need to do is talk to Patricia Gilbert."

"No," he said strongly.

"Maybe she can help. I know . . ."

"*No!*"

Morgan was silenced by the sudden sharp response. Kent jumped to his feet.

"I don't want to talk to her about *anything.*"

Morgan stared at the boy and slowly sat forward again. "Why? Has something happened?"

Kent became agitated. He flounced away, turning his back. "I already told you, nothing."

"You think I'm going to believe that? I mention Patricia Gilbert's name and you go ballistic. Since when can't you talk to her openly?"

Kent wheeled around. "Since I found out about the two of you."

Morgan was on his feet. "Kent," he said unconsciously in warning.

"To her I'm just another stupid kid

with problems. I thought she . . . cared about me. But she's only interested in my *problems.*"

Morgan suddenly felt overly warm. He spoke carefully. "She does care about you, Kent. Patricia's always been there for you."

"Not anymore," Kent said bitterly, his eyes sparkling with anger. "Now she's got you," he said scathingly.

Morgan could only stare. Suddenly it was clear why Kent was feeling both hurt and outraged. Morgan knew that neither he nor Patricia would have had the power to prevent what was happening: Kent's sexual awareness. Patricia had tried to warn him.

"You want to tell me what you mean by that?" His tone was even, deceptively calm.

"You're sleeping with her, Dad," Kent said, as if it were perfectly obvious to one and all.

Morgan hoped to God it wasn't. He had another realization. He'd inadvertently made his son his rival. He knew that everything he said now was crucial.

"Be careful what you say," he continued in that warning tone. "I admit that

Patricia Gilbert means a lot to me. I consider her a very good friend. Knowing her has helped me to be a better father to you. It's helped me to learn a few things about myself. Do you object to that?"

Kent took several steps closer to his father and then stopped himself. His face was flushed with suppressed rage. "She was *my* friend first. She liked me *first*," he said loudly.

"She still does. But I don't think she sees the need to fuss over you all the time, like she was your mother or something."

"That's good, 'cause I don't need a mother. I already have one."

"Then what do you want from her?" Morgan asked quietly.

Kent visibly swallowed and looked trapped. Morgan's heart went out to the boy, suddenly caught unprepared with real adult feelings.

"I . . . I thought I was . . . really special to her. I thought . . ." he fumbled to explain, his voice shaky with anger and confused emotions.

"Kent, you are special. You're more special to her in ways no one else, even me, could be to her. I know that."

"Did she say that?"

"I know by the way she talks about you . . ." Morgan tempered gently. "In your own way you love her, and there's nothing wrong in that."

"I don't," Kent said forcefully, clearly upset at the suggestion. "Don't you say anything to her," he further demanded in a panic.

"I won't. But I want to know why you think . . ."

"I found her hair clip. I know she was here in your room." Kent shook his head in frustration. "You're sleeping with her. I know it."

"That's the second time you've said that. It's none of your business. Patricia Gilbert and I have been doing nothing to be ashamed of, Kent. *Nothing.* That's all I'm going to say about it."

Kent looked steadily at his father. "You love her?"

The unexpected question caused a peculiar knot to form in Morgan's gut. He told his first lie in the conversation. "I haven't thought about it much. Love is pretty complicated." He watched the emotions shift in Kent as the unspoken challenge died.

Kent looked sharply at his father once

again. "What about that other woman?"

Morgan frowned. "What other woman?"

"The one in your office that day. Beverly . . ."

Morgan shook his head, bemused, realizing how unwise it was to believe that children didn't know what was going on around them. He told the truth. "She and I were seeing each other. Last summer, before you came to New York. You never had a chance to meet her then, but that's been over for a while."

Morgan stood still, fighting the desire to physically comfort his son and knowing that's not what Kent would want from him. "Do you still believe that Patricia no longer cares about you?"

He lifted his shoulders. "I don't care." Then he headed toward the door. "Can I go?"

Every fiber of Morgan's being wanted to force Kent to stay put. He was afraid of what his son would do out there in the streets with all his resentment. But his instincts told him to let the boy go.

"Sure. Don't stay out too late."

Kent didn't respond, one way or another. He kept moving until he was out the front door, closing it loudly behind him.

It was almost one in the morning when Morgan heard the front door open and close. He listened and eventually heard Kent's slow and heavy footsteps on the stairs.

"Kent?" he called out.

"Yeah, it's me," came back the muttered reply.

Morgan waited. He decided not to make the lateness an issue.

"Where'd you go tonight?"

"No place."

"Tomorrow's a school day. I don't want this to become a habit." There was no response. "Did you hear me?"

"Yeah, I heard."

"Good night."

" 'Night."

Morgan lay still and listened until the town house was still and quiet. He finally got out of bed and walked down the hall to Kent's room. Morgan quietly opened the door and peered in. Kent had gotten his clothes off and dropped everything on the floor. He was already in a deep sleep. Morgan bent over to pull the covers over his son, listening to the gentle snore.

And he felt his insides tighten when he got a warm wafting of the smell of alcohol.

The auditorium was packed. All assistants, and three fourths of the school staff were there.

There were nearly four hundred parents and, surprisingly, quite a number of students in attendance. Patricia already knew that Morgan would not be in the audience. He had flown to Los Angeles for two days, arranging for Kent to stay with one of his school buddies, and within an easy call of herself or Connie Anderson. Patricia knew, however, that it was unlikely that Kent would call her for anything. The talk he'd had with his father had not resolved his conflict with her.

The school administration was forced to schedule the parent meeting in response to the growing chorus of worried parents who had heard a half-dozen versions of the school's crises: Kyra Whitacre's abortion, the fight between the two boys . . . the distribution of condoms.

When Patricia entered the large room

it was noisy and the atmosphere was charged. She anxiously looked around the auditorium for Jerome. She had not seen him the whole day. She herself had been busy deflecting as much gossip and curiosity as possible. Someone had even hinted that the press would be on hand.

The school officials arrived on stage together as a block, as if for safety. The audience began to quiet down. Jerome finally appeared to take the last seat on the stage, his demeanor and posture separating him from everyone else. Patricia knew it was deliberate. She reluctantly took her place at the far end of the line of administrators. Mr. Boward, the principal, finally got up to the podium to quiet the audience and begin the meeting.

"On behalf of the staff at Duncan I want to welcome you and to thank so many of you for coming out this cold evening. Unfortunately, the reason for this meeting is not a pleasant or easy one. We have tried to answer many of your questions by phone, but that became impossible when we found it tied up staff time. Therefore, this meeting became necessary. We realize that you've raised some disturbing questions about Duncan's ability to protect your children, and there have been rumors about events that supposedly took place here at the school. The allegations, however, are false and without merit. We hope to answer all of your questions by the end of the evening. Right now, let me introduce . . ."

The audience was attentive for the next thirty minutes, and then grew restive. All the following comments only served to put the school administration in the best possible light. They were conscientious. They were doing a good job. The school had the second-best reading scores in Brooklyn. But those remarks didn't address the immediate concerns of the parents. Through it all Jerome remained silent and seemingly inattentive. Patricia, peeking down the line of staff members and colleagues, wondered what was going through his mind. Someone from the audience finally stood up and interrupted.

" 'Cuse me. Now that all sounds nice and fine, but we want real answers. We understand a girl here got an abortion recently. I want to know how that could happen."

The audience laughed and someone else shouted out, "We *know* how it happens!"

Mr. Boward responded quickly, "Yes, it's true that one of our girls found herself in trouble. But there is absolutely no evidence to support your fear that any sexual activity actually took place on school grounds, during school hours, or that anyone on Duncan's staff would aid a student in an abortion."

"My daughter got pregnant while attending this school three years ago. What kind of supervision are these kids getting anyway?"

"I think we're getting off the point . . ." Mr. Boward said formally.

Jerome rose and stepped up to the mike. He leaned in front of the principal and talked directly to the parent.

"Maybe she got pregnant in your own living room some night while you were out. Where was the supervision then?"

The audience gasped. Patricia moaned and gnawed her lip. Mr. Boward whispered something strident to Jerome. He slowly sat down. The principal again faced the group.

"I think the point is, there are some things which happen to and between the students which school authorities don't have control over. It's, of course, regrettable that our young people make poor decisions at times . . ."

Jerome stood up again and shouted, this time without benefit of the mike. "At which point it's too late to start blaming each other. The question is, how do we prevent it from happening again? What do we do to help the kids? They're the ones we're talking about."

There was a surprising burst of supportive applause from the audience. Patricia glanced around and saw it was mostly Duncan staff and some of the students. There was also a low hissing of disapproval. Jerome was once more waved to his seat, while those on the stage cast disapproving glances in his direction. He ignored them all.

Patricia felt the ambivalence with which she'd arrived at the meeting begin to die. Jerome was right. No one yet was really addressing the issue of the best way to be of help and available to the students. She looked at Jerome and caught his attention. Patricia nodded, hoping he'd know she was on his side.

"I heard the girl got an abortion," one woman began. "Did she do it in the bathroom? Who helped her?"

"Did anyone at Duncan tell her parents what was going on? Are you now advocating abortions as a solution to teen pregnancy?" someone else shouted out.

Patricia failed to follow the logic of the argument or question.

"I'm afraid we did not know the young girl was pregnant right away. We, therefore, had no knowledge of her abortion until afterward. But that is not the issue here."

"No the issue is we can't even trust that our children are going to be safe and given good advice in their own school!" a father angrily voiced.

"I think we're going overboard with this," yet another father said, trying for calm. "After all, even as parents we know our kids sometimes don't listen to a thing we say. Sometimes they do what they want to do, no matter what."

"Not *my* son. He's a good boy who's well behaved and does exactly what he's told to do. He knows what'll happen if he doesn't."

A little heckling began with the first speaker and continued through all the responses thereafter. Patricia had no idea what people were for or against, other than their own individual authority. She began to detect a disturbing problem that had not fully occurred to her before. She looked at Jerome to see how he was responding. His impatience was barely contained.

Mr. Boward used the gavel a little too forcefully and the noise caused the microphone to squeal. He tried to focus the audience once again, and finally Patricia saw that the entire purpose of the meeting was only damage control. The school was taking a defensive position, but so were the parents. The talk continued to meander unfruitfully for ten more minutes around the pregnancy, with Mr. Boward trying to absolve the school of any responsibility. The fight between the two students was glossed over quickly as a fight over a girl. The audience, with no further need for explanation and apparently with an understanding all their own, let it go. A mother stood up and held out her hand.

"I found these in my son's schoolbag. They're condoms."

"Why were you going through his schoolbag?" an unidentified voice shouted. For a second there was silence in the auditorium. The mother ignored the interruption and rushed on. "When I asked him where he got them he said from a friend, and that the friend got them from school."

This got instant attention from everyone. Patricia again looked at Jerome. He was listening carefully, not very concerned.

"What is your question?" the principal asked patiently.

"Well, I want to know when did Duncan start giving out condoms to the students? And why weren't the parents told about this?"

"There was nothing to tell you because Duncan does not distribute condoms. We are not health care providers, we're educators."

"Isn't it the same thing?" Jerome asked clearly. He was ignored, too.

"My daughter told me that lots of kids at school can get condoms when they want."

"That can't be true. We have no official policy regarding that. We . . ."

"Well, maybe we should." It was Jerome again.

Patricia knew he was not going to stay

put much longer. She felt afraid for him.

"The school doesn't have the right to make decisions to give condoms to our kids. Why wasn't it discussed with the parents?" an angry mother spoke up next. The agitation of the audience was quickly gaining momentum, and people shouted and spoke out of order.

"Who gave you the right to tell kids it's okay to have sex any time they want? And look what happens. Some girl goes and gets pregnant and then kills her baby!"

Patricia got up from her seat and made her way to the mike. Jerome stood, too. He reached the podium before she did and took physical control so that Mr. Boward had no choice but to stand aside and let him talk. He held up his hand for silence.

"Excuse me, please. I'd like to try and answer that question . . ." The parents quieted down. "My name is Jerome Daly. I'm one of the guidance counselors here at Duncan. I can hear that many of you parents have real concerns about your kids. But I think in order to answer the questions and deal with the problems, we first have to accept that there is a shared responsibility involved here."

Patricia sat in Jerome's vacated seat on the stage, and sighed with relief. He had gotten a handle on the situation. People were listening. He was making sense.

"I think we first have to realize as both parents and educators that our first obligation is to do everything we can to give our kids the best and most reasonable information we can, to help them make smart decisions for themselves.

"Maybe if they knew and understood more about sex, perhaps they would also have more respect and concern for the consequences. Perhaps if we didn't make them feel guilty, or as though sex was some unnatural thing that you only get to do with approval — and who's to say whose approval that should be — they'd feel less pressure to explore it too early."

A little rumbling went through the auditorium. Patricia glanced anxiously at Jerome, wanting him to be careful, wanting him not to be so brutally honest.

"Are you saying that it's perfectly okay for our sons and daughters to run around having sex any time they get the urge?"

"Absolutely not," Jerome said firmly. "But I am saying let's recognize that they *will* get the urge. Rather than try to squelch it, or to pretend like it doesn't exist, or even that it's wrong, why not give our kids as much help and information as they need to handle it responsibly?"

"You're talking about giving them condoms!" a mother concluded, outraged.

"Yes," Jerome said.

Patricia closed her eyes against the inevitability of what was going to happen next. The fervor picked up steam. Jerome again got control.

"Look, none of you want to see your children having children. They haven't even had a chance to grow up or have their lives and find out what it's all about, or what they might want to do with it. Suddenly, *wham!* they make a mistake that changes everything forever. The wrong decision is preventable and we can teach them how."

It seemed so reasonable. No one was listening. The parents had been challenged on a level that Jerome could not begin to understand. Voices from the audience rose in indignation and self-defense. Comments came from all over the auditorium. But very few were willing to agree with Jerome. Patricia was disappointed, but not surprised.

"You don't have the right to decide for me how I'm going to raise my child. I don't want you deciding what they will learn or not learn. Sex shouldn't be taught in the schools, period!" A round of applause broke out.

"Fine!" Jerome shouted over the noise. "Are you teaching your kids about it at home? Are they getting the information from you, or from their friends?"

"I'm certainly not going to teach my kids how to go around having sex. That's the only reason they want condoms."

"How about to prevent disease? AIDS? To save their lives? How about to *prevent* pregnancy and abortion?" No one was listening. Jerome grew angry and lost it. "Hey! Have any of you considered asking your kids what they wanted? Do you even talk to your kids? Hasn't it occurred to you yet that if you're finding condoms in their pockets and knapsacks and wherever else you're searching, that maybe there's something going on that you *should* know about? Why not ask yourself why your kids are sneaking around and getting condoms behind your back!"

Mr. Boward and the other administrators were beside themselves. Everyone was trying to get Jerome away from the microphone, away from the raw nerves he'd exposed.

"I'm not finished yet," he cried at the principal with such menacing intent, he backed away.

Jerome turned to the audience again. They must have sensed his anger because it was more curiosity than consensus that kept them listening.

"I gotta tell you that you people don't get it. You don't really care about your kids at all. Sometimes you make hard decisions to protect them, not yourself, because there are so few choices. If you all weren't so invested in treating your kids like some sort of property that you have an exclusive right to, we wouldn't be here tonight talking about how offended *you* are. Dammit to hell. What about the *kids?*

"You want to know where your kids got the condoms? From me, that's who. Because if the girl who got pregnant had made her boyfriend use one, she might not have gotten pregnant, and there would have been no need for an abortion, right? Right . . ."

To the sounds of boos and cries of outrage, Jerome walked away from the microphone. He was headed off the stage and toward the exit when Patricia calmly approached the microphone and tapped.

"Excuse me, may I have your attention?" People looked at her suspiciously. She recognized many of the parents. "Thank you. I'm Patricia Gilbert. I'm the other counselor at Duncan. Many of you know me. We've had meetings together and talked and worried over your children. I hope you know and believe that I would not do anything . . . *anything* that would deliberately jeopardize your children's health or safety. Or their future. But I want to say right here and now that I fully and completely support Jerome Daly. We're both aware that there's no official policy on the issue of condom distribution at Duncan. But there *is* a necessity for them, and I'm desperately sorry that so many of you don't agree. I respect your position as parents, but

I also hope you won't close your minds completely to alternatives."

The disapproval was now heaped upon Patricia. But she could sense the surprise as she left the stage. Her heart was pounding in her chest, and her hands were shaking. But she also felt an enormous relief. Patricia knew she'd done the right thing, and so had Jerome.

But they were never going to hear the end of this.

Jerome stood in front of her. His eyes were bright and thoughtful. He was grinning at her. "That was a stupid thing to do."

"You ought to know."

"Thanks, Patty."

"Well, I felt I owed you big. This was a good time to give up the marker."

"You know what's going to happen, don't you?"

"I don't want to know, and I'm certainly not interested in knowing this moment. I just want to say, I admire what you did. And I was sincere when I said I agree with you. I do."

"I appreciate your support," he said with a shrug.

"You were pretty good out here. I'm a

little late again."

"I was unfair. I had no right to criticize you."

"Maybe. So, now that we've totally disrupted the meeting, what should we do?"

"Stick it out till the bitter end. Then I'd say let's go get drunk, but that's not setting a good example."

"I could use a glass of wine, and a quiet place to talk," she said.

"You got it," Jerome said.

The next crisis didn't happen until the next week when Morgan's housekeeper reported that she was sure Kent had been drinking beer in his room after school. Then Morgan was called into a Brooklyn shop, on a Saturday afternoon, because his son had been caught shoplifting. He was with Eric Patton.

Feeling more angry than dispirited, Morgan took his son home. And he issued an ultimatum. Then he called Patricia with the bad news.

But she could only handle one problem at a time. For the moment, it involved the fallout from the faculty-parent meeting. That Monday morning she came into the office and found

Jerome with a stack of empty boxes. He was slowly filling each one with his belongings.

"Oh, no . . ." Patricia murmured.

Jerome looked up and smiled sadly. "Oh, yes."

"They can't fire you."

"They probably can, but they didn't. I quit."

"But, Jerome . . ."

He held up his hand. "Patty, I appreciate your support and stuff, but it's okay. Really. I think I've known since before Christmas I was going to have to make this decision."

She frowned. "Christmas?"

"My leaving has almost nothing to do with that meeting. But it was sort of the final straw."

"Jerome, I'm so sorry."

His gaze on her was even more sad. "Yeah, me, too."

"Miss Gilbert?"

Patricia turned around at the sound of her name and faced two of her colleagues. Mrs. Teasdale looked stern but uncomfortable. Mrs. Forrest didn't have to say anything. Her expression of self-righteousness spoke for her.

"Yes?"

"We've been asked to have you come down to the office. There's something the principal would like to discuss with you."

Patricia grimaced at her colleagues' stern expressions. "I won't try to escape. Do I get a blindfold?"

"I don't think your attitude is going to help you," Mrs. Forrest uttered with stiff dignity.

Mrs. Teasdale apologized all the way out the door. With a nod of encouragement to Jerome, Patricia followed the two women knowing full well that bad news always traveled in pairs.

Patricia also considered, during the silent march to the principal's office, that the only thing missing was a drumroll. Mrs. Teasdale and Mrs. Forrest flanked her with a kind of stiff formality that made Patricia want to laugh. Except that, she suspected, it had to be serious to warrant an escort.

Mr. Boward, the principal, muttered a hello when they entered his office.

"Sit down. Sit down, ladies."

"I think I'd rather stand," Patricia stated. "I suppose this is all about the parent meeting and Mr. Daly's admission."

"Patricia, please sit down," the principal implored. "This is not an inquisition."

But Patricia noticed that Mrs. Teasdale had found something on Mr. Boward's desk to stare at which occupied her attention from the more immediate problems. Gertrude Forrest stared at Mr. Boward as if daring him to say anything other than the reprimand she expected her to receive. "But this is official. Have I done anything wrong?"

"I'm sure you know better than *we* do," Mrs. Forrest said with exasperation. "We only want to confirm some very damaging information which has come to our attention."

"Now, Gertrude," the principal began.

"Well, I certainly hope it will be more than confirming your worst fears. I assume I'll get a chance to tell my side."

"This whole business is unfortunate," Mr. Boward said. "We'd like to keep it just between the parties in this room."

Patricia frowned. "It's a little late for that. The whole school is talking about that meeting. And I just left Jerome Daly, remember? I understand he's resigned."

Suddenly all eyes turned to her. Even

Mrs. Teasdale was sufficiently interested to look blankly at her.

"This isn't about Mr. Daly," Gertrude said. She looked to Mr. Boward, who also hadn't expected any misunderstanding.

"Patricia, I'm sorry but . . . I had to call you in to ask you about something entirely different. It concerns one of the students."

Finally, Patricia did understand. The blush on Mrs. Teasdale's face was a giveaway. Gertrude Forrest's primly set mouth and her squared-back shoulders spoke of indignation. Mr. Boward's furtive glances said the rest. Patricia decided she would sit down after all.

"What is it?" she asked flatly. But her own suspicions were already tightening her stomach muscles.

The principal cleared his throat. "Well . . . we've received a letter stating that . . . er . . . that you're involved with the parent of one of our students."

Patricia knew that Gertrude was watching her carefully. But instead of blushing, under the circumstances, she felt suddenly chilled as the blood seemed to drain right out of her face.

"Who sent you that information?" she asked.

Mr. Boward shook his head. "It was sent anonymously. But you understand we have to check it out."

"Does it mention who the student is?"

"So you're not denying anything," Gertrude charged.

"Does it?" Patricia asked the principal.

"No, but it's pretty specific in other details. Too many to just see it as a crackpot letter. I'm sorry, but I have to ask. Is the accusation true? Have you been . . . involved with one of the parents?"

The first thing that came to Patricia's mind was how could she avoid identifying Kent . . . at all costs. Her concerns about her relationship being private notwithstanding, she'd gone into her affair with Morgan Baxter always knowing there was a very delicate balance between her personal and professional life.

Patricia remembered that awful meeting with Beverly McGraw and her none-too-subtle threats. But Patricia couldn't figure out what the woman hoped to gain by this disclosure . . . other than her public humiliation.

She looked at the principal, and thought of her work with the students at Duncan. Work for which she had been praised and rewarded, as much as it had been frustrating and, a few times, disappointing. She'd found a place at this high school because she'd worked hard and had believed in the children and the system, even when it didn't always work well on their behalf. Patricia thought briefly of Jerome and recognized that despite everything that had happened, he only had the welfare of the students in mind.

But Patricia knew that she, too, had crossed the line. And she had no excuses to fall back on.

"On my own time away from Duncan, I have been seeing someone. That relationship has not interfered with me doing my job for the students here."

"But does that *someone* have a child in this school? And did you know that?" Mrs. Forrest pushed.

Now Patricia could feel the blood rush back. She felt trapped. She could think of no way out of this short of lying. She couldn't do that, nor did she want to. "Yes," Patricia said.

Mrs. Teasdale closed her eyes and sighed.

Mrs. Forrest gasped. "I told you so," she addressed to the principal.

Mr. Boward shook his head. "You've just made my job very difficult, Patricia," he said sadly.

"Why? I tell the truth and I'm executed? I have a right to a private life."

"Of course. But you have no right to bring any of the students into the circle of your private life. It . . . doesn't look good. If this gets out it raises all kinds of questions that I can't answer.

"Now, I think I should have a talk with this parent and . . ."

"No. I'm not going to tell you who it is. I'm not going to do anything to compromise a student here."

"Patricia," Mr. Boward said patiently. "You've already done that. If you tell me everything, we can have the child transferred to another school, and that will be the end of it."

"No, it won't. Why should one of the students have to pay for my indiscretion? Why should he or she have to wonder what went wrong to cause them to be shipped somewhere else? Why should that child's parent be penalized for making a private adult decision?"

The principal sighed. "Because the minute it involved the school it wasn't private any longer. You certainly should have seen that. And unless you cooperate this whole thing is going to grow much worse. There's a hint that a copy of the letter could be sent to the central board. Now, I don't intend for this high school, *any* of its students or faculty, to be embroiled in an embarrassing scandal."

The word scandal brought back unfortunate memories to Patricia. It seemed ironic that she'd survive one damaging episode in her life while a student at Stanford only to end up involved in another at a high school where she counseled. She'd lost her scholarship to medical school because she'd been involved with a man who had no integrity and had used her, completely derailing her childhood dream of becoming a doctor. Was she about to risk another chance, and a young boy's reputation . . . a man's love, in order to protect a principle?

"What are my options?" Patricia asked.

"Mr. Boward," Gertrude interrupted.

"I don't think we should be bargaining. This is a serious matter."

"The only other one that I can think of, and I'd hate to do this, is that *you* transfer out," the principal suggested uncomfortably.

Patricia stood up. She looked around the gathering that was the official representation of the welfare of the students of Duncan High School. "I would have liked to have finished out the school year, but . . . I'll leave."

"You'd rather give up all you've worked for here than tell us what was going on?"

Patricia smiled at the irony. "If I tell you I will lose everything that's important anyway."

Chapter Seventeen

Morgan came up to the podium as the applause continued. He nodded briefly in the direction of the audience of some three hundred employees of the Sager Electronics Company, and waited until silence took over. Morgan glanced briefly behind him where five men and two women sat, all having spoken about expected changes in their departments within Sager now that Ventura was the parent company. David Sullivan had also been among those to speak. He'd drawn laughter from the audience and demonstrated a knowledge and camaraderie of the staff that was impressive. Morgan faced the large group knowing, however, that he would have the final word.

"I want to congratulate every one of you for your expert input during the negotiations, and for your cooperation and willingness to accept change. I think we all agree this was a better alternative to selling Sager Electronics and putting so many people out of work. That was never my intention.

"Sager is a well-established company with years of product excellence and customer satisfaction to pride itself on. But even the best of companies occasionally needs tweaking and upgrading, needs to plan long range and change their focus. Just ask Bill Gates." The audience laughed quietly. "That is what we're going to do. Change our focus. Sager will survive a major transition which will take it successfully into the next millennium." More applause.

"You will need a captain at the helm of this great ship. Someone with knowledge and insight to steer the course. It will not be me. I will remain the overseer, if you will. Big Brother." There was more laughter. "I am here today to announce the person who will lead you from within" — Morgan knew that heads and eyes shifted to the seven people to the right and slightly behind him — "someone you all trust and know. Mr. George Tanner."

Surprise fleetingly rippled through the audience and was quickly covered by enthusiastic applause. Morgan joined in as he stepped away from the microphone and nodded in George's direction. The man rose to the occasion. He hid his own surprise well, and behaved like someone in charge. He stood and came forward. Morgan reached out for his hand and found the grip was firm, but not grateful. His thank you was quick and heard by only Morgan before he stood in front of his staff.

Morgan didn't have to look to David Sullivan to know that his regional director was, to put it in the vernacular, pissed.

David stood in the doorway and quietly watched Morgan who was seated in front of his PC studying the monitor and occasionally entering information.

"You wanted to see me?" David asked casually. He stood with his hands in his pockets, and his usually pliant athletic body was stiff with unaccustomed tension.

"Yes. Come in," Morgan responded absently. He kept his attention focused and maneuvered the mouse through the on-screen program.

David pursed his mouth and slowly

approached the desk. Morgan hadn't invited him to sit down, but David did so anyway. Morgan continued to work at the keyboard, using his save function and clearing the screen to the main menu. He turned to face David. Morgan looked at the younger man carefully, finally taking a sheet of paper from a folder on his desk and handing it to David.

"I'm sure you recognize what this is."

David spared the sheet a brief glance but didn't take it. "It's my resignation."

Morgan sat back. "I can't accept it."

For the first time since Morgan had hired David Sullivan to work for him, he saw his assistant speechless.

"You can't accept it," David repeated flatly, as if trying to understand.

Morgan was relaxed. Comfortable in his chair. He smoothed the lay of his tie and regarded David's every move. He had never seen David surprised at anything before. "That's correct."

"You do understand why I turned it in, don't you?"

"I would guess it was over the Sager transactions and the fact you didn't get the exec spot. Also because of the way you attempted to get the top position."

David kept his expression bland. "Did someone talk to you?"

"Not a word," Morgan said without hesitation. "Not giving you that position, David, was *my* decision. It had nothing to do with your strategy. By the way, there was essentially nothing wrong with the strategy."

"Except that it failed," David said wryly, still trying to gauge and read into Morgan's calm exterior and his assessments and insights.

"It was bound to fail for several reasons."

David's normal persona and self-confidence returned. "Did you know what I was doing all along?"

"No, not right away," Morgan admitted easily. "I figured it out after I gave you the go-ahead to finish the negotiations. You seemed a little too gung ho."

"That was bad?" David frowned.

"Not in itself. But you never told me everything. You were having meetings that weren't called for and had no purpose in what I wanted to accomplish. But you also never lied to me, which was a good move on your part."

"I don't see how you could know that," David prevaricated.

Morgan shrugged. "I had a totally clear game plan of how the acquisition and negotiations should go for Sager. I knew how long it should take and the points that would be hardest to achieve. I knew what Sager wanted from me. Any deviation from the plan had to be due to your own input and spin on the circumstances. Or influences on the Sager committee. The changes were subtle, but I noticed. And you did something pretty obvious. You led people to believe that your being exec was a done deal."

David laughed lightly, crossing an ankle over his knee. He gave a new consideration to Morgan Baxter, viewed him — now that it was too late — with more appreciative eyes. "I guess I got caught with my hand in the cookie jar."

Morgan nodded, but his eyes narrowed dangerously as he stared at David. "I didn't mind that. I would have been surprised if you didn't have some self-interest. The trouble began when you got greedy. You thought you could empty the cookie jar."

David made an indifferent gesture, denying nothing. "I saw an opportunity that would get us both what we wanted."

"But it was *my* cookie jar. You should have asked how much you were allowed to take."

David shook his head with a dry smile. "Somehow I can't really see you saying, oh, sure, David, go right ahead and make yourself director of Sager."

"You're right. I wouldn't have. Not under any circumstance would I have made you director. Let me be perfectly frank on that."

David was intrigued and, oddly, annoyed. He tightened his lips again thoughtfully. "Why not?"

Morgan's smile was almost imperceptible. He began to play idly with a star-shaped paper weight on his desk, rolling it point over point. "Because you would have been a lousy director."

David sat up straight. "Look, I know as well as you do what Sager has going for it . . ."

"But you would not have been able to make the best use of the company. You would have missed obvious opportunities to expand its capabilities. You would have lost interest eventually, run it into the ground. In the long run the company would have ended up with exactly what I wanted to avoid. A hostile takeover attempt by a stronger outsider, or the stockholders."

David grew tense again at the explicit criticism. "So, you're saying I'm not as good or as smart as George Tanner."

Morgan smiled. "You may be smarter, but George will make a better director, and be good for the company."

"Why?" David shot back.

Morgan looked at him carefully. "Because George cares what happens to the company, its future, and the three hundred or more employees who depend on it for their living. You don't."

"Then I don't get it. I knew the jig was up when George got the position. I thought you'd be happy to get rid of me."

"Well, you were wrong." Morgan gave up his laid-back posture and leaned over his desk toward David. He put aside the paper weight and used his hand and fingers to make his point as he explained. "Look, David . . . you're not the least bit interested in being in charge of anything. But you do like power. You haven't handled it very well so far, but that's because you've been operating with your ego and not your head.

"I don't accept your resignation because you haven't done a thing to hurt me or my company, my interests." Morgan slowly made a steeple of his fingertips and seriously regarded David over the point. His gaze narrowed speculatively. "It crossed my mind that you may have seen me as a dumb uppity nigger who'd gotten this far on luck and entitlement programs and that I wasn't capable of holding on." Morgan watched David flush a deep pink but remain silent. "I paid attention to white CEOs and learned how it was done and I did them one better. If you forget that I'm black, what's happening shouldn't be unfamiliar to you," Morgan said smoothly. "The fact is, you're very smart and very clever, but not smarter or more clever than I am."

David never batted an eyelash, never squirmed, never got angry. He looked at Morgan with total fascination and riveted attention.

"I know your strengths and your weaknesses. Probably better than you do. It's my business to know. I want you right here at Ventura. I have plans for you."

David chuckled, incredulous. "What do I get out of it?"

"Almost anything you want. It's up to you. As long as you don't try to go through, around, or over me to get it. You want the attention. You want to manipulate. You like working the room, holding out the carrot for the top deal. Fine. You were excellent at the Sager negotiations once you took over. I got what I wanted, so did the people at Sager. The only person who lost out was you. Your focus was too short-term.

"If you stay here you can continue as you have been. Probably do more traveling. The fact is, you stand a better chance with me, because I'm willing to give you your head . . . in most cases. You might even get busier than you really want."

David chuckled. "You mean, I might actually have to work hard now and then." Morgan nodded. "And if I stay you can also keep an eye on me." Morgan smiled. David shook his head and frowned. "I don't get you," he said, bewildered.

"Good," Morgan drawled.

"Another man would have crucified me."

"There's no advantage in revenge and I don't have the time for that. And I'm waiting to see if you'll eventually prove me wrong on something. This is a second chance. But it's still up to you."

David lifted the page from the edge of Morgan's desk and stared at it for a long considering moment.

"So . . . what's your decision?"

David scanned the single sheet. He slowly stood up and began tearing the page in half, and then in half again.

When the door shut behind him, cutting off the loud music, Kent felt relief. He zippered his varsity jacket and looked at his watch. It was already after midnight. He didn't care.

"We're going to hang out in the Village. You coming?"

Kent turned to Pete, his girlfriend Tiffany, and another boy he didn't know as well, Taz. He felt a buzz from the beer and tequila. He couldn't knock back as many as Pete or Taz, but his stomach was starting to react to all the junk he'd eaten, drank, and smoked at the party. But he wanted to handle it. He wasn't going to punk out. And he didn't want to go home. His father might be there . . . with Patricia Gilbert.

Then Kent glanced at Gabriella, who was waiting for him to make the decision. He could see she wasn't hot on the idea of a trip into Manhattan.

"Her father's not going to like that. He's real strict with her," he said, referring to Gabriella. She gave him an impatient look.

Tiffany made a disparaging gesture. "That's what you get for making it with someone like her. Drop her off and come with us."

"We got wheels, man," Taz boasted.

Kent was tempted. Maybe nothing was going to happen. Whenever he was with Eric and WeeGee, he had to be careful. They sometimes got into some funny stuff and he didn't want his father to find out. He looked at Gabriella and felt mild impatience. He'd promised.

"I don't know, man. My ass will get mowed."

"Let's just go, already," Pete said impatiently. He headed toward a black Mazda.

Kent turned to Gabriella as he started following the other three to the car. "Come on. We don't have to stay long."

"Okay," she agreed quietly.

They reached the car where the front seat was pulled forward so they could climb into the back. Gabriella sat between Kent and Tiffany, with Pete and Taz in the front.

"Whose car?" Kent asked.

"My brother's," Taz said.

Kent squinted at Taz, becoming a little uneasy. Taz was only a year older than he was. "You got a license?"

Laughter erupted in the front seat.

"License!" Pete said scathingly. "Shit, we don't need no fuckin' license. We never get picked up."

Kent and Gabriella exchanged looks. "I can drive," he offered. "I didn't drink as much as you."

Taz scoffed. "Forget that shit. I ain't letting you drive my brother's car. What if something happens?"

"Chill," Pete said from the front. "Ain't nothing gonna happen. I'm tellin' you."

Kent felt like he needed to say something else. He felt his head rattle with the sideways jerking of the vehicle. He'd had about three beers but Taz had had more. Kent thought of his father and the way he would sometimes stare at him when he came home from a party.

And he remembered the promise he'd made that he wouldn't drink beer again. He had some second thoughts, but already the car was started with the radio turned on loud. It pulled away from the curb, and shot off too fast down the residential street. When Gabriella slipped her hand into his, he held it.

The music from the console blasted into the night, and Kent wanted to ask Taz to turn it down. He began scanning the streets. If he saw a cop car he would at least warn everyone. The Mazda stopped for a light at the traffic circle at the western end of the Parade Grounds of Prospect Park. Another car was in front and one pulled up next to them. It, too, had music booming from the speakers, the bass from the rap song sounding like shots of thunder.

The occupants began screaming at them, trying to get their attention. Kent glanced at the car and immediately recognized Kamil Johnson, sitting on the passenger side in the front. Kent couldn't believe it. His stomach tightened in alarm as Kamil stared back.

"Shit," Kent mumbled to himself.

"What?" Gabriella asked nervously.

"Look, let's forget about Manhattan. I

don't feel like it . . ."

The light changed and all the cars started forward. The car in front of theirs went left and up Prospect Park West. The Mazda continued on the drive into the park from the right lane. The other car with Kamil followed. There was almost no one else around.

"Who the fuck is that?" Pete asked as the other vehicle began to keep pace with them.

"Kamil Asshole Johnson," Taz cackled. "They trying to do us, man."

Then the other car swerved threateningly in their direction before quickly straightening out. But Taz maneuvered to prevent getting hit.

"Jesus Christ!" Tiffany shrieked. "What are they doing?"

"Kent . . ." Gabriella whispered fearfully.

"Hey, cut it out. Just let them go," Kent ordered.

"No way. Keep going," Pete said.

Taz pressured the accelerator and the car surged forward with a screech of its wheels. The S-turn roadway challenged him as the other car came alongside again, driving recklessly in the empty oncoming lane. A bottle was thrown at them out the window of the other car, but fell short and smashed on the road.

"Kent, I'm scared . . ." Gabriella whimpered.

He couldn't say anything. He was too busy watching the other car and wondering if Taz could really keep them on the road and out of an accident. Kent tapped Taz roughly on the shoulder. "Hey, back the fuck up . . ." he shouted.

"I'm gonna show that asshole," Taz said, laughing.

The car veered dangerously as an unexpected sharp curve appeared. Gabriella screamed. Tiffany was silent, clutching the back of Pete's seat for balance. The car went into the turn too fast, and the entire right side of the vehicle lifted from the road. Kent automatically threw his weight in the opposite direction to counter the pull. But it wasn't enough.

The car rolled over to the left and Kent continued to twist in the other direction as Tiffany's and Gabriella's bodies dumped on top of him. The other car ran into the left side of the Mazda as it fell into its path. The impact bent metal, split plastic, and shattered glass. With the momentum the car rolled over completely to the left.

Gabriella screamed again.

Patricia sat at her dining table considering the official letter in her hand. It was the report from the central Board of Education on the charge of inappropriate behavior. She'd argued that her personal life, her time away from Duncan and its students, was not inappropriate and not up for discussion. That was not the way the New York City Board of Education viewed the matter.

She had been given a choice. Resign or be disciplined and assigned to another school. Either way Patricia realized that she'd be leaving Duncan or starting somewhere else at the end of the school year. Other than a certain protection of her ego and reputation, what was the point?

Patricia didn't resign. She instead negotiated for the rest of the year as part of a sabbatical to finish her degree and to begin clinical work. Over the summer she would worry about another job. She would try to figure out if she had a personal life anymore. And she would decide if the respect and love she'd developed and nurtured for Morgan Baxter meant anything.

For now, there seemed nothing to do but plan for the next week. And what she would say to Morgan about her decision. The truth. And then what? She hadn't heard from him all day, and the void made Patricia feel especially lonely right now.

When the phone finally did ring, she felt such relief that her hands were trembling when she answered and she heard Morgan's tired voice.

"Hello?"

"I'm lonely," he opened. "It's Friday night and I don't have a date."

She laughed. "You didn't ask."

"I thought you knew it was a standing order."

"I assumed no such thing."

"You're not going to work with me on this, heh? Kent's at a party and I have the house to myself. Come on over."

"It's already so late . . ."

"Are you telling me you don't want to be with me tonight?"

Patricia smiled. "I'll be right over."

She was glad. No. She was desperate.

The night was cold, so they ordered in from a nearby Szechuan house and ate in the kitchen. Patricia looked across the table at Morgan Baxter, watching the animation and intelligence in his face, feeling safe and happy . . . and knew that she was in love with him. It seemed less a startling discovery than an admission of the facts. The realization warmed her, made her feel grounded as a woman. And it felt . . . curious. It had been more than ten years since Patricia had held any feelings for a man remotely approaching the depth of what she knew was in her heart for Morgan.

It was wonderful. And it was very scary.

After dinner, Morgan and Patricia came slowly together. Their kiss was nothing more than a warm sealing of unspoken vows, and their tongues were erotically playful with each other. He began to knead her back and shoulders. She heard the slow heavy breathing, the sensual rise of his desire and intent. Patricia pressed into him, aligning her body against Morgan's.

She let out a soft sigh, feeling a sudden urgency to make love with him, as if it might be the last time. Morgan began to kiss Patricia with a need that matched her own. His mouth completely captured hers. He slid his warm hands under her sweater, circling her slender torso, feeling the heaving of Patricia's chest. His fingers released the clasp on her bra and his hands came forward to close over her breasts.

Patricia moaned, wanting to tell him to hurry. Morgan was about to suggest, in a voice already husky with passion, that they go upstairs when the phone began to ring.

Morgan reluctantly released Patricia to answer. She felt dazed and languid. She rearranged her clothing. It was late and she was already alert to the call.

By the time Patricia reached Morgan's side he had finished the call. He turned to her, his mouth a grim line, and his eyes were filled with dread.

"Oh, my God," Patricia found herself whispering. "It's Kent, isn't it?"

Morgan merely turned away, hurrying to get his jacket and her heavy knit cardigan from the hall closet. "That was the hospital. There was an accident . . ."

Typical of hospital personnel, no details of the accident or the victims were given over the phone, but Morgan had at least been assured that there were no fatalities.

They took his car. During the entire car trip to Maimonides not a word was said between them. Morgan's concentration was absolute and Patricia remained silent, simply resting her hand on his thigh, where the muscles were taut with tension, to show her concern and sympathy.

Morgan gave his name at the emergency-room desk, where an exhausted resident on duty directed him and Patricia to a triage area. There were several police officers talking with hospital personnel, while filling out preliminary reports. Patricia spotted the mother of one of Duncan's sophomore girls, Tiffany, although she couldn't remember the woman's name. She was pacing anxiously outside a curtained room and crying softly. Patricia saw Pete Connors's parents and older brother. She also recognized Timothy . . . Taz . . . Sheppard, on a gurney and in a discussion with a police officer. His neck was still in a brace from the EM service, and there was blood staining his shirt and pants. Patricia didn't immediately see Kent or any other teenager who may have been involved, and Patricia found herself slipping her hand into Morgan's. He gripped it tightly. Morgan got the attention of a passing aide.

"My name is Morgan Baxter. I got a call about my son Kent, and a car accident."

The woman walked a few feet to a wall secretarial and looked through a list. "Let me just check if the doctor is finished."

She walked away before Morgan could ask another question. Patricia stroked Morgan's arm as the aide went into a nearby cubicle. A moment later a young female doctor came out. Patricia noticed at once there was blood splattered on the doctor's white medical coat. Morgan's hand crushed hers.

"Are you Kent's parents?" the doctor asked, looking between them.

Patricia let go of Morgan's hand.

"I'm his father," he responded.

"Kent's okay. He has a broken hand and wrist and a dislocated shoulder. There are cuts and bruises around his face and head and some swelling. I think he might have a concussion. We'd like to keep him at least overnight for observation."

"What happened?" Morgan asked.

The doctor shook her head. "I don't have all the facts. You should talk to the officers over there." She nodded to her right. "They all had been drinking, and the alcohol levels were above normal. I don't know who was driving, but I understand that the driver misjudged a curve. The car flipped over. He and your son were hurt the worst, but nothing life-threatening. Some broken bones, lots of bruises. You can go in to see him now."

Morgan nodded as the doctor turned to a staff member. He looked at Patricia but she spoke first.

"You go on in and I'll wait here."

Morgan didn't question the decision. He swept aside the curtain and went in to his son. Patricia stared at the curtain as it fell back into place. She could hear nothing beyond it, and she stood feeling isolated and out of place. She had a brief conversation with Pete Connors's family to try to find out what had happened. It was Peter who told her about the other car and Kamil Johnson. The police were trying to find him now. Patricia watched as Taz was wheeled down a corridor toward radiology, but she took a position near Kent's treatment room to wait for Morgan and more information. She stood out of the way, leaning against a wall, listening to the sounds of near tragedy all around. Tiffany's mother had stopped crying, and the doctor had given her a signed release form for her daughter who had escaped with minor cuts.

"Miss Gilbert?"

Patricia turned at the tentative mention of her name. She found herself facing Gabriella Villar's father. "Mr. Villar . . ." she began in surprise, and then frowned. "Gabriella?"

He shook his head and smiled. "She is fine. A little bit shaken, but she did not even get a scratch."

"I'm so glad."

"My wife and I, we are most grateful to the young man. Mr. Baxter's son."

"You are? What did he do?"

"Gabriella said she and Kent were in the back seat of the car. When the car went off the road and began to turn over, young Baxter protected my daughter with his body. He held her in her seat."

"He did?"

"*Dios mio.*" Mr. Villar nodded and

sighed. *"Es posible que . . ."*

"No, no. Don't even think of it. She's fine. Kent is fine, thank goodness."

"Please. You will see Gabriella? Her mother is helping her to get dressed and we will take her home."

Patricia walked into the cubicle and introduced herself to the woman quietly talking to Gabriella in Spanish. The woman was slender and petite. No taller than her daughter, but nearly as youthful-looking. Her smile acknowledged Patricia and her connection to Gabriella.

Patricia touched the young girl's arm and Gabriella smiled wanly. "Are you okay?"

"Yes, thanks to Kent. Is he hurt?"

Patricia could hear the relief, and a great deal of adoration in the remark. "Yes, but not seriously."

Gabriella looked doubtful. "Are you sure?"

Patricia smiled. "I promise."

"I would like to say thank you . . ." Gabriella said, stepping into her shoes and taking a sweater from her mother to pull over her head.

Patricia reached out to help her. "Maybe you should wait. Kent's father is with him right now, and I think your parents would like to get you home."

Mrs. Villar sided with Patricia and Gabriella finally agreed.

"But you will tell him for me, yes? I cannot thank him enough. And I am sorry he got hurt."

When Patricia left the Villar family, Morgan was in the corridor looking for her. She went to him. "Mr. Villar's daughter was one of the passengers."

Morgan nodded. "Kent told me. He's a little close-mouthed about the accident. I didn't want to push for details right now." He shook his head. "The boys were high."

Patricia touched his chest. "Do you want to stay with him awhile? I can call a car service to take me back for mine. You can call me later."

"No, stay with me. He's in a little bit of pain and they can't give him too many painkillers until they know how bad the concussion is. They're going to send him up to a ward pretty soon." Morgan looked into her face. "He asked if you were here. Do you want to see him?"

"Maybe that's not such a good idea right now."

"Afraid?"

"Yes," she admitted.

Morgan nodded in understanding. "I want to talk with the officers who arrived at the scene. Wait for me at the nurses station."

Patricia watched him walk away. The emergency area soon emptied of Gabriella and her parents, Tiffany and her mother. Kent was wheeled up to a ward for the night. The doctor on duty had moved on to another emergency. The officers finished their conversation with Morgan and left him next to the nurses station looking thoughtful and stern. Patricia went to him and wrapped her arms around his middle. Morgan hugged her and glanced down into her upturned face.

"I heard about what Kent did for the Villar girl."

"I know you think you need a stiff drink, but why don't we go home?"

"Hummm . . ." Morgan grumbled dryly with a comical lift of his brows. He looked at Patricia for a long considering moment and then sighed deeply as he took her hand and they walked from the hospital to the parking lot. "I have to call Melissa. She has to know."

"Yes, of course," Patricia said.

Morgan unlocked and opened the passenger door and Patricia climbed in. He leaned down to whisper to her.

"Stay with me tonight?"

She nodded.

At the town house she roamed the living room restlessly while Morgan went upstairs to the privacy of his room to place the call to Kent's mother. Patricia had second thoughts and considered leaving after all. This was a family crisis . . . and she was not family. She wasn't sure what she was to the Baxters. Kent's counselor and his first major infatuation. Morgan's friend, his lover. But that seemed too tentative, not solid enough to count on. Patricia felt herself a strange sort of appendage to Kent and Morgan. Belonging . . . but not really. The ties could be cut at any time. In a way she was about to.

She heard Morgan come down the stairs. Slowly. He was tired and no wonder. Patricia saw the signs of emotional strain and held out her arms to him. Morgan accepted the comfort like it was a lifeline. He held her close, kissed her as if it was the only thing that made sense. It was insistent. Aggressive. There was urgency in the play of his lips and tongue, his soft breathing and the heat of his body. Patricia tried to take the fear right out of him.

"Melissa wants to fly to New York." Patricia stopped stroking his jaw, but Morgan caught her hand and kissed the fingers. "I tried to tell her Kent was okay. She doesn't need to come."

"Yes, she does. Kent's her child. Of course she'd want to see for herself that he wasn't seriously hurt. *I* would want to know."

Morgan nodded and sighed. "Well, she's coming. Brad, too, her husband. I offered to put them up here but they opted for a hotel." He hugged Patricia again and sighed. "Something about my privacy and everything."

The strangeness came back, but Patricia smiled despite the sense of inevitability that seemed to drape over her. "Why don't you go to bed? The kids are fine and you need some sleep."

"I need you," he said softly.

Patricia let Morgan lead her back up the stairs to his room. They didn't need the lights, didn't need to talk. They didn't need to strip beyond underwear because they didn't make love. They kissed and held each other in the dark.

Morgan curled against her back, burying his face in the sweet scent of her skin, covering her breast with his hand and being lulled by her heartbeat. Everything was okay. And it was going to get better. Morgan fell asleep with a mantra repeating in his head. He didn't know where it came from, all of a sudden. It was hypnotic, sending him into a deep sleep, comfortable in the knowledge that his son was okay and Patricia was with him. *Love her love her love . . .* came over and over. He had to remember to say so. When Kent was home. When Melissa and Brad were gone.

When it was just the two of them.

Chapter Eighteen

It was only when Patricia reached the ward where Kent had been assigned at Maimonides Hospital that she again felt apprehension. She wanted to see him because she cared and was concerned. But she wondered if once with Kent she would become painfully transparent in her feelings for his father, and her secrets would be exposed and laid bare. Her vulnerability leaving her defenseless. Here, she would cease to be a counselor or even a friend, but someone who had become a part of Kent's life through a deeper emotion known as love. Was she only asking for more heartache?

Patricia stopped before the open door to the room. She could hear voices. She listened and heard Kent and a woman. Not a nurse or doctor.

His mother.

Patricia turned away, her stomach

muscles clenching. She couldn't intrude. And she was suddenly scared. Leaning against a wall, as staff and visitors and ambulatory patients moved around her, she became aware of a tremendous sense of isolation, like the first time she'd gone to Kent's football game.

She changed her mind and walked to the nursing station. A young woman glanced up indifferently.

"Yes?"

"I just wanted to find out how one of your patients is doing. Kent Baxter?"

The woman looked down a list of names and then located Kent's patient book. She leafed through a number of pages. "He's stable. You can go in. He's allowed visitors."

Patricia shook her head. "I don't want to interrupt. I think he's with family."

The young woman behind the desk shrugged. "That's up to you. You can always come back if you want."

"That's a good idea. Is there someplace where I can get some coffee?"

"On the third floor."

"Thanks," Patricia said, turning away. Suddenly her path was blocked.

"Are you Patricia Gilbert?"

Patricia felt all of her nerves coiled tighter now as she stared at the woman in front of her. There was no time for her feelings to find a place that would make her comfortable with the knowledge that Kent's mother and Morgan's ex-wife faced her.

"Yes," Patricia said automatically. Her voice seemed thin.

The woman didn't smile. She didn't have much of any kind of facial expression except a sort of staring curiosity. Patricia had no idea what she was thinking. And for the life of her, as obvious as it seemed, she could do nothing but stare right back. The woman was perhaps two inches taller than herself, with short light brown hair cut into a stylish bob. Large gray eyes, a squarish jaw, and a mouth that was full. Her makeup was subtle but applied to emphasize her cheekbones.

She wasn't at all what Patricia had expected, and she was quickly forced to confront her own stereotype of a white woman who had married Morgan and given birth to their child of mixed race. Patricia had imagined someone pretty but superficial. Friendly but unsophisticated. Sweet but unchallenging.

It had meant something abstract, Patricia realized now, to know previously that Kent's mother was white. But seeing Melissa now meant something entirely different. She was simply a woman somewhere in her mid to late thirties who was Kent's mother and Morgan's ex-wife, who happened to be white. And she was in an advanced state of pregnancy. That awareness had more of an effect on Patricia than anything else about her. That and the fact that Melissa was irrevocably tied to Kent and Morgan's past and even their future.

Patricia inclined her head slightly. "Yes . . ."

"I heard you ask about Kent. I'm his mother."

Now there was a smile. A surprisingly confident one, without guile or suspicion. Her gaze swept boldly over Patricia.

"Kent described you perfectly."

Patricia moved swiftly away from the subject of herself. She didn't want to hear about what else Kent may have said to his mother about her.

"How's he doing?"

Melissa sighed and nodded in relief.

"Just fine, thank God. I think he's done all the things a teenager can to drive his father and me crazy, but he's going to be okay. I think the accident scared him quite a bit. Let's hope it scared some sense into him."

Patricia tried to grin but her mouth only felt distorted and unnatural. She wasn't sure how friendly she could be with this woman. Not because she couldn't like her, but because she represented so much of what Patricia suddenly recognized she wanted. She felt envious of Melissa, and the knowledge made her melancholy.

"You don't have to worry too much about Kent. It's been a little rough for him this year, but he's bright and he's got a good sense of himself."

Melissa's eyes fluttered and she nodded. "There were a lot of things on his mind. Things I couldn't help him with."

"I understand that," Patricia said honestly.

"Did you come to visit?" Melissa asked, still assessing Patricia.

"I don't want to interrupt. You should be with him."

"Well, right now I want to find out when he's going to be released. And he's hungry. He says hospital food sucks. He's ready to go home." Melissa chuckled easily.

Patricia was confused. Home where? Home with her to Colorado, or to the Heights with his father?

"Go on in. Kent will be happy to see you. He's talked a lot about you."

"Really?"

Melissa slowly nodded. "He said you were the only black teacher at Duncan who seemed to understand how he was feeling about himself."

It was such a simple statement, but one which clarified exactly what Melissa knew about her. And Patricia had to admit that she could detect nothing more in Melissa's announcement than acceptance . . . and relief. Patricia sighed to herself and felt her body begin to finally relax.

"I'm glad you came."

"I'll only say hello and stay a few moments," Patricia said with a nod.

"Maybe you'd like to meet me afterward. We could get something to eat and . . . just talk." She glanced at her watch. "My husband and Morgan are supposed to pick me up in another hour or so. They wanted to give me time alone with Kent."

Patricia started to decline. She couldn't be here to witness that gathering. "I don't think . . ."

"Oh, please . . ." Melissa laid her hand on Patricia's arm. "I would really like to get to know you. You mean so much to both Kent and Morgan. I want to find out how Kent *really* is doing."

"Why would you think I'd know any more than you do?"

"Because I'm his mother, and I'm going to love him and accept him no matter what. Just as he is. But I want to know that my son is going to be okay out there in the rest of the world. You did it. I guess I want the assurance that Kent can manage, too."

Melissa's honesty was hard to ignore or deny, and Patricia realized she was curious, too. She slowly smiled, somewhat ruefully.

"Sure. I'll meet you at the entrance in fifteen minutes. There's a coffee shop across the street."

Patricia watched as Melissa walked away before she again approached the wardroom. Kent was in the bed nearest the door. The far bed had another teen, who was in conversation with a number of family members. Kent was watching the TV, positioned on a mechanical extension arm coming from the wall next to his bed. There were several magazines, his Walkman, some cookies all mixed up in the bed linens with him. His left hand was plastered up to the elbow. His right hand rested under his head.

She silently watched him. Seeing more clearly now the parts and physical features that were Kent's mother or his father. Patricia was paralyzed. She couldn't go in. Kent's infatuation notwithstanding, his difficulty in accepting her relationship with his father aside, she found that she had succumbed to the emotional trap of wishful thinking, and too many dreams unrealized.

What if . . .

Kent were her own son?

Patricia hesitated just a second too long, intending to leave. She wasn't sure she would be able to talk around the emotional lump in her throat. If she tried, she was afraid she'd start to cry.

She adored this boy.

She loved his father. And, in a way, she knew she was about to lose them both. Perhaps not the physical Kent and Morgan Baxter, but the emotional and troubled people who'd first come to her attention back in October. Now everything was changed because they had changed. And so had she. Now, there was a relationship and alliances and history between them all. Now there was all this love. Patricia still didn't know what would become of it all — *them* — in the future.

Kent saw her.

His eyes brightened in surprise. "Hi," he said.

She could not retreat, but still looked for any sign that Kent didn't want to see her.

"Hi," Patricia murmured, her smile wavering. She gestured awkwardly over her shoulder to the corridor. "I . . . I just saw your mother."

"Yeah, she was just here. Did you come to see me, Ms. Gilbert?"

She was encouraged by the quizzical lift of his brows. She realized that Kent was probably feeling funny about seeing her, too. "If it's okay. I won't stay long. Just wanted to see how you were doing."

Patricia walked to his side. The hospital bed was higher than a normal bed surface, and its mattress height not only made her feel small, but made Kent seem larger. His feet hung off the end an inch or two.

"How's the hand?"

He wiggled the fingertips. "Okay. They're going to put something smaller on next week and take this cast off. And then everything comes off in about a month."

"Wow," Patricia said with a grin, duly impressed with the medical advancement and shortening of time in his recovery.

"Yeah," Kent said, chuckling.

Suddenly neither of them knew what to say. Patricia observed that Kent seemed to be holding up better than herself. *Youth,* she mused. Everything was momentary. It was either a great tragedy, the best thing in the world . . . or no big thing at all.

"Did my mom say anything to you?" he asked quietly.

"We introduced ourselves. I'm going to meet her for coffee after I leave you. We're just going to chat."

Kent groaned. "Not about me, I hope."

She merely smiled. He knew very well

that they would.

"You know, you're quite a hero to Gabriella and her family." He shrugged. "If you won't get too embarrassed, I'm pleased and proud of the way you handled yourself during the accident. Except . . ."

"Yeah, I know. We were drinking and smoking and shouldn't have been in the car . . ." His eyes widened. "You didn't tell Mr. Villar everything, did you? He'll never let Gabriella do anything again if he knew."

"On the other hand, if you're honest and apologize — after all you saved her from getting hurt — he might forgive you and trust you all the more."

Kent thought about that and nodded. "You're right."

"Well, I'd better go. I only wanted to . . ."

"Ms. Gilbert? I gotta tell you something," Kent interrupted on a rush. His voice was strained.

Patricia stared at his struggle and suddenly feared an outright confession and declaration. She watched the way Kent shifted, cleared his throat, and avoided her gaze.

"Remember when there was that

meeting in school, and Mr. Daly got into trouble, and then the principal got on you?"

"I know about Mr. Daly. How did you know about Mr. Boward wanting to see me?"

"I knew about it. I . . . I knew it was going to happen."

"How?"

" 'Cause . . . I was the one who sent the letter to the office."

Patricia just stared at Kent. She didn't know what to say. She didn't even know what to feel or think. "You mean . . ."

He nodded. "The one about you seeing my father. I didn't say it was my father, I just said you were going out with the parent of a student. I didn't sign my name or anything. I . . . just sent it."

Patricia wasn't angry at Kent. She was numb — but not angry. She'd believed that Beverly McGraw had been responsible for the letter, but it occurred to Patricia now, when she thought about it, that it was a very immature thing to do. Beverly McGraw might be accused of a lot of things; acting childish and vindictive was not on the list.

"What did you think would happen once it was read?"

He still wouldn't look at her. "I don't know. I thought maybe they would talk to you and tell you to stop. I didn't know you'd get fired."

"But you did want something to happen to me?" she asked.

Kent was silent for a moment. Then he shrugged. "I thought I did." His face grew flushed. "I thought you liked me and . . . I was so mad when you and my father started seeing each other, and I felt like . . . you weren't paying any attention to me anymore."

"Oh, Kent . . ." Patricia murmured.

"I know I was just a stupid kid, but I thought maybe you were making fun of me, and . . ."

"I'd never do that."

"Yeah, I know, but I just had to do something. I'm sorry you got fired. It was all my fault."

"Why are you telling me this now?"

" 'Cause, I want you to still like me. And I thought if I told you, maybe you could talk to the principal and he'd hire you back."

"I can't go back. But I want you to know that I do still like you. And it wasn't all your fault. I . . . handled things badly."

"My father really likes you, Miss Gilbert. I was going to tell him about what I did, but then I got scared."

"You thought he'd send you back to Colorado?" Kent nodded. "He wouldn't. He might be a little mad, but he'd never send you away from him again."

"Do you think I should tell him?"

"What do you think?" she asked.

He sighed, like a martyr. "I guess."

Patricia looked kindly on the boy. "I would have liked to finish the year at Duncan. Maybe I would have been gone next fall anyway, once my degree was through. But I'm not mad at you, Kent. As a matter of fact, I have a great deal of respect for the fact that you told me what you'd done."

"I'm really sorry."

"I know you are. So am I."

"I was a real asshole . . . I mean . . ." he stammered.

Patricia shook her head. "We won't talk about it anymore. Deal?"

"Deal," Kent agreed with relief.

And then there was a moment when it seemed there was something else he wanted to say or do. Patricia wasn't sure what, until she realized Kent was debating whether or not to hug . . . or kiss her. He leaned forward, and then pulled back. The decision was apparently too overwhelming. He fell back against the pillow instead and framed a weak, boyish smile.

Chapter Nineteen

"What are you thinking?" Morgan asked as he placed the wooden tray on Patricia's bureau. They'd had a rather romantic snack of wine, cheese, and bread. That had come after they'd made love. He could see Patricia's reflection in the mirror over the dresser. She lay languishing and dreamy.

"I wish you didn't have to go," Patricia confessed in a quiet voice.

Morgan turned and smiled at her. He stood naked, with his hands on his hips. "I like to hear you say it. Do you mean now or tomorrow?"

"Yes," she sighed.

Morgan laughed lightly and returned to the bed. He sat on the side facing her and she slowly sat up. The blanket and sheet dropped away from her bare breasts. Morgan reached for her and Patricia came forward into his arms. He kissed her in a leisurely gentle way.

There was no urgency anymore. Then he gazed into her eyes.

"That frown is not because I have to get home in a while, or because I'm leaving for Europe tomorrow. Are you worried about your orals and your committee decision?"

Patricia closed her eyes and laid her cheek against his chest. "Uh-huh. I was thinking . . . I can't believe I've finally gotten this far. I'm still waiting for the other shoe to drop . . . for something terrible to happen to stop me again."

"You mean, like that guy you knew in school?" She nodded. Morgan hugged her closely. "Hey, that's all over. I know it was hard. Frankly, I'm surprised you don't hate the guy, but you know what they say in a situation like that?"

"What?"

" 'Success is the best revenge.' "

She smiled against his warm firm skin. Patricia felt such an overwhelming rush of love and pride and gratefulness that she didn't know what to express first. So she just kissed Morgan's chest and smiled at him.

"I'm going to miss you so much," she admitted honestly.

"It's only for about ten days." Morgan kissed her forehead and cuddled her in his arms. He loved the feel of her slender body. "Want to change your mind about coming with me to Germany?"

"I'd love to, but I can't. The test . . ."

"Wishful thinking."

"Besides, I think it's a good idea to take Kent with you."

"I was surprised he wanted to when I asked. I think he just liked the idea of being out of school for a while."

"I think he just wanted to be with you. I'm so glad that things have worked out for you both."

"Just like you said they would."

"Well . . . let's just say I'm glad I wasn't proven wrong," she said dryly.

"There is still one thing," Morgan suggested.

"What?"

"Us."

Patricia was silent. Yes, there was that.

She and Morgan hadn't actually had a conversation about their relationship. There'd been no plans, no declarations, no commitments. There had just been the mutual silent agreement that they needed each other, that they liked being together. And the "us" that they might be still hung out there in midair, left stranded as one crisis after another occurred around them.

"We need to talk about it, Pat. We need to decide about . . ."

"I know."

"Soon?"

"Yes."

"Now?"

"No," she said emphatically. "You have to go soon to get home before Kent does."

"He knows where I am. He knows you and I have a relationship. It's time to bring it out in the open and deal with it together."

"Not tonight, Morgan," she said. "Let's not start a conversation we can't hope to finish in a few minutes or an hour."

"And I wouldn't want to. But I want you to understand something." He looked into her face, lifted her chin with his fingers so he could press his lips to hers. "Everything is going to change when I get back."

Patricia blinked at him, the implication of his words spurring first a moment of hope and then one of anxiety. "Can I ask how?"

"Let me give you a hint," he whispered.

And then Morgan began to make love to her again.

As if they had all the time in the world.

Chapter Twenty

Morgan thought, in an abstract run of his mind, that university reception areas were similar to dentists' offices. Not really uncomfortable, but no place you want to hang around in for very long. Morgan had already been in this one two hours. He'd read the annual report twice, and several outdated copies of *Time*. He'd walked the corridor and stared out the window across the campus at Columbia where the spring semester was in its second month and the campus grounds were crowded with students.

Morgan turned his head sharply as the door next to the secretary's desk finally opened and Patricia slipped out. She didn't immediately see him, and for the moment seemed a bit unfocused and dazed. The exam had lasted almost three hours. She was dressed in an off-white linen dress, belted at the waist. No dangling eccentric earrings today, but small pearl ear studs and the single strand of pearls she'd worn at Christmas.

It was only as Morgan stood up from the vinyl sofa that Patricia seemed to realize there was someone else in the small area. Then she suddenly blinked at him, peering through her glasses as if he were an apparition.

Morgan began walking toward her. He reached to pull her glasses from her nose at pretty much the same time Patricia walked into his arms. The familiar scent of her hair and her cologne made him smile foolishly.

"What are you doing here?" Patricia asked.

"I came to be with you. My business was finished so Kent and I flew home a few days early."

"I'm so happy to see you."

"How's it going?"

Patricia grimaced in agony. "It was tough. The committee dug for every bone and then proceeded to scrape each one clean. How's Kent? Where is he?"

"Boat show at the Javits Center. He's thinking of flying out to Colorado for

Easter. He has to face his grandfather with the news that he's not interested in a military life, or in entering the Academy in Colorado Springs." Morgan kissed her forehead and slid his hands up her back. "He says to tell you hello, and he hopes you want to marry me."

Patricia stared at Morgan. "You haven't asked me yet. We haven't even said . . ."

Morgan smiled at her. "That we love each other? Pat, that's a given at this point. We've said it in so many ways that I'm not in any doubt. But, I love you. I want you and me and Kent to be a family."

Her eyes misted over and she took a deep breath, too overcome to attempt more than a heartfelt, "I love you, too."

He hugged her, wanting to do a little more, but aware of their surroundings. "We'll discuss it later." He glanced at the closed door. "What happens next?"

"Oh . . . the committee goes into a huddle to discuss the merits of my paper. If I've convinced them I know more about the subject of adolescent psychology than they do, I win. I'll know in a few minutes or a few hours."

"I told Kent you were almost a doctor.

I think the official word he used was 'cool.' "

Patricia's smile broadened. She started to speak but the office door opened once again. A tall, middle-aged woman came out. Just behind her were two more women and two men. Patricia turned quickly from Morgan, but holding on to his hand. The woman gave Morgan a brief acknowledging nod before holding out her hand to Patricia.

"Congratulations, Dr. Gilbert," she said heartily.